Denise N. Wheatley loves happy endings and the art of storytelling. Her novels run the romance gamut, and she strives to pen entertaining books that embody matters of the heart. She's an RWA member and holds a BA in English from the University of Illinois. When Denise isn't writing, she enjoys watching true-crime TV and chatting with readers. Follow her on social media: Instagram, @Denise_Wheatley_Writer; Twitter, @DeniseWheatley; BookBub, @DeniseNWheatley; Goodreads, Denise N. Wheatley

A *USA TODAY* bestselling author of over one hundred and five novels in twenty languages, **Tara Taylor Quinn** has sold more than seven million copies. Known for her intense emotional fiction, Ms Quinn's novels have received critical acclaim in the UK and most recently from Harvard. She is the recipient of the Readers' Choice Award and has appeared often on local and national TV, including *CBS Sunday Morning*. For TTQ offers, news and contests, visit tarataylorquinn.com!

DANGER IN THE NEVADA DESERT

DENISE N. WHEATLEY

ON THE RUN WITH HIS BODYGUARD

TARA TAYLOR QUINN

MILLS & BOON

First Published in Great Britain 2023
by Mills & Boon, an imprint of HarperCollins*Publishers* Ltd
1 London Bridge Street, London, SE1 9GF

www.harpercollins.co.uk

HarperCollins*Publishers*
Macken House, 39/40 Mayor Street Upper,
Dublin 1, D01 C9W8, Ireland

Danger in the Nevada Desert © 2023 Denise N. Wheatley
On the Run with His Bodyguard © 2023 TTQ Books LLC

ISBN: 978-0-263-30727-6

0523

MIX
Paper | Supporting
responsible forestry
FSC™ C007454

This book is produced from independently certified FSC™ paper to ensure responsible forest management.

For more information visit: www.harpercollins.co.uk/green

Printed and Bound in the UK using 100% Renewable Electricity at CPI Group (UK) Ltd, Croydon, CR0 4YY

DANGER IN THE NEVADA DESERT

DENISE N. WHEATLEY

This book is dedicated to my fifth-grade teacher, Mrs Myra Blouin, who convinced me that I could accomplish anything.

If you want to know what a killer looks like, go look in the mirror.

—Lieutenant Tony Mullins, Memphis Police Department

Prologue

Police Sergeant Charlotte Bowman climbed down the trail of Glacier Lake's campsite, careful not to roll her ankle on the rugged terrain like she had the last time.

The sun was setting on the beautiful grounds, nestled in between the majestic River Mountains. Beams of light glistened off the shimmering blue water, illuminating the canyon's colorful wildflowers and crystalline gemstones.

The lake's surroundings made for the perfect afternoon getaway. Charlotte wished she were there for one. But instead, she was investigating the latest murder committed by the Numeric Serial Killer.

Tendrils of jet-black curls stuck to her perspiring neck. Charlotte swiped them up toward her bun and fanned her face. The one-hundred-degree temperatures of River Valley, Nevada were unrelenting. She'd dressed for the police station's air-conditioned office, not an impromptu trip to the scorching crime scene.

While pulling off her denim jacket and tying it around her waist, Charlotte lost her footing. She skidded along the jagged gray dirt, the thick soles on her hiking boots kicking up clouds of dust. A nearby boulder saved her from falling to the ground.

Charlotte steadied herself, then proceeded down the path.

A surge of adrenaline coursed through her body when a desert willow appeared up ahead. Its twisted, forty-foot-tall trunk opened into an elaborate canopy of stunning dark pink blooms. Long, slender twigs fluttered in the breeze, blowing fragrant waves of violet through the air.

The tree's beauty was overshadowed, however, by the memory of Brad Ellington's lifeless body lying underneath its branches. The circumstances surrounding his death were peculiar. There was no trauma to the body. He was fully clothed, without a speck of dirt on his pristine gray Polo shirt, khaki pants and white sneakers. His wallet, keys and identification were still in his pockets, making him easily identifiable.

And proving this was no robbery. So, what was it about?

The biggest oddity was the number nine that had been carved into his left cheek. Its edges were jagged, as if cut with a dull object. Charlotte had seen a lot during her fourteen years in law enforcement, but there was something about the barbaric scar that chilled her to the core.

You're doing it again. No emotions, remember? Stick to the business at hand.

Charlotte pulled on a pair of latex gloves and approached the tree. River Valley's chief of police, Ethan Mitchell, had sent her back out to the scene to try and collect more DNA. She'd tried to tell him that the team had combed the area numerous times. The only evidence worth gathering was a few clumps of blood-soaked dirt. The results came back identifying only one profile, and that was Brad's.

"There's got to be something more out there," Chief Mitchell had insisted, his bushy silver eyebrows shooting up toward his receding hairline.

Charlotte knew that look. It meant an order had been given and the conversation was over.

And now here I am, trying to pull off a magic trick and make evidence appear that just isn't here...

A dark cloud drifted in front of the setting sun, blocking its fading light. Charlotte grabbed a flashlight from her black cargo pants and turned on her body cam.

"This is Sergeant Bowman, reporting from the Glacier Lake campgrounds where Brad Ellington's body was found. Per Chief Mitchell's request, I am searching the scene for additional evidence—"

Loud footsteps thumped behind her. Charlotte stopped abruptly and pivoted. No one was there.

Am I hearing things?

The campsite had cleared out now that dusk was settling. Fishermen's boats were docked, jet skis stored and charcoal grills extinguished. There were no visitors in sight.

Charlotte turned her attention back to the hollow at the base of the tree trunk. *Just see what you can find and get the hell out of here...*

"I am standing near the desert willow where the deceased victim was recovered, attempting to collect anything that will link our suspect to the scene. I'll be scanning the soil and gathering additional samples for blood evidence, bodily fluids, footprints, hair, fibers..."

Everything that we've already searched for, she resisted the urge to add.

Charlotte bent down and scooped up a clump of earth. She shined her light on the specimen. Nothing jumped out at her. She packed it inside of a plastic bag anyway.

Creak!

The sound of crackling bark screeched overhead. Charlotte leapt to her feet, hoping to avoid a falling branch. The air grew still. And silent, except for the leaves swishing in the wind. Nevertheless, Charlotte spun a one-eighty in search of a lurker. No one was there.

You're being paranoid...

She bent down and scooped another sample of soil.

Bam!

"Dammit!" Charlotte yelled, gripping the back of her head.

She tumbled onto her knees. Her eyes darted in search of the branch that had knocked her to the ground. Charlotte attempted to roll over and pull herself back up. But she was stopped by a pair of hands.

An excruciating squeeze to her shoulders pushed her into the dirt. Charlotte released a piercing scream but was quickly silenced when a hand covered her mouth.

A heavy body pounced on top of her. Pressed her face into the ground.

"Stop!" Charlotte attempted to yell before being muffled by the soil.

"You're coming with me," a deep, trembling voice sputtered in her ear.

"The hell I am!" she barked.

The assailant grabbed a chunk of her hair, pulling her face out of the dirt.

"What did you just say to me?" he growled.

She choked, spitting a mouthful of soil onto the ground. "I said I'm not going with—"

He shoved her face into the dirt. Charlotte reached back, struggling to jab him with her elbow. He didn't budge.

Her passageways constricted as she gasped for air. Particles of dirt invaded the sparse streams of oxygen trickling down her throat. Charlotte felt herself fading to black. Just when she thought she might pass out, the man grabbed her arm, forcing her to stand.

"Go," he spat. *"Move!"*

He shoved her up the terrain toward the parking lot. Charlotte's slim wrists were bound behind her back, held together within his tight grip.

You have got to get away from this man. He is going to kill you. Fight!

Her head swiveled when a family climbed inside a nearby car. The attacker's grasp tightened.

"Don't even *think* about calling for help. Try it and I'll snap your neck right here on the spot."

The sobering threat dampened Charlotte's will to fight. A scream crept up her throat, but she suppressed it. She had no doubt this man would not only kill her but that innocent family, too, if she resisted. She swallowed, craning her neck to get a better look at the assailant. His baggy black clothing and dirt bike mask made it nearly impossible. The only two things Charlotte could make out were his tall frame and dark, dead eyes.

"You won't get away with this," she uttered. "Do you realize who I am?"

He emitted a sinister chuckle. "Of course I do. You're Sergeant Charlotte Bowman."

A burst of fear detonated inside her chest. Charlotte's knees buckled underneath the weight of him speaking her name. She almost fell to the ground before he yanked her back up.

"*Walk!* Don't make this harder than it has to be."

Tears of anger burned Charlotte's eyes. She knew better. Her guard should've been up. But stress and fatigue had gotten the best of her. Charlotte had naively shown up at the crime scene alone, thinking the visit would be just as uneventful as all the others, despite the numerous threats she'd been receiving.

The harassment had begun the moment she was promoted to sergeant and revved up once she took over the serial killer case. Suspicions of her fellow law enforcement officers swirled in the back of her mind. But now Charlotte realized she could've been wrong. Maybe it had been the suspect she was after threatening her all along.

Just as the assailant dragged her toward the middle of the parking lot, a little girl hopped out of a car.

"Mommy! I left my bucket down by the water!"

"Isabella!" a woman yelled, running after her. "Come back here!"

"Get down!" Charlotte's attacker hissed, forcing her to duck behind a pickup truck. Before Charlotte could bend over, the woman turned in their direction.

"Ma'am?" she called out. "Are you okay?"

"Shut your mouth!" the suspect insisted.

A man climbed out of the car. His eyes darted back and forth between Charlotte and her assailant. "What's going on here? Miss, do you need some help?"

The assailant pushed Charlotte to the ground and ran off. The couple charged toward her.

"Kurt," the woman yelled. "Call 9-1-1!" She helped Charlotte to her feet. "We'll stay with you until the authorities get here."

"Thank you," Charlotte panted, too overwhelmed to tell the woman that she herself was law enforcement.

Chapter One

Miles slammed his laptop shut and glanced down at his watch. It was almost seven o'clock. He grabbed his cell phone and texted his mother, letting her know he'd be late for their family dinner.

Just as he hit the send button, the phone rang. The call was coming from a Nevada area code. He didn't recognize the number but picked up anyway.

"Hello?"

"Hi. Um—Officer Love?"

The woman's soft voice sounded somewhat familiar. "It's Detective Love, actually. I was recently promoted. May I ask who I'm speaking to?"

"Oh. Congratulations on the promotion. This is Charlotte. Charlotte Bowman."

The phone almost slipped from his hand.

"Char-*Charlotte*? Hey…hi—hello," he stammered, his chest tightening. "What a surprise. How are you?"

"I'm okay. I could be better. Which is why I'm calling you."

Miles paused, his skin prickling with curiosity as he thought back on the moment they'd met.

The pair crossed paths a few years ago at the Southwestern Law Enforcement Education and Technology Conference.

Charlotte was attending on behalf of River Valley PD. They were partnered up during a combative suspect training session, and the energy between them was magnetic. Miles could still remember the shivers of excitement that shot through his body when Charlotte spun him around, patted him down and placed him in handcuffs.

That partnership led to dinner later that evening, which led to a nightcap in her hotel room and, ultimately, the pair making love. Afterward, Miles found out that Charlotte was recently divorced. She wasn't ready for a relationship. Once the conference ended, so did their brief yet passionate tryst.

Upon returning to Clemmington, Miles found himself pining after Charlotte. He couldn't get her off his mind. But he'd resisted the urge to contact her and they never spoke again. Until now.

"I'm shocked to hear from you," he said.

"I know. A lot of time has passed. And a lot has changed in my life since we met."

She hesitated. Miles held his breath, eager to hear where this conversation was going.

"Plus," she continued after several beats, "I need you."

He shot straight up in his chair. "You need me? Why? What's going on?"

"I don't know if you've heard, but we've got a serial killer on the loose in Nevada. His last two murders occurred right here in River Valley."

"Oh, wow. No, I hadn't heard. We'd been busy here working to catch that California serial killer who attacked my sister, Lena."

"Yeah, I read about that. I'm so sorry, Miles. But good on Lena for putting up an amazing fight. And congratulations to your entire family on the arrest. You were a pretty integral part of that takedown, weren't you?"

"Thank you. And yes, I was."

Miles stood up and walked over to the window. Fall was approaching, and the black oak tree leaves were already turning a deep reddish orange. The park district's decorating committee had propped their giant scarecrow near the wrought iron entryway gates. Faux jumbo pumpkins and square bales of hay had been scattered throughout the lawn.

His gaze drifted toward a family heading to the playground, lovingly holding hands. A deep longing twitched inside his chest. He quickly turned away. "So, you mentioned something about needing me?"

"Yes. I did. I was recently promoted to sergeant, and—"

"Wait, you were? To *sergeant*? That is huge, Charlotte. Congratulations are in order to you, too."

"Thank you. But you know how the saying goes. 'To whom much is given, much is expected.' Shortly after I was promoted, this serial killer case landed on my desk. And honestly, I feel like I'm in over my head. Since you just went through a similar investigation, I was hoping you could lend me your expertise. Maybe develop a partnership of sorts."

A flurry of emotions hit, sending Miles back down into his chair. Partnering up with Charlotte would mean reconnecting, talking on a regular basis, possibly meeting in person…

"I was hoping you'd consider flying out to River Valley and spending some time here in town," Charlotte continued. "If you can, of course. You're probably swamped after being promoted—"

"I'm not, actually," Miles interjected faster than he'd intended. "I mean, things have slowed down quite a bit since the big arrest. Now that summer's come to an end, it's pretty dead around the station. So…"

"*So*, does that mean you'd be willing to come on board with me and help catch this killer? I've already gotten the approval from my chief."

Miles paused. Charlotte could have consulted with an expert whose primary focus was serial killers. Yet she'd chosen him.

A wave of exhilaration swelled in his chest.

Could this be about more than just business?

"Of course I'll come on board with you," he blurted out before squeezing his eyes shut.

Slow down. She already hurt you once. Don't leave yourself open for it to happen again.

Instead of lamenting over his zealous reaction, Miles scooted closer to the desk and pulled out a notebook. "Tell me about the suspect. What do you know about him so far?"

"He's very similar to the serial killer you just arrested. Organized, premeditated and mission oriented. But the difference is he's murdering young women *and* men. The victims are athletic, professional, and seem to go missing during nights out on the town. But a number of days will go by between the time they disappear and the time they're found."

"What's the main cause of death? Shooting? Stabbing? Strangulation?"

"That's what we're trying to figure out. There's been no trauma to the bodies. So we're thinking that they've been poisoned with an undetectable substance. But here's where things get strange. All of the victims have been found near bodies of water. And there's a number carved into one of their cheeks. In every case, that figure has equaled the number of days between the victim going missing and their date of death."

"Damn," Miles uttered, frantically taking notes. "This guy sounds pretty twisted."

"He is. And much like your killer, there is virtually no evidence left at the crime scenes. That's been our biggest challenge." Charlotte inhaled sharply. "So, what do you think? Are you up for this?"

"Yes. I am absolutely up for this."

"Thank God," Charlotte breathed. "How soon can you get here?"

The excitement in her voice ignited a tingling that coursed through Miles's entire body.

Take it easy. Deep breath...

"First, I have to talk to my chief and the rest of the department," he said. "Make sure my absence won't be a problem."

"Is your father still the chief?"

"He is. I'm surprised you remember that."

"I remember a lot..."

Miles didn't respond immediately. Instead, he sat in silence, relishing the flirtation in her tone.

"Are you still there?" Charlotte asked.

"I'm here. Sorry. I, uh—I'm actually heading to my parents' house now for dinner. I'll run all this by my dad while I'm there and see what he says. If he's down with it, then we'll take it from there."

"And by *take it from there*, I'm hoping you mean you'll hop on a flight and meet me here in River Valley first thing in the morning."

"I don't know about all that," Miles rebutted, chuckling at her enthusiasm. "Let's start with me locking in your number and calling you as soon as I know more."

"That sounds good. I'm looking forward to hearing back from you. And hopefully working with you, Detective Love."

"Same here, Sergeant Bowman. Talk soon."

Miles disconnected the call and stared up at the ceiling, his breathing quickening at the thought of reconnecting with Charlotte.

Bring it down. Remember, it's just business...

Chapter Two

"How's the case coming along, angel?"

Charlotte looked up from her desk. Corporal Walter Kincaid, her colleague and ex-boyfriend, was hovering in her office doorway. His rumpled expression reeked of faux concern.

"Don't you mean Sergeant Bowman?" she snapped. "We talked about this, Corporal. Please show me some respect."

"My apologies, *Sergeant Bowman.* I guess I haven't shaken that adorable little pet name I gave you back when we were dating. Permission to enter?"

Charlotte cringed at the sarcastic tone in his voice. Walter's resentment toward her had been unrelenting ever since she'd been promoted.

"Sure. Come in."

She slammed her laptop shut, not wanting him to see that she'd been reading the latest article published by the *River Valley Voice* on the Numeric Serial Killer. It was scathing, just like all the others.

River Valley's most prolific serial killer in history strikes again as he continues to elude the town's bumbling police department.

Reading that felt like a swift uppercut. Charlotte and her team had been working overtime trying to capture the killer.

Nevertheless, they were failing. And the media refused to let them forget it.

Miles, please get here. Fast!

"*Hello*, earth to Charlotte," Walter said, waving his hands before plopping down into a chair. "You still with me? Looks like you drifted off into space or something."

She glared at him, wondering what she'd ever seen in the smug wise guy. Walter had been with the force for almost two years before Charlotte joined. The moment she laid eyes on the Taye Diggs doppelgänger, there was an immediate attraction. But she'd fought it. In the beginning, at least.

Charlotte had promised herself that she'd never date a coworker. But Walter's constant flirting and dry sense of humor eventually wore her down. After months of turning him away, she'd finally agreed to coffee. That mocha latte at Drip & Sip led to weekly lunches, which led to dinners and drinks, and eventually, a relationship.

But after a year of petty arguments over whose turn it was to do the dishes, to more intense jealousy and control issues, Charlotte realized that she'd made a mistake. She cut things off with Walter and never looked back.

He, however, insisted that he could change and begged for a second chance. When that didn't work, he tried partnering with her on the Numeric Serial Killer case. Charlotte turned down his offer. Walter had been on her ever since, offering up unsolicited advice on how to handle the investigation in an attempt to worm his way back into her life.

"What can I do for you, Corporal Kincaid?" she asked, flipping open a file and focusing on it rather than him.

"Why so formal? Let's not act like you and I weren't sharing the same bed almost every day of the week, and—"

"*Walter!*"

"Ahh, that's more like it. I love hearing you call me by my first name."

"Keep it up and I'll be filing a complaint against you with Chief Mitchell. Now, once again, why are you in my office?"

"*Damn* you're a hard nut to crack," Walter muttered under his breath while scrolling through his cell phone. "Speaking of which, I know you're having a tough time trying to crack this case, and the media's been eating you alive with all the negative reporting."

He's trying to get a rise out of you. Don't let him...

"Where are you going with this?" she asked.

"Just let me finish. I know you don't want my help with this case—"

"Hold on. That is not true. Help is one thing. But you asked if we could partner up on the investigation. That's a completely different scenario. Now, please continue."

The right side of Walter's neck began to pulsate. Charlotte remembered how that would happen every time he became agitated.

"I've been doing some research on the Smiley Face Killer," he said. "Have you heard of him?"

"Of course I have. And I don't think it's just a *him*. I believe those murders are being committed by a group of people who're scattered all over the United States. They've been at it since 1997."

Walter rolled his eyes. "Here you go with one of your deep dive rants..." He slid his cell across the desk. A Wikipedia article titled "*Smiley Face Murder Theory*" appeared on the screen. "Look, my point is, the Smiley Face Killer could be committing these murders here in Nevada. Think about it. All of our victims have been found near bodies of water. They all went missing days before the dates of their deaths. The cause of their deaths has been undetermined. All of that sounds like the work of the Smiley Face Killer to me."

"Thanks for the input," Charlotte said, pushing the phone back across the desk, "but I do not think this is the work of the Smiley Face Killers. First off, they only murder young men. Our suspect is murdering men and women. Secondly, their victims are usually found floating in water with smiley faces drawn somewhere nearby. Our victims have been placed on the shores with numbers carved into their cheeks, and not a smiley face in sight. Third—"

"*Okay*, okay," Walter grunted, snatching up his cell. "I get it. You think I'm wrong. What else is new? Anything to keep me from working this case with you."

The shrill ringing of her phone interrupted the conversation.

"I'll let you take that," he muttered before jumping up and heading toward the door.

It was another trait of his that Charlotte had gotten used to—him running off whenever he felt wronged or embarrassed.

She picked up her cell and answered without checking the caller ID.

"Sergeant Bowman speaking."

"Hello, Charlotte. It's Miles."

She jolted forward and gripped the arm of her chair. "Hey! Please tell me you're at the airport and on the way here."

"Umm, I'm fine. Thanks for asking. How are you?" he asked, chuckling softly.

That quiet laughter awakened a sensation in Charlotte's mind. She remembered hearing it throughout the weekend they'd spent together during the conference.

Stop it. Focus!

"I'm sorry, Miles. Glad you're well. I'm okay. But I'll be a lot better if you're calling with good news."

"And by good news, do you mean—"

"Look," Charlotte interrupted. "Will you please stop stalling and tell me what's going on!"

Walter cleared his throat. She looked up, not realizing that he was still hovering in the doorway.

"Who is that?" he whispered.

She ignored him.

"All right, all right," Miles said. "I'm calling to tell you that yes, I can get the time off and come to River Valley."

Charlotte slammed her hand against the desk. "Miles! You just made me the happiest woman in the world. Thank you, thank you, thank you!"

"Miles," Walter muttered. "Who the hell is Miles?"

"Hey, hold on a sec," Charlotte said before pulling the phone away from her ear. "Corporal Kincaid, if you have anything else to discuss with me, you'll have to table it for later."

He threw her a look of irritation before taking his time walking off.

"Okay, I'm back," she said into the phone.

"Listen, Charlotte. You don't have to thank me. I'm happy to help in any way that I can."

"I'm sure you can guess my next question. How soon can you get here?"

"This weekend. I would try and make it sooner, but I've got a few case files to close out."

"Understood. I'm just glad you're coming. Do you need help booking flights or a hotel or anything?"

"No, I've got all of that taken care of. I booked a one-way ticket there since I didn't know how long you'd need me. And I'm staying at the River Valley Inn."

"Perfect. Be sure to send me your receipts so I can have the department reimburse you. Oh, and, Miles?"

"Yes?"

"I really appreciate this. I know things between us didn't end on the highest note after we met. I could've handled the situation differently. But I was in a bad place after a really bitter divorce. So… I apologize."

"Listen, I appreciate the apology. But that's old news. Let's start over fresh and just focus on the investigation."

"Point taken. Send me your trip details when you get a chance. I'll pick you up from the airport and we'll get to work as soon as you arrive. In the meantime, if there are any new developments in the case, I will let you know. I'll send you copies of the case files, too."

"Good. That'll be helpful. Talk soon."

Charlotte disconnected the call and jetted toward Chief Mitchell's office. On the way there, Walter jumped in front of her.

"Hey, what was that phone call abo—"

"I don't have time to chat, Corporal," she interrupted, brushing past him. "I've got some big news to report to the chief."

Chapter Three

Miles followed Charlotte along the shoreline of Lake Lise. He stepped cautiously across the desert floor, careful to avoid the deep cracks nestled between gravel and sand.

He'd arrived in Nevada late that morning. Thinking back on the moment he stepped off the plane, Miles chuckled to himself, remembering how his calf muscles quivered with anticipation as he made his way through Harry Reid International Airport. When he exited the terminal and laid eyes on Charlotte, the detective was hit with a flood of emotions.

She was just as stunning now as she'd been back when they first met. The way her silky black hair framed her slender face, offsetting dimpled cheeks and piercing brown eyes. Her lips, the bottom slightly fuller than the top, shimmered in her signature pale pink gloss. When they parted, he recalled how soft they'd once felt pressed against his.

He'd greeted her with a long embrace, melting into the warmth of her body. The spark was still there, shooting up his back when her hands glided across his shoulder blades. Just as he'd inhaled the rose-scented perfume pulsating from her neck, she pulled away, rushing him off to the crime scene where the first victim's body had been found.

Miles had tried to make eye contact. Read into her gaze. See if it would reveal what her words wouldn't—that she still had feelings for him. But Charlotte wasn't having it. Her nervousness was apparent, as was her avoidance.

When he'd suggested they catch up over brunch before diving into work, just to get reacquainted and iron out any awkward kinks between them, Charlotte turned him down. She wanted to get to Lake Lise well before the sun set. During the fifty-minute drive there, she'd been all business. Miles tried to interject a little small talk in between the details of the case. But Charlotte managed to avoid discussing anything personal.

Now, as they continued along the water's edge, the conversation remained solely on the investigation.

"What many people don't realize," she said, "is that there are a number of water sources throughout Nevada. Folks think of this state as some dry, barren flatland. But there are miles of lake beds flowing between these vast mountain ranges."

"It's interesting that your suspect is leaving his victims near random bodies of water in a state known for its drylands. Is he trying to send some sort of message?"

"Well, one of my colleagues thinks the Smiley Face Killer could be behind the murders. I'm not buying into that theory. There are too many differences in the cases. But I do believe our killer may have copied that aspect of the Smiley Face Killer's modus operandi."

"Why? To try and throw you off into thinking that this could be their work?"

"Could be..."

Miles watched as Charlotte skipped over a trail of eroded gray stones. Her waist twisted, causing her slim-fitting jeans to move against her curvy hips. He pressed his fingertips against his eyes and turned away.

"Well, I have to agree with you," he said. "Between what you've told me about this case and everything I've read in the files, I highly doubt that the Smiley Face Killer is behind these murders."

"I honestly think my colleague is just trying to insert himself into this investigation any way he can. *He* may not really even believe that theory. You'll understand why I say that once you meet him."

Charlotte led Miles toward a dilapidated picnic table near the edge of a seventy-foot cliff. "Here's where River Valley's first victim's body was found. Underneath the table. Her name was Brandy Graves. Twenty-five years old. Just graduated law school. She was out with her girls, celebrating a new job. Got separated from the group and went missing for twelve days."

"I remember reading her case file. Like the other victims, she had a number carved into her cheek. Eleven, if I recall correctly." Miles slowed down as they approached the table. Only two of its splintered legs were still standing. Both benches on either side were lopsided like a seesaw. "And what about the cause of death? You mentioned that there was no trauma to the bodies."

"Right." Charlotte sighed. "Which makes this case that much more complicated. There's been no viable evidence left at the crime scenes, and no obvious causes of death."

"So what are you and the medical examiner thinking? Poisoning, maybe?"

"Definitely. We're still waiting on the toxicology reports to come back. But succinylcholine is a possibility."

"Ahh, the popular muscle relaxant, better known as sux," Miles said. "That makes sense. It can cause respiratory paralysis if too much is administered, which will quickly lead to death. Plus, sux oftentimes goes undetected during autopsies."

He pulled out his cell phone and snapped several photos of the scene, then began shooting videos of the surrounding area. The camera caught a glimpse of Charlotte, watching him intently. When Miles pulled the phone down, she quickly turned away.

"You all right?" he asked, the question chased by a smile.

"Yep…yeah. I'm fine. Why?"

"No reason." He shrugged, deciding against calling her out for gawking.

"Listen, I wanna check out the other crime scene in River Valley at some point. Glacier Lake, right?"

Charlotte ran her hands up and down her arms. Despite the steamy temperature, her body appeared to shiver. "Right. But, um… Miles, there are a couple of things that I didn't share with you during our initial phone call."

"I'm listening."

"I was attacked a few weeks ago."

"You were *what*?" Miles yelled so loudly that a couple walking near the shore stopped and looked their way. "Why didn't you tell me that? I would've come here sooner had I known. Who attacked you?"

Charlotte stared down at the silver bracelet on her wrist, fiddling with the geometric-shaped charms. "I don't know. He hasn't been caught yet."

"I'm so sorry." Just as Miles raised his arms to embrace her, she fell into his chest. "Were you hurt?"

"No. Just a little banged up. And shaken up, of course."

"Sure. That's to be expected. I'm glad you're okay."

The pair slowly pulled away from one another.

"And, uh, that's not all," Charlotte continued. "I've been getting harassed, too. What started off as petty little occurrences turned into more serious threats."

"What kind of threats?"

"My car being keyed, tires being punctured, strange text messages, emails and phone calls. That type of thing. I've felt like I'm being followed, too. So, with all that happening, plus juggling my promotion and this investigation, I'm in over my head. Which is another reason why I called you here."

The look of fear in Charlotte's distant gaze sent a streak of anger through Miles.

"You already know I'm gonna do all that I can to protect you. And I'm assuming you've already reported this to the department."

"I have. But, honestly? I don't know if anyone's taking it seriously. Chief Mitchell is so focused on solving this case that I think he's let that investigation slip through the cracks. Unintentionally, of course."

"Do you have any idea who might be behind the threats?"

Charlotte expelled an exasperated sigh. "I'm thinking it could be the killer, or a jealous colleague."

"Or it could be both."

She nodded, staring out at the rippling blue water. "I've thought about that, too. That's where you come in. I need an unbiased person by my side to help figure it all out. Someone who I know will have my back."

"You already know I'll be holding you down every step of the way." Miles paused, inching closer toward her. "Can I ask you something?"

"Of course."

"Is this investigation the only reason why you called me here?"

Charlotte's lips parted, but she remained silent. Every muscle in Miles's face tensed as he stared her down.

"In all honesty," she said, "yes. If anything, I resisted at first because of our personal history, but ultimately the job is more important than that, and we're both adults."

The swell of hope that had been pounding inside his chest plummeted to the soles of his feet.

"But, full disclosure?" she continued.

"Yes. Please."

"Being in your presence again has brought back emotions that I didn't expect to feel. And... I don't quite know how to process that."

Here it is. Your second chance...

Miles took Charlotte's hand in his. Her fingers remained limp within his grasp.

"However," she began, "with that being said, I think we should keep things professional. I've gotta stay focused. As River Valley's new sergeant, not to mention first female sergeant, I can't make any missteps. The entire department is looking to me to solve this case, right along with the media and these victims' families. So, the heat is on. I've got my work cut out for me and cannot afford any distractions."

"Oh, so I'm a distraction?"

"You know what I mean, Miles. Plus, I already made the mistake of dating a coworker. That ended in disaster. Now that you and I have partnered up, I don't want history to repeat itself."

"Okay, so I'm a distraction *and* a mistake in the making. Wow." His arms fell by his sides. "This is taking me right back to when we first met. But I get it. I guess..."

Charlotte stood there silently, which Miles took to mean that the conversation was over.

"Are we done here?" he asked.

"Please tell me you're not upset."

"Upset? No. I'm just keeping it professional, per your request."

"Touché. Okay then, why don't you let me treat you to lunch, then we'll stop by the police station so you can meet the team?"

"Sounds like a plan," Miles conceded, his gait heavy with disappointment as he followed Charlotte back to the car.

Chapter Four

Charlotte and Miles walked side by side through the police station's parking lot. She peered at him from the corners of her eyes, thinking the same thoughts she'd had throughout lunch—that he had somehow grown even more handsome over the years. His dark, close-cut, wavy hair appeared thicker. His well-defined features and reddish-brown complexion were flawless, as was his toned, trim physique.

"Ready for me to meet all of your comrades?" Miles asked.

"Yep," Charlotte chirped despite feeling somewhat reluctant. "Let's do it."

The moment they entered the station, she made a beeline toward Chief Mitchell's office. Charlotte could feel everyone's eyes on them. But no one's glare was more penetrating than Walter's.

He'd been standing near the reception desk when they walked in. She held her head high and hurried past, acting as if she hadn't seen him.

Please don't try and pull a stop and chat, she'd thought. Luckily, he didn't.

During their lunch at The Capital Grille, Charlotte told Miles about her relationship with Walter. He appeared to lose his appetite, picking over his salmon Caesar salad while questioning whether she'd been in love with him. The question took Charlotte by surprise. She'd danced around a clear response.

"We, um…we were pretty close."

"Was he angry when you broke up with him?"

She hesitated, then slowly nodded. "He was."

"Is he trying to win you back?"

"He is."

"Okay, well, I guess that solves the mystery of who's been threatening you."

She didn't like to jump to the conclusion that it was Walter, but the thought had crossed her mind.

"Whoever it is, my hope is that we'll catch him soon," Charlotte said before quickly changing the subject.

And now, as the pair walked through the station, she prayed that Walter wouldn't approach them.

Miles took his time while trailing behind her, casually glancing around the department. His eyes danced inquisitively as he checked out his surroundings.

Charlotte, however, saw right through his doe-eyed curiosity. She knew he was trying to figure out which officer she'd dated.

When Walter came sauntering toward them, she held her breath, bracing herself for an awkward exchange.

"I see we've got an unfamiliar face around here," Walter said just as Chief Mitchell exited the break room.

"Hey, Chief!" Charlotte yelled, waving him down.

Chief Mitchell jumped back so abruptly that he spilled hot coffee on his hand.

"Dammit, Charlotte! You scared me. What is going on?"

She grabbed Miles's arm and pulled him toward her boss. "My apologies. Can we please go to your office and talk? *Now?*"

Miles snorted, leaning into her ear. "I've gotta meet Walter at some point. No better time than the present, right?"

"Wrong," she hissed under her breath.

Chief Mitchell's rotund belly jiggled as he charged back inside the break room and grabbed a stack of napkins. "I've only got time for a quick chat. I have a call with the medical examiner's office in fifteen minutes." He did a double take. "Is this the detective from Clemmington you were tell—"

"I'll tell you all about it in your office," Charlotte interrupted while herding the men down the hallway. The moment they stepped inside the chief's office, she closed the door so fast that it clipped the back of Miles's shoes.

"Sorry," she muttered. "Chief Mitchell, this is Detective Miles Love. And yes, he is the investigator I've been telling you about who works for Clemmington PD. Detective Love, meet Chief Mitchell."

Miles shook his hand. "It's nice to meet you, sir. Thank you for allowing me to assist in this case."

"Thank you for being here. That was great work you and your family did back in California, catching the maniac committing all those twisted murders. Please, have a seat."

"I appreciate that. I think the case of the heart-shaped murders might be the one to send my father into retirement. Which wouldn't be a bad thing considering my mother's been wanting him to turn in his badge for the past couple of years."

"Tell her to join the club. My wife's been begging me to retire for the past *ten* years. But…" The chief's voice trailed off as he glanced around his spacious yet cluttered office. Stacks of cardboard boxes filled with old case files lined the walls. His worn cherrywood desk had been there since the day he started, right along with the tattered, mismatched chairs surrounding it. "I'm not ready to trade all this in. Not yet. But anyway, enough about me. What's the game plan between you two?"

"Well," Charlotte said, "I've spent the afternoon catching Miles up on all the case details. We visited the crime scene out at Lake Lise, and he took plenty of photos and notes. We're planning to review the autopsy reports of the murder victims and see if anything jumps out at Miles that the department may have overlooked."

"That sounds like a good place to start," the chief said just as someone knocked on the door.

"Uh-oh," Charlotte muttered, already knowing who it was.

Walter cracked open the door and stuck his head inside. Chief Mitchell continued talking while he stood in the doorway with his mouth hanging open.

"The medical examiner is supposed to have the toxicology results back on Brad Ellington and Brandy Graves this afternoon. I'm curious to find out what'll show up, if anything. Sergeant Bowman, you should join me on that call. Detective Love, would you like to sit in on it as well?"

"I'd love to. Thanks."

"Chief," Walter interjected, "that sounds like it'll be an interesting discussion. Would you mind if I sit in on it as well?"

Chief Mitchell turned to Charlotte. "Sergeant? This is your case, so it's your call. Did you change your mind about partnering up with Corporal Kincaid?"

Oh, hell no, she almost blurted out. "No, I did not," she replied instead. "And now that Detective Love is here to assist in the investigation, I don't think it's necessary for Corporal Kincaid to be a part of the conversation with the medical examiner. I'd prefer to limit the participants."

"Humph," Walter grunted before stepping inside the office. "Well, since things have been somewhat quiet around the station, I've been reviewing the case files. I was thinking that maybe the killer's been using GHB to poison his victims."

The room fell silent.

"You know," Walter continued, "the date-rape drug?"

"We know what GHB is," Charlotte replied through tight lips. "The medical examiner tested both victims' blood and urine during the initial autopsies. There were no traces of it found in either of their systems."

"I wasn't offering up a definition for you," he shot back before pointing at Miles. "I was doing it for your friend here. Figured he may not know what I'm talking about."

Miles turned in his chair and faced Walter. "I actually discovered that GHB, better known as gamma hydroxybutyric acid, had been ruled out early on in the investigation when I reviewed the case files myself. Charlotte and I have moved on to more sophisticated drugs of choice. Succinylcholine, perhaps, or maybe even tetrahydrozoline. Could even be propofol."

Walter shoved his hands inside his pockets while looking down his nose at the detective.

"Have you heard of those drugs, Corporal?" Chief Mitchell asked.

"Uhh, I believe I may have—"

"Are you aware of the effects they'd have on the human body if administered improperly?"

"I, umm… Actually, no, sir."

The chief glanced down at the silver watch clinging to his chubby wrist. "I'll tell you what. Why don't you go study up on those drugs while Sergeant Bowman, Detective Love and I handle the call with the medical examiner?"

Walter hesitated, his eyes narrowing while glaring at Charlotte and Miles. "Yes, sir," he finally said through clenched teeth that sent his temples pulsating. His anger was palpable as he shuffled into the hallway.

"Nice meeting you!" Miles called out.

Walter responded by slamming the door behind him.

"Looks like somebody's feelings are hurt," Chief Mitchell said.

Charlotte had already revealed her past with Miles to the chief so everything was aboveboard, and he'd said he trusted her judgment. So rather than address his comment, she pulled out her notebook and opened it to a blank page. "Oh, well. Let's get down to business, shall we?" she suggested right before the chief's phone rang.

"Here we go." He tapped the speakerphone button. "Chief Mitchell speaking."

"Good afternoon, Chief Mitchell. This is Dr. Peterson."

"Hey, Doc. I've got Sergeant Bowman and Detective Love from Clemmington, California, here with me. What have you got for us?"

"Nothing new, unfortunately. There were no positive results in Ms. Graves's and Mr. Ellington's toxicology report."

Charlotte slid her chair closer to the desk. "Hello, Dr. Peterson. So there didn't appear to be any drugs in either of the victims' systems?"

"So far, no. And that was after we analyzed their blood, urine, hair, sweat and saliva."

"Dr. Peterson, this is Detective Love speaking. Is there a more extensive analysis you could administer that would pick up traces of drugs this test may have missed? Such as succinylcholine and tetrahydrozoline, for example?"

"There is, actually. I can go back in and perform a spinal tap, then collect fluid from the victims. Hopefully that'll identify and diagnose the exact cause of death. Problem is, drugs like succinylcholine and tetrahydrozoline don't stay in the system very long, which can make them difficult to detect. But we'll see what the test results reveal."

Chief Mitchell gave Charlotte and Miles a thumbs-up. "Sounds good, Doc. How long do you think it'll take to get those results back?"

"Well, in some cases, I can tell the cause of death right away depending on what comes back. But it usually takes at least forty-eight hours to get the full results."

"Please keep us posted," the chief said.

"I certainly will. As soon as I know more, I'll give you a call."

Disappointment churned inside Charlotte's stomach. She'd hoped the results would offer up some sort of information that would bring them one step closer to solving the case.

And getting this killer off my trail...

Miles slid his chair toward hers, as if sensing her distress. "In the meantime," he said, "Sergeant Bowman and I will analyze the crime scene at Glacier Lake, continue reviewing the case files and maybe visit some of the places the victims were last seen before they went missing."

"Good idea," Chief Mitchell told them. He pushed his silver bifocals toward the tip of his nose, staring at them over the rim. "While you two are at it, Sergeant Bowman, be sure to show Detective Love around River Valley so that he can get a sense of the town. Let him see some sights. Try some of our great restaurants." He pointed at Miles. "Bowman's been through a lot with this investigation. I don't want her to overdo it. And while the department is working to protect her, I'm glad you're here. There's no harm in having an extra set of eyes on my sergeant."

Miles wrapped his arm around the back of her chair. "Trust me. I will do all that I can to keep her safe."

The chief reached inside his drawer, pulled out an envelope and slid it in front of Charlotte.

"What's this?" she asked.

"A gift card to Havana's Bistro. I've been holding on to it since my birthday. Why don't you two take it and go have dinner there? Decompress over a couple of marinated steaks. Or chicken breasts baked in plantain leaves. And you've gotta try their vanilla cream caramel flan." He sat back and licked his lips. "Ooh, now I'm getting hungry. Maybe I should keep that—"

Charlotte snatched the gift card off the desk. "Don't even think about it!"

The chief stood and chuckled, pulling his cracked black leather belt over his belly. "Fine. Take it. Is there anything else you two need to discuss before I go outside for a quick smoke break?"

"Smoke break," Charlotte rebutted. "I thought you quit. Does Mrs. Mitchell know you're smoking again?"

"No, she does not. And I'd like to keep it that way. Now stop acting like the feds and get out of my office before I take back my gift card."

"Thanks, *Chief,*" Charlotte said fondly. He'd always been like a father figure to her, looking out for her when she needed it the most. For that, she would always be grateful.

"It was great meeting you, Chief Mitchell," Miles said.

"Likewise. If you two discover anything new, no matter how small, be sure to let me know. We have got to get this bastard off the street before he takes another life."

"Will do, sir."

Charlotte led Miles to her office. "Ready to look over these files and see what we can find—"

She paused when Walter came running up from behind.

"So how did the call with the medical examiner go?" he panted.

"It went well," Charlotte responded, her tone as dry as the Sahara. "Miles, would you like a bottle of water or cup of coffee before we get started?"

"I'm good for now. Thanks."

Walter hovered in the doorway, eagerly tapping his foot. "Oh, were you going to the break room? Because I can walk with you. I'd love a cup of—"

"Detective Love and I are about to get to work. So, no. I'm not going to the break room."

Walter pointed in Miles's direction. "You got the whole

office buzzing about you, man. Is it even legal for a California law enforcement officer to be working a case here in Nevada?"

The detective turned to Charlotte. "Do you wanna take this one? Or should I?"

"Be my guest," she replied, her lips curling into a mischievous grin.

"Thank you. Corporal Kincaid, according to the California-Nevada Compact for Jurisdiction on Interstate Waters, law enforcement officers in both California and Nevada are allowed to arrest suspects who've committed crimes on Lake Tahoe and Topaz Lake."

Walter's head tilted as he side-eyed Miles. "Really? Huh… and, uh—where did you get this information?"

"From the Nevada State Legislature," Charlotte responded coolly. "Title 14, Chapter 171." She could sense the defeat drifting off Walter's heaving chest. *Finish him*, she thought as Miles continued.

"And I'm not sure just how much you know about this case, Corporal, but the Numeric Serial Killer's first victim was found on the shore of Lake Tahoe."

Walter snorted loudly. "Yeah, I know. Wanda Osborne. I could never forget her story."

"That is incorrect. It was actually a man named William Oglesby."

"And on that note," Charlotte said, sauntering toward the door, "Detective Love and I need to get to work. Did you have any other questions, Corporal Kincaid?"

He rocked back on his heels, posturing as if he wanted to say more. She didn't give him the chance.

"Enjoy the rest of your afternoon," Charlotte told him before closing the door.

"That's cold," Miles said, bursting out laughing.

"Trust me. It's well deserved." She pulled several folders

from her drawer and placed them in front of Miles. "Ready to get started?"

"I am. But now Chief Mitchell has me fiending for some chicken and marinated steak."

"Work now, eat later." Charlotte cracked open her laptop. "Now let's get to it."

Chapter Five

Charlotte pulled in front of the River Valley Inn. "I am absolutely stuffed. You should've stopped me at the chargrilled skirt steak and Latin fries. But *nooo*. You just sat there and watched me run wild with the sweet potato pudding!"

"At least give me credit for stopping you at one mojito since you're driving. But as for the meal? No. You deserve to indulge. I remember how strict you are with your diet. Organic this, keto that. Live a little. You look great. A comforting meal every once in a while isn't gonna hurt you," Miles insisted before glancing at his watch.

"Why do you keep checking the time? Is there somewhere you need to be?"

"No. I'm concerned about you driving home by yourself this late."

"This late? It's not even nine o'clock yet."

"I know. But it's pitch-black out here. You have to drive through some pretty deserted areas to get home, don't you?"

"I do. However, I've driven these roads thousands of times. And my house is only fifteen minutes away. I'll be fine."

"Are you sure?"

"I'm positive. Plus, did you forget that I am a River Valley police sergeant?" Charlotte patted her purse. "And I'm carrying a loaded Glock 22?"

"No, I didn't. But did *you* forget that a serial killer is running around town who we suspect may have attacked you? Not to mention those threats you've been receiving."

"Of course I haven't forgotten. But what do you want me to do? Stay here and spend the night with you?"

Miles threw her a sly grin.

"Okay now!" She swatted his arm. "You know I didn't mean it like that."

"Look, I'm going to get a rental car tomorrow. I don't like the idea of you driving me around, then dropping me off and going home alone."

"Suit yourself."

Charlotte stared out the window. Aside from the dim yellow light shining down on the two-story inn's white brick exterior, the surrounding area was eerily dark. But knowing Miles was in town made her feel safe. News of his presence would spread. Everyone in the department already knew he was here. So if she were being harassed by a jealous colleague, Charlotte expected the threats to cease.

"I'll tell you what," Miles said. "Why don't you pick me up in the morning, we'll go have breakfast, then head to the rental car company? Tonight will be the last time you play chauffeur. It should be the other way around."

Charlotte thought back on her days of dating Walter. She'd driven them everywhere the majority of the time. He would blame wanting to ride shotgun on a bad right knee, never caring about her being behind the wheel alone late at night. She had eventually caught on to his motive—wanting to indulge in limitless cocktails.

"Thank you, Miles. I appreciate that. Pick you up at seven?"

"Sounds good. See you then. And be careful. Call me as soon as you get home."

"Yes, Dad," she joked.

Miles planted a lingering kiss on Charlotte's cheek. A rush of air seeped through her parted lips. She closed her eyes, taking in the feel of his soft, warm lips.

"Don't forget to let me know you made it in," he said before climbing out.

Charlotte watched as he headed inside. His sexy, athletic swagger had her tingling in places that she shouldn't.

Girl, go home!

Instead of following her command, she continued to sit there, ogling Miles. Right before entering the lobby, he turned and waved, then gestured for her to get moving.

"The shower will be running cold tonight," she muttered before driving off.

Dense layers of fog rolled across her windshield. Charlotte switched on the bright lights and made a right turn onto Peak Avenue. She glanced over at the empty passenger seat, already feeling the void of Miles's absence.

The urge to call him suddenly hit. Charlotte shook it off. He was already worried that she was alone. No need to exacerbate his concern. But that wasn't the only reason. She also didn't want to appear clingy.

Charlotte switched on the satellite radio and hit channel 104. A classic Steve Harvey stand-up routine was playing. She turned up the volume, sinking into her seat as the jokes put her mind at ease.

Until a pair of headlights flashed erratically behind her.

Charlotte's head swiveled back and forth between the rearview and side-view mirrors. The billowing smog prevented her from getting a good look at the vehicle.

"Can you please get off my bumper!" she yelled, as if the driver could hear her.

The car sped up, now inches away from hers. It swerved wildly from right to left. The headlights continued to flash. Then its piercing horn blew erratically.

"What in the hell are you doing?" Charlotte screamed, tightening her grip on the wheel.

The vehicle darted over into the left lane, despite it being a two-way street. Its engine roared as the car picked up speed, quickly catching up to Charlotte.

They rode side by side. She slowed, and it slowed, so she pressed down on the accelerator while struggling not to run off the road. Charlotte reached for her phone to call Miles. But it was inside her purse, which had flown into the back seat. She contemplated lunging for it, remembering she'd yet to sync the cell with the car's Bluetooth, then reconsidered. One wrong move and she'd veer off into the desert, ending up blinded by a flurry of sand.

The car crept closer to Charlotte's. She screamed, jerking her vehicle away from the assailant's. She skidded over the edge of the desert. A blanket of gravel enveloped her sedan. She veered back and forth, the steering wheel taking on a life of its own. The passenger side of her car rode the shoulder. The attacker's vehicle was inches away from the driver's side. He had her hemmed in. A collision was looming, unless she drove farther into the pitch-black desert.

Charlotte slammed on her brakes. The assailant zoomed down the road. She spun out of the sand and hit the accelerator, driving off in the opposite direction.

Within seconds, the assailant made a U-turn. Then suddenly, the road became crowded. Headlights flashed everywhere. Charlotte grew disoriented. But the one thing she could still make out was her attacker, back on her tail.

Charlotte sped up, weaving through the traffic until the road cleared.

"Please tell me I lost him. *Please* tell me I lost him…"

One glance in the rearview mirror proved that she hadn't. Whoever was chasing her came up the rear, then pulled up on the side. He veered toward her in yet another attempt to run her off the road. She sensed the move coming and swerved to the right, barely avoiding a collision.

I should've listened to Miles. I should not have driven home alone...

But it was too late for regrets. Charlotte had to save herself.

An eighteen-wheeler came racing down the street, heading straight toward the assailant's car. Its booming horn blared into the foggy night air.

Charlotte's attacker slammed on his accelerator, almost crashing into her.

"Get away from me!" she screamed, wiping a sheet of sweat from her forehead.

The car rammed into her bumper. Charlotte jolted forward, her head banging against the steering wheel. She moaned, sitting up slowly. Through her muddled vision, she saw the driver pull up next to her.

Find your gun! Shoot him!

A flash of silver shone off the passenger seat. Charlotte's Glock 22 must've fallen from her purse. She grabbed it and rolled down the window. Stuck her arm out and pointed the gun at the car.

The driver slammed on his brakes. He lost control and spun out in the middle of the street.

Pop!

"Good!" Charlotte yelled, hoping he'd blown out a tire. She pulled over and scrambled for her cell phone, her fingers trembling as she dialed 9-1-1.

"Nine-one-one, what is your emergency?"

"Cindy! It's Sergeant Bowman. Listen, I am on Peak Avenue near the corner of Willow and Circle Drive. Send backup. Now! I'm being chased by some lunatic."

"I'm calling for backup right now, Sergeant. Stay on the line with me. Is the assailant actively chasing you?"

"No. I pulled my gun on him and he lost control of his

car. Got stuck in the middle of the road. I don't want to try and apprehend him alone, because if he's our Numeric Serial Killer, he may be heavily armed. But I'll have eyes on him until the rest of law enforcement gets here."

"Ten-four, Sergeant. Help is on the way."

Charlotte peered into the side-view mirror. Her attacker was gone.

"Wait," she uttered. "Where'd he go? Where did he go!"

She stumbled out of the car and stared down the street. It was empty.

"Dammit!"

"What's happening now, Sergeant Bowman?"

"My assailant! He…he got away. But…*how*? He'd lost control of his vehicle and blew out a tire, and…" Charlotte fell against the door, her legs weak with frustration.

"Did you get a look at the vehicle?" Cindy asked. "Or the license plate?"

"No. It's too dark and foggy out here. It looked like a dark sedan, but that's all I could make out."

"I've still got law enforcement heading your way. How are you doing? Do you need medical attention?"

Charlotte gritted her teeth and flung open her door, falling into the seat. "No. I'm okay. Tell the officers they don't have to come out here. There's no need. The man is gone."

"Well, should I at least send someone to escort you home? What if he heads back that way and finds that you're still out there?"

"He won't."

"How do you know?"

"Because he got a good look at my Glock when I pointed it directly at his car."

"Oh," Cindy replied. "Gotcha. That'll do it."

"I'm leaving the scene now. I'll check back in with you

once I make it home, and fill out a report tomorrow. Not that it'll do any good."

"Don't get discouraged. Maybe he'll be apprehended this time. But in the meantime, be careful out there."

"I will."

Charlotte disconnected the call and dialed Miles's number. He picked up on the first ring.

"Hey," he said. "I was just thinking about you. It's been more than fifteen minutes since you dropped me off. Did you take the long way home?"

"I never made it home. Pack an overnight bag. I'm heading back to the inn to pick you up. You're staying with me tonight. If you don't mind," she quickly added.

There was a long pause on the other end of the phone.

"Do you mind?" Charlotte asked.

"No. Of course not. I just— This is so unexpected, that's all. What happened to make you want me to stay the night?"

"It's a long story. I'll explain everything when I get there."

Chapter Six

Miles sat at Charlotte's white marble kitchen island, watching as she cleared their plates.

"I would've been happy to take you out to breakfast, you know," he told her.

"I know. I wasn't in the mood to sit down at a restaurant and be seen in public. But thank you for offering. And for staying here with me last night. I really appreciate it."

"You don't have to thank me. That's why I'm here. To help you in any way I can. So if it means getting homemade scrambled cheese eggs, extra crispy turkey bacon, perfectly toasted bagels and a delicious cup of cappuccino, then hey, I'm all in."

Charlotte pulled a lock of hair behind her long, delicate neck and smiled softly. "Thanks. Glad you enjoyed it."

"You're welcome. Can I help you clean up?"

"Absolutely not. Sit back and enjoy your coffee. You've done enough just by being here."

Miles reclined against the back of his gray suede stool, watching Charlotte as she fluttered about the kitchen. She could be so tough, yet she had a gentle way about her that he found extremely appealing. The way her slender fingers wrapped around the glasses, and her lithe legs moved gracefully as she went back and forth between the island and the sink. Not to mention the sweet scent of her vanilla and lavender lotion wafting through the air.

Charlotte's three-story townhome was glamorous yet homey with its plush neutral furnishings, fur rugs and colorful abstract artwork. Framed photographs of her family and friends were scattered around the house, as were exotic souvenirs she'd collected while vacationing over the years.

I could get used to this, Miles thought as he plucked a grape from a midnight blue Murano glass bowl.

"A memento from Venice," she'd said earlier when he mentioned the dish's beauty.

Being in Charlotte's presence made him realize that his feelings for her never waned. If anything, they were even stronger this time around.

When she bent down to pick up a napkin that had fallen to the floor, Charlotte's pink romper rose toward the top of her thighs. Miles turned away, knowing that if he kept looking, something of his might rise as well.

Her phone pinged. She hopped up and tapped the screen, then burst out laughing.

"What's so funny?"

She handed him the phone. "Check out this text message Cindy just sent me."

Char, you won't believe this. Word around the station is that Walter's pissed you brought in an outsider to assist in the serial killer investigation. So now he's planning to single-handedly make an arrest so that HE can be the hero and win you back. LOL!

Miles didn't find the message amusing. It was actually quite annoying.

"Walter is such a clown," Charlotte said.

Couldn't have said it better myself, Miles thought. But he kept the comment to himself. He didn't want to appear petty or as if he was in competition to win Charlotte back.

He set her phone on the island, drained his cup and stood. "I guess we should head to the station."

"I was thinking we could stop by Glacier Lake first. I want you to check out that crime scene. See if anything sticks out at you—"

Her cell phone pinged again.

"Ugh," Charlotte groaned. "I don't wanna hear about Walter anymore, Cindy."

She read the text, then dropped her phone. It crashed onto the island. Miles jumped at the loud thump.

"What's wrong now?" he asked. "Did Walter say something even more irritating than he did in the first message?"

Charlotte didn't utter a word. She just stood there shaking, staring at Miles through watery eyes.

He hurried around the island and wrapped his arm around her. Her skin was covered in goose bumps.

"What is going on?" he asked.

"Chief Mitchell just texted me. We've got another murder on our hands."

Miles grabbed her cell and scanned the message.

I need for you and Det. Love to get to the Hoptree River ASAP! Stephen Seymour's body was found near the shore this morning. Considering he's the district attorney's son, this is going to be a high-profile case. The media is already out there. Let me know when you're on the way.

"Oh no..." He tried to hand her the phone. She turned away.

"I can't," Charlotte murmured. "Not yet."

"I got you," Miles said before sending a response. As

he typed, Charlotte leaned into him, her body trembling against his.

"I can barely process one murder before another one is committed," she whispered into his chest.

"I know. But I'm here now. So together, we're gonna go hard and do whatever it takes to catch this bastard." He pulled away and raised her chin, staring directly into her eyes. "Come on. You're good. Take a deep breath, regroup, and let's get to the crime scene."

MILES AND CHARLOTTE walked along the shoreline of the Hoptree River. He looked out at the crisp blue water, its calm waves washing over colorful rocks and course tan sand. Lush greenery grew from the majestic cliffs bordering the lake. Docks housed sleek motorboats and jet skis. And now, yellow caution tape blocked off a good portion of the area.

The river would've normally been bustling with visitors. But instead, it was swarming with law enforcement officers.

The medical examiner stood over Stephen's body, frantically scribbling notes in a pad. Crime scene photographers took pictures of the victim. A forensic investigator slowly moved about the area, searching for evidence. Policemen stood guard over several news outlets, who'd been relegated to the back of the crime scene. Chief Mitchell was in the near distance, holding his head while talking on the phone.

"How are you feeling?" Miles asked Charlotte.

"Good. No fear. I'm in sergeant mode now, ready to take over."

"That's my girl."

Charlotte pulled a box of latex gloves and shoe covers out of her duffel bag. She and Miles slipped them on, then made a beeline toward Chief Mitchell.

"Okay," the chief said into the phone. "Again, I am so sorry for your loss, sir. My sergeant, who's heading up the investigation, just arrived on the scene. Trust me, we're doing everything we can to catch this killer. Yes, I will absolutely keep you posted. I'll be in touch soon."

The normally cool head of River Valley PD appeared pale and discombobulated. Streams of sweat ran down his temples. His jittery hands were clenching in and out of tight fists.

"Glad you two are here," he grumbled in Charlotte and Miles's direction. "That was Thomas Seymour. Stephen's father. I really feel for that man. He lost his wife to cancer a few years back, and his oldest daughter in a car accident last year. And now," he choked out, pointing over at Stephen's body, "*this.*"

"Chief Mitchell," Charlotte said, "I promise we're going to step up this investigation and catch the killer. Stephen will be our last victim. Trust me on that."

"Good. That's what I want to hear. And just so you know, the number four was carved into Stephen's left cheek."

"Had he been reported missing?" Miles asked.

"No, which is strange. His father could barely talk, so I didn't wanna ask too many questions. I figured he'd be in a better position to speak to me once a little time passes by."

"Let's hope." Charlotte ran her hand along the back of her neck as it burned under the hot sun. "I'm going to take a look at the body. Miles, can you join me?"

"Of course."

They approached the victim. Stephen's body lay peacefully in the sand, as if he'd positioned himself there to take a nap. His arms were down by his sides. His skin had turned a shade of purplish blue, while small blisters covered his legs. Stephen's white denim shorts and pale blue T-shirt were spotless. He wasn't wearing shoes, and the bottoms of his feet were completely clean.

"No bloating," Miles said. "Looks like he's only been dead about a day or so."

"I agree. There doesn't appear to be much decomposition to the body at all. Looks like somebody carefully placed him in this spot, too. My guess is that he was carried out here, hence the dirt-free feet."

The forensic investigator circled the body, studying the ground while collecting samples. "Sergeant Bowman, I've found some pretty decent evidence. There was a glass bottle and a pair of sunglasses stuck in the sand near the victim. The gravel I gathered may contain biological evidence. I'll head to the crime lab as soon as I'm done and turn everything over for testing."

"Great. Thanks, Virgil. Let's hope they can pull some DNA from it. Fingerprints, blood, sweat, saliva, *something*. Can you ask the lab director to put a rush on that analysis?"

Virgil sealed a plastic bag filled with sand. "I'm already one step ahead of you, Sarge. I called down to the lab on the way here and told the director to clear her schedule. She knows how important it is to get this case solved. So she's already expecting me."

"Awesome. Thanks."

Miles pointed over at the herd of reporters shouting questions and shoving microphones at law enforcement from behind the caution tape. "The media is in a complete frenzy."

"After word gets out about this murder, the entire town will be. I can literally feel the pressure to catch the killer closing in on me like cement walls." She turned to the medical examiner. "Dr. Peterson, thank you for getting here so quickly. Any initial thoughts on the cause of death?"

"It looks very similar to the other victims. No apparent trauma. The body is well-preserved. And there's that infamous number carved into his cheek."

"Are you thinking this victim was drugged, like the others?"

"I am."

Charlotte slipped a surgical mask over her nose and mouth and hovered over Stephen's body. "Have you performed the spinal taps on the other two victims and had their cerebrospinal fluid tested yet?"

"I have. The first round of toxicology reports came back inconclusive. So I told the lab to run them again. I'm still waiting on those results."

An earsplitting scream ricocheted through the air.

Charlotte leapt to her feet and grabbed hold of Miles, watching as a young woman charged toward them. Her curly blond ponytail flew through the air, while mascara-stained tears streaked her face.

Law enforcement stopped her just as she came crashing into the caution tape.

"Where's Stephen?" she shrieked. Where's *Stephen*?"

"Ma'am, please stand back!" one of the officers insisted.

"Should we go and find out who that is?" Miles asked Charlotte.

"Yes, we should."

The woman locked eyes with Charlotte as they approached.

"Hey! Can you *please* help me?" the woman begged. "I think that's my boyfriend over there!"

"What is your boyfriend's name?"

"Stephen. Stephen James Seymour. My cousin is a news reporter, and she just called and told me his body was found out here. Is it him? Please tell me it isn't him…"

Charlotte reached for the woman's hand. "I am so sorry."

"Stephen's *dead*?" she wailed, collapsing against Charlotte and almost knocking her down. Miles steadied them both.

"What is your name, ma'am?" he asked softly.

"Phoebe Daniels. Stephen's soon-to-be fiancée. He was my everything. *Everything.* We were gonna get married. Soon! I mean, as soon as he stopped with all the partying. That's what probably took him out, you know. The partying…"

Charlotte allowed Phoebe past the caution tape. She and Miles led her over to a nearby picnic table. Miles pulled out his notebook while Charlotte began questioning her.

"When was the last time you saw Stephen?" she asked.

"About a week ago. I begged him to stay home that night, too. But he insisted on going out with his boys."

"Do you know where they went?"

"Probably to every single bar on Rush Street."

Miles looked up from his notebook. "Where is Rush Street?"

"You must not be from around here," Phoebe said.

"He isn't," Charlotte told her before turning to Miles. "Rush Street is one of the most popular strips in downtown River Valley. It's where the majority of the town's bars and clubs are located."

"And it can get wild," Phoebe added. "Especially on a Saturday night."

"So Stephen went out with his friends last Saturday?" Miles asked.

Her eyes fell to the ground as she tapped her fingertips against her chin. "Yes. Last Saturday for sure. He left the apartment at around eight o'clock. And that was the last time I saw him—"

Her voice broke. As she sobbed into her hands, Miles leaned into Charlotte. "Last Saturday was exactly five days ago," he whispered.

She nodded and ran her hand along the left side of her face. They were on the same page. The number four that had been carved into Stephen's cheek represented the number of days between him being kidnapped and murdered.

"So it only took a day for his body to be found," she whispered. "We'll see what Dr. Peterson says once the autopsy results come in, confirming the exact date of death."

Phoebe sniffled, wiping her eyes with the neckline of her

yellow tank top. "You know, I figured Saturday would be a wild night for Stephen and his friends. Every time they get together, things get outta hand. But who knew it would lead to his death?"

"Why didn't you report him missing to the authorities?" Miles asked. "Or anyone else for that matter?"

"Because Stephen was a party boy. Everybody knew that about him, including his own family. He'd go off on binges for days without contacting any of us. I figured he'd show back up at some point, just like he always did. But not this time. Because he…he was dead!"

Charlotte patted her back. "I am so sorry, Phoebe."

"Don't be sorry. Just catch this killer!"

"We're working on it."

"Well, work harder!"

"We will," Charlotte replied calmly. "I promise. Now, can you give us the names of Stephen's friends who he was with that night?"

Phoebe stared out into the distance, her eyes bulging as her body shook. Charlotte followed her gaze. The coroner had begun swabbing Stephen's fingernails.

"I can't look at that," Phoebe said, covering her mouth as she spun around on the bench. She moaned while taking in a rush of air. *"You can do this. You can do this,"* she muttered to herself before pivoting toward Charlotte. "Okay, Stephen was out with his best friend, Hunter Stout. And Rob Lee, who's another close friend. And Josh. Josh…" Phoebe pulled out her cell phone and scrolled through the contacts. "Josh Tillman. Those are the three guys who he always hung out with. They probably met up with other people at some point, but you should start with them."

"And the bars?" Charlotte asked. "Are there any particular ones that they frequented often?"

"Absolutely. The Blue Lagoon, Eden's Den, and The Bottomless Bar. But Stephen and his friends like to barhop. So if I were you, I'd check the surveillance footage at every single spot on Rush Street."

A commotion ensued near Stephen's body. The autopsy technicians were placing him inside of a body bag.

Phoebe screamed, bolting from the table. "Wait! I wanna see him before you take him away!"

Charlotte gently clutched her arm. "Hold on, Phoebe. Calm down. Trust me, you do not want to see him like that. The best thing you can do for Stephen is stay put and answer our questions."

She slouched back down onto the bench, burying her head into the table just as Chief Mitchell approached.

"Sergeant Bowman, Detective Love, can I speak with you two? Privately?"

Charlotte patted Phoebe's shoulder. "Give us a sec, sweetie. We'll be right back."

She responded with a nod, her head still tucked away in her arm.

"Listen," the chief said once they were out of earshot, "Dr. Peterson is going to perform the autopsy on Stephen's body as soon as they get to the morgue. If there's a drug in his system that dissipates quickly, I'm hoping the rush will improve our chances of detecting it."

"Good," Charlotte said. "Are you satisfied with the amount of evidence that forensics collected?"

"I am. Are you?"

"Yes. And Virgil's already contacted the lab to ask that they put a rush on the DNA analysis. So hopefully we'll be getting some answers soon."

"That would be great," Chief Mitchell grunted, clawing at the red splotches covering his forearms.

"Here we go with the stress flare-up." Charlotte reached

inside of her duffel bag, pulled out a bottle of oat serum and handed it to him. "Here. Try some of this."

"Did my wife tell you to pack this for me?"

"She sure did. Mrs. Mitchell knows how tense you get. Especially when we visit crime scenes."

"That woman," he griped, slathering it over his skin. He nodded in Phoebe's direction. "Who's that young lady?"

"Her name is Phoebe Daniels. She's Stephen's girlfriend."

"Poor thing. Must be tough, seeing him out here like this. Was she able to provide any pertinent information?"

"She was," Miles replied. "The last time she'd seen Stephen was Saturday night, before he went to hang out with a group of friends on Rush Street."

"Humph. Interesting…"

"Miles and I are going to stop by the bars they visited and view the surveillance footage, then call the friends in for questioning."

Charlotte crossed her fingers behind her back as she spoke. She'd interviewed friends and family of the other victims, and it had never turned up any good leads. She had a feeling about this one, though, that she might find a thread….

Chief Mitchell gave them a thumbs-up. "Good plan." He wiggled the bottle of serum in the air. "I'd better hold on to this. I don't see the day getting any less stressful for me."

Footsteps pounded behind the group. Miles and Charlotte glanced over their shoulders, rolling their eyes simultaneously at the sight of Walter.

"Sorry I'm late, sir," the corporal panted while dusting sand off his navy slacks.

"Who called you here, Kincaid?" Chief Mitchell asked. "I thought I instructed you to stay back and keep an eye on things at the station."

"Well, I, uh—I figured you all could use some extra help. When the DA's son turns up dead, it's all hands on deck, right? We've gotta get this case solved. And it looks to me that the investigation is dragging, so—"

"Chief Mitchell," Charlotte interrupted, "Detective Love and I are going to head over to Rush Street now." She grabbed Miles's arm and slowly backed away. "We'll keep you posted."

"Wait, what's happening on Rush Street?" Walter asked.

"That's where my boyfriend was last seen before he went missing!" Phoebe yelled from the picnic table.

Walter stepped in front of Miles. "Sergeant Bowman, I know that area well. *Very* well. It's my stomping ground. Why don't I go with you? We can tag team the bar owners and review surveillance footage together, just like we used to."

"I've got a better idea," Miles interjected, pushing past him. "Why don't you fall back, and let us—"

"Hold on, hold on." Chief Mitchell pulled the men apart. "I've got the *best* idea. Sergeant Bowman, Detective Love, you two go on. Talk to the bar owners. View the footage. See what you can find. Corporal Kincaid, since you're here now, why don't you help me clear the crime scene?"

"But shouldn't I be a more *active* part of this investigation?" Walter huffed defiantly.

"Corporal, that's an order!" the chief barked.

Walter's eager expression crumpled into a frown as he stormed off toward the forensics team.

"What about Phoebe?" Charlotte asked Chief Mitchell.

"I'll take care of her. You two just go and get me some evidence."

Chapter Seven

Charlotte approached The Blue Lagoon's foggy glass door and glanced inside. All the lights were out. Unoccupied dark wooden chairs were pushed neatly beneath the tables. Sunlight bounced off the mirror hanging behind the bar, highlighting dusty glasses and bottles of alcohol.

"Looks like they're closed," she said to Miles. "Should we knock anyway?"

"Might as well. Maybe the manager's hiding out in the back."

She tapped on the window. No answer. She tried again, a little harder this time. Still no answer. They waited a few minutes, then moved on.

"Why don't we try The Bottomless Bar since it's just a couple of doors down," Charlotte suggested before leading the way.

The charming, old-school street, known for its redbrick road, once housed cozy diners and specialty shops. But as River Valley's tourism grew, so did the mayor's desire to collect vacationers' dollars. Bakeries and barbershops were replaced with bars, twenty-four-hour fast-food restaurants and boutique hotels. The winding Rush Street had transformed into a mini Las Vegas Strip, minus the casinos. Both Nevada residents and visitors were known to frequent the town for the water adventures, live music and cheap, well-crafted cocktails.

The Bottomless Bar's blacked-out windows and steel metal door prevented Charlotte from seeing inside. She crossed her fingers, hoping someone would answer as Miles banged on the door. After several seconds, it cracked open.

"Closed!" a deep voice croaked from the other side.

"Sir, it's Sergeant Bowman with the River Valley PD. I need to ask you a few questions. May I please come in?"

The door swung open. Charlotte jumped back at the sight of the man standing before them. He was at least six foot five, with biceps as big as thighs and a snarl that rivaled a pit bull's.

"Good afternoon, Sergeant," he boomed, rubbing his tattooed hand over his bald head. "What can I do for you?"

"Good afternoon. Detective Love and I are working a homicide investigation and need to take a look at your surveillance footage from last Saturday."

"Is this about the DA's son, Stephen? Wasn't he found floating in the middle of Lake Tahoe, butt naked and high on cocaine?"

"Where in the world did you hear all that?" Miles asked.

The man sized Miles up with a smirk that revealed his missing front teeth. "You must not be from around here. Word travels fast in this town."

"Yeah, well, it also travels incorrectly," the detective rebutted. "Nothing you just said is true."

Charlotte grabbed the edge of the door. "I'm sorry, what's your name?"

"Menace. And before you ask, yes. That's what my mama named me."

Fitting, Charlotte thought.

"Okay, Menace. Nice to meet you. May we please come in and take a look at that footage?"

He backed away slowly and held open the door. "Sure. But

I can tell you now, you won't find anything that useful. As soon as I heard Stephen was murdered, I remembered seeing him here last weekend and reviewed the footage myself. I was a private investigator before I started managing this place. Investigative work is in my blood. So I couldn't help but to check the surveillance and see what I could uncover."

Charlotte and Miles stepped inside the dark bar. Black cement walls surrounded black tile flooring. Everything was black, from the steel tables and chairs to the bar and leather stools.

The CCTV equipment was set up behind a DJ booth. The pair watched as Menace played around on the computer, double-clicking the mouse until footage of bar patrons appeared on the screen.

"So you did see Stephen here last Saturday night?" Charlotte asked.

"Yep. He got here right before midnight and wasn't around for long. But I'll tell you this. While he was here? That kid drank his ass off. And I'm not just talking beer. He and his boys were downing silver bullets for about twenty minutes straight."

"Silver bullets?" Miles asked. "What are those?"

"They're shooters, also known as mixed shots that contain gin and scotch.

"Whew!" Charlotte breathed. "I could pass out from the thought of drinking a lethal combo like that."

"Tell me about it," Menace quipped. "Don't let my burly stature fool you. I may be all brawn, but even I have my limits. And a silver bullet is where the buck stops for me. I don't know how those guys were even able to walk out of here." He paused. "Well, actually they weren't walking. They were stumbling. Especially Stephen. He went crashing into one of the windows on the way out. I thought I was gonna have to call an ambulance. But he swore he was okay and left, bloody nose and all."

"Oh, boy," Charlotte uttered, thinking about how Stephen's father would feel once he learned all of this.

"Do you have cameras set up to record the exterior of the bar?" Miles asked.

"I do. And as for the night Stephen was here, that's where the footage gets interesting. *After* they left. Just watch." Menace pointed at the screen. "Okay, here we go. Do you see Stephen? He's right there, doing shots with his boys."

Charlotte studied the group of men. "I do see him. And he looks to be dressed in the exact same outfit he was wearing when his body was found."

"Mmm," Miles muttered, "he sure is."

The pair watched as Stephen and his friends downed drinks, grabbed women and danced around wildly.

"Just so you know," Menace said, "Stephen stopped by The Blue Lagoon before he came here. So he was already pretty drunk when he walked through the door."

Charlotte pulled a thumb drive out of her bag and handed it to Menace. "Would you mind saving a copy of that footage for me?"

"No problem." He slid the device inside the USB port, then poked the monitor so hard that it almost toppled over. "Look! Here we go. Stephen and his friends are about to leave."

"Wow," Miles said. "You were right. Stephen can barely walk. He's bumping into almost everybody he passes."

"And his friends can't help him because they can barely stay on their own two feet," Charlotte added.

Menace enlarged the screen that highlighted the outside of the bar. "Now watch. Stephen and his friends are gonna cross the street and get in line at Eden's Den. Then Josh approaches the door and talks to the bouncer. He's probably asking if they can skip the line. The bouncer checks out the friends and nods. Josh signals them over."

Charlotte's eyes narrowed. "Okay, now they're all going inside." She paused. "Wait, go back."

Menace rewound the footage a few seconds. "You saw correctly. Stephen never entered the bar. Just Josh, Hunter and Rob."

"When you replay the video," Miles said, "first we see two of the friends practically carry Stephen toward the back of the line. Then they're out of frame. Josh talks to the bouncer and waves the guys over. Two of them show up. But Stephen doesn't."

"Exactly," Charlotte said. "Where did he go?"

Menace paused the tape and spun around. "That's the million-dollar question. When I watched the footage earlier, I saw that he never reappeared. He must've wandered off, then met with foul play, obviously."

"Are you sure he never came back into the frame?" Charlotte asked.

"Positive. And my guess is that the other guys were so drunk they didn't notice he wasn't with them."

"We need to talk to someone at Eden's Den," Charlotte told Miles. "Find out if anyone saw Stephen show up there at some point during the night."

"Hold on." Menace jotted something down on a napkin before handing it to her. "This is the owner of Eden's Den's number. Her name is Sasha. She should be able to help you."

Charlotte stood on her tippy toes and stared across the street. "I wonder if she's there now."

"Not yet. She drove to Vegas this morning to check out the nightclub and bar convention. She won't be back in River Valley until later tonight. But give her a call anyway. She can connect you with the manager, Bronson. He's usually around every Saturday and may have seen something that night."

Miles shook Menace's hand. "We can't thank you enough, man. You've been a huge help."

"Anytime." He pulled the thumb drive from the computer and handed it to Charlotte. "I want this killer off the street just as bad as everybody else."

"We're getting closer," Charlotte replied, following him to the front of the bar. "I can feel it."

"Good luck."

A blast of hot, dry air hit Charlotte and Miles the moment they stepped outside. They sauntered up and down the street, peering inside windows and knocking on doors. No one answered.

"Looks like the only help we're gonna get here today is from Menace," Miles said.

"Why don't we head back to the station? We can debrief with Chief Mitchell, make sure the evidence was submitted to the crime lab, and put in calls to Sasha and to Stephen's friends."

"Let's do it. The challenge will be getting all that done without being bombarded by Walter."

"One can only hope…"

CHARLOTTE HUNG UP the phone and stared across her desk at Miles. "So, Eden's Den is a dead end."

"Stephen didn't show up in any of their surveillance footage?"

"According to Bronson, no."

"Well," Miles said, "we should still take a look at the video when he sends it over."

"We definitely will. I'll have Officer Haney contact the other businesses on Rush and see if any of their cameras captured Stephen entering their establishments or walking past them."

There was a knock at the door.

"Come in!" Charlotte called out.

Virgil stuck his head inside. "Sorry to interrupt. I just saw your text. I did drop the evidence off at the lab. The director has already submitted everything for processing."

"Excellent—" Charlotte paused when she heard rubber soles screeching along the floor outside of her office.

"Excuse me," Walter said, peering over Virgil's shoulder.

Virgil ignored the interruption. "Do you need anything else on my end, Sergeant?"

"No. You're good. Thank you for everything today. Awesome work."

"Thanks. If I hear anything from the lab, I'll let you know."

He could barely make his way out of the office as Walter hovered in the doorway.

"Here we go," Miles muttered.

Walter didn't wait for an invitation before stepping inside. "What's up, Sarge?"

"How can I help you, Corporal?"

His back stiffened. "May I sit?"

Charlotte held up her hand just as he reached for a chair. "Actually, Detective Love and I are in the middle of contacting witnesses. Do you need something?"

"Do *you* need something is a better question. I overheard Chief Mitchell talking to Stephen's girlfriend, Phoebe, back at the crime scene. She mentioned a few of the friends Stephen was out with the night he went missing. Hunter, Rob and Josh? I play softball with those guys. I know 'em real well. I can get any information that you want outta them. Just as long as you reconsider partnering with me on this case."

A shooting pain exploded inside Charlotte's head. She closed her eyes, wishing there were a trapdoor in the floor for Walter to fall through.

"Listen, Corporal Kincaid," Miles said. "Sergeant Bowman has had a long day. Why don't you report back once you actually speak with Stephen's friends—"

"Excuse me," Walter interrupted, "but who are you again? And why are you even addressing me? I was talking to the sergeant of the *River Valley* Police Department. You know, the one that you have absolutely no jurisdiction over?"

"Corporal Kincaid!" Charlotte said, slamming her hand against the desk. "First of all, show some respect. Second of all, as an officer of this department, you are obligated to assist in the investigation however you can. Third of all, you cannot blackmail me into doing anything. Keep this up and I will file a formal complaint against you. Is that understood?"

Walter's frontal vein protruded from his forehead. "Whatever you say," he muttered. "You know, this promotion really changed you." Just as he turned to walk away, Chief Mitchell approached.

"Bad news," the chief said. "I just got a call from Freelain & Associates. All of Stephen's friends have lawyered up. They've refused to come in for questioning. So, time to come up with a new strategy."

"Oh," Walter breathed, his lips spreading into an arrogant smirk. "Is that so?" He wiggled a finger at Charlotte. "That changes things, now doesn't it? Let me know if you wanna partner—*oops*—I mean team up with me when I go talk to Stephen's friends."

Before Charlotte could respond, Walter strutted off.

"What was that all about?" Chief Mitchell asked. "Does Corporal Kincaid know Stephen's friends personally or something?"

"That remains to be seen, sir," Charlotte said. "In the meantime, I'll put in a call to Freelain & Associates. See if I can talk the attorneys into bringing their clients in for a chat."

Chapter Eight

"I really needed this night," Charlotte said.

Miles nodded. "Same here. Glad we decided to kick back and have some downtime."

He and Charlotte were sitting out on her spacious wraparound deck, grilling snapper and corn on the cob. She'd had a mini meltdown that afternoon when Stephen's friends refused to come in for questioning, despite her pleas to their attorneys. Miles suggested they call it a day and offered to cook her dinner. She agreed without hesitation.

Charlotte refilled their glasses of pinot grigio. "I really wish we could have talked to Stephen's friends before they lawyered up. They probably would've been a lot more open and vocal. What do they have to hide?"

"Good question. We'll find out once they agree to talk to us. If they do..."

"Can you imagine Walter making that happen before I do? We'd never hear the end of it."

Miles turned the fish, then took a long drink of wine. "Well, if he's the one to pull information out of them that'll lead us to the killer, I'm sure we can find a way to endure his boasting."

"Very true. He better not mess things up, though. What if one of the friends is connected to the killer? That testimony might get tossed if Walter gets it without their attorney present." Charlotte tapped her fingernails against her glass and stared up at the sky. The sun was setting behind stunning layers of lavender and orange clouds. "It's getting a little chilly out here. Should we light the firepit?"

"Sure. That would be nice."

She grabbed the torch lighter and tinder, then stood over the circular bronze pit, her yellow sundress blowing in the wind. The breeze pulled her dress forward, silhouetting every curve of Charlotte's shapely figure.

Look away, a voice inside Miles's head spoke a moment too late. While he was still ogling her, their eyes met. Hers danced with amusement. He'd been caught.

Miles quickly turned away, closing the grill, then switching on the deck's heat lamps. "These should help warm you up, too," he blurted, his voice cracking with embarrassment.

"They will. Thank you."

He spun around just as she reached for her chair. They collided, his shoulder brushing against her breasts. Miles grabbed her before she went tumbling to the floor.

"I'm so sorry!" he breathed, his arms wrapped around her waist. "Are you okay?"

Charlotte nodded. "I'm fine."

Her gaze traveled from his lips to his neck, down to his chest. Miles moved in closer. Ran his hands down the curve of her back and rested them on her hips. Charlotte's body pressed against his. A stirring deep in his stomach pushed him to go further. He lifted her chin. Their lips touched. Miles savored the lushness of her kiss as vanilla-flavored gloss lingered on his tongue.

Just as his hands slid down farther, the doorbell rang. Charlotte pulled away from his grasp.

"Who is that?" she panted, straightening her dress. "I'm not expecting anybody."

"I've got a surprise for you."

"You've got a what?"

"A surprise!"

Miles hurried inside the house, leaving a baffled Charlotte standing on the deck. A few moments later, he returned with someone hiding behind him.

"Who is that?" she asked.

A woman hopped out and charged toward her.

"Ella!" Charlotte screamed, embracing her sister. "When did you get to River Valley?"

"I just drove in from Reno. Came straight here after my assignment ended at Saint Mary's Hospital. They'd been short on nurses in the neonatal unit for weeks but recently brought on a few new hires. So, I've finally got some time off in between gigs."

"I am so happy to see you. You have no idea how much I need you here right now."

"I heard. A little birdie reached out and told me that you could use a little pick-me-up."

"Oh, I wonder who that could've been," Charlotte said, giving Miles a wink. "How did you manage to pull this off without me knowing?"

"Easy. I looked Ella up on Facebook and sent her a private message asking if she could come see you."

Charlotte gave his arm a gentle squeeze. "Thank you." She turned to Ella and spun her around. "You look good, girl. Your skin is glowing, your curls are luscious, your curves are curving. What's his name?"

"Now, what does me looking good have to do with a man?" Ella asked, wiggling her hips joyfully in her fitted denim dress. "Maybe I'm happy because I'm single."

"Well, if I had been dating that ex of yours, Nate, then I'd be a happy single woman, too. I was *so* glad when you two broke up."

Ella rolled her eyes. "Here we go. Number one, his name is Noel. And number two, he wasn't that bad. Just a little overbearing. And needy."

"And number three," Charlotte said, "if you add controlling and insecure, you'd be on point."

"Ha!" Ella poured herself a glass of wine and sat on the edge of a teal deck chair. "Well, none of that matters anymore. I listened to my big sis and broke things off with him—"

"*After* she found out he'd been cheating on her," Charlotte added, pointing in Miles's direction. *"She's always had bad taste in men..."*

He kept his eyes on the fish searing on the grill. "I'm staying out of this one. I do not get involved in disagreements among siblings. Including my own."

"As you should considering my sister's being overly dramatic," Ella said. "Anyway, Noel and I only dated for a few months, so it wasn't hard to move on. Now that I've dismissed The Cling-On as Charlotte used to call him, I'm happy, loving my job as a traveling nurse and enjoying an active, healthy dating life."

"Yeah, thanks to me." Charlotte began before Miles nudged her. "I pretty much orchestrated that breakup."

Miles brought the food over to the table. "Listen, why don't we give Ella a break and eat?"

"Good idea," Ella said. "Otherwise, my big sis would never let up."

As the group prepared their plates, Ella reset the conversation and threw Charlotte in the hot seat.

"So," Ella began, "enough about me, sissy poo. What's going on between you and Miles?"

Charlotte choked on a mouthful of corn while a piece of snapper fell from Miles's fork.

"What do you mean?" she asked. "We're working on this investigation together. You know that."

"Is that all you two are working on?"

"Yes," Charlotte confirmed, shooting her sister a look of death. "Now drop it, will you?"

"Okay, okay. No need to get snippy. Speaking of the investigation, what's the latest on it?"

"We're making progress," Miles said. "Slowly but surely."

"I heard about the DA's son being murdered. That was a shocker."

Charlotte set her fork down, her upbeat demeanor fading. "It was. But more evidence was recovered from that crime scene than any of the others. We're hoping something will come of it, and in the meantime, just trying to remain optimistic."

"Is that ass clown you used to date still trying to take over the case? What was his name, *Falter*?

"Wait, wait," Miles sputtered. "I almost spit out my wine. What did you call him?"

"Falter," Charlotte snorted. That's her nickname for Walter."

"It sure is. Because he was a misstep. Am I wrong?"

"Not to criticize my girl's judgment or anything," Miles said, "but no. You are not wrong at all."

"See," Ella said, "I'm not the only one in the family with a questionable dating history…"

"Listen, you two are not about to sit here and chastise me over a relationship that didn't work out. Especially when you both live in glass houses."

"Wait, why are you dragging Miles into this?" Ella asked.

"Yeah," he chimed in, clutching his chest innocently. "How did I get involved? I'm Finland. Switzerland. *Neutral* when it comes to all this drama."

"Oh, please," Charlotte snorted. "Don't sit here and play coy. I remember a few dating disasters you told me about when we first met. Remember the woman who tried to talk you into having a threesome with her and her husband? And you didn't even know she was married? Or what about the one who—"

"All right, all right." Miles waved his white napkin in the air. "I surrender. Can we please get back to Falter—I mean Walter?"

Ella cackled, pinching Charlotte's arm. "I like this guy."

"Yeah," Charlotte replied, locking eyes with Miles. "I do, too…"

His mouth went dry from her response. Rapid-fire questions flew through his mind. Had he heard her correctly? Did she just profess her feelings for him? Was it just a friend thing, or something more?

Gotta be more than friends. She did just kiss me…

Miles waited to see if she'd say more. Instead, Charlotte turned her attention back to Ella.

"As for Walter, he's as obnoxious as ever. Butting into the investigation, trying to partner up with me, trying to take it over."

"Hating on me," Miles added. "Trying to win Charlotte back…"

"Which will never happen," she quipped. "But anyway, we found out that Walter hangs out with a few of Stephen Seymour's friends. Which is weird."

"Very weird," Ella said. "Those guys are at least ten years younger than him. Can you say early midlife crisis? I'm telling you, Char, that man hasn't been right since you broke up with him. I've always thought he was the one behind those threats you've been getting. And to hear that he's connected to Stephen and his friends? That's suspicious."

"So what are you saying?" Miles asked. "That Walter might have something to do with Stephen's murder?"

"Yes," Ella confirmed while casually slathering butter on

her second ear of corn. "I am. The man is a quintessential narcissist. With a sprinkle of sociopathy on top."

Charlotte's head slowly tilted. "You know what, Ella? You may be onto something. I always suspected he could be behind the threats against me. But the murders? I didn't go that far."

"Why would you? In your mind, he's Corporal Kincaid, here to serve and protect. You'd never think to entertain the idea of him being a criminal."

"Wait, I'm still trying to digest all this," Miles said. "You two actually believe that Walter could be the Numeric Serial Killer?"

"Yes," they shot back in unison.

"Wow. Well, maybe we need to take another look at that Rush Street surveillance footage from the night Stephen went missing. See if Walter shows up on any of it. Since he said that area is his stomping ground, he may have been out there that night."

"Forget all that," Ella said. "Just go and arrest him now!"

"I wish we could," Charlotte said. "I'd lock him up in a heartbeat."

Ella's cell phone rang. "Oh, no," she moaned.

"What's wrong?"

"That's Elijah texting me. I told him I'd be back in River Valley today. We made plans to go out for drinks tonight, but I was so excited about coming to see you that I totally forgot about them."

"Aw, does that mean you have to leave?"

"I probably should. I've got to wash my hair, touch up my manicure, redo my makeup, the whole nine."

"Well, it was so good seeing you," Charlotte said. "Next time, it has to be longer."

"It will. I promise."

Miles followed the sisters out to Ella's car, watching as

they clung to one another. He thought about his siblings, Lena and Jake, and realized just how much he missed being with them in Clemmington.

Ella threw her arms around him. "It was so nice meeting you, Miles. Thank you for being here and taking care of my big sis."

"I'm happy to do so. Thank you for coming by and surprising her on such short notice."

After Ella climbed inside her electric-blue jeep and drove off, Miles and Charlotte walked back inside the house arm in arm.

"Should we finish off that delicious bottle of pinot grigio?" she asked.

"Absolutely," Miles murmured, leading her to the deck.

CHARLOTTE'S PHONE PINGED.

"Chief Mitchell is texting me. Maybe he's got a case update."

"Let's hope so," Miles replied, looking over her shoulder.

The pair were curled up on her cream suede sofa in the family room, listening to John Coltrane's *A Love Supreme* album while finishing up a second bottle of wine.

"Ooh, *yes!*" Charlotte squealed. "The chief just received an email from Freelain & Associates. The attorneys are going to bring Stephen's friends in for questioning. I've gotta reach out to them and schedule dates and times."

"Good job." Miles gave her a high five. Their fingers intertwined. She leaned in and kissed his cheek.

The unexpected move stiffened his body. He quickly recovered, loosening his back so not to appear as thrilled as he felt.

"See?" he said. "What did I tell you? I knew we would still get a sit-down with those guys even though they lawyered up."

"Yes, you did. And I appreciate you reassuring me. Because I was about to lose it." Charlotte set her phone on the coffee table and reclined back on the couch. "This day really took a turn for the better. Thanks to you. I know I say this all the time, but I appreciate you being here, Miles. So much. I don't know if I could've continued working this investigation without you."

"Of course you could have. But like I always tell you, I'm happy to be a part of it. And even happier to have reconnected with you."

Just as Charlotte nestled her head against his chest, her phone pinged again.

"That's probably the chief replying to my message." She examined the screen. "Hmm, this isn't him. It's a text from an unknown number."

"What does it say?"

Charlotte didn't respond. A long line creased her frowning forehead.

"What's wrong?" Miles asked her.

She handed him the phone.

FYI, you got lucky escaping that car chase. Next time I'll succeed in running you off the road, kidnapping you and torturing you for twelve days straight. I'll carve a #12 into your cheek, then leave your perfectly preserved body on the shores of the Creosote River. Your days are numbered, Sergeant Bowman...

Charlotte nestled against him, as if needing to feel protected. "What are the chances of you staying here with me permanently? Or at least until we catch the killer?"

"You already know the answer to that."

Chapter Nine

Charlotte tapped her pen against a notebook and stared across the desk at Stephen's friend Josh. His icy blue eyes appeared puffy and dull, as if he'd been crying. There was a glint of defiance, indicating he didn't want to be there.

A miniature fan propped on the corner of her cluttered desk did little to cool the stuffy office. A pipe had burst in the interrogation room early that morning, forcing Charlotte to question Josh in her small space. Despite stacking plastic bins filled with evidence and research files in a corner, it was still overcrowded. The area wasn't equipped to house five people. But she wanted Miles and Chief Mitchell there as she faced off with Josh and his attorney.

Charlotte spun her laptop around and pointed at the screen. "Is this you in the video?" she asked Josh.

He brushed his floppy blond curls away from his face, his eyelids jumping uncontrollably. "Is that Eden's Den?"

"Yes, it is."

"Then, yeah, that's me."

"So you, Stephen, Hunter and Rob were together when you arrived at the bar. Is that correct?"

"Uh, lemme think. Umm…"

Josh ran his hands down his sunburned arms. He looked like a surfer ready to catch a few waves in his white tank top, palm leaf Bermuda shorts and flip-flops. Charlotte was surprised that his attorney hadn't asked him to dress more appropriately. But she shouldn't have been, considering he was the son of a real estate mogul who owned half of River Valley. The trust fund crowd tended to do whatever they wanted.

"So when we got to Eden's Den," Josh said, "yeah, Stephen was with us. I went to talk to the bouncer, Darryl, because I know him. He works security at one of my dad's shopping centers. He told us we could jump the line, and we did."

"*Who* did?" Miles interjected.

"*Meee*," Josh drawled while counting on his fingers, "Hunter, Rob and..."

He paused for several seconds.

"And?" Charlotte asked.

Josh fidgeted with his grubby fingernails. "I don't know, man. When we got inside the place, it was packed. I mean, wall to wall. And *full* of smoke. We could barely, like, see a thing. So we just went straight to the bar and grabbed some shots or whatever. We downed those and lost each other in the crowd. To be honest with you, I don't even remember how I got home that night."

"Hold on, son," Chief Mitchell said, his right brow lifting. "Back up. Does that mean you don't remember whether or not Stephen ever entered the bar?"

"Yeah. I really don't, sir."

"Oh, boy..." the chief growled, pulling off his glasses and rubbing his eyes.

Charlotte slid her open hand toward the middle of the desk. "Is it okay if we take a look at your phone?"

"Why do you need to see his phone?" Josh's attorney asked.

"Just in case there's something on it that could lead to some answers. Info Josh may have missed because it didn't seem important."

"There isn't," Josh shot back.

"Let us be the judge of that," Charlotte retorted. "We're the experts here. Stephen may have mentioned something in a text message that could allude to where he ended up, or even left a voice-mail message that contains vital information."

Josh sat straight up and pounded his fist against the desk. "I am not a suspect here! I shouldn't have to turn over anything to you—"

His attorney placed his hand on Josh's shoulder, quieting him down. "Would it be possible for you to collect whatever information you need from Stephen's phone, Sergeant Bowman?"

"Stephen's phone was never recovered, Mr. Brown."

He turned to Josh. "I thought Corporal Kincaid told you that Stephen's cell was in police custody."

"Who the hell is Corporal Kincaid?" Josh asked.

"Corporal *Walter* Kincaid."

Miles and Charlotte shot one another curious glances. She studied Josh, who was staring off into space with his mouth hanging open.

Mr. Brown appeared flustered as he ran his hand across his chubby bearded face. "Josh, you mentioned being softball teammates with Corporal Kincaid, who's with the River Valley PD. Do you not remember telling me that?"

"Ohh!" he yelled. "You mean Big Walt? Yeah! Hell yeah. I know who you're talking about now. That's my boy. He's the Savage Sliders' left fielder. He likes to come out and party with us, too."

A tense silence circulated through the office. Chief Mitchell's pale complexion turned a deep shade of burgundy as he clawed at his forearms. Charlotte slid open her drawer and discreetly handed him a new bottle of oat serum. "Thanks," he muttered, slathering it on while nodding at Josh. "Was Corporal Kincaid out with you the night that Stephen went missing?"

"Lemme think, lemme think…umm… You know, I don't remember. He may have been. But listen, dude. I was drunk. I mean *drunk* drunk—"

"Josh," his attorney interrupted. "They don't need all that detail…"

"I would appreciate it if you addressed me as Chief Mitchell. Not *dude*."

Josh tugged at the hem of his shorts. "Sorry…"

"Back to your cell phone," Charlotte said. "We aren't interested in any of your personal information. We won't search through your photos or contacts, nothing like that. We're only interested in information that could assist in finding out what happened to Stephen."

Josh turned to his attorney. "Do I have to do this?" *I have nudes on my phone*," he whispered loud enough for everyone to hear.

"You're not going to look at photos or anything unrelated to the case, correct?" Mr. Brown asked law enforcement.

"That is correct," Charlotte replied.

"Wait," Josh pressed, "don't they need an eviction notice to confiscate my cell?"

The attorney placed his hand on Josh's shoulder. "You mean a search warrant. And no, not if you give them the phone voluntarily. If you don't, they'll obtain a warrant and take the phone anyway."

Josh stared straight ahead, silently rocking back and forth in his chair. Mr. Brown leaned toward him and whispered, "They just want to take a look at the last communication you had with Stephen before he was met with foul play. Since you don't have anything to hide, I'd advise you to go ahead and hand over the phone in good faith." He looked at Charlotte and continued, "They won't use anything on that phone to incriminate you."

Several moments passed before Josh pulled the cell from his pocket and tossed it onto the desk. "Fine. Here. Take the damn phone. Just don't look at my nudes. And if you can't resist, *please* don't share them with anybody. My mom would kill me if she knew I was sending naked pictures to my friends."

"Trust me," Charlotte said, "we won't be the least bit tempted."

She called the digital forensics investigator in to take the phone and download the data while Miles pushed the interrogation forward.

"Josh, is there anything else you can tell us about the night that Stephen disappeared? Do you remember encountering anyone strange? Someone who may have followed you guys from The Bottomless Bar to Eden's Den?"

"Not really, no. Looking back, I wish I hadn't gotten so wasted. I would've been more alert. Better able to look out for my boy, you know?"

It was the most sensible thing Josh had said all afternoon.

"I do know," Miles said. "But don't blame yourself. Just do all you can to help us with the investigation."

"I'm trying. I'm trying…"

Charlotte observed Josh as his left leg bounced rapidly. He tugged at his earlobe, mouthing words but not saying anything.

"What's on your mind?" she asked him. "Is there something you're not telling us?"

Josh shrugged and slid forward, resting his elbows against his knees. "Something hit me about that night. But it's probably not important, so…never mind."

"Anything you can tell us about that night is important," Miles said. "So go on. We're listening."

"I remember Stephen stumbling around pretty bad. I mean, *really* bad, after we left The Bottomless Bar. And don't get me wrong. We were all messed up. But Stephen was way worse than the rest of us, even though he drank the least. It got me to thinking. What if somebody roofied him? Do you think that could be a possibility?"

"It certainly could," Charlotte replied just as she noticed Walter loitering near her office.

Please do not try and come in here...

Chief Mitchell seemed to notice him, too. When Walter peeked through the window, the chief stood and headed for the door. "Sergeant Bowman, Detective Love, I'll let you two wrap this up. I need to have a quick chat with someone."

Get him! Charlotte wanted to shout. But instead, she responded, "Thank you, sir. We'll circle back with you once we're done."

"Sounds good. Mr. Tillman, Mr. Brown, thank you for coming in today. We really appreciate it."

Josh hopped up from his chair and saluted Chief Mitchell. "Nice meeting you, Admiral Michaels. Thank you for your service here today."

The chief ignored him and walked out into the hallway. "Corporal Kincaid! In my office. I need to talk to you. *Now.*"

"Do you two have any further questions for my client?" Mr. Brown asked.

"If Josh can't think of anything else that would be helpful," Charlotte said, "then I think that's it. Forensics should be done with the cell phone data download. We'll return it to you on the way out."

"So that's it?" Josh asked, holding his hands up over his head. "You're not gonna arrest me?"

"Do we have reason to?" Miles asked.

Mr. Brown gripped Josh's arm and pulled him out of the

chair. "Son, let's go. I pray your father doesn't ask to see a copy of this interrogation video."

Charlotte led them toward the front of the station, her legs heavy with disappointment.

Back to the drawing board, she thought as Josh didn't appear to be their killer.

Chapter Ten

"These dinners of ours keep getting better and better," Charlotte said to Miles from across her dining room table. "But you have to keep your promise. No talk of the investigation."

He glanced down at his plate. "With this helping of sautéed scallops, Parmesan pasta and grilled asparagus you cooked? Trust me. I won't be doing much talking at all."

"Now, that would defeat the purpose of me preparing this special meal for you. This is supposed to be a thank-you, a night off and a chance for us to catch up on things *outside* of work."

"I'm only kidding with you," Miles said, opening a bottle of Ribolla Gialla.

He filled Charlotte's glass and handed it to her. Their fingers brushed lightly against one another's. She shifted in her seat, adjusting the deep sweetheart neckline on her fitted magenta dress.

"Hey, can I ask you a personal question?" he said.

"Sure. Ask away."

"Why did you and your ex-husband split up?"

Charlotte froze mid-swallow. She coughed, a piece of scallop catching in her throat.

"Wow," she said after several sips of wine. "I didn't see that one coming."

"I'm sorry. Are you okay?"

She nodded but didn't proceed in answering the question.

"When you and I first met at that conference," Miles said, "you refused to discuss your divorce. I assumed it must've been pretty intense. I mean, it drove you to use me for my body all weekend long, then kick me to the curb as soon as the last session ended."

"Will you stop it with all the dramatics!" Charlotte insisted, grabbing a dinner roll and pretending to aim it at his head. "If I recall correctly, you had a pretty good time that weekend, regardless of what I would or wouldn't share with you."

"Damn right I did."

His sexy lips pulled into a half smile. Charlotte resisted the urge to swipe everything off the table and pull him on top of it.

"That's why I was so disappointed when you ended things," Miles continued right before his smile faded.

Charlotte took a long sip of wine, then exhaled slowly.

Time to open up. He deserves to know...

"So, I was married to an attorney. A very slick criminal defense attorney whose practice was based in Las Vegas."

"Oh, boy. I can already see where this is going."

"Yeah, and you'd probably be right about everything you're assuming. My ex and I were basically in a long-distance relationship. He spent most of his time in Vegas while I was here in River Valley. Eventually he bought a condo there, and his trips home became less and less frequent. Unfortunately, he fell into all the stereotypical Sin City trappings. High-stakes gambling, escort services, heavy drinking, recreational drugs..."

Miles reached across the table and took Charlotte's hand in his. "I am so sorry you had to deal with that. I figured whatever happened must've been rough. But damn. I didn't expect it to be that bad."

"Thank you, Miles. Believe it or not, things got worse. I found out he and a couple of judges were taking bribes to help their clients get lighter sentences or skip jail time altogether. There were also rumors that he'd gotten caught up with the mob. After I heard all that, I just cut ties, started seeing a therapist and worked to move on."

"Good for you. That couldn't have been easy. And after hearing it, I can understand why you didn't want to share your story. We barely knew one another."

"Plus, it was still fresh when you and I met. I wasn't ready."

"Yet you found it in you to date a clown like Walter, huh," Miles quipped.

"Look, you are not allowed to judge the decisions made by a brokenhearted woman. After that divorce, I was not in my right mind. And in all honesty, my divorce is the reason why I made the mistake of dating Walter. He knew I was vulnerable and took advantage of it."

"What even attracted you to him? He's such a jerk."

Charlotte could hear the pain in Miles's strained tone. She knew he was wondering why she hadn't reached out to him. Charlotte was too embarrassed to tell him that she hadn't been ready for real love back then. She knew deep down that Walter was just something to do. Someone to keep her mind off her ex. At that time in her life, that was all she could handle.

"I don't know," she replied quietly. "But trust me, if I could turn back the hands of time and do things differently, I would."

"So looking back, you have regrets?"

Charlotte looked Miles directly in the eyes. "I do."

She swirled a cluster of noodles onto her fork and nibbled at them. The conversation had managed to disrupt her appetite. The pair remained silent for several moments before Miles finally spoke up.

"I can understand how you felt."

"You can?"

"In a way. I mean, I've never been married obviously, so I can only relate to your experience to a certain extent. But you were in survival mode. And Walter was like low-hanging fruit. He was right there. In your face, every day. Probably sweating the hell out of you to date him."

"That he was."

"What man in his right mind wouldn't be?"

"That was an awfully nice thing for you to say. Thank you. But can we please change the subject? As a matter of fact, how about we turn this conversation around and focus on *your* dating history."

"Oh, no…"

"Oh, no, nothing," Charlotte shot back. "Come on. Spill the beans. Tell me why you're single, and what went wrong in your last relationship."

Miles let out a low moan, stalling as he piled more pasta onto his plate. "I despise the hot seat."

"Well, you made me sit in it long enough, so now it's your turn. And I'm sure your story isn't worse than mine."

"You're right. It isn't. But it's similar. Because in the end, I did get my heart broken."

Charlotte's stomach dropped at the pain on his fallen expression. "I'm sorry, Miles. Listen, you don't have to talk about it if you don't want to."

"No, no. I'm good. I forced your story out of you. It's only fair that I share mine. Bottom line? She cheated."

He shoved a piece of asparagus inside his mouth as if he were done talking.

"Wait, that's it?" she asked. "You're not gonna share any details with me?"

"Do I have to?"

"Of course you do! I just poured my heart out to you. You're obligated to spill every drop of your tea."

"All right. Fine. I just… I can't stand rehashing the situation. But anyway, on one of my visits to LA to visit my sister back when she still lived there, I met a bartender who worked at a spot near the police station."

"Ooh, a bartender. I bet she was pretty, wasn't she?"

Miles shrugged. "She was attractive. As you can imagine, dating someone who works in that industry is tough. She got hit on constantly. Ballplayers, actors, musicians… I was surprised she was even interested in me. I was just a cop."

"So she hit on you first?"

"She did. I figure she was tired of dating industry men. But in the end, turns out she was just like many of them."

"What do you mean?"

"Well, she got so drunk one night that she forgot I was driving in the next morning to see her. When I got to her place, I was knocking on the door, but there was no answer. I realized the door wasn't closed all the way, so I went inside. Called out her name. Didn't get a response. Walked into the bedroom, and *boom*. Caught her in bed with another man."

Charlotte's mouthful of wine went down so hard that it burned her throat. "*What?* That must've been a horrible experience."

"It was. After that happened, I found solace in serial dating. Took me a minute to realize that I'm a one-woman man. So, I've committed to remaining single until I meet the right person."

The statement lingered in the air. Charlotte remained silent, unable to take her eyes off him.

In that moment, she realized that something had changed within her. Charlotte was having a hard time controlling her attraction toward Miles. Maybe it was everything he'd poured into her investigation. Or that he was still just as fine as he'd been the day they met. The fire between them had never died. They'd simply quelled it for the sake of the case.

"Listen," Miles said, taking their plates. "Enough sad talk about cheating and breakups and therapy. Didn't I see a salted caramel cheesecake from Beatrice's Bakery around here somewhere?"

Charlotte followed him into the kitchen. "You sure did. It's right there on the counter."

"But wait, you didn't clean your plate, young lady. I don't know if you're allowed to have dessert."

"I can't just have a tiny little piece?" Charlotte asked, her silky tone laced with flirtation. She blamed it on the alcohol and kept going. "I thought you were dying to give me a taste.

Okay, too far. Rewind...

"Wait, wait," she stammered. "That didn't come out right."

"It came out exactly how it was supposed to. Because you're right. I am dying to give you a taste."

Miles opened the box of cheesecake, dipped his finger in a dollop of whipped cream and licked it off.

"Don't do that," Charlotte murmured, every nerve in her body buzzing.

"Don't do what?" he asked, repeating the gesture.

"That."

He slid a fork into the cake and held it to Charlotte's mouth. When her lips parted, he slipped it inside.

"Oops," Miles whispered. "I got a bit of graham cracker crust right here in the corner of your..."

He leaned in and kissed her. Charlotte sucked in a breath of air. Her mind told her to take a step back. But her heart told her to stay put. Her heart won.

She melted into the kiss, their lips in perfect sync. Her hands clutched the back of his neck as his held her waist, leading her out of the kitchen.

They stumbled up the stairs, his mouth moving to her ear, then down to her neck. When they reached the bedroom, he paused, staring at her intently as if asking for permission to enter. She responded by pushing him inside, unbuttoning his shirt on the way to the bed.

Chapter Eleven

Miles awakened to the feel of Charlotte's smooth back pressed against his chest. She was still wrapped in his arms, her shoulders moving to the rhythm of her deep breathing.

A satisfied smile lingered on his lips despite the dull pain throbbing over his right eye. It may have been the lack of sleep. Or too many glasses of wine. Either way, he didn't dare get up to search for a bottle of aspirin. He'd dreamed of being back in this position for so long and refused to disrupt the moment.

Charlotte stirred slightly. Miles kissed the back of her neck, hoping she'd awaken for another round of spontaneous lovemaking. But her fluttering eyelids remained closed.

He glanced at the clock. It was almost 6:00 a.m. The alarm was set to go off in thirty minutes. Miles tightened his grip, her body aligning perfectly alongside his. Sleep or awake, he'd relish their last minutes together until it was time to head to the station.

Miles had lain awake most of the night. Being with Charlotte incited an adrenaline rush he couldn't suppress. But their explosive evening wasn't the only cause of his insomnia. While they'd promised to bury all talk of the investigation, their avoidance didn't negate the fact that the clock was ticking and they still had a case to solve. One that might be linked to the threats she herself had been receiving.

A cell phone screen lit up from the mirrored nightstand. Miles raised his head, eyeing its pale pink case. It was Charlotte's.

The buzzing didn't disturb her. He ignored it, resting his face against her hair as he lay back down.

He inhaled the sweet scent of coconut serum. Just as he sprinkled her shoulder with tender kisses, her phone lit up again. And again.

Miles popped up and gently shook Charlotte's shoulder. "Hey, your phone is blowing up. Maybe you should check it. See what's going on."

"Ugh," she groaned, gripping her temples. "My head is pounding. How much did I drink last night? Wait, what even happened last night?"

"You really don't remember?" he breathed, his lips nuzzling her ear.

"Ooh," she sighed sexily, reaching for the phone. "It's all coming back to me now."

He continued running his lips lightly across her shoulder as she checked her cell.

"Oh *no!*" Charlotte hopped up, knocking Miles in the mouth with her elbow.

"*Ow!* What's wrong?"

"Chief Mitchell has been trying to reach me for over two hours! Another body was found. This time at Angler Canyon Reservoir. Female victim. We need to hurry up and get to the crime scene! *Damn*, I hope they haven't transported the body to the medical examiner's office yet," she swore before storming into the bathroom and slamming the door.

Miles rolled out of bed and slipped into his boxers. "I'll meet you downstairs in fifteen minutes!" he called out.

She didn't respond.

This wasn't the way he'd hoped to start their morning.

MILES PULLED INTO the Eagle County Medical Examiner's parking lot. "This is the part I hate most about our job."

"Which part?" Charlotte asked. "Finding out we've got another murder on our hands? Or having to examine the body with the coroner?"

"Both."

The pair had just left Angler Canyon Reservoir. Their victim was identified as Nalah Coldon, a twenty-nine-year-old woman last seen over two weeks ago leaving a bar in downtown River Valley.

"So Nalah definitely fits the description of our killer's other victims," Charlotte said as they entered the gray cement two-story building. "Young, fit, attractive and successful."

"Correct. And she disappeared during a night out with friends, just like everyone else who's turned up dead."

Miles could see the veins protruding from Charlotte's neck. The stress of the case had already kicked back in. She'd been strictly business ever since they left her house earlier that morning, as if their night together never happened.

What do you expect? She's got another homicide to contend with, Miles told himself. Nevertheless, the reminder didn't kill the sting of rejection burning inside his chest.

"Our victim had just made partner at her law firm before she was killed," Charlotte said. "I can't imagine what that poor woman went through in the days leading up to her death."

"Or all of the victims for that matter. It'll be interesting to hear what the medical examiner knows so far."

Charlotte flashed her badge at the receptionist before leading Miles down a long, sterile hallway and onto a set of elevators. A blast of freezing air hit them when the doors opened onto the lower level.

The temperature failed to mask the putrid scent of decomposition. A rush of nausea rumbled inside Miles's stomach.

He covered his nose and mouth. But the foul odor still managed to seep through his fingers.

"I'll ask the coroner for masks once we get to his office," Charlotte told him.

He nodded, keeping his mouth tightly closed. She led them through a heavy metal door past a wall of mortuary chambers and into the autopsy suite.

"Hello, Dr. Peterson," Charlotte said.

"Sergeant Bowman. Good to see you."

The medical examiner stood behind a steel table covered with a white body bag. Miles was able to get a better look at him now than he had at Stephen's chaotic crime scene. Dr. Peterson couldn't have been more than five feet tall. Wiry white hair protruded like small bushes from a blue skullcap, while a potbelly poked out from underneath his surgical gown. Droopy jowls, close-set hazel eyes and a toothy grin made him appear more like a comedic actor than a pathologist.

The examiner pointed toward a small wooden closet. "You know where to find the gowns, gloves and masks." He acknowledged Miles with a head nod. "Detective Love, correct? We met out at the Hoptree River, during the recovery of Stephen Seymour's body."

"Yes, we did. Good to see you again, Doctor. Though I wish it were under more pleasant circumstances."

"Most definitely." His eyes lowered as he unzipped the bag. "I'm really hoping you can assist River Valley PD in finally catching the killer, like you did back in California. This is getting to be a real problem that our police department can't seem to handle on their own."

"We're all working hard to make an arrest, sir."

Miles reached over and gave Charlotte's arm a reassuring squeeze. Her muscles tensed underneath his touch. He could tell by her drawn expression that she hadn't taken kindly to Dr. Peterson's statement.

The pair pulled on their protective gear and approached the body.

"This definitely looks like the work of our killer." Charlotte said.

Dr. Peterson nodded, pointing to the victim's left cheek. "I'd say so. Especially considering she's got the number eight carved here."

The scent of rotten eggs drifted from the victim's body. Her skin had already turned a pale shade of gray. Dried blood resembling streaks of rust stained the left side of her face, neck and collarbone.

"Are you suspecting another poisoning?" Miles asked.

"I am. I already drew specimens and sent them off to the forensics lab. The toxicologist promised to put a rush on testing. Maybe we'll luck out this time and something will be revealed in the results."

"Wait," Charlotte said, pointing at the victim's neck. "What about the bruising along her throat? This is the first time I've seen that type of scarring on one of the bodies. Could the cause of death be asphyxiation this time?"

"I don't believe so," Dr. Peterson replied, running his fingertip along her neckline. "The bruising is fairly light. There was no bleeding around the throat, and the hyoid bone at the base of her tongue isn't fractured."

"Were there any splotches in her eyes or on her lungs?" Miles asked.

"No. Nor was her heart enlarged. Further proof that asphyxiation probably wasn't the cause of death. But these are just my initial findings. Once I perform the full autopsy, I'll know more."

Charlotte slowly studied the body from head to toe. "I really hope that the toxicology report comes back positive this time. We need a win in this case. Desperately."

"It's coming," Miles said, wanting nothing more than to reassure her after sensing dejection in every word she spoke.

"Thank you, Dr. Peterson," Charlotte said. "Please contact me with any updates."

"I certainly will."

She ripped off her protective gear and was out of the autopsy suite within seconds. Miles rushed to keep up with her. Charlotte didn't utter a word as she walked two steps ahead of him all the way to the parking lot.

"Hey, are you okay?" he panted.

"I'm fine."

"Look, I know it seems like this investigation is going from bad to worse. But you're doing everything that you can to solve it."

Charlotte's black pumps screeched along the asphalt as she stopped in the middle of the lot. "Am I? Because last time I checked, I was laid up in bed sound asleep this morning while the rest of River Valley PD was at *my* crime scene. Then when I got there, Walter had taken the lead on the investigation, and Chief Mitchell was asking where the hell I'd been for the past two-plus hours! Do you know how humiliating that was? It was as if he knew you and I were together last night. Meaning, *together* together."

"Listen, Charlotte. You're overthinking this. There's no way the chief would know that. Not to mention, you're human. I'm sure you didn't even realize you'd turned off your ringer."

"False. I did realize it. Because I turned it off on purpose."

"Why would you do that?"

"Because for the first time in a long time, I just wanted to enjoy a night off with some good food, good wine and good company."

Her words pulled him in closer. "And I get that," he said

softly, placing his hands on her shoulders. "Everybody's entitled to a break. It's normal. And healthy."

Charlotte pulled away. "Not when you're pursuing a serial killer. In my case? It was nothing short of stupid." She paused, shaking her head while looking straight through him. "I'm sorry, Miles, but I don't think we should—"

"Please," he interrupted, backing away. "I already know where this conversation is going. You don't have to say it."

Her head fell. "I didn't mean to lead you on. I didn't even expect for things to go as far as they did last night. But I've got to stay focused. No distractions."

"Understood," he told her, his voice straining against the knot stuck in his throat. He wanted to address the whole distraction statement, but at this point, he didn't have the energy. Or the emotional bandwidth.

Fool me twice, shame on me...

"Where to now?" Miles asked. "Angler Canyon Reservoir?"

"Yes—"

Charlotte stopped at the sound of her buzzing cell phone. She scanned the screen, cringing at the message. "Scratch that. Chief Mitchell just texted me. He wants to meet back at the station. ASAP."

"But what about the crime scene? Shouldn't you be there processing it?"

She threw open the passenger door and collapsed into the seat. "Walter is handling it."

Chapter Twelve

"What happened to you this morning?" Chief Mitchell asked Charlotte.

She sat across from him, her jittery knees banging against the edge of his desk.

"Sir, I am so sorry. When I fell asleep last night, my ringer was off, and I didn't hear your call coming in."

"Your *ringer* was off?"

Charlotte picked at her cuticles, wishing she could dissolve into the floor. "Yes, sir."

"Sergeant Bowman, may I remind you that you're investigating one of the deadliest cases this town has ever seen? Your ringer should be on at all times. Is that understood?"

"Absolutely. It was my mistake, and it'll never happen again."

He downed several gulps of piping hot coffee, despite the sweltering temperature inside his office. "What's going on with you, Bowman? Is everything all right?"

"Yes," she insisted, sliding toward the corner of her chair. "Everything is fine. I've been working this case to the bone. Detective Love and I are constantly reviewing the surveillance footage we've collected, constantly poring over the case files, and revisiting the crime scenes over and over again. As a matter of fact, we were leaving the coroner's office and

heading back to Angler Canyon right before you called me back here."

"Speaking of Detective Love..."

Charlotte grimaced beneath the scrutiny in his squinting eyes.

"Do you think it's benefiting you having him here? Or has he become more of a distraction than an asset?"

See, I knew it!

Charlotte cleared her throat, choosing her words carefully before speaking them. "Detective Love has definitely been an asset to this investigation, sir. I value his input as well as his skill set. Plus, he's acted as a great sounding board. And I certainly appreciate his protection. I've felt much safer knowing he's got my back, which is a lot more than I can say for some of my colleagues around here. Half of them don't even seem to believe I've been threatened. A couple even have me wondering whether they're behind the threats."

"That's an awfully bold statement to make, Sergeant Bowman."

"Bold, but true."

A stare down ensued as neither of them spoke a word for several moments.

Did I go too far? Charlotte asked herself as the chief's bushy brows arched into his rumpled forehead.

"Sir, may I ask what sparked these questions? Was it the fact that I showed up late to the crime scene this morning? Or is it something else?"

"Well, since you brought up your colleagues in the department, I will share this with you. Some of them think that this case is too complicated for you to handle. Arriving late to the crime scene today, appearing flustered and disheveled, only fueled their argument. You're a sergeant now, and as you know, to whom much is given, much is expected."

"Chief, rest assured that I *can* handle this case. I am confident that this latest victim is going to lead us to the killer. While we were at the medical examiner's office, I took a close look at Nalah Coldon's body. Her murder appears a bit different than the others, starting with the fact that she has some bruising around the neck. Maybe our suspect is slipping. I have yet to fully process the crime scene myself. Once I do that, question the victim's friends, and receive the full autopsy and toxicology reports, I will have some definitive answers."

Chief Mitchell grabbed a pile of papers sliding off his desk and stacked them neatly. "I believe in you, Bowman. And I do trust that you'll solve this case. That's why you were promoted to sergeant and assigned to it over everybody else in the department—"

He was interrupted when Walter came bursting into the office, panting like a rabid dog.

"Chief!" he yelled. "Sorry for the interruption, but I need to speak with you. Immediately."

Charlotte leapt from her chair. "*Excuse* me, Corporal Kincaid. Chief Mitchell and I are in the middle of a meeting."

He grinned arrogantly. "That's why I pardoned myself first. Plus, it's good that you're here. I was planning on sharing this with you, too." He shoved his hands inside his pockets and sauntered toward the desk. "Sir, I found a syringe near the crime scene."

"You *what*?" Charlotte uttered.

"*I* found a syringe near the crime scene," Walter repeated, much louder this time. "I'll send it off to the lab for testing this afternoon."

While Charlotte was happy for the discovery, she wanted to slap the sneer off his smug face.

Chief Mitchell broke out into a slow clap. "Good work, Corporal. That syringe may be the first piece of viable evidence collected at any of the crime scenes."

"I know, right?" Walter jabbed his crooked index finger in Charlotte's direction. "Maybe it wouldn't have been such a bad idea to partner up with me after all."

"How about we wait and see what forensics reports back before you break out the champagne?" she suggested.

"I don't know, Sergeant," Chief Mitchell said. "Corporal Kincaid might be right. Maybe you should rethink teaming up with him on this investigation."

Just as Charlotte opened her mouth to object, Miles appeared in the doorway.

"Sorry to interrupt. Detective Bowman, the manager of The Tipping Point just called. She pulled the surveillance footage from the night Nalah was there."

Charlotte turned to Chief Mitchell. "Sir, are we done here? I need to get back to my investigation."

"You mean *our* investigation?" Walter quipped. He nudged Miles. "Did you hear the news? I found a syringe at the crime scene today. Already sent it off to the lab for testing."

Miles nodded, his poker face in full effect. "Great work, Corporal Kincaid. I hope it leads us straight to the killer."

"*Us?* Don't you mean *me*? Because at this point, I feel like I'm carrying this entire case all by myself."

"You *cannot* be serious," Charlotte spat just as Chief Mitchell rose to his feet.

"Hold on, hold on. Let's reel it in. Sergeant Bowman, I know you're anxious to review that footage from The Tipping Point. Why don't you and Detective Love head there now, then go by Angler Canyon once you're done?"

"Yes, sir—"

"Wait," Walter said, stepping in front of Charlotte as she tried to walk out. "Why don't *I* go to The Tipping Point with Sergeant Bowman since I wanna see the surveillance, too, then escort her to Angler Canyon? After all, I am the one who examined the scene this morning."

Charlotte held her breath, praying Chief Mitchell wouldn't go for it.

"Well…" the chief began right before her phone buzzed. She checked the calendar notification, then smiled.

"Oh, look," she said, shoving the screen in Walter's face. "Your in-service training session on traffic and parking enforcement is scheduled to begin in fifteen minutes. Have you set up the conference room and sent a reminder to the attending officers yet?"

"Dammit," he muttered. "Can't you get somebody else to do it—"

"Oh, *no*. I certainly cannot. As the corporal of River Valley PD, it is your responsibility to conduct those sessions."

Walter pushed past Miles on his way out the door. "I still wanna review that surveillance footage once you retrieve it!"

"Of course you do!" She snickered at the sight of him storming down the hallway.

"Sergeant Bowman?" the chief said. "Don't let today's hiccup happen again."

"I won't, sir. You have my word."

THE TIPPING POINT was bustling during downtown's happy hour. Patrons spilled out of the nautical-themed bar's heavy wooden door and onto the street.

Before heading there, Miles had insisted he and Charlotte spend some time looking into phone records to see if they could trace any of the threatening calls she'd been receiving. Nothing useful turned up. Whoever was making those calls used an untraceable burner phone.

On the way inside the bar, Miles wrapped his arm securely around Charlotte and led her through the rowdy crowd. They weaved their way around the packed tavern, squeezing between white high-top tables filled with groups of friends and coworkers toasting drinks and gyrating to the beat of techno music.

Colorful mainsails hung from the ceiling, and surfboards lined the walls. Shirtless male servers wore captain's hats and white trunks, while the women sported tank tops and mini wrap skirts.

"This place looks like *The Love Boat* meets *Too Hot to Handle!*" Miles yelled over the music.

"Yeah, it's a lot to take in! I think that's the manager in the back, hanging the anchor on the wall."

"I'll lead the way." Miles's grip on Charlotte's waist tightened as they made a beeline toward the petite blonde. Last night's memory of his hands gripping her hips flashed through her mind.

Shake it off, she told herself as they approached the manager.

"Hey!" the woman chirped, flipping her bouncy bob over her shoulder. Her bright green eyes and neon white smile appeared innocent, almost angelic. But her muscular biceps and six-pack abs served as a warning that she was far from fragile. "I'm Piper. You're Sergeant Bowman, right?"

"Yes, that's me." Charlotte shook her extended hand.

"I just got a call from your partner," Piper said. "Corporal Kincaid?"

Charlotte and Miles threw one another looks of annoyance.

"Interesting," Charlotte responded. "Was he asking about the surveillance footage you have of Nalah Coldon?"

"He was. He asked if I could email it to him. But our internet is down, so I wasn't able to send it." She reached into the back pocket of her white denim shorts and pulled out a USB flash drive. "I saved the footage on this. Oh, and by the way, the two friends Nalah was with the night she went missing are here now."

"They are?" Miles asked. "Where?"

"Over at the bar. See the redhead with the high ponytail and the girl next to her with the platinum buzz cut? Those are her girls."

"We should go and talk to them," Charlotte suggested to Miles.

Piper pointed across the room toward a faux porthole hanging on the wall. "While you're at it, you might wanna talk to Nalah's ex-boyfriend, too. Unfortunately, he's also here."

"Which one is he?" Charlotte asked.

"The jerk with the short mohawk dressed in the tight orange T-shirt, hanging off those two women who clearly don't wanna be bothered with him. His name is Tommy. He was here the night that Nalah went missing. He harassed her from the minute she walked through the door until the minute she left. You'll see it all on the surveillance video. Watch closely. When Nalah left the bar, he followed her out."

"Did he ever come back in?" Miles asked.

"No. He didn't."

Charlotte shook Piper's hand. "Thank you for that information. If we need anything else, we'll be in touch."

She and Miles headed toward the front. "Who should we tackle first?" Charlotte asked. "The friends or the ex-boyfriend?"

"Definitely the ex. But I don't want the friends to leave before we get a chance to talk to them."

"Good point." Charlotte reached inside her purse and pulled out a couple of business cards. "Why don't you go over to the friends, introduce yourself and give them my card? See what they're willing to share. While you do that, I'll go talk to the ex."

"You got it."

Charlotte watched Miles walk toward the bar. He moved with ease as the crowd parted a path for him. Women's gazes lingered on his handsome face and fit physique. He ignored the attention, focusing on reaching Nalah's friends.

That cool demeanor was what attracted Charlotte to him the moment they'd met, and what drew her into the bedroom the night before. For a brief moment she softened, realizing that she'd been too rough on him. But then Chief Mitchell's words popped into her mind.

Don't let today's hiccup happen again...

The reminder sent Charlotte straight across the bar toward Tommy.

Nalah's ex stood with his shoulders slumped, holding a beer in each hand and swaying his hips in between two women.

"Aw, come on, ladies!" he yelled. "I don't see nothing wrong with a little threesome—"

"For the tenth time," one of the women interrupted, "would you please get the hell away from us?"

Tommy held his finger to her head. "I've got a better idea. How about you suck my—"

"*Excuse* me," Charlotte cut in. "Tommy, I'm Sergeant Bowman with the River Valley PD. I'd like to speak with you regarding your ex-girlfriend, Nalah Coldon. Can we go outside and talk?"

He propped his elbow on the table and eyeballed Charlotte from head to toe. "Mmm...a police sergeant, huh. Sweetheart, you're way too fine to be working in law enforcement."

"Oh, am I?" Charlotte asked, casually opening her dark green blazer and exposing her holstered Glock 22.

"What the..." Tommy flinched, falling back into a stool.

"I would advise you to show some respect, young man," she continued. "Now, do you want to step outside and talk to me? Or should I place you in handcuffs and take you down to the station, where you can be formally interrogated?"

The two women Tommy had been harassing snickered and walked off. His long, gaunt face fell sheepishly. "Can we go out back? I don't want everybody to see me talking to the cops."

"Sure. Show me the way."

Charlotte stopped by the bar and grabbed Miles, and together, they followed Tommy out to a patio that was closed to the public due to construction. He rested against a metal guardrail and crossed his arms, staring down at the ground. "If you're gonna ask whether or not I killed Nalah, the answer is no."

Charlotte pulled her cell phone from her purse, opened the Voice Memos app and hit the record button. "According to video surveillance, you were the last person seen with her before she went missing. Didn't you follow Nalah out of this bar that night?"

"I did. But that's because I was pissed off after she walked away while I was in the middle of a sentence. You can't just disrespect me like that."

"Were you yelling at her and getting physical, too?" Miles probed. "Because according to eyewitnesses, you two were in the middle of a pretty heated argument before she left. And is it true that you tried to restrain her before she was able to get away?"

Tommy chuckled condescendingly. "Sounds like Nalah's girls have been in your ear. I saw you over at the bar gossiping with them."

"Gossiping?" Charlotte said. "That's not what we call it. Detective Love and I are here to gather information in hopes of making an arrest."

"What's up with you, dude?" Tommy asked Miles. "You can't speak for yourself? Gotta have a chick talk on your behalf?"

Charlotte snatched a pair of handcuffs out of her pocket.

"Okay, okay!" Tommy threw his hands in the air. "I'll cool out. Look, I was drunk that night. *Really* drunk. Nalah and I had just broken up. I saw her dancing with some dude, and it set me off. So I confronted her about it. And that...that turned into a big blowup."

"What happened after you followed her out?" Miles asked.

"We stood on the street and fought."

"For how long?"

Tommy shrugged, digging his thumbnail into the gap between his two front teeth. "I don't know. Ten, fifteen minutes?"

"How did the argument end?"

"Nalah had the valet guys pull her car around and left."

"Do you remember which direction she went?"

"East on Silver Street. I assumed she was heading home."

"And where did you go?" Miles asked.

"Back inside the bar. Partied till it closed at three in the morning, then took some chick home with me."

"Hmph, that can easily be proven true or false once we review the surveillance footage," Charlotte told Miles before turning to Tommy. "Wait, what do you mean, *some chick*?"

"I—I'm drawing a blank on her name."

Miles's notepad fell to his side. "Let me get this straight. You were upset with Nalah for dancing with someone else but spent the night with a stranger whose name you can't recall?"

"You make it sound so...*salacious*. But yeah. That's what happened."

"No judgment. Just making sure we've got the story straight. I'd advise you to try and remember who she is. We'll need to contact her and confirm your alibi."

Tommy pulled at the wooden beads on his bracelets, his confident smirk twisting into a scowl. "I will."

"Here's my contact info," Charlotte said, handing him a card while Miles jotted down Tommy's number. "If you think of anything, call me. Either way, Detective Love and I will definitely be in touch."

Tommy flicked the card along the edge of his palm. "Look,

I may be guilty of a lotta asinine crap, but like I said, I didn't kill Nalah."

A cool blast of air blew onto the patio when the door swung open. Several patrons spilled out onto faux grass.

"Hey!" Piper yelled from inside. "You all aren't supposed to be out there!"

Charlotte turned to Miles. "Do you have any more questions for Tommy?"

"I think that's all I've got. For now."

"We'll be in touch," she told him. "And by the way, your behavior inside the bar? The excessive drinking, harassment and whatever we *didn't* see? Cut it out. Next time I won't hesitate to lock you up for disorderly conduct."

"Yes, ma'am."

On the way back to the car, Charlotte kept her Voice Memos app going. "So what did Nalah's friends have to say about her and Tommy?"

"They backed up everything Piper told us. Neither of them approved of their relationship. He was controlling from the very beginning. Verbally abusive, which eventually turned physical. They'd encouraged Nalah to press charges on numerous occasions, or at least take out a restraining order. For whatever reason, she always refused. But what's interesting is that they don't think he killed her."

Charlotte paused. "We'll see what comes of the surveillance footage. If Tommy's story doesn't check out, let's bring him into the station for questioning and collect his DNA."

Miles nodded. She tried to make eye contact when he opened the passenger door. He turned away, his expression dark. She knew he wanted to talk more about their night. They needed to. She didn't want the situation to spiral into a repeat of what happened after their first fling.

But now wasn't the time. She'd already gotten called out by the chief for losing focus. Charlotte couldn't let it happen again.

Chapter Thirteen

Miles sat alongside Charlotte behind her desk, watching the surveillance footage from The Tipping Point. His eyes darted back and forth between the computer screen and her side profile. It was the same view he'd had the night before while lying next to her. The subtle slant of her eyes, straight edge of her nose, gentle curve of her lips…

You're doing it again!

The detective propped his hand against his face, blocking the view of hers while watching the screen. He was itching to continue the discussion about their night together. But he couldn't. They were both deep in investigation mode. Plus, Charlotte had already made her stance clear. He wondered whether she regretted what happened between them. He'd find out at some point. Just not now.

"Okay, so there's Nalah," she said, pointing at the monitor. "See her sitting at the bar between the two friends?"

"I do. And you can see Tommy in the frame, too. He's at that table about six feet over, slowly inching his way toward her."

"Yep, *aaand* here he comes. He's tapping her on the shoulder. Look at how she waves him off. A clear indication that she didn't want to be bothered."

"Yet he just stands there, continuing to harass her," Miles said.

The pair watched as Tommy grabbed Nalah's waist and twisted her body back and forth.

"So he's just gonna force her to dance with him?" Charlotte asked.

"Looks like it."

Nalah pressed her hands against Tommy's chest. He held on to her as she writhed back and forth, struggling to escape his grip. Her friends jumped in and tried to pull him off. He pushed them away. The redhead fell back against the bar. Nalah went completely still, then slapped Tommy across the face.

"Whoa!" Charlotte exclaimed. "Okay, things are getting intense. This is when the police should've been called. I wonder if Piper saw any of it."

Tommy grabbed Nalah by the shoulders and pulled her out of the frame.

"According to her friends," Miles said, "they were regulars at The Tipping Point, and everyone was used to seeing them fight. It was a normal occurrence. So my guess is that people just turned a blind eye to it."

Nalah reappeared in the frame, approaching her friends as if nothing happened.

"She seems pretty unaffected by Tommy's behavior, too." Charlotte tapped the screen. "Look, now she's talking to some other guy."

"Maybe he's the one Tommy was referring to when he mentioned getting upset over her dancing with someone else."

As soon as the words were out of his mouth, Nalah hugged the man. Her hands glided over his broad shoulders, ripped pecs and biceps, which were bulging through a fitted white T-shirt. He brushed her bangs away from her face. The pair began swaying back and forth. Then Tommy reappeared in the frame.

"Uh-oh," Miles uttered. "Here we go."

Tommy stood inches away from the man. Nalah tried to hold him off. He shoved her, prompting the man to grab the straps of Tommy's tank top and knock him back. Tommy fell to the floor.

"Wait," Charlotte said. "Why is Nalah running over to help Tommy?"

Miles's eyes narrowed as he watched her help him up off the floor. She held him back as he tried to confront the man. Her friends shook their heads while backing away.

"Ugh," Charlotte groaned. "I hate to see this. Nalah's girls don't seem to wanna get involved at this point. They're probably used to witnessing this vicious cycle of abuse and are tired of getting in the middle of it."

"Can you blame them? So many women end up hurt or dead trying to defend their friends from abusive partners."

The man who Nalah had been dancing with shook his head before walking off. She didn't seem to notice as her focus remained on Tommy, who was now flapping his hands in her face.

"Oh, look," Charlotte said. "After Nalah helped him get back on his feet, he's going off on her again."

"This is unreal. And to know that it all ends with Nalah turning up dead is chilling. I'm fighting the urge to jump through the screen and warn her. Save her. *Something*."

"I feel the exact same way."

Tommy grabbed Nalah's arm and pulled her toward the back of the bar. They were out of the frame for a few minutes before returning. He put in her a headlock. She ducked down and managed to wriggle out of it.

"I cannot believe everybody is just standing around watching these two go at it like this without doing anything," Charlotte said.

"Including the bartender. He's back there flirting with women and serving drinks as if nothing's happening. And I know it's nobody's responsibility, but damn. Whatever happened to helping out a fellow citizen?"

"Like we said earlier, maybe they're all just used to it. Not to mention they seem too drunk to care."

Miles rubbed his chin, focusing on Tommy as he wrapped his hand around Nalah's throat. "Judging by the looks of this video, Tommy is way more violent than I'd expected. I'm curious to see if the story he told us about Nalah leaving without him holds up."

No sooner than the words were out of his mouth, he caught a glimpse of Nalah running for the exit.

"Look, she's leaving the bar. And Tommy is following her out. Can you zoom in? We can see what's going on outside through the window."

Charlotte expanded the screen. The valet stand was in clear view. Nalah stormed the attendant, shoving her ticket into his chest. She frantically pointed down the street and pushed the man in that direction. Tommy stood inches away from her with his arms behind his back, talking in her ear.

"He's trying to be discreet now that they're outside," Charlotte said. "But it's obvious he's still harassing Nalah. She's trying to get away from him, but he's holding on to the back of her dress so that she can't move. And look at how she's wincing, pulling her head away from his. She can't escape his grasp."

"This is so hard to watch."

A white convertible pulled in front of the bar. Nalah jerked away from Tommy and ran around to the driver's side. She dug around inside her purse, pulled out several bills and practically threw them at the attendant.

Miles sat straight up, trying not to blink as he studied the screen. Nalah climbed inside the car. Tommy approached the passenger door. Right before she pulled off, he hopped inside.

"Hold on!" Charlotte boomed. "What the hell just happened?"

"Tommy lied to us. That's what happened. It'll be a half-truth if he reappears in this footage, walks back inside the bar, then leaves with some other woman."

"I highly doubt that's gonna happen."

The video lasted another 27 minutes. Nalah's car never reappeared. Neither did Tommy.

Charlotte slammed the laptop shut. "And there you have it. Time to bring Tommy in for questioning and a cheek swab."

Chapter Fourteen

River Valley PD's tiny interrogation room still smelled of fresh paint. Tommy sat on one side of a wobbly wooden table, staring down at his hands while pressing his fingertips together so hard that they trembled. Charlotte was seated across from him, looking on intently with her chin propped against her fist. Miles sat in between them, his black metal chair positioned inches away from Tommy's.

"Thank you," she said to Officer Haney after he collected Tommy's DNA. The second he left the room, she went in.

"So, Tommy, why did you lie to us?"

"I didn't lie. I just… I didn't tell the whole story."

She glanced down at her recorder, making sure the red light was on. "And what was the whole story again?"

He groaned, his lean frame slumping down into the chair. "Me and Nalah got into a huge fight inside the bar. She stormed out during the middle of it. I followed her out because I wasn't done talking. She called for her car, and by the time it arrived, I *still* wasn't done. So I got inside the car with her so I could finish what I was saying."

"And that's a completely different story from what you told Sergeant Bowman and me at The Tipping Point," Miles reiterated. "Which, once again, means you lied."

"Look," Tommy said, slamming his fist into his palm as

he spoke, "after Nalah pulled off, she drove around the block a few times while I said my piece. Once I was done, she dropped me back off at the bar."

"We have eyewitness accounts from people who saw you leave the bar with Nalah but never return."

"*Eyewitnesses?* What eyewitnesses? You still talking about Nalah's hatin' ass friends? Or The Tipping Point's manager, Piper? Also known as Piper the Pill Popper. You can't trust a word that woman says. If she isn't drunk, she's high. Or both. Half the time that chick doesn't know whether she's coming or going."

"She seems pretty reliable to me," Charlotte told him. "And sober. Unlike you, she didn't waver on her memory of what took place that night."

Miles spun the laptop around and played the footage of Tommy riding off with Nalah. "Not to mention the surveillance footage doesn't lie. We saw you leave with Nalah, but according to the footage, you never returned."

Silence fell over the room. Charlotte tapped the tip of her pen against the table. Tommy's eyes diverted from her piercing glare to the drab olive carpet.

He's breaking. Keep pressing. The confession is coming...

"You can't even look at me, can you?" she asked.

His bulging pupils slowly rolled back up. He stared directly at her. "Look, Nalah was an attorney. I know how all this works. I didn't even have to come down here and talk to you if I didn't want to. I could've lawyered up. But I didn't. Because I'm innocent."

Miles scooted closer to Tommy and pointed in his face. "Then tell us what the hell really happened that night. What are you hiding from us?"

"Nothing!" A lone tear trickled down his cheek. "Look, I know I ain't right. I know I wasn't a good boyfriend to Nalah. But I didn't kill her. I loved her. I just…"

"You just what?" Charlotte asked, softening her tone at his show of emotion.

"I can't help but blame myself for what happened to her. And that's killing *me*."

"Why do you blame yourself?"

"Because had I not gotten drunk and acted a fool that night, she...she never would've left the bar," Tommy sputtered, choking on his words. "And whoever did this to her never would've gotten ahold of her to begin with, because she would have been with me."

"All right, then," Miles said. "Once again, tell us what really happened. Because if you didn't do it, then Sergeant Bowman and I need to get back out there and investigate who did."

Tommy's chest expanded as he sucked in a breath of air. "The reason I didn't show back up in that surveillance video is because Nalah dropped me off in the back of The Tipping Point. Not in the front."

"By the patio, where we questioned you?" Charlotte asked.

"Yeah, back there. Before I could go inside, this chick stopped me. She was standing outside smoking a blunt. She was flirting real heavy, asking if I wanted to take a hit. She was cute or whatever. Smokin' hot body. And Nalah had pissed me off. So I took a hit and chilled with her."

"Is this the woman you took home, whose name you can't remember?"

"Yes. Her."

Miles flipped to a blank page in his notebook. "Do you remember her name now?"

"I do. It's Candy."

"Candyyy..." Charlotte said, holding out her hand. "Do you know her last name?"

"Yeah. Cain."

"Cain?"

"Right. Cain."

"The woman's name is *Candy Cain*?" Charlotte repeated.

"Yes. According to her. Now, is that her government name? I don't know. You'd have to ask her."

"Trust me," Miles said, "we will. Have you been in touch with her since Nalah's murder?"

"I have. We're, um...we're kind of dating now."

"In a new relationship already, huh." Charlotte pointed at his cell. "Would you mind passing along her phone number so we can reach out and confirm your alibi?"

"I'll do you one better. I was gonna stop by her job when I left here. Why don't we go there together? You two can talk to her in person and acquit me now or whatever you call it. Declare me innocent, reverse the charges..."

Miles turned to Charlotte. "What do you think?"

"I think that would be great. Keep this investigation moving forward."

"Cool," Tommy said, jumping up from the table. "I'll drive."

"*I'll* drive," Miles shot back, leading them out of the station.

Chapter Fifteen

Miles let up on the accelerator.

"There it is," Tommy said, pointing at a run-down shack on the left side of the road.

"There *what* is?" Charlotte asked.

"Candy's office."

"Office?" Miles snorted. "That looks more like an oversize outhouse to me. Where the hell are we, anyway?"

"Right outside of River Valley," Charlotte told him. "In a town called Gunderson. It's unincorporated, with a population of less than a thousand. And this is no office, obviously. It's a strip club called Razzle Dazzle. Patrons love this place thanks to the inconspicuous location and unassuming exterior. Hence no sign outside."

The parking lot was jam-packed. Miles found a space in the very back and glanced at his watch. "Two fifteen in the afternoon during the middle of the week, and this place is completely full."

"Hey, what can I say," Tommy replied, jumping out and skipping giddily toward the entrance. "The music is good, the buffalo wings are even better, and the dancers? *Whew!* They're the best."

"I'm guessing Candy Cain is a dancer here?" Charlotte asked.

"Candy Cain is the *top* dancer here."

Miles rolled his eyes, following Tommy inside. He almost choked on the streams of smoke billowing through a long, dark hallway.

Tommy approached an overly tanned shirtless man standing near the bar. His bony chest and frail arms were on full display underneath a dusty black leather vest, likening him to an aging rock star.

The man gave Tommy a high five and pointed toward the stage. A dancer dressed in a red-and-white thong was sliding down a pole, swinging her legs to the beat of a bass drum. An array of rowdy men, from suit and tie types to rugged cowboys, stood around the rickety stage, cheering her on while tossing money in the air.

Tommy blew the woman a kiss, then waved frantically at Miles and Charlotte. "Come on!"

The aging rocker tipped his cowboy hat at the pair when they walked by.

"Looks like Tommy's trying to turn this interrogation into a social hour," Charlotte muttered in Miles's ear.

"Yeah, he needs to reel it in. Don't worry. I'll keep him on course."

Multicolor strobe lights swirled overhead, turning Tommy's pale complexion into varying shades of yellow, purple and blue. He pivoted at least three times, staring excitedly around the tiny club before pointing at an empty table. "Do you all wanna grab seats near the stage? Or hang out at the bar until Candy's set is over—"

"We'll wait over by the bar," Miles quickly replied, diverting his attention away from the scantily clad women scattered everywhere.

Tommy shoved his hand inside his pocket and pulled out a wad of dollar bills. "All right, I'll bring Candy over as soon as she's done."

Two stools sat empty on the far end of the bar. Miles led

Charlotte toward them, keeping his eyes fixated on the dingy burgundy carpeting along the way. He could feel her watching him while she giggled softly into her collar.

"What's so funny?" he asked.

"You! It's so cute how stiff and uncomfortable you are. Not much of a strip club guy, huh?"

"Um, *no*. Not at all. The only time you'd catch me in a place like this is if I absolutely had to be there."

"Under what circumstances would you absolutely have to be at a strip club?"

Miles threw his arms out at his sides. "Moments like this! Or if I had to celebrate a friend's bachelor party, or birthday party, or...*whatever*. Some men try and find any reason under the sun to hang out at strip clubs."

"Humph. Well, I'm glad you're not one of them."

Miles almost asked why she'd care either way. It didn't seem as if she wanted anything to do with him beyond business. But he steered clear of the subject.

Get out of your feelings. She's not on that. So you shouldn't be, either. Stay focused on the case...

Tommy came dancing over with Candy by his side.

"Sergeant Bowman, Detective Love, I'd like for you to meet my future wife, Mrs. Candy Cain dash Thompson."

"Nice to meet you both," she purred, extending her hand.

Miles wrapped his fingers around her flimsy grip, careful not to cut himself on her bloodred acrylic nails. She pulled away quickly without making eye contact.

"Is there somewhere quiet we can talk?" he asked. "Sergeant Bowman and I don't want to take up too much of your time. We just have a couple of questions."

"Not really," she said, running her fingers through her spiky platinum-blonde wig. "And I can tell you right now, Tommy didn't kill that girl. He was with me that night. And *ooh*...what a night it was..."

Miles flinched at the sight of her biting Tommy's cheek.

"Ouch!" Tommy squealed, chomping his teeth toward her neck. "Come on, babe. This is serious. We can get to the good stuff later."

"Sorry, snooks. You're just so irresistible—"

"Look," Charlotte said, "Detective Love and I need your official statement that you and Tommy were together that night, for the *entire* night, in order to clear his name."

"Here it is. My official statement. Thomas Thompson was with me the entire night that the girl went missing. He did not kill her... *Wait!*"

Candy paused, then pulled away from Tommy and punched him in the shoulder.

"Ow!" he howled. "Babe, what was that for?"

"Babe! Don't you have a Ring security system at your house?"

"Yeah. Why?"

"Duh. Because! It should've recorded us going into your house that night your ex disappeared, then leaving the next day."

Tommy broke into a round of applause. "Girl, you are good. I mean, *really* good."

Miles glared at Tommy as he toyed with Candy's peppermint-shaped earring. "You mean to tell me you've had a recording that could prove your whereabouts this whole time and didn't say anything?"

"Dude, I didn't even think about—"

"Detective Love," Charlotte corrected.

"Sorry. *Detective Love*, I've been so caught up in the rapture of Candy Cain that I didn't even think about it."

"Tommy, you do realize that you're a person of interest in Nalah's murder investigation, don't you?" she asked.

He shrugged, focusing on Candy rather than Charlotte. "I guess I just assumed you all would get that I'm innocent."

"Well," Miles began, "that's not how this works. We can't assume anything. If you want to profess your innocence, then we need solid proof. How soon can you get that footage to us?"

"Tonight. I'll grab it the minute I get home." He turned to Candy. "Which will be after my girl gets off work."

"We'll be on the lookout for it," Miles said. "You've got our email addresses. Send it to us ASAP, or else we're going to have another conversation down at the station that won't be as pleasant."

Tommy threw him a salute. "Aye aye, captain!"

Charlotte looked on, shaking her head in disgust. "He really thinks this is a joke."

A commotion erupted near the entrance. Three young men who looked like they'd just stumbled out of a frat house were hurdling over one another, racing toward the stage.

"Why do those guys look so familiar?" Charlotte asked.

Candy rolled her eyes and hid behind Tommy. "Ew. We refer to them as the Rich Boys of River Valley. They throw a lot of money around the club. But they like to get sloppy drunk and way too touchy-feely with the girls."

"Yooo," Tommy breathed, pointing at the group. "Those are Stephen Seymour's boys. That's Hunter in the Gucci joggers, Josh in the long denim cutoffs and Rob in the khakis. They were out with him the night Steph went missing."

"How do you know that?" Miles asked.

"Because I was out that night, too. As a matter of fact, they hit a few of the bars the night Nalah went missing, too." Tommy froze, then rotated back and forth like a robot. "Wait, are you all thinking what I'm thinking?"

"And what would that be?" Charlotte inquired.

"That those guys might be your killers! They were at the exact same spots that Stephen *and* Nalah were the nights they went missing."

"Yeah, and so were you."

Tommy's arms fell by his sides. "Damn. I didn't even think about that…"

The group watched Stephen's crew blow smoke from their mouths as they puffed on cigarettes.

"Hey!" Candy yelled in their direction. "You're not supposed to be smoking in here!"

The aging rocker manning the door held his finger to his thin, cracked lips, signaling for her to shut up. Candy rolled her eyes and turned away.

"They just let those guys run wild in here. Preppy jackasses. Looking like they stepped straight off the set of *American Psycho*. You all have no idea how twisted they are."

"No, we don't," Miles replied. "How so?"

"They think they can just have their way with anybody. Especially women. Hunter's parents own a vacation home that they use to throw freaky parties and whatnot. I've heard some pretty shady things have gone on out there."

Tommy nudged Candy. "Babe, don't you think you're talking a little too much?"

"No, let her speak," Charlotte said.

"I just don't want my girl getting in too deep. Those guys are trouble."

"You're speaking to the authorities. There is no such thing as getting in too deep. Now, Candy, what types of shady things are you referring to?"

She hesitated, shifting her weight from one silver platform stiletto to the other. "Well… I haven't been to any of the parties personally. But some of the girls from the club have. Those dudes hire them to entertain their friends. They tell them they're just expected to dance, but things usually go way beyond that. Of course, alcohol and drugs are involved. And once a bunch of rich, arrogant douchebags get drunk and high? It's game over."

"What do you mean, game over?" Charlotte asked.

"What I mean is, anything goes. Things get dangerous. Violent, even."

"Okay," Tommy interrupted, wrapping his arm firmly around Candy. "You've said enough. Now you're just speculating. I've been to a couple of Hunter's parties, and they're not that bad. You don't wanna start accusing people of things based on hearsay. Especially dudes like them. They all come from powerful families. Running your mouth can get dangerous. And I don't want those sexy lips of yours getting you into any trouble."

"Where exactly is Hunter's house located?" Miles asked, ignoring his warning.

Tommy tapped his index finger against his chin. "You know, I can't recall…"

"But we can probably find out for—," Candy chimed in just as Tommy broke into a fit of loud coughs. She turned to him, recoiling when his eyes bulged at her.

"Sorry," she muttered. "I don't know where it is."

Pulling a card from her purse, Charlotte threw Candy a knowing look and handed it to her. "If you happen to recall the address, please, give me a call. Tommy, are you sure you don't want to ride back with us?"

"No," Candy answered for him. "He wants to stay here with me."

"You're not wrong," Tommy gushed, nuzzling his nose against hers, then pointing at Miles and Charlotte. "The lady has spoken. I'm staying here."

Miles lobbed a stern head nod in Tommy's direction. "We'll be waiting on that Ring camera footage. Don't make us have to chase you down."

A piercing scream rang out over the music. The group turned toward the stage. Hunter was standing near the edge, tugging at a dancer's leg.

"You know what?" Candy said. "I might remember where that house is after all."

"Babe," Tommy screeched, tightening his grip on her waist. "What do I always tell you? Snitches get stitches!"

She glared at the stage, then at Tommy. "Looks to me like Darlene's the only one who's gonna need stitches. You see the way Hunter's flinging her around that stage!"

"Can-Can," Tommy muttered in her ear, "didn't I tell you to never go against me? Especially in front of company? It's disrespectful."

"Hey, Candy!" the aging rocker yelled from across the bar. "This isn't a rest stop. Your break's over. Get your ass back up on that stage! Big money just walked through the door, and Darlene can't handle them alone."

She pulled away from Tommy and focused on Charlotte, her eyes tearing up. "I'd better go. Sorry I couldn't be more help."

"We appreciate you speaking with us. If you think of anything else you want to share, you have my number."

"Thanks for the ride," Tommy interjected before Candy could say another word. "See ya." He grabbed her hand and pulled her away.

Miles leaned against the bar, watching the pair walk off. "I will never understand why any woman would want to date a man like that. He is a controlling bully. Would barely let Candy speak."

"I agree. But stay tuned. I have a feeling we haven't heard the last of Candy."

Chapter Sixteen

"Are you sure you have to go?" Charlotte asked Miles.

"I wish I didn't. But yes, I do."

Miles rolled his suitcase toward the front door. He'd received a call from his brother that morning with news that a Clemmington cold case was heating back up. Their father asked that Miles get back to town as soon as possible to help sort through the recent developments.

A mix of panic and sadness churned inside Charlotte's stomach as the pair said their goodbyes. She'd gotten used to Miles being there. The thought of him leaving, even if he would only be gone for a few days, wasn't sitting well with her.

"You'll be fine while I'm gone," he said, as if sensing her distress. "Just stick close to home and make good choices. Chief Mitchell is going to make sure you've got extra detail on you. And Officer Haney promised that he'd keep a close eye on you, too. So you're good."

"It still won't be the same. But thanks..."

Miles's cell phone pinged. He checked the notification, then peeked through the blinds. "My car is here. I'd better get to the airport before I miss my flight."

A streak of anxiety shot through Charlotte's rigid body. Her racing heart implied that this was about more than just

Miles's protection. Emotions were taking over. She was having an *absence makes the heart grow fonder* moment before he'd even left.

Shake it off! her inner voice insisted, knowing now was not the time to get emotional. She blinked back the mist in her eyes as he walked out the door.

"I'll be back as soon as I can," he said.

"Good. Don't let your family talk you into abandoning me. At least not before we solve this investigation."

"I won't. The only reason I'm going back is because this cold case means so much to my father."

"What's it about?" Charlotte asked. The question was a combination of curiosity and stalling. She wasn't ready for Miles to leave. They hadn't had a chance to discuss his case since he got the call.

"There's a popular winery located in Clemmington called Vincent Vineyard. The owner and my father were really good friends, until Mr. Vincent turned up dead. He was murdered, and law enforcement never caught his killer."

"Oh, no. I'm so sorry. When did this happen?"

"A little over a year ago. He was stabbed to death at the vineyard, and a knife was recently found buried in the field. So, we're going to question the family again and see what my sister finds after she runs the weapon through forensics."

The car horn blared so loudly that it rattled the bay window.

"Let me get going before this guy leaves," Miles said.

Charlotte grabbed his arm and went in for a kiss on the cheek. He turned his head before it landed. Their lips ended up connecting.

A moment of stunned silence swirled around them. Miles broke into a curious grin. "Wow. What was that for?"

She shrugged. "I don't know. I guess I'm gonna miss having you around. Even if it is only for a few days. When you do come back, we, uh…we should probably talk more about what happened between us the other night."

"I'd like that."

They embraced for several moments, neither of them wanting to pull away.

"I'll call and let you know when I make it to Clemmington."

"Please do. Safe travels."

Charlotte stood in the doorway, watching as Miles climbed inside the car and pulled off. She stayed there until the vehicle was out of sight.

The buzz of her cell phone pulled Charlotte back inside the house. It almost vibrated off the fireplace mantel before she grabbed it. A text message from an unknown number appeared on the screen.

Stephen's friend Hunter is throwing one of those parties tonight. 8421 Ace Lane. Some of the girls from the club are going. You didn't hear any of this from me. ~ Candy

She paced her living room floor, the soles of her bare feet pounding against the warm wood.

What to do, what to do…

Miles was gone. But there was no way she could miss going to this party. It could lead to finding out more about Stephen's murder. And possibly Nalah's.

She replied to Candy's message.

This will stay between us. Are you planning to attend?

Not sure. Depends on how much Hunter is willing to pay. And whether or not I can sneak away from Tommy. Are you?

I'm not sure either…

While she appreciated the lead, Charlotte didn't want to share her next move with Candy.

She went into her bedroom and slid open the frosted glass closet doors. The brunette bob wig that she'd worn last Halloween was sitting on the top shelf.

"Are you really about to do this?" Charlotte asked herself, knowing that Miles wouldn't approve. Neither would Chief Mitchell. But she couldn't miss out on an opportunity to catch Stephen's friends in action. Plus, if she went in undercover, chances of her being found out were slim to none.

Charlotte pulled the wig down and slipped it over her hair. She turned to the mirror on her bronze vanity table and adjusted the bangs.

"Yep. You're really about to do this."

CHARLOTTE MADE A left turn down Ace Lane. She'd spent the day tracking down dead ends, reaching out to friends of the victims, even ones she'd interviewed before, hoping to find something they'd all missed. Then she'd heard from Miles, who reported he arrived in Clemmington just in time for a major breakthrough on his case, so he hoped to wrap it up ASAP.

The block was dimly lit and fairly calm, with the exception of one house near the corner. She assumed it belonged to Hunter.

She let up on the accelerator, eyeing the luxury cars parked along the curb. The few homes lining the block were lavish, with sprawling lawns and unique, intricately designed architecture.

"In five hundred feet," the navigation system announced, "your destination will be on your right—8421 Ace Lane."

Tires screeched behind her. Charlotte looked in the rearview and saw headlights speeding toward her. The engine roared as a horn blasted. She quickly pulled over just as a neon green Lamborghini sped past.

"Jerk," she muttered.

Charlotte hit the accelerator and drove closer to the party spot. Young women dressed in barely there bikini tops and miniskirts spilled out of the ostentatious wrought iron front door. Shirtless cat-calling men carrying bottles of alcohol chased after them.

"What in the world is going on here…" she uttered, realizing her black maxi dress wouldn't blend in with this crowd.

A cream Rolls-Royce pulled up next to her car. Charlotte froze at the sight of four young men hanging out the window.

"Hey, baby!" one of them yelled. He pointed toward Hunter's house. "You going to the party or what?"

She quickly slipped on a pair of cat-eye sunglasses. "Thinking about it."

"Cool. Meet me out back by the pool for a little drink and a little…you know…" he said with a wink.

Charlotte kept her head down and grabbed her clutch, ready to pull out her Glock if necessary. She waited for the car to pull off before parking and climbing out.

Hunter's contemporary three-level, glass-encased house was surrounded by lush trees and greenery. It was lit up from top to bottom, with gyrating bodies on display in every window. A DJ bopped from side to side in the front of the great room while playing hip hop music that blared through six-foot-tall speakers.

Charlotte walked the perimeter of the property. The infinity edge pool and Jacuzzi out back were packed with topless women and frisky men. Four dancers who she recognized from the Razzle Dazzle stood inside an elaborate white gazebo, passing out drinks to a group of men laid out on gray herringbone wicker club chairs. Charlotte slid her sunglasses down her nose to get a better look. Candy didn't appear to be among them.

"Hunter, *stop*!"

The scream came from the house's second-floor balcony. Hunter was standing dangerously close to the railing, struggling to balance a woman on his shoulders. She gripped his head as he swayed back and forth, clearly intoxicated.

"Put me down!" the woman yelped. "I'm gonna fall!"

"Will you *stop*?" he insisted. "I got you!"

Just as her upper body jolted forward, Hunter's friend Rob swooped in from behind and grabbed her. The woman collapsed into his arms.

"Come on, man, cut it out!" Rob yelled. He clutched Hunter's shoulder and tried to pull him back, but Hunter jerked away.

"I'm coming in hot!" Hunter yelled, climbing up onto the railing.

"Dude! You're gonna kill yourself!"

Before Rob could get him down, Hunter spread his arms out at his sides and jumped off the balcony. Everyone cheered as he flipped through the air and crashed into the pool.

These people are out of their minds...

Charlotte continued through the yard, stopping when two familiar-looking women emerged from the Jacuzzi.

Where do I know them from?

And then it hit her. They were Nalah's friends, the ones she'd been with at The Tipping Point the night she disappeared. Charlotte wondered if Nalah had ever been to one of Hunter's house parties, and just how well the pair knew one another.

She grabbed her phone, eager to tell Miles about the connection between Hunter and Nalah's girls. But then she paused.

I'm not supposed to be here.

The only person who knew Charlotte was attending the party undercover was Cindy, the station's 9-1-1 dispatcher.

But she wouldn't understand the significance of Nalah's friends being here.

Charlotte slid her phone inside her purse, then pulled it right back out. "You have got to take photos of all this," she whispered to herself.

She shot several pictures, then slowly pivoted while recording a video of the expansive yard. She stopped on someone who was climbing up an eighty-foot palm tree. It was Stephen's friend Josh.

Out of nowhere, Hunter ran over to the tree and joined him. "Race you to the top!" he called out.

As Charlotte continued taping the shenanigans, a pair of hands slid across her hips.

"Hey, baby," a whiny voice whispered in her ear. "Instead of you standing over here talking to yourself and snapping shots of all the fun, why don't you put that phone away and join in?"

Charlotte jabbed her elbow deep into the person's bony chest and spun around.

"How about you get your hands off me instead?" she asked the short, scrawny kid who looked to be about sixteen. His frizzy red hair flopped in his face when he doubled over in pain. His glasses fell to the ground as he held his stomach.

"Oww," he groaned. "Why'd you do that?"

Charlotte almost felt sorry for him. Almost...

"Because you need to learn some respect, that's why. Maybe then injuries like that won't happen again." She slapped him hard on the back and walked off.

An animalistic howl echoed through the yard. Charlotte cringed while watching Hunter and Josh slide uncontrollably down the palm tree, their bare arms, chests and legs scraping against the bark.

"Somebody help me!" Josh yelled, stopping in the middle of the trunk. "I'm not gonna make it!"

His eyes landed on her. She pulled her bangs farther down her forehead. He tapped Hunter's shoulder, then pointed at her.

"Hey! I think that's the chick who tortured me down at the police station!"

"Where?" Hunter asked, glancing in her direction. "And why the hell would she be at my house? Hey!" he yelled into the crowd. "Somebody bring me a ladder! I've gotta get down from here and bounce five-O up outta my house!"

Within minutes, Rob ran over with a ladder. Charlotte took advantage of the disruption and hurried out of the backyard. She squeezed her clutch, feeling for her Glock. Relief hit knowing it was still there.

Charlotte peered over her shoulder on the way to the front of the house, making sure she wasn't being followed. Between the sunglasses and the wig, she thought she'd disguised herself well enough. Apparently not.

Dread hampered her movement as she shuffled toward the street, her platform wedges dragging along the rutted asphalt.

Just get to the car. Just get to the car...

"Hey!" someone called out. "Wait up!"

Charlotte sped up. But the screech of rubber soles drew nearer. She reached inside her purse, looped her index finger around the gun's trigger, then spun around.

"What do you want?" she screamed.

"Sorry!" someone yelled into the dark space between them.

Charlotte lowered her head, peering over the rim of her glasses. The wimpy redhead she'd encountered by the pool was standing in front of her with his arms outstretched.

"I just wanted to say goodbye. I hope you're not leaving because of me. Maybe I could...get your number?"

The laugh creeping up her throat was stifled when she bit her tongue. "I'm leaving because I need to get home," she said, backing away from him. "And you're way too young for me. I'm sure there are plenty of girls at that party who you could talk to, *if* you're even old enough to be here."

"Roman!" someone yelled from Hunter's front lawn.

"Delilah," the young man talking to Charlotte called out. "I'm in the middle of something here!"

"See!" Charlotte said. "There's one now—" She paused when Hunter and Josh came running to the front of the house. "Oops, gotta go!"

Charlotte hopped inside her car and sped off. The whole way home, she envisioned being hunted down by another vehicle. Her muscles tensed at every red light as she sat there, waiting for a strange car to pull up next to hers. Her eyes darted from the rearview to the side-view mirror. Anxiety rumbled through her stomach. She grew faint at the thought of being attacked again.

"You shouldn't have done this," Charlotte told herself. "You should not have come out here alone, without Miles."

She couldn't shake the feeling that she was being followed. Or watched. When her house appeared up ahead, Charlotte hesitated to pull into the driveway for fear that someone would jump out from behind the bushes and pounce.

The car's bright lights shone along the road, displaying empty sidewalks and front lawns. Neighbors' homes were pitch-black. All was quiet. Charlotte reluctantly crept into her driveway. Her headlights beamed through the shrubbery. No shadowy figures appeared to be lurking in the pink oleander hedges.

She drew her gun and climbed out of the car, hurrying inside of the house without incident.

See, you were just being paranoid...

Charlotte secured the top and bottom locks, kicked off her shoes and headed to the kitchen. After pouring a glass of wine, she set up shop in the living room and scanned the photos she'd taken at the party.

How in the hell am I gonna tell Miles about all this?

She grabbed her laptop and connected the USB cord to her phone. As the photos downloaded onto the computer, she clicked open the case file and added a few notes on the evening's events.

Once she was done, Charlotte double-clicked the folder that contained photos from Nalah's crime scene. She shuffled through the pictures, studying images of the medical examiner standing over Nalah's body, the forensics team placing evidence inside of brown paper bags, and Chief Mitchell, who was busy giving police officers directives.

And then there was Walter. He'd somehow managed to appear in almost every photo.

"No surprise there..."

Charlotte tapped on a picture of Chief Mitchell speaking to someone in the crowd. A man standing near him caught her eye. She zoomed in on the image.

Her glass of wine almost slipped from her hand. Charlotte knew that face. It was Hunter.

"What in the hell was *he* doing there?"

She grabbed her phone, so tempted to call Miles and tell him everything. But it was late. And she didn't want to disrupt him while he focused on his father's investigation.

"Just be patient," she told herself, setting the cell aside and turning her attention back to the computer.

Just when the download was complete, the lights went out.

"Oh, come on!"

Charlotte glanced around the room. The glare from her computer screen created a creepy glow that spanned the vicinity. The entire first floor of her house looked like a scene straight out of a horror movie.

Where was the flashlight? And the fuses? And the fuse *box*?

"Miles chose the wrong time to leave me here alone..."

She stood and turned on her cell phone's flashlight. It barely shone through the darkness. Charlotte pitched it, not wanting to waste the battery that needed recharging, and felt her way toward the kitchen.

On the way there, a dark figure hurried past the living room window. She stopped, holding her breath while staring outside. Another figure rushed by.

Where is my gun?

A hushed commotion stirred outside the front door. Charlotte's head swiveled as she searched the living room for her weapon. It wasn't there.

You left it in the kitchen!

She remained stuck in that same spot, watching the window as voices seeped through the cracks.

"Hey, Linda!" someone yelled from the street. "Are your lights out, too?"

"Yes!" her next-door neighbor hollered back. "Are yours?"

Charlotte tiptoed to the window and peeked through the blinds. Linda, who lived two houses down, was standing out on the curb pointing up at her house. Their other neighbor Randall approached.

"Looks like a few neighbors' lights are out," he said.

Charlotte pressed her palm against her forehead, blowing a sigh of relief. She walked outside and joined them near the curb.

"What's going on?" she asked. "Have we all lost power?"

"That's what it looks like." Linda sighed. "But our houses are the only three on the block that appear to be hit."

"Hmm. That's weird. Has anyone called the electric company yet?"

"My wife just did," Randall said. "Do you have a flashlight? Or candles?"

"I have both. I was so thrown off when the lights went out that I didn't grab either."

Linda handed Charlotte a pink bedazzled flashlight. "Do you want to borrow mine while you go back inside to grab yours?"

"No. I'll be fine. If I can't find the flashlight I keep in the kitchen, I'll just grab one from the trunk of my car."

"Randall!" his wife called out from their front lawn. "I just got a text from the electric company. They're on the way. They should be able to get us back up and running in no time."

"Great. Thanks, hon!"

A cool breeze settled over Charlotte, giving her a sense of calm. "I'm so relieved that this was a mini blackout, and not an attack on me." She paused when her neighbors threw her looks of concern. "I mean, you know, with me being a police sergeant and all, you never know if someone could have something against me, or…"

Linda slowly backed away. "I'm gonna go back home and make sure the kids are okay."

"Yeah, me, too," Randall chimed in. "Hopefully it won't be too much longer before NV Energy gets here."

Charlotte waved sheepishly, embarrassed after realizing that she'd said too much. "Stay safe!" she called out to their backs as they hurried off.

That wasn't much better…

She went inside and closed the door, blinking rapidly as her eyes adjusted to the darkness.

Maybe I should've taken Linda up on that offer to use her flashlight.

The back of her cream leather couch appeared in the distance. Charlotte tiptoed toward it, gliding her hand along the edge on her way to the kitchen.

She stopped at the sound of footsteps stomping across the floor.

What the...

"Miles?" she called out. "Is that you?"

Silence.

That feeling of dread came rushing back. She thought about her gun. It was still in the kitchen.

Dammit!

The footsteps were now clumping through the hallway. Charlotte felt her way toward a corner in the living room and crouched down. Her eyes were fixated on the white walls. A shadowy figure hovered near the living room's entrance. The silhouette's hand slowly rose to his head. He appeared to be holding a gun.

"Chaaarlotte," a shrill voice called out. "Come out, come out wherever you arrreee."

She covered her mouth, stifling a scream. Charlotte wanted to crawl underneath her console table but feared she'd make too much noise. So she sank farther down, praying the blackout would help to hide her.

A stream of light shone into the living room. It bounced from wall to wall like a disco ball, disorienting her as she followed the beam. The clumping soles commenced, moving in closer until the intruder was inside the living room.

Through the darkness, Charlotte could see that he was wearing a ski mask and dark clothing. His feet were covered in black combat boots. A flash of silver in his left hand confirmed that he was, in fact, gripping a gun.

"I found your Glock inside your purse," he whispered, attempting to disguise his voice. "As you very well know, I'm no gunslinger. Shooting victims isn't my modus operandi. But *oh* how satisfying would it be to pop you in the head with your own weapon. I'd hold on to it as a souvenir afterward.

And if River Valley PD wanted it returned? They'd have to get it back in blood."

He stopped. Rested against the railing. Then switched off the flashlight. The room went completely dark.

"So, what'll it be, Charlotte? A bullet to the head? Or do you finally wanna find out how I murder my victims? That's what you and your idiotic cohorts have been dying to know, isn't it?"

She dug her fingernails into her calves, racking her brain for a way to escape. If she tried to run for it, Charlotte knew the man would shoot her right there on the spot.

"Hey!" he yelled. "Are you listening to me?"

She screamed, unable to hold it in any longer.

"Ahh, there she is. I finally got a rise out of the goody-goody, newly minted *Sergeant* Charlotte Bowman. Where's your little bodyguard tonight? Did he get sick of your failure to catch me and back out of the investigation? If he did, who could blame him? River Valley PD is *pathetic*. Especially now that it's being run by the likes of you."

As he rambled on, Charlotte stared up at the silver ballerina statue sitting on the edge of the console table. It appeared blurry through her tears. She considered grabbing it, charging the intruder and ramming it upside his head.

But then she thought otherwise. A bullet would reach her before she reached him.

How in the hell am I going to get out of this?

"Ooh, this is fun!" the man said. "When I cut those power lines, I had *no* idea taunting you would feel this good."

"You're *sick*!" Charlotte uttered. "Why are you doing this?"

The man began pacing the floor. "Why am I doing this? Because I want you to suffer, just like I did!"

He bolted across the room. His knee struck the edge of the coffee table, but he managed to stay on his feet. Charlotte jumped up and tried to run. He dived over the love seat and grabbed the back of her dress, tossing her to the floor. She groaned in pain, rolling over and pulling herself up onto her elbows.

Charlotte could hear the man wheezing as he stomped back and forth.

"See what you made me do? I didn't wanna attack you yet! I'm trying to relish in your fear. I wanna hear it. Smell it. *Taste* it."

She waited for him to turn around and pace toward the window. When his back was to her, she hopped up, grabbed the ballerina statue and struck him across the head.

"Ow!" he hollered, falling onto the couch.

She darted across the room. But he stuck his leg out and tripped her before she could get away. Charlotte grabbed hold of an end table, spun around and kicked him in the groin.

Her foot barely made contact. He grabbed her ankle and twisted it until she fell to her knees.

"This isn't going as planned," he grunted, climbing on top of her. "Now I'm gonna have to kill you!"

Charlotte felt the cold metal tip of the gun graze her left temple. "No, no, no," she muttered, shuddering underneath the weight of his body.

"No, no, no," he mocked, sliding the barrel along her jawline, her neck, then her chest. "How do you want to die, Charlotte? A bullet to the head? To the heart? Or should I just strangle you with my bare hands? I think I'd enjoy that method the most. The feel of your throat constricting in my grasp while your eyes bulge and your body convulses…"

His hand gripped her neck. It was covered in a latex glove.

So no fingerprints. He's going to kill me, and there will be no evidence left behind…

The attacker's jagged fingernails poked through the thin rubber, digging into her flesh. "I wonder how long it'll take you to die once I start squeezing the life out of you. Two minutes? Three minutes? But wait, you're a feisty one, sooo… *Five* minutes?"

Charlotte choked as his grasp tightened. Her eyelids fluttered. Breathing shallowed.

Hold on. Don't give in. Hold on…

She sputtered as a tiny stream of air caught in her throat. Just as she felt herself passing out, a pair of headlights flashed through the window.

Her attacker's grip loosened. After a few moments, the front door opened slightly.

"Thanks, Linda! I'll let Charlotte know that your power is back on and ours should be next."

Miles!

The killer leapt to his feet. Her gun fell from his hand and slid underneath the couch as he ran to the back of the house.

"Miles!" Charlotte attempted to scream. She barely had any voice left.

"Charlotte?" Miles called out.

"Here," she gasped. "Down here!"

He shined his flashlight along the floor, then rushed toward her. "Charlotte! What happened to you?"

She took in a deep breath and exhaled, crying out, "The killer! He was here!"

"He was *here*?" Miles asked, helping her stand. "When?"

"Just now! He ran to the back of the house."

Miles wrapped his arm around her and drew his gun. He handed Charlotte the flashlight, then led her to the kitchen. The back door was wide open. They rushed out onto the deck. The yard was empty. The wooden gate leading to the alleyway swung in the wind.

"He's gone. I let him get away!" Charlotte sobbed, collapsing against Miles.

"This is not your fault. Whichever officer was scheduled

to sit out front and keep an eye on things should've been here, watching over the house. Let's go call the station and report this—"

"Wait, Miles. There's something I have to tell you. Officer Haney was scheduled to be here tonight. But… I told him it wasn't necessary."

"Why would you do that?"

Charlotte clutched his arm and led him back inside. "We need to talk. I've got a lot to share with you. And I have a new lead on a suspect."

Chapter Seventeen

Miles handed Charlotte a hot cup of green tea, then took a seat next to her on the couch.

"Thank you," she mumbled.

Charlotte didn't look up from her lap. Miles figured she was too embarrassed to make eye contact after admitting that she'd gone to Hunter's party.

He'd had a strong urge to get back to her after wrapping up his work in Clemmington. So he hopped on the first flight to Nevada without even bothering to unpack or to let her know he was coming. Good thing he followed his gut.

"You know I'm holding back on just how upset I am with you, right?" Miles asked.

"I do. And I appreciate it. Because I don't have it in me to be reprimanded right now—"

"But, Charlotte," he interrupted, "you have got to stop with these rogue solo missions. Seriously."

"I know. And I will."

"Are you sure you don't wanna go to the hospital, just to get checked out and make sure everything's okay?"

"No. I'm fine. I'd rather be out there with the rest of law enforcement, searching for the killer."

"Well, Chief Mitchell wants you to take the night off. Focus on your mental health while they do the heavy lifting."

"I wish I could've gotten a better look at the guy. But he was covered from head to toe and disguising his voice. Plus, it was pitch-black in here. I was completely caught off guard…"

Miles sat back and took a sip of his rum and Coke. "I can't believe the turn this case has taken after that night we were…"

"Together," Charlotte finished after his voice trailed off. "I agree." Her head fell against the back of the couch. "I am juggling so many emotions right now. I'm exhausted yet riled up, discombobulated but laser focused, terrified but feeling fearless. I think I should call Chief Mitchell and tell him that I'm fine. I need to hit the streets and help look for—"

"No, you don't." Miles ran his thumb along the edge of his highball glass, struggling to keep calm despite his anger. "Listen, you've had a long, rough day. It's late, and you're tired. The last thing you should be trying to do is jump into investigation mode after what you went through tonight."

Charlotte sighed, her expression softening. "You know what? You're right."

"I am?" he asked, shocked that she agreed.

"Yes. You usually are."

Her eyes fell to her lap as she fiddled with a cushion zipper. Charlotte wasn't the fidgety type. Something was on her mind.

"What are you not saying to me that you want to say?" Miles asked.

"How is it that you know me so well?"

"I guess I've been around you long enough to sense when something's on your mind. Is it?"

"Yes," Charlotte replied softly. "It is."

"I'm listening."

She sat straight up, running her hands along the sides of her legs. "Full disclosure, when you left for Clemmington, I felt something that I didn't expect to feel."

"Something meaning…"

"Something personal. Emotional. And that got me to thinking about us actually being together."

"Really? I—I'm surprised to hear that. Especially after the conversation we had outside of the medical examiner's office. What brought this on?"

"Having you here in River Valley has enabled me to see you in a different light. The way you go to such great lengths to protect me and make sure I'm okay. That is one of the most attractive traits a man could have."

"It comes naturally. Because I really care about you."

"And I really care about you, too, Miles. But I've found myself fighting my feelings. Because this time around, it's not a divorce that's standing in my way. It's this investigation. I'm so focused on capturing this killer that I can't see beyond it. Plus, what if we got involved and people in the department found out? Chief Mitchell already thinks my head isn't in the game. A relationship between us would only add to that theory. And even if we start something up and try to keep it a secret, that would be too much pressure. Can you understand what I'm saying?"

"I can. My heart says otherwise, but I get it. I came here to help you solve this case. That hasn't changed. Now, do I wish something more could happen between us? Of course. Because my feelings for you aren't going away. But at the same time, I do realize our focus needs to remain on the investigation."

She leaned in and kissed him tenderly on the cheek. "Thank you for that. And who knows what may happen once the killer is behind bars."

"Don't make any promises you can't keep."

Charlotte pinched his nose. "That wasn't a promise. It was simply a statement."

He reached over and ran his fingertips along her throat. "How does your neck feel? Still sore?"

"A little. But the pain is easing up."

"Good." Miles drained his glass, then stood. "I think I need a refill. Can I get you another cup of tea?"

"No, thanks. But you can pour me a rum and Coke, too. I think it's time for something a little stronger."

"You got it."

Charlotte's cell phone buzzed.

"Can you get that?" she asked him. "I'm too tired to get up."

"Sure. We should probably check in with Chief Mitchell. See if any officers were able to find Hunter, or spot someone who may be linked to your attack."

"Good idea."

Miles grabbed her phone off the mantel and tapped the text notification. A message from an anonymous number popped up on the screen, bolded and in all caps.

TRUST THAT I'M COMING BACK FOR YOU, SERGEANT CHARLOTTE BOWMAN! NEXT TIME, THERE WILL BE NO INTERRUPTIONS. I'LL BE COMING IN HOT. GUNS BLAZING!

His mouth went dry as he reread the message.

"Oh, no," Charlotte groaned. "You look like you're about to be sick. What is it?"

Miles handed her the phone. "Another threat."

She read the text, then sprang to her feet. "*I'm coming in hot, I'm coming in hot...* Where have I heard that? Hold on!" Charlotte pulled up the video she'd filmed at Hunter's party.

"What is this?" Miles asked.

"Just watch."

He looked on as an image of Hunter climbing onto a balcony appeared.

"I'm coming in hot!" Hunter yelled before diving into the pool.

Charlotte stood frigidly, visibly shaking. She stopped the video and dialed Chief Mitchell's number. "We need to bring Hunter in for questioning. *Immediately.*"

Chapter Eighteen

Officer Haney escorted Hunter inside the interrogation room.

"I found him passed out on his front lawn," the policeman said. "Brought him straight here."

Charlotte rolled her eyes at the sight of Hunter, dressed in nothing but yellow swim trunks and flip-flops. His bare, muscular chest was completely sunburned, as were his peeling cheeks. One of his puffy eyes had been blackened, and his lower lip was split open.

Hunter winced as he walked toward the chair across from her and Miles. Charlotte peeked down at his inner thighs. Just as she'd suspected, they were covered in bright red scrapes, along with his stomach and arms.

Shouldn't have been climbing up that palm tree, idiot...

"Have a seat, Mr. Stout," Miles said.

He slammed down into the chair. "Ooh," he moaned, pressing his hands against his legs.

"Long night, huh?" Charlotte asked, surprised that his attorney wasn't there with him.

"Yeah. A long night that never ended." Hunter squinted, covering his eyes while staring up at the ceiling. "Is there any way you could turn down those fluorescent lights?"

"This is a police station," Miles said. "Not a spa. The lights aren't on dimmers."

"What the hell am I doing here, anyway? Is this about Stephen's murder? I already told Chief Mitchell everything I could remember about the night he went missing—"

"This isn't about Stephen's murder," Charlotte interrupted. "At least not yet." She slid a photo of Nalah across the table. "Do you recognize this woman?"

The black plastic chair that Hunter was sitting on wobbled back and forth as he scooted closer. "Um, she looks a little familiar. But I don't know. I have a lot of parties at my house. She may have stopped through one or two of them."

Charlotte studied his broad shoulders and tone of voice, wondering if he was the man who'd attacked her last night.

"What about now?" she continued, slamming a photo of Hunter at Nalah's crime scene down in front of him. "Do you remember seeing her at Angler Canyon Reservoir the day she turned up dead?"

His mouth fell open. A shallow gasp was all he could muster.

"What were you doing out there?" Miles asked.

Hunter rubbed his hands together, then ran them up and down his scruffy beard. "I, um… Wait. It's starting to come back to me now…"

"*What's* starting to come back to you?"

"How I know her."

Several moments of silence passed.

"Are you planning to share that information with us sometime today?" Charlotte asked.

Hunter slid down in his chair and crossed his arms over his chest. "Yeah. She was dating one of my boys."

Charlotte glanced over at Miles, wondering if Hunter was referring to Josh or Rob. "Which one of your boys?"

Another long pause.

"Answer the questions, Hunter," Miles insisted.

"T-Tom," he muttered underneath his breath.

"Who?"

"Tom," he repeated a little louder.

"As in Tommy?"

He shrugged. "Yeah. I guess."

"So you're friends with Tommy," Charlotte said, nudging Miles. "Funny, Tommy never mentioned that to us."

"It is, isn't it? And the perfect opportunity would've been that day we all saw Hunter at the Razzle Dazzle."

"You saw me at the strip club?"

Charlotte held up her hand. "We're not here to answer your questions. Now, where were you last night?"

Hunter sat straight up and looked her in the eyes. "I was at my parents' vacation house. Throwing a party. And you know what's funny? I saw an uninvited guest there who looked just like you."

"Oh, did you? Hmm. That's interesting. You must have me mistaken for someone else. But you know what's even funnier than what you *think* you saw? The fact that I was attacked last night by a man who looked just like you!" Charlotte retorted, knowing she was exaggerating but wanting to see his reaction.

"You were *what*?" Hunter yelled, leaping to his feet.

"Hey, sit down!" Miles commanded. "Before I have Officer Haney come back in here and place you under arrest."

"For what?"

"Disorderly conduct, for starters. Now, do we need to have you restrained?"

"No," Hunter mumbled, slinking back down into his chair. "Look," he said to Charlotte, "I didn't attack you. I was at the house all night, up until that stupid ass policeman picked me up and brought me here."

"Can you prove to us that you didn't leave?" Charlotte asked.

"Yes. I have hundreds of eyewitnesses who can vouch for me."

"What about the security cameras? And your neighbors' cameras? Will the footage tell us a different story?"

Hunter didn't respond. Miles held his hand to his ear and leaned into the table. "I'm sorry, Mr. Stout. I don't think I heard you. What was that you said?"

He pushed forward in his chair, balancing himself on its two front legs. "I didn't say anything..."

"And why is that?"

"Because you all are trying to pin something on me that I didn't do! And I *may* have left the house for a few minutes or whatever. But the reason why isn't any of your business."

"The hell it isn't," Charlotte shot back. "The reason why you left could have you serving a twenty-year sentence for attempted murder."

"Or multiple life sentences if you had anything to do with all the other murders that've recently taken place," Miles added.

"Wait a minute!" Hunter roared. "Are you actually accusing me of being a damn *serial* killer?"

Charlotte pulled her cell phone out of her navy blazer pocket and opened the video of Hunter jumping into the pool. "Is this you?"

"See!" he exclaimed, bouncing up and down in his seat. "I knew that was you at my party!"

"Answer the question! Is this you?"

Hunter flopped back so hard that his chair almost toppled over. "Yes! It's me. And you already know that. So why are you asking?"

"This phrase that you used before jumping into the pool, *I'm coming in hot*. Is that something you say on a regular basis?"

"I don't know. I guess. Why?"

Charlotte pulled up the text sent to her by the killer. "Did you send this to me?"

Hunter's eyes darted across the screen, his lips moving as he read the message. "No. I didn't. *I'm coming in hot* is a popular hip hop phrase. People use it all the time. And I hate to break it to you, but I'm not the nutjob killer you're looking for. Sorry you two can't seem to get the job done and catch him, but you're coming after the wrong guy."

"But you admit that there was a time during the party when you went missing," Charlotte reiterated. "Where did you go?"

"To buy drugs, okay? Are you happy now? And don't even bother trying to find out who my dealer is, because I'll never tell."

"Would you be willing to let us take a look at your cell phone?" Miles asked.

"Yeah. I would. Because my biggest secret is out of the bag now. I do drugs. Can you arrest me for that?"

"Do you have any on you?"

"Nope."

"Then let's just focus on you handing over that phone. We've got bigger things to deal with right now."

Hunter snatched the cell out of his pocket and slid it across the table. "Open the camera roll at your own risk. There may be a sex tape or two in there."

"Believe me," Charlotte mumbled as she scrolled through his text messages, "we are not interested in seeing that."

Nothing in his phone appeared suspicious. Just messages to and from family and friends. Charlotte stood and handed him the cell.

"Hunter, please excuse us. We'll be right back." She gestured for Miles to follow her out. As soon as the door closed behind them, Charlotte breathed a sigh of frustration.

"I don't think it's him," she said.

"Are you sure?"

"Not a hundred percent. But my gut is telling me that it isn't."

"I don't think we should let up on him just yet."

Charlotte threw her arms out at her sides. "Well, we can't hold him. We don't have anything on him."

"True. Let's shift our focus, then. Follow up with Tommy and see if he'll admit to selling drugs to Hunter."

"That, plus we need to follow up on that Ring camera footage he never turned over."

Miles nodded, brushing a stray curl behind Charlotte's ear. "How are you feeling? You doing okay?"

"I am. I'm feeling pretty strong."

"Glad to hear it. Should we go back in and tell Hunter he's free to go?"

"Yes, we should." She hesitated. "Miles, I know you've heard this from me before, but I have to say it again. Thank you for being here. I could not have gotten through any of this without you. Actually, I wouldn't even be here right now if it weren't for you."

"Once again, you do not have to keep thanking me. There is nowhere else I'd rather be. And you're welcome."

When Officer Haney walked by, Miles signaled him over. Charlotte instructed the policeman to swab Hunter's cheek for DNA, then take him home.

On the way out, Hunter approached her and Miles.

"You all need to talk to Tommy. He's the one who had me out at that crime scene. Before you two even got there."

"How do you know that?" Charlotte asked.

"Because I saw you running up the canyon, past the caution tape, while I was out in the crowd. How did Tommy know that Nalah had been killed, *and* where to find her body, so early in the game?"

Charlotte stood silently for several moments, then instructed Officer Haney to take him away.

"What's our next move?" Miles asked, following her down the hallway.

"It's time to pay Tommy a visit."

"I agree. If he doesn't have that security camera footage, we should arrest him right there on the spot. We've got enough probable cause, especially considering he was the last person seen with Nalah the night she went missing."

"And I won't even bother asking a judge for a warrant. We'll just take him right into custody."

Chapter Nineteen

Miles made a left turn onto Buckhorn Lane and tapped the brake. He jerked the steering wheel, barely missing a huge ball of tumbleweed rolling across the road.

"This literally looks like a scene straight out of an old Western," Charlotte muttered.

After leaving the police station, she and Miles drove to Tommy's house. He wasn't there, so they tried Candy's apartment. Neither of them were there. They figured the pair must be at the Razzle Dazzle and headed straight to the club.

Miles pulled into the parking lot. It was packed, as usual. There appeared to be some sort of commotion near the entrance. He stopped the car and saw Tommy shove the old rocker who manned the door against a wooden railing. Candy attempted to squeeze her skinny body in between them. Tommy pushed her away, knocking her to the ground.

"Hey!" Charlotte yelled, bolting from the car and running toward them. "What is going on out here?"

"Buster is tryna charge me thirty dollars to get inside the club!" Tommy yelled before pushing him again.

"I already told you," Buster heaved, his gravelly voice barely audible, "no more freebies! Your tab is already over a thousand dollars!"

"Man, go to hell—"

Before Tommy could finish, Buster grabbed him by his wifebeater's straps and slammed him against the splintered front door.

"That's enough!" Miles said, pulling the men apart.

Just as Buster bent down and dusted off his jeans, Tommy lunged at him. His fist almost clipped Buster's jaw, but the old rocker ducked right before it connected. The miss caused Tommy to lose his footing. He stumbled across the cedar decking board and hit the floor. On the way down, a small plastic bag fell from his pocket.

"Ohh," Charlotte breathed as Miles restrained him. She grabbed the bag and studied the powdery white substance inside. "What do we have here, Tommy?"

He rolled over onto his side and clutched his rib cage.

"Tommy," Charlotte repeated. "What is this?"

"Baking soda," he moaned.

She handed the bag to Miles. "How much are you willing to bet that Tommy is Hunter's drug dealer?"

"Not a dime. Because I don't like to lose, and that would be like handing over free money."

Candy bent down and cradled Tommy's head in her hands. "You okay, baby?"

"No. I think I'm dying!"

Buster stepped over his body and threw open the door. "I'm going back inside to call the police."

"Sir," Miles said, "we are the police."

"Good! Then arrest this asswipe for attempted murder!"

"I don't think we can go that far," Charlotte said. "But he will be coming with us. Get up, Tommy. Let's go."

"Let's go. Go where?"

"Down to the police station."

He rolled over onto his other side and cried out, "I think I need an ambulance. Take me to the hospital!"

Miles grabbed him by the arm and pulled him to his feet.

"Careful!" Tommy shouted. "My arm feels like it's broken. And most of my ribs, too. *Owww.*"

"Candy!" Buster yelled. "You'd better get your butt back in here before you lose your job. The DJ is calling you to the stage!"

She grabbed Tommy's face and showered it with kisses. "I gotta go, baby. Are you coming back when you're done with the cops?"

"Wait," Tommy whined. "You're not coming with me to the station?"

"I can't, babe. My big performance with Nikki Nonstop is tonight. Plus a few of my regulars are here, and I owe them—"

"I don't give a damn who's here! I need you!"

"All right," Miles said. "That's enough. Let's go."

"Bye, cuddles!" Candy called out, blowing kisses in the air. "I love you!"

"No, you don't!" Tommy cried. "If you did, you wouldn't be abandoning me right now. It's so obvious that love don't live here anymore."

Charlotte stopped Buster before he went back inside. "Are you okay, sir?"

"Yeah. I'm good. But I'll be even better once that punk pays the club what he owes us. Yo!" he shouted in Tommy's direction. "Just in case you hadn't guessed it, you're officially banned from the Razzle Dazzle until you pay up!"

Charlotte caught up with Miles as he placed Tommy in the back of the car.

"So," Miles said to him, "whatever happened to that Ring camera footage you were supposed to turn over to us?"

Tommy didn't respond.

"Trust me," the detective continued, "now is not the time

to go silent. You've got a lot of explaining to do. And you'll have plenty of time to do it once we get inside that interrogation room."

"PLEASE, DETECTIVE LOVELACE," Tommy begged. *"Please!"*

Miles glared in the rearview mirror. "It's Detective Love. And we do not have time to stop by your house. We've already shown you more than enough grace. The niceties stop here."

Charlotte turned in her seat, watching as Tommy broke down in tears. "How much time did we give you to turn over that footage?"

He rolled his neck, staring out the window rather than responding.

"*A lot.* My guess is that you don't have it. Because if you did, you would have handed it over by now. Apparently, it's more important for you to start fights at a strip club with drugs in your pocket than to prove your innocence in a murder investigation."

"Exactly," Miles agreed. "Therefore, to the police station we go."

A loud bang echoed through the car. Charlotte spun back around. Tommy was slamming his head against the window, cursing under his breath.

"Do you want me to have you committed under an involuntary seventy-two-hour hold?" Miles threatened.

"No! I'm just… I'm *frustrated.* Because I dropped the ball and didn't send you that damn footage. But I'm in love, dude! Can't you understand that?"

"Please!" Charlotte shouted. "For the last time, it's Detective Love. Not *dude*. Show some respect."

"Sorry, *Detective Love.* Anyway, like I was saying, I'm in love. Candy's got me outta my head. Like, in a chokehold or something."

"Candy?" Miles asked. "Or cocaine?"

"Du—I mean Detective, I am not on coke. Come on. Just give me a chance to prove what I'm saying is true. Take me to my house and let me pull up the footage. I promise that'll show you I wasn't involved in Nalah's murder."

"You know," Charlotte cut in, "you keep proclaiming your innocence. If you really are, then how did you know Nalah was dead so early on in the investigation and where her body could be found?"

"What are you talking about?" Tommy asked.

"Hunter told us that you were the one who informed him of Nalah's murder and sent him to the crime scene."

"That snitch," he muttered under his breath. "Look, here's the deal. There's an underground group of guys who listen to River Valley's police scanner faithfully. Hunter and I are both in it. Whenever a call comes in to 9-1-1 reporting a crime, at least one of us rushes to the scene to film it for our YouTube channel."

"Your *YouTube* channel?" Miles repeated. "Ugh, that is ridiculous. Sounds to me like you all have way too much time on your hands."

"Don't knock it. We've got over a hundred thousand sub-scribers, and we're making a whole lotta money off all our sponsors and ads. But anyway, the day that Nalah's body was found, I couldn't make it to the scene because I was, uh...*pre-occupied* with Candy. So Hunter went instead. At the time, I didn't even realize that it was Nalah out there. We just knew a body had been found. And obviously we heard the location being transmitted over the scanner."

"This case is getting stranger and stranger by the day," Charlotte said. "So, this YouTube channel. What's the name of it?"

"The Hunter and the Hunted. Get it? It's like, we're on the hunt for crime scenes, and the victims have been hunted down by some perp. The name is a play on words, too, since Hunter is a founding member of the group. See what we did there?"

Miles snapped his fingers. "Yeah, back to Hunter. Why didn't you tell us that you know him so well the day he showed up at the Razzle Dazzle?"

"Because, you know my motto. Snitches get stitches. So what's up? Don't you wanna free me so you can go after the real killer? All you gotta do is turn the car around, slide through my crib and let me show you that video footage!"

Miles tapped his fist against the steering wheel. Tension crept up his neck as his temples ached with frustration. "What do you think?" he asked Charlotte. "Should we take a quick detour and stop by his house?"

"Yes!" Tommy hollered. "Let's do it!"

Charlotte ignored him. "It wouldn't hurt. For once, Tommy actually has a point. If he can prove that he returned home that night—"

"Which I did," he interrupted.

"—and stayed there until the next day," she continued, "then we can check him off our list of suspects."

"Might as well. At this point, what do we have to lose?" Miles glanced in the rearview mirror. "Tommy, you'd better not be wasting our time."

The detective made a U-turn and sped down Beaumont Street.

"If he is guilty," Charlotte whispered, "he's doing a great job of hiding it. Because if nothing else, the man is confident."

"Yeah, let's see how confident he is once he gets behind the computer and has to pull up that footage."

When they arrived at the house, Tommy skipped up the walkway as if he didn't have a care in the world. The second he opened the door, Charlotte and Miles were hit with the stench of musty clothes mixed with stale marijuana smoke.

Black curtains were drawn, making it almost impossible to see through the living room. But the clutter was apparent. Take-out containers, cardboard boxes and dirty dishes were strewn everywhere. A futon, folding chair and set of crates acting as a coffee table were the only pieces of furniture in the room.

"Are you in the process of moving out?" Miles asked.

"Nah. Candy hates the place, so I boxed up a bunch of my stuff so we could do some decorating." Tommy pointed at the futon. "Have a seat. I'll go grab my laptop. Can I get you all something to drink? Alls I've got is beer, Red Bull and hard seltzer. And tap water."

"No, thank you," Charlotte replied, holding her finger to her nose. "Just go get your computer so we can grab the footage and get out of here."

A peeling plaid blanket covered the futon. Miles and Charlotte threw one another looks of disgust before sitting as close to the edge as possible.

"This little pit stop had better be worth it," he warned.

"Agreed. I'm beginning to feel nauseous."

Tommy shuffled back into the room with his computer. He plopped down in between Miles and Charlotte and logged into his Ring account.

"All righty," he said, rubbing his hands together. "Here we go."

Tommy clicked on the History tab. Nothing appeared on the screen. "Wait," he mumbled, hitting the enter button on the keyboard. Still nothing. "What the hell is happening right now?" He pounded the touchpad, then the enter key, then the touchpad again.

"Where are your recorded videos?" Miles asked.

"I don't know. I must be doing something wrong here. I've never tried to go back and review old footage. I usually only watch the live views."

"Hold on," Charlotte said. "Tommy, do you have a Ring protection plan?"

"No. It costs extra. Why?"

"Because that's what you need in order to record surveillance footage! If you don't have a protection plan, then your camera won't tape anything. It only streams live videos." She headed for the door. "Miles, cuff him so we can get down to the station and move forward with the interrogation. I also wanna run the drugs he had on him through a chemical test kit so we'll know whether it's cocaine, or heroin, or—"

"Hold on," Tommy said. "It's none of those things! And I can prove it!"

Miles waved him off. "Here we go with the false promises again. Just like you were gonna prove via surveillance footage that you were here with Candy all night when Nalah went missing, right?"

"Wrong."

Tommy scrambled to his feet and ran to the back of the house. Charlotte and Miles chased after him.

"Where are you going?" she yelled.

"To the bathroom! The proof is in my medicine cabinet!"

The pair stood outside of the cramped powder room, watching as Tommy knocked every bottle inside the cabinet into the sink. "It's here," he panted. "Somewhere…"

"What's here?" Miles asked.

"The meds that are in that baggie you all confiscated!"

The detective stepped over the threshold, struggling to avoid brushing up against the filthy pedestal sink. "You know what? That's enough. Your time is up. Let's go." He pulled a pair of handcuffs from his back pocket.

"Wait!" Tommy said, shoving a bottle in Miles's face. "See? Here it is. Those are not illegal drugs in that bag. It's crushed up OxyContin. I've got a prescription. My name is on it and everything."

Miles grabbed the bottle and handed it to Charlotte, then handcuffed him.

"Come on, man!" he cried.

"Detective Love," Miles reiterated, pushing him out of the bathroom.

"Come on, Detective Love! And Captain Berkin!"

They ignored him, hauling Tommy out to the car.

"I'm gonna prove you both wrong," he grumbled. "Watch me."

"Yeah, well, until then," Charlotte said, "you'll be in police custody."

An elderly woman stood on the curb across the street, checking her mailbox. "Hello, Tommy," she called out. "Thank you so much for mowing my lawn this morning."

"You're welcome," Tommy responded, barely looking up at her. Right before he climbed inside the car, he popped back up.

"What are you doing?" Miles asked.

"Just gimme a second. Hey! Mrs. Milton?"

"Yes?"

"Don't you have a Ring surveillance system?"

"A what?"

"A Ring camera security system!"

"I do. Why?"

"Does your camera record video footage?"

"I think so."

"Where are you going with this?" Charlotte asked him.

"Mrs. Milton lives directly across the street from my house. Her camera may have recorded me the night Nalah went missing."

Miles grabbed the top of Tommy's head and nudged him toward the back seat. "That's quite a long shot. Too bad you weren't that interested in retrieving the footage when we initially requested it."

Tommy pushed back, resisting Miles's effort to get him inside the car. "Mrs. Milton! If you can pull up footage of me from two weeks ago, call and let me know!"

The woman stepped into the street. "From two weeks ago? I'll see what I can do, hon. Is everything all right?"

"Everything is fine, ma'am," Charlotte said. "Thank you." She nodded in Miles's direction. "Come on. Let's hurry up and get him to the station."

Chapter Twenty

Miles clutched the steering wheel as he drove toward Charlotte's house. After another long, exhausting day at the station, the pair were finally heading home.

It'd been nearly three weeks since Nalah's murder, and the investigation had been inundated with false leads. Intense pressure was closing in on the entire force. But no one felt it more deeply than Charlotte, which caused tensions to build between her and Miles.

"Once again," she began, her tone trembling with frustration, "we need to meet with Chief Mitchell and share our suspicions about Walter."

Choose your words wisely, Miles told himself.

"Charlotte, I know you're anxious to tell the chief what you think you know about Walter's involvement in—"

"What I *think* I know? Come on, Miles. The writing's on the wall. This investigation has hit one dead end after another. Every other suspect on our list has checked out. All roads lead back to Walter. *Now's* the time for us to put together a formal report and present it to Chief Mitchell first thing in the morning."

Miles let up on the accelerator as he turned down Charlotte's block. "I still think you're jumping the gun. We'll only get one shot to explain why we think the corporal of River

Valley PD is a serial killer. When we do, our presentation has got to be well-thought-out and chock-full of facts."

"And it will be. Now let's go inside and get to work!"

"No," Miles argued, "it won't be. We still don't have enough evidence to prove Walter's guilt."

Charlotte reached for her door handle as he pulled in front of the house. Before he could bring the car to a complete stop, she jumped out.

"Really?" Miles asked. "So you're just gonna storm off rather than talk things out?"

"Yes! Because this conversation is over," Charlotte shot back before rushing up the walkway.

Miles sat there, his head falling against the back of the seat.

"I can't do this," he muttered before driving off.

THIRTY MINUTES LATER, the detective found himself turning into Angler Canyon Reservoir's parking lot. Miles took his time before climbing out of the car. His calf muscles stiffened as he stood—the result of spending way more time behind a desk than in the gym.

The setting sun cooled the air blowing through the canyon. He rolled up the sleeves on his pale blue shirt and inhaled, almost tasting the fragrant white flowers blooming from lush ash trees. Miles was grateful for the much-needed time alone, even if it was being spent at a crime scene.

Despite Charlotte's angry delivery, she'd been right about one thing—their investigation had certainly been hit with one dead end after another. All of the victims' autopsy and toxicology reports came back negative for foreign substances. Neither Tommy's nor Hunter's DNA matched evidence at the crime scenes, and their YouTube channel checked out. Results from the forensic sweep performed on Charlotte's house the night she was attacked came back inconclusive.

Law enforcement was able to retrieve surveillance footage from the night of Hunter's party that showed him leaving and returning to the property. But he hadn't been gone long enough to have assaulted Charlotte. Ironically, his drug dealer alibied him, admitting that he'd sold marijuana to Hunter at the reported time.

The powdery white substance they'd confiscated from Tommy turned out to be oxycodone, just as he'd claimed. His neighbor Mrs. Milton handed over the Ring camera footage from the night Nalah went missing. Just as he'd claimed, it showed Tommy and Candy entering his home that evening and reemerging the following day.

Once Hunter and Tommy were cleared, Charlotte and Miles had grilled Walter on whether he'd told Josh that Stephen's cell phone was in police custody. Walter denied it, and Chief Mitchell believed him. When Charlotte asked Walter what happened to the inside information he'd sworn he could pull from Stephen's friends, she discovered they'd cut him off after rumors swirled he was trying to frame them. Nevertheless, the chief refused to question Walter's integrity.

Maybe all that is what brought me out here, Miles thought. Because at this point, he was willing to do whatever it took to solve the case so he could return to Clemmington. Even if it meant scouring crime scenes alone. Because being in such close quarters with the woman he cared about yet continually clashed with was becoming too much to bear.

The detective trekked down the rocky terrain toward a cluster of sagebrush shrubs nestled in the hillside. It was the exact spot where Nalah's body had been found. Wind whipped across the canyon, breezing through tree leaves as sunlight slipped behind the mountains. Chirping songbirds and gurgling waves made for serene surroundings. Most fishermen, boaters and sunbathers had already vacated the site.

A calm filled the air, contrasting with the violence of the heinous crime that had taken place there weeks ago.

Walter's initial report indicated that just like the other victims, there was no trauma to Nalah's body. But her lavender tank dress had been pulled up around her shoulders, while the rest of the bodies remained fully clothed. She'd been found completely nude from the neck down. According to the medical examiner, she hadn't been sexually assaulted. Charlotte believed the killer left her in that position to taunt the River Valley PD. Miles feared that if they didn't capture him soon, his attacks would come faster and become more brutal.

Kicking a cluster of rocks aside, Miles pulled out his cell and snapped several photos of the shrubs. Just as he zoomed in, it vibrated. The buzz startled him, sending the phone tumbling into a tangle of gray branches.

"Ugh," Miles huffed, scraping his hand as he reached into the jagged twigs and retrieved it.

Charlotte's name flashed across the screen. "Hey, what's up?" he asked, not bothering to disguise the irritation in his voice.

"Hel-help me..."

Miles shot straight up. "Charlotte? What's wrong?"

She gasped into the phone. And then silence.

"Charlotte!" he yelled, charging back toward the parking lot. "Are you okay? What's going on?"

"Heee..."

The phone went dead.

Miles jumped inside the car and sped off toward her house.

WHY DIDN'T YOU call 9-1-1?

It was too late now. Miles burst through Charlotte's front door, rushing from room to room in search of her.

"Charlotte! Where are you?"

Silence.

"Charlotte!"

The stench of burning meat drifted through the house. Miles ran to the kitchen. It was filled with smoke, but Charlotte wasn't there. The patio door was open. He ran outside.

Haze smoldered across the deck. Three feet of fire burned from the grill. Miles stumbled down the stairs, choking as fumes filled his lungs.

"Charlotte!"

His eyes stung as he struggled to see. Grabbing a bag of sand from underneath the deck, he dumped it onto the grill and put out the fire. Through the billowing smoke, he caught a glimpse of Charlotte.

She was sprawled on the ground with her arms out at her sides and eyes closed. He rushed over and fell to his knees.

"Char, wake up," he pleaded, pulling her onto his lap. "Come on, wake up!"

She didn't budge. A heightened sense of panic stifled his breathing. He checked her pulse. It was weak.

At least she's alive...

"Who did this to you?" Miles lamented, wrapping her in his arms and rushing her to the hospital.

Chapter Twenty-One

"So, you weren't attacked?" Miles asked Charlotte.

She shook her head, pulling at the cannula tube tangled in the IV line. "No. Or... I don't think so."

He reached across the hospital bed and clutched her hand. "You don't remember what happened? Or how you ended up fainting?"

"Not really. I just know I wanted to surprise you with a special dinner since things have been so strained between us lately. I remember firing up the grill, throwing on the steaks, and then *boom*. I hit the ground, called you, and now I'm here at the hospital."

"Well, first off, thank you for the dinner gesture. I really appreciate you doing that. But I'm so confused. Did someone come in and hit you over the head, and now you can't remember? Or did you get overheated from all the smoke?"

"I just— I don't know." Charlotte pressed her palm against her pounding forehead. "I do feel a migraine coming on, though. And my stomach is killing me."

"It could be that the stress of this case is catching up to you. We'll see what the doctor says once your lab results come back."

The anguish in Miles's unsteady tone was apparent. Charlotte stared into his bloodshot eyes. He looked as though he hadn't slept in days.

"I'm sorry," she whispered.

"For what?"

"For the way I've been treating you. This case has got me bugging out. I know I haven't been the nicest person to deal with. So for that, I apologize."

The hurt that had been riding Miles's shoulders lifted a bit. "Thank you for saying that. And I get it. You're anxious to catch this killer before he commits another murder. You've been attacked. And threatened. Our leads are going cold before they even catch any real steam. It's enough to break anybody's spirit and alter their behavior."

"You're always so diplomatic. And you know all the right things to say." She tightened her hold on his hand. "I'm glad you understand."

The moment was interrupted when Charlotte's cell phone buzzed.

"Can you see who that is?" she asked. "I'm being held captive by all these lines."

"Charlotte, why don't you rest instead of worrying about who's contacting you? You're under enough stress. I don't want you to—"

"Miles," she interrupted. "I don't want a repeat of what happened the last time I ignored my phone. Now please, can you just see who it is?"

A low grunt preceded him grabbing the phone off the wooden nightstand. "It's a text from Chief Mitchell."

"See, there may be something important going on." She took the phone and scanned the message. "Oh, wow…"

"What did he say?"

"The chief just got a call from the forensics lab. The results came back on that syringe Walter collected from Nalah's crime scene."

"And?"

"There were traces of heroin inside of it. The fingerprints were run through CODIS and matched up with a man named Otis Fielding."

"Does that name ring a bell?" Miles asked.

"It does. Otis is a well-known drug addict here in River Valley who's got a lengthy criminal history. His rap sheet is filled with petty crimes, though. Nothing serious."

"Up until now, possibly. What's the next move? Is he being brought in for questioning?"

"No. Because Otis is in jail right now for attempted armed robbery. He's been locked up for almost three months. There's no way he could have killed Nalah. Angler Canyon is a popular hangout spot for drug addicts. We try and keep the area clean, but they know how to hide within the terrain."

"So in other words, you don't think the syringe is connected to Nalah's murder."

"No. I don't."

Miles nudged her arm. "Why do I get the feeling you're a little pleased with this news?"

"Stop that." She snickered, swatting his hand away. "I just want this case to be solved, even if it is at the hands of Walter. But it won't be."

"I know. Because you're convinced that he's the killer."

"Exactly."

The doctor entered the room. "How are you feeling, Ms. Bowman?"

"A little better, I guess. My head and stomach are still bothering me, but I'm not feeling quite as woozy as I did when I first came in. Maybe I just needed to sit still and get some fluids in my system."

"Could be…" The doctor, who appeared to be in his late sixties, scratched his balding head while shuffling over to the monitor. "Your blood pressure has gone back up since you first arrived, which is a good sign."

"That's a great sign," Miles said. "And by the looks of that big grin on your face, Doc, I'm guessing Charlotte's lab results came back okay?"

"Oh, yes. Ms. Bowman's lab results look good. Really good."

"So what do you think is wrong with me?" she asked. "Why did I fall out like that?"

The doctor held her file to his chest and rocked back on his heels. "The reason you fainted was due to a drop in your blood pressure, which was caused by a hormonal release. When that happens, the blood vessels in the body relax, preventing the proper amount of blood from reaching your brain."

"Okay," Charlotte said slowly. "What does all that mean, then? Am I going into early menopause?"

"Quite the opposite, Ms. Bowman. You're pregnant."

She emitted a cackle so shrill that it rattled her pounding head. "I'm sorry. I thought you said I was pregnant. So, perimenopause, huh? You think that's what's happening here?"

"No, not perimenopause. You are *pregnant.*"

The room faded to black. Charlotte's brain buzzed with disbelief. She turned to Miles, blinking rapidly until he came into view. His eyes were bulging out of his head. And his bright smile was filled with joy.

Miles's fingers intertwined with hers. Charlotte's remained limp, unable to grasp his hand or the pregnancy news.

"How far along is she?" he asked.

"Not far, but the gynecologist will talk to her about that," Charlotte thought she'd heard through the white noise ringing in her ears.

Miles moved from the chair to the bed. The corners of his

eyes were damp with tears. Every tooth inside his mouth was on full display as he wrapped his arm around her.

"This is...this is unreal!" he exclaimed.

'Yeah," she squeaked. "It sure is."

The doctor patted Charlotte's shoulder. "Congratulations, you two. I'll leave you alone for a bit so you can digest the news. In the meantime, if you need anything, just buzz the nurse and she'll be right in."

"Will do," Miles said. "Thank you, Doctor."

The moment the door closed behind him, Charlotte burst into tears. Miles was holding her so tightly that he didn't seem to notice.

"Please," she gasped. "I can't breathe!"

"Oh! Sorry."

Charlotte grabbed a tissue and cup of ice water, avoiding his gaze. He slowly pulled away.

"You're not happy about the news, are you?" Miles asked.

"I just... I'm *shocked*. This is the last thing I expected. A baby? I'm not prepared to have a baby. I just got promoted to sergeant. I'm in the middle of the biggest investigation of my career. You and I aren't married. We're not even dating—"

"Charlotte," Miles interrupted. "Listen to me. This is a surprise for us both. And I understand how you feel. A baby doesn't fit into your plan. But you know what? I see this as a blessing. A light to brighten all the darkness surrounding us. We're going to bring new life into the world. I hope this doesn't sound selfish, but I've always wanted to be a father. And I can't think of anyone I'd rather share that honor with than you."

Tears trickled down Charlotte's cheeks. Her body grew numb with fear. And doubt. She flung the stiff white blanket off to the side as her entire body began to sweat.

"I hear you, Miles. But you're gonna have to give me some time to process all of this. It's a lot..."

"I know it is. And I will. It goes without saying that I will be here with you every step of the way."

She nodded, unable to respond. He leaned in and kissed her forehead. Overcome by a bout of vulnerability, she rested her head on his chest.

"I've got you," he whispered, stroking her hair. "I've got *us*."

Charlotte thought of Chief Mitchell. If he found out about the pregnancy, he would want to take her off the case.

"I don't want anyone in the department to know about this," she told Miles.

"Not even the chief?"

"*Especially* not the chief. At least not right now. I'll tell him eventually."

"You should. Sooner rather than later. Because obviously this pregnancy is going to affect your involvement in the investigation."

She sat straight up, pulling away from his embrace. "How so?"

"What do you mean, *how so*? The long hours you've been working, the grueling crime scene examinations, visits to the morgue, suspect interrogations—all of those things take a toll on your mental and physical well-being. Not to mention your stress level. Keep in mind what happened to you today. I know you don't wanna hear this, but you're going to have to pull back on this case, Charlotte."

She fell back onto a pillow, pressing her fingertips against her throbbing temples. "Here we go. See, this is what I mean. I'm not ready to stop. Now is not the time to let up on this case, Miles. Pregnant or not, we need to go harder."

"Well, sorry to break it to you, but you can't. I won't let you risk your life or the life of our child for this. There are plenty of capable law enforcement officers in the department who can step up and assist in the investigation."

Charlotte closed her eyes, counting to ten while taking deep breaths. The pain in her stomach began to subside. She placed her hand over her belly as Miles's words replayed in her head.

He was right. This was a blessing. But what should've been the best moment in her life couldn't have come at a worse time.

Chapter Twenty-Two

Charlotte knocked on Chief Mitchell's door.

Please let this go well...

"Come in!"

She stuck her head inside. "Hey, you got a minute?"

"I do. But make it quick. The digital forensics guys are coming in to beg for updated tools and software. I've been avoiding them for weeks because I have yet to figure out how to work it into the budget."

"Don't worry. This won't take long."

Charlotte almost fell into a chair as a rush of nausea hit her square in the gut. She didn't know if it was the pregnancy, the fact that she'd let Miles talk her into sharing the news with the chief or the stench of old coffee wafting through the office.

Maybe it's a combination of all three, she thought, eyeballing several paper cups scattered along the desk.

"Any updates on the investigation?" he asked.

"Nothing that I haven't already reported. I'm actually here to discuss something else with you. But before I do, I'd like to ask that you keep it between us. At least for the time being."

"Your secret's safe with me. What's going on?"

Just say it. And hope that he doesn't ask a bunch of questions. Like who's the father.

"Chief, I, um... I'm pregnant—"

Crack!

Charlotte stopped abruptly when the sound of breaking glass smashed against the door.

"What the hell was that?" Chief Mitchell yelled.

"Sorry, sir!"

Charlotte rushed to the door and threw it open. Walter was crouched down on his knees, picking up pieces of a shattered coffee mug.

"What are you doing?" she hissed.

He looked up at her, his eyes red with anger. "Just trying to get to my desk. I must've slipped on something and dropped my cup in the process."

"Right outside of Chief Mitchell's office, huh? Just as I'd come in here to have a private conversation. How coincidental." She crossed her arms in front of her chest and leaned against the doorway. "Maybe you got tripped up after overhearing my conversation. Were you standing out here eavesdropping on us?"

"*Eavesdropping?* Why would I care about whatever it is you two are talking about?"

"Oh, please. Let's not act like you haven't been overly concerned with every move I make since my promotion. Not to mention our failed—"

Charlotte stopped herself.

"Not to mention our failed *what?*" Walter asked, standing straight up as a crowd began to gather. "Our failed relationship? You sound a bit paranoid, Bowman. Could it be that those threats you *allegedly* keep getting are throwing you off? Or maybe it's the fact that you have yet to solve this case."

An audible gasp rippled through the area. Charlotte ignored the instigators, focusing solely on Walter while fighting the urge to punch him in the throat.

"Walk away, Corporal Kincaid," she warned.

Instead of taking heed, he moved in closer. "Or maybe

you're finally realizing that you're in too deep, thanks to that premature promotion, *Sarge*."

"Go to hell, Walter—"

"Hey!" Chief Mitchell barked just as the digital forensics team walked up.

"You ready for us, Chief?" the director asked.

"Yeah, come on in, guys. Sergeant Bowman, let's reconvene later this afternoon. And, Corporal Kincaid? Watch it. That's a superior you're talking to."

"Yes, sir," Walter said, his exaggerated tone far from sincere.

Charlotte slipped past everyone and hurried toward her office. She grabbed the door to slam it shut. A hand forced it back open. She pivoted, almost slamming into Miles.

"Hey, you okay?" he asked.

"No, not really." She grabbed a tissue and patted the back of her damp neck. "I was just in Chief Mitchell's office, sharing the news that I'm pregnant. Walter was loitering right outside the door. I think he may have overheard our conversation."

"Wait, I ran out to the parking lot for five minutes and missed all of that? Let me go and have a word with Walter—"

"No!" Charlotte insisted, pulling him back inside the office. "Walter is already questioning my capabilities as a sergeant. I don't want him thinking I can't fight my own battles, too. I appreciate the gesture, though."

"Of course. That's what I'm here for. Don't worry about that clown. You've got way bigger things to think about. So, how did Chief Mitchell react to the news?"

"He didn't get a chance to. As soon as the words *I'm pregnant* were out of my mouth, Walter smashed a mug right outside of the office. Then the digital forensics guys came in for a meeting. It was just chaotic. The chief and I are going to reconvene later this afternoon."

"Okay, well, at least he's aware of what's going on. Now, grab your purse. I've got a surprise for you."

"A surprise? What kind of surprise?"

"The kind you'll find out about in fifteen minutes. Let's go!"

"UM, I DON'T mean to burst your bubble or anything," Charlotte said when Miles pulled in front of the Drip & Sip Coffee Shop, "but coming to this place is not a surprise."

"Woman, just get out of the car and follow me."

The scent of frosted cinnamon rolls hit well before they entered the café. Charlotte clutched her grumbling stomach.

"On second thought, maybe this little coffee run is exactly what I needed."

"Trust me," Miles said, holding open the door, "it is."

"Charlotte!" someone screamed the moment they stepped inside. She swiveled and almost tipped over at the sight of Ella charging toward her.

"El! What are you doing here?"

"I was just assigned another temp job in Reno. So of course I had to stop through River Valley again and see my big sis on the way there."

"Aww, I'm so glad you did." Charlotte squeezed her watery eyes shut as she embraced her sister. "Miles was right. I did need this surprise, and he seems to always know where to find you. There's been so much going on. The stress of this investigation has taken over my entire life."

"Don't let it. You've got my little niece or nephew to think about," Ella insisted now that Charlotte and Miles had shared the pregnancy news with their immediate families.

"That's exactly what I've been telling her," Miles said.

"I'm working on it." Charlotte glanced around the quaint shop, eyeing its long rustic tables, antique bookshelves and old album covers hanging from the walls.

"I love this place," Ella gushed. "Nice choice, Miles. I found an empty table near the back by the window for us."

"Cool," he said. "Why don't you two have a seat and I'll place our order? Charlotte, should I get your regular? A decaf caramel macchiato and cinnamon roll?"

"*Two* cinnamon rolls. Don't judge me."

"Never would I do that. Ella, what are you having?"

"I'd like a mocha latte and everything bagel, please."

"Got it. Be right back."

Ella clutched Charlotte's hand and led her to their table. "Okay, so, how wonderful is Miles?"

"He's… Yeah. He's a great guy."

"Uh-oh."

"Uh-oh, what?"

"I know that tone. It's the same one you had back when you first met Miles, then dumped him after three days of pure bliss!"

"You are so dramatic. That is not how it happened."

"That's exactly how it happened. And now, I already know you're about to go into the whole *I'm going through too much to even think about a relationship* spiel. Only this time, the excuse will be your case rather than the divorce, which was your excuse the last time."

"I hate that I share everything with you." Charlotte stared down at the table, running her nails along its rigid grooves. "Look, it's not that simple. I've already explained to Miles that this case is my number one priority. I can't get distracted by a relationship right now."

"Seriously?" Ella pointed at her belly. "Seems like you're already past that point. You and Miles are in each other's lives permanently now. Plus, it's not all about you anymore. That man dropped his entire life back in California to be here for you. That says a lot. And he's so excited about becoming a father. Shoot, I wish I could find a distraction that wonderful."

Clanking dishes rattled behind Charlotte. "Look, he's on his way back here. Let's table this conversation for later. Better yet, let's just drop it altogether."

"Whatever you say…"

Miles approached balancing a tray and his cell phone. "You're looking good, big bro," he said to the screen. "You been hitting the gym behind my back?"

"No doubt," Miles's brother, Jake, replied, flexing his biceps.

Charlotte passed their drinks around and leaned into the phone. "Hey, Jake. How are you?"

"Hey, I'm hanging in there. How are things going out there in the desert? Any new leads on the case?"

"Things are moving. We've got a few interesting bites we're looking into."

"Who is that?" Ella whispered.

"My brother," Miles told her.

"Who is that?" Jake asked.

"My sister, Ella," Charlotte said.

Miles turned the phone in Ella's direction.

"Damn!" Jake uttered. "Oh, wait, sorry. I shouldn't have— I was just…"

"Taken aback by my sister's beauty?" Charlotte finished for him.

"Yeah, actually. I was. Let me check my schedule real quick and see when I can take a trip to River Valley. You know, to check on my baby brother. See if he needs a little of my Clemmington PD expertise."

"Oh, so you work in law enforcement, too?" Ella asked.

"I do. I'm a detective."

"Mmm, interesting. It just so happens that I love a man in uniform."

Charlotte side-eyed her sister, then tapped Miles's arm. "Sorry Ella hijacked your video chat," she whispered.

"No worries. It's actually nice to see Jake vibing with someone. His dating life hasn't been the smoothest, to say the least."

"Listen, guys," Jake said, "I need to get going. Duty calls. Miles and Charlotte, let me know if there's anything I can do to help out on my end. And I mean that. The investigation, the pregnancy, whatever."

"Thanks, man," Miles said. "We appreciate it."

"And, Ella," Jake continued, his voice dropping several octaves, "it was a pleasure meeting you, albeit digitally. Hopefully next time we can do so in person."

She flipped her hair and flashed a red-carpet smile. "Yes, that would be nice."

The pair grew silent while gazing at one another through the screen.

"Bye, Jake," Charlotte interjected.

Miles disconnected the chat and took a sip of his chai tea. "So, what'd I miss? I saw you two sitting back here gossiping while I was up at the counter."

"Who, *us*?" Charlotte glanced around the café in mock confusion. "Gossiping? Why, we'd never…"

"Actually," Ella cut in, "we were talking about how wonderful you are, and how I am so looking forward to being an auntie."

"Aww, thanks. But not as much as I'm looking forward to being a dad."

"Sweet." A line of worry suddenly creased Ella's forehead. "Speaking of parenthood, Charlotte, I'm assuming you're going to back off this investigation and focus on your pregnancy now, right?"

Charlotte picked up a napkin and fanned her face as the air in the room grew warmer. She could feel Miles's eyes on her, awaiting her response.

"Listen," she began, "I know how much you both care

about me. And I appreciate it. But I'm committed to seeing this case through to the end. Nothing either of you say is going to change that. Plus, I'm healthy, the baby is healthy and the doctor hasn't mentioned anything about me needing to dial it back. So don't worry. I'll be fine. *We'll* be fine."

"I hope you're not doing this because you think you have something to prove," Miles said.

"Not at all. Proof of my abilities was validated when Chief Mitchell promoted me over everyone else in the department. Now, am I bothered by the fact that I have yet to solve this investigation? Absolutely. Is the media pressure getting to me? Definitely."

"See," Ella said, shaking her head so hard that her curls slapped against her face. "I don't like that. You're stressing yourself out, Char. Listen to me. I'm a nurse. You're gonna end up jeopardizing yourself *and* the baby over this case. You've got to take into consideration what all that pressure could do to your body. There's the threat of gestational diabetes, preeclampsia and premature birth, just to name a few."

The fanning of the napkin was no longer working. Charlotte had broken out into a full-blown sweat. "But imagine the amount of stress I'd be under if I let this case go. Some of my colleagues are waiting on me to fail. So much so that one of them has been threatening me to try and throw me off."

"We don't know that for a fact," Miles said.

"Well, what we do know for a fact is there are people in that department who resent me."

"And by people," Ella said, "do you mean Walter?"

"Not just Walter. But he's certainly number one on my list."

Ella brushed a few flyaways out of Charlotte's eyes. "I'm getting the sense that you're irritated."

"That's because I am. And I'd love to change the subject. A surprise visit from my sister is supposed to be enjoyable.

I'm not enjoying this tag-teaming interrogation you two are putting me through."

"You're right," Ella said just as the bell over the shop's door jingled. A commotion erupted near the entrance.

"Stephanie!" a male voice boomed. "How's the owner of my favorite coffee spot in town doing?"

Charlotte groaned, immediately recognizing that loud, irritating voice. "What in the hell is Walter doing here? Do you think he followed us?"

"I certainly hope not," Miles responded. "But if he did, it wouldn't surprise me. Either way, don't worry about it. Just relax and enjoy your coffee and cinnamon rolls."

"I've suddenly lost my appetite."

"Oh, no," Ella said, sliding the plate toward her. "Eat up. Don't allow that man to get to you. Let him see you back here having a good time."

Charlotte stared at the rolls. Buttercream icing oozed down the sides of the warm pastries. "You're right. What was I thinking?"

The moment she bit into the gooey dessert, Walter came strolling over.

"Hey, what's up, everybody? Did my invite to this little shindig get lost in the mail or something?"

"Hello," Ella grumbled while Miles and Charlotte ignored him.

"I just so happened to be driving by and saw you three sitting in the window. So I figured I'd come in and say hello. Especially to you, Ella. It's been a long time. How've you been?"

Ella glared up at him, her lips twisted with disgust. "Wonderful. Especially after hearing the news that Charlotte and Miles are expecting—"

Charlotte gave her a swift kick underneath the table.

"*Ouch!* What was that… *Ohh.*"

"Wait," Walter said. "Expecting what? Go on and finish what you were saying, Ella. Charlotte and Miles are expecting…"

A ringing cell phone disrupted the moment.

"*Thank* you," Charlotte whispered, ecstatic for the disruption.

Ella scrambled for her phone and turned away from the group.

"So, what news is your sister referring to?" Walter pressed.

"Charlotte and I are anticipating a visit to Reno once Ella starts her next temp job there," Miles told him.

"Really?" Walter questioned, his smirk reeking of skepticism. "Are you sure that's what it is?"

"Positive," Charlotte shot back.

Ella grabbed her things, interrupting the debate. "Sorry to break up the party. But that was the hospital administrator. I need to get to Reno. Stat." She hugged Charlotte and Miles. "So good seeing you two. Char, I'll call you later tonight."

"Better yet, text me and let me know you made it!" she called out as Ella rushed toward the exit.

"Hey, wait up!" Walter ran after her, bumping into several chairs along the way. "I'll walk you to your car!"

"Look who's trying to be a gentleman," Miles said.

"Please. More like he's trying to pry information out of her. That was a close call."

"Sure was. You shut Ella down just in time."

Charlotte drained her cup and wrapped a half-eaten cinnamon roll in a napkin. "Miles, I really appreciate you setting this up. Thank you."

"Of course."

"Why don't we head back to the station? I wanna take another look at the surveillance footage from The Bottomless Bar. See if we can figure out where Stephen could've ended up. Afterward, maybe we can drive over to Rush Street and retrace his steps."

Miles remained quiet while piling their dishes onto the tray.

"You know," Charlotte continued, "let's walk that backstreet near Eden's Den, just to see what we might find."

Still nothing. She studied his somber expression as he stood, then followed him out of the shop. When they reached the car, he stopped her.

"May I make a suggestion?" Miles asked.

"Sure."

"Why don't we review the surveillance footage at the station and have Officer Haney walk the area?"

"I know what you're doing," Charlotte retorted. "And it's not gonna work."

"Think of it this way. If you start passing some of the caseload on to other officers, whoever's threatening you may back off, and—"

"That's not gonna happen." She flung open the car door and climbed inside. "So just drop it."

He stood there, gripping the door frame. Charlotte stared straight ahead, her stony expression unflinching.

"Okay, then. Consider it dropped."

Chapter Twenty-Three

Charlotte knocked on the guest room door. There was no answer. She stuck her head inside. Miles was lying across the bed sound asleep, the remote still in his hand.

She glanced at the clock. It was a little after 8:00 p.m.

Just don't wake up within the next hour, she thought before grabbing her purse and tiptoeing out the front door.

Charlotte hurried inside the car and headed straight to Rush Street. Miles had refused to take her earlier that afternoon, insisting that she needed to dial it back. While he may have won that battle, he hadn't won the war. Because now that he was out cold, she was determined to press on toward the goal of gathering new evidence with or without him.

She made a right turn down Cottonwood Lane. The narrow, two-lane street was surrounded by a nature preserve, filled with diverse flora and fauna. Charlotte switched on the bright lights as darkness enveloped her car.

Anxious to get to the other side of the preserve, she rammed her foot against the accelerator. She hadn't been out driving alone in quite some time. It evoked an eerie sense of vulnerability. She'd taken for granted the comfort of Miles's presence as memories of the Peak Avenue car chase flashed through her mind.

Turn around. Go back home. You promised, no more solo missions...

But Charlotte refused. She was feeling defiant after the confrontation with Miles outside of the coffee shop. She didn't need to prove to him she was still capable even while pregnant. She felt the need to prove it to herself. At this point, her determination trumped all sensibility. Backing down wasn't an option.

"You should at least call him," she muttered to herself. "So he'll know where you are. *Somebody* should."

Charlotte tapped the phone button on the car's touch screen.

"Miles Love."

His name appeared in the contacts list. She reached out. Her fingertip hovered over the selection. As she contemplated placing the call—

Bam!

Charlotte's head snapped back, slamming against the headrest. The car jolted forward before careening into a ditch and burrowing in the shoulder of the roadway.

Brakes screeched behind her. Bright lights shone through the back windshield, illuminating the interior of the car. Charlotte peered through the window, struggling to blink through the dizziness and adjust her blurred vision.

This cannot be happening...

"Ma'am!" a high-pitched voice called out. "I am so sorry! Are you okay?"

Relief hit when Charlotte realized she'd been rear-ended by a woman rather than the killer. She rolled her window all the way down. "I'm fine. I think. My head is a little woozy, but other than that, I'm good."

"Looks like I did a number on your car's bumper," the driver said, keeping her distance as she surveyed the damage. "Mine, too. I should not have come out here..."

"What do you mean?" Charlotte asked.

"I recently had a retinal detachment surgery. Guess I should've waited a little longer before getting back behind the wheel."

Charlotte climbed out of the car and stumbled, falling against the door.

"Oh, no! Are you sure you're all right?"

"I am. Just trying to steady my legs. They're a little wobbly." She continued toward the back of the car. "Whoa. You're right. You did do a number on my bumper. The left side is completely hanging off."

The woman covered her mouth, whimpering into her palm. "Ooh, I am so, so sorry. Let me grab my insurance info. They'll take care of everything."

Charlotte watched as the driver jogged toward her car. Her vision was still hazy, but she was able to make out a black baseball cap and oversize black windbreaker.

Several moments passed before the woman stepped back out of her car. She switched off the headlights, then slowly approached. Charlotte tried to get a better look at her face but couldn't see well through the darkness.

"Here you go," the driver said, handing her a piece of paper.

Charlotte looked down at her hands. They were hidden beneath motorcycle gloves.

"Again, my apologies."

The voice sounded a bit deeper this time.

Or are you just hearing things because you're out of it?

Charlotte's skin prickled with alarm. Something wasn't right.

"Thank you," she said, taking the paper with one hand while reaching into her waistband with the other. It came up empty. Her gun must've slipped out when she was hit.

"You're welcome, Sergeant Bowman."

Run!

Charlotte pivoted, charging toward her car. Hot, sticky leather scraped against the back of her neck. The driver grabbed her by the collar and knocked her to the ground.

"Time to finish what I started!"

The voice now resembled the attacker who'd broken into her house.

"No!" Charlotte screamed, the soles of her sneakers digging into the dry dirt as he dragged her into the preserve. "Let me go!"

He flung her body against a tree trunk. She moaned, sliding to the ground as bark tore through her shirt. Charlotte clutched her back while struggling to her knees.

A pair of headlights shone in the distance.

"Help!" she screamed, praying someone would hear her. *"Help!"*

The car got closer. Beams of light flickered through the trees. Charlotte caught a glimpse of her attacker pulling a syringe from his pocket. She kicked her foot in the air, desperate to knock it from his hand.

"Stand down!" he yelled, grabbing her leg and pulling until she fell backward.

Charlotte screamed, her head pounding the hard soil as she bit down on her tongue. The taste of metal filled her mouth.

Get up. Don't you give in. Get up and fight!

She pulled herself onto her elbows, expelling a chunk of blood before wiping dirt from her eyes. When her vision cleared, she watched in horror as the assailant raised his foot high in the air. A heavy black boot hovered over her stomach.

My baby! a voice screeched inside of her head.

And then...

Boom!

"Ahhh!"

The man yelled out in pain after his foot slammed against

a stone buried beneath the dirt. Charlotte had managed to roll over seconds before his boot made contact. She flinched at the sound of his cracking bones.

He lost his balance, stumbling backward. Charlotte kicked her foot high in the air. The firm tip of her shoe landed right between his legs. His animalistic howl reverberated through the preserve as he toppled over in agony.

"You bitch!"

Charlotte hobbled to her feet and bolted toward the car.

"Do *not* let him get away this time!" she cried out, throwing open the door and frantically searching for her gun.

Got it.

Charlotte stumbled back into the preserve. She pushed her way through branches, desperate to find her attacker.

A dark shadow whizzed by in the distance.

Pop! Pop!

She fired a couple of shots. They ricocheted off a tree truck and disappeared into the distance.

Keep going!

Charlotte made her way toward the area where the assailant had lain clutching his groin. He was gone.

No, no, no!

"Where the hell are you?" she yelled.

Silence.

She ran to the left, then right. There was no sign of him anywhere.

An engine roared from the road. Charlotte hurried back toward the street. When she reached the area where their cars had been parked, hers was the only one there.

"He's gone," she sobbed, spinning in circles as tears burned her eyes. "I cannot believe this. He's gone!"

Charlotte stared down Cottonwood Lane. Taillights flickered in the far distance. She jumped inside her car and sped toward the vehicle. But after driving over two miles, she realized that it was too late. Her attacker had gotten away once again.

"Nooo!" she screamed, banging her fist against the dashboard.

Charlotte's fingers shook as she jabbed the phone button on the touch screen and hit Miles's name. He picked up on the first ring.

"Hey, where are you?" he asked. "I didn't know you left the house. I've been calling you—"

"I messed up, Miles. Bad. Really bad."

"What do you mean? What happened?"

"I was attacked!"

"What? When?"

"Just a few minutes ago. I was heading to Rush Street and got rear-ended on Cottonwood Lane. When I got out to check the damage on my car, the driver attacked me. It was the killer, Miles. I was able to fight him off, but I almost died!"

Charlotte heard a car door slam through the phone.

"Are you still on Cottonwood Lane?" he panted.

"Yes. But I'm on my way to the police station. Just meet me there."

"No! I want you to go straight to the hospital. You and the baby need to get checked out before we do anything else."

"But I'm okay, Miles. *We're* fine."

"This is not up for debate, Charlotte. You have got to see a doctor, just to be safe. You're not a superhero, contrary to what you seem to believe. Something might be wrong and you just don't know it yet."

The road ahead blurred as Charlotte's eyes filled with tears. "Okay. I'll head to River Valley Memorial now. If nothing else, I think I need stitches in my tongue."

"You what?"

"I'll tell you about it later."

"All right. I'll call Chief Mitchell and let him know what

happened. Were you able to get a look at the suspect or his vehicle this time?"

"Not really, no. It was so dark, and I was completely disoriented after he crashed into me. Plus, in all honesty, I had my guard down. At first, I thought it was a woman—"

Charlotte paused.

"Hello?" Miles said.

"I'm here. Something just dawned on me. When I was being attacked, the killer seemed to be laser focused on my stomach. He tried to stomp me right in the middle of it. Why would he do that? Of all the areas on my body, why was he concentrating on my stomach?"

"I think I know where you're going with this. Walter overheard you telling Chief Mitchell that you're pregnant, and he's the one who's behind the assault?"

"Exactly!"

"But wouldn't you have known if it was Walter who attacked you?"

"My car had just been hit, Miles. *Hard.* I was completely disoriented and could barely see through the darkness."

His throaty sigh whooshed through the car speakers. "Maybe it's time for you to discuss your suspicions about him with Chief Mitchell. And we should find out where he was tonight. See if he can be accounted for."

"I totally agree. It's long overdue..." Charlotte's voice faded. She'd managed to cheat death yet again, at the hands of someone she was once so close to. "Hey, can you stay on the phone with me until I get to the hospital?"

"You don't even have to ask."

Chapter Twenty-Four

Charlotte sat on Ella's couch, holding her sister as she wept in her lap.

It had been three days since Charlotte's attack. After much resistance, Miles and Chief Mitchell were able to talk her into taking a break, at least for a short period. The chief was adamant that she do so considering the pregnancy. His wife even called to express her concern.

The pain of stepping away hurt Charlotte worse than the actual assault. But she needed the time to recover as they awaited Chief Mitchell's response to their findings on Walter.

That evening, she and Miles had been sitting out on the deck relaxing when Ella called. They'd assumed she was reaching out to check on Charlotte. But the terror in her voice said otherwise.

"Somebody tried to kill me!" she'd screamed into the phone.

Within minutes, Charlotte and Miles were inside the car, heading to Reno. And now, as he spoke quietly with police near the doorway, Charlotte struggled to comfort her inconsolable sister.

"I cannot believe this happened to me," Ella whimpered.

Charlotte's jaw tightened as anger burned through her body. "Neither can I. I should've had that man locked up a long time ago. I am so sorry, El." She studied the red strangulation marks lining Ella's throat and the small scar sliced into her left cheek.

"I'm so glad you were able to get away from that maniac before he was able to do any more damage. But I really wish you would've gone to the hospital. You have got to stop being so hardheaded."

"For the tenth time," Ella argued, "I feel safer here at the apartment rather than some wide-open, public place. Victims are the most vulnerable inside of hospitals."

"Yeah, maybe in the movies. But not in real life."

"Okay, everyone," one of the policemen said. "We're gonna join the other officers down in the parking lot who are examining the scene. Let us know if you need anything, or if Ella remembers something that's not already in the report."

"Will do," Miles said. "Thank you." He closed the door and took a seat on the arm of the couch. "How are you feeling, El?"

"Sore. And pissed off. But I'll be all right."

"She's finally calming down," Charlotte whispered.

Miles nodded. "Aside from Charlotte, do you realize that you're the first victim who's managed to get away from the killer?"

"I do. I fought him off like my life depended on it, because it did. That man sliced at my face, and I saw a syringe almost fall from his pocket. Who knows what was inside of it."

"That's what we're trying to figure out," Charlotte said. "What could this man be using to kill his victims?"

Miles pulled out his notebook. "Ella, I know you've been through a lot and you're probably still in shock. But do you feel up to telling us exactly what happened, from the time you left work to the time you were assaulted?"

"I do," she moaned, slowly sitting up. "I wanna do whatever I can to help end this nightmare."

"Can I get you anything before you start?" Charlotte asked. "Water? Tea? Something stronger?"

"I'd love something stronger. But I've got to be in my right mind when I tell this story. So no, thanks."

Miles tapped his pen against the pad. "Ready when you are."

Ella took in a deep breath of air. "Okay, so I left work a little after seven o'clock. I stopped at Dickerson's and picked up a salad on the way home. It was going on eight o'clock by the time I pulled into the apartment complex. I parked my car, and right before I reached the stairwell, somebody snatched me up and dragged me into the wooded area behind the complex."

"Did you get a look at the guy?" Miles asked.

"Not really. He was dressed in all black and wearing a ski mask."

"What about his height and size?"

Ella wiped her eyes, smearing navy blue eyeliner across her cheeks. "It's all a blur, really. I was so flustered. And of course terrified. From what I could see, he was pretty tall. Definitely over six feet. And his clothes were baggy. But if I had to guess, he appeared more on the slim side."

Miles took rigorous notes before glancing over at Charlotte. "Sounds like the description you gave of your attacker."

"I definitely think it's the same per-person." Her voice cracked. She wanted to be strong for Miles, and especially for Ella. But she was beginning to unravel under the weight of the situation.

"Okay," Miles continued, "so your attacker was tall, thin, dressed in all black and wearing a ski mask. Did you get a look at his eyes?"

"No. Not really. I just remember seeing two dark, evil slits."

"So dark eyes, possibly."

Ella coughed, then cringed while clutching her throat.

"You need some hot tea," Charlotte told her.

"Hot tea? I need some drugs. Can you grab the bottle of oxycodone out of my purse?"

"Didn't you just take an oxy about thirty minutes ago?"

"Look," Ella said, rolling off the couch and limping toward the kitchen counter, "I took one over an hour ago. Did you forget that I'm a nurse? I know what I'm doing. I promise you, I will not overdose or become addicted."

Charlotte rolled her eyes and looked to Miles for backup.

"She's been through a lot," he whispered. "Just let her be."

Charlotte nodded and walked over to the window. "Looks like there are several more squad cars down in the lot. And dozens of officers examining that wooded area."

Ella came back into the living room carrying a piece of paper. "Do you all want to see the police report?"

"Definitely," Miles said while Charlotte rejoined him. As they skimmed the report, Ella let out a loud groan.

Charlotte sprang from the couch. "What's wrong?"

"I missed three calls from my boss. She is freaking out on my voice mail. Word must be getting around about the attack. I'm gonna go call her back. Can you give me a few minutes?"

"Of course. Take your time."

The second she was out of the room, Charlotte collapsed onto Miles's shoulder.

"I cannot believe what I'm reading," she whimpered, the police report shaking in her hand. "My sister was *brutally* assaulted. Dragged, kicked, strangled, cut…"

Her voice trailed off as the soft cry turned into a full-blown sob. Miles wrapped his arm around her. "But you know what? Ella survived. To the point where she's turned down medical attention. The woman is tough. And so are you. Keep pushing. We've come too far in this investigation to let it get the best of us now."

"I won't…"

Charlotte's cell phone buzzed. It was a text from Chief Mitchell.

Anybody seen or heard from Corporal Kincaid? He's been MIA since this morning. If anyone knows of his whereabouts, let me know ASAP!

"Miles!" she hissed, handing him the phone. "Look at this."

He scanned the message, then propped his head in his hand. "My God…"

"That psychopath has been in Reno all day, stalking Ella so he could attack her! But listen, don't say anything to her about this just yet. I want Ella to focus on recovering—"

She stopped abruptly when Ella walked back in.

"My boss is so sweet. She offered to come and stay the night with me so I wouldn't be alone."

"But I was going to stay with you," Charlotte told her.

"You don't have to do that. I'll be fine. Plus, you need to get back to River Valley. You *are* the sergeant, after all. And don't you two wanna hit the streets and find the monster who did this to me?"

"Absolutely," Miles affirmed. "That's our number one priority. That, and making sure you're okay."

When Ella sat back down on the couch, Charlotte stared at the bandage covering her cheek. Thoughts of torturing Walter, then shooting him dead crossed her mind.

"I wish I could thank that group of teenagers who pulled into the parking lot blaring their music," Ella said. "I think that's what threw off my attacker. He didn't drag me far enough into the wooded area for us to totally go unseen, because I was fighting too hard."

"My girl," Charlotte said, giving her hand a squeeze.

Ella jumped when the doorbell rang.

"You're okay," Miles told her. "That's probably your boss, isn't it?"

"Ugh. It's gonna take me a minute to work through this PTSD."

As Ella headed to the door, Charlotte leaned toward Miles and whispered, "I'm texting Chief Mitchell right now, letting him know that I think Walter is behind Ella's attack. I'll wait until we leave to call him. I don't want her to hear the conversation and get more upset than she already is."

"Good. While you do that, I'll take screenshots of the police report so we'll have a copy of it."

Ella stood in the living room's entryway embracing a short, chubby redhead who looked to be in her early sixties.

"You know you didn't have to come over," she told her.

"Don't be ridiculous, sweetheart. I had to make sure you were okay. Plus, being here with you means I can enjoy a night away from my snoring husband. *And*," she continued, holding up a plastic bag, "I bought snacks on the way here that I'm not supposed to be eating. Chocolate, Cheetos, Chex Mix…"

Charlotte and Miles stood when Ella walked her boss into the room.

"Patrice, this is my sister, Sergeant Charlotte Bowman, and her partner, Detective Miles Love. They're investigating the Numeric Serial Killer case."

"Nice to meet you both," Patrice said, bypassing their extended hands in exchange for hugs. "Thank you for your service. And don't worry. I'll keep a close watch on the place tonight." She nudged Ella's arm and patted her purse. "I packed my…you know…just in case—"

"Okay," Ella interrupted. "Char, Miles, why don't you two head back. I know you've got a lot of work ahead of you."

"Are you sure you'll be okay without us here?" Charlotte asked.

"Positive. I've got Patrice with me, and the cops have the place under surveillance."

Patrice held her handbag in the air and gave the group a wink. "Don't forget what's in here!"

"And on that note," Ella said, walking Charlotte and Miles to the door. "Before you even ask," she whispered, "yes, Patrice has a license to carry."

"Wasn't gonna say a word," Charlotte replied. "Listen, if you need anything, *anything*, just call me and we'll turn the car right back around. Do you understand me?"

"Yes, I understand. And I thank you. But I'll be fine. Thank you for getting here so fast, and for putting me back together. Because I was in shambles when you two got here."

"Understandably so," Miles told her. "And like your sister said, if you need us, call us."

"I will. Be careful. And keep me posted."

Charlotte waited for the door to close behind her before she let the tears fall. She swiped them away, not wanting Miles to see her crying. When they reached the parking lot, she approached the police chief and gave him her card, asking that he reach out with any updates.

"Should we head straight to the station?" Miles asked on the way to the car.

"Definitely." She checked her phone. "No response from Chief Mitchell. I'll try calling him now."

Miles looked on expectantly.

"Voice mail," she told him before leaving a message.

"Chief, it's Sergeant Bowman. I need for you to call me as soon as you get this message. Corporal Kincaid needs to be located and apprehended immediately. We're positive that he's behind these attacks."

She shoved the phone inside her purse and looked to Miles. "We need to get to River Valley in record time and join in on the search."

"I'll drive as fast as I can."

Right before he opened the passenger door, Charlotte noticed a flash of metal glimmering off the asphalt a couple of spaces over. "Wait," she said, pointing at the ground. "What is that?" She led Miles toward a maroon Toyota Camry. "I just spotted something near that car's left rear tire."

He turned on his cell phone's flashlight while she pulled a pair of latex gloves from her purse. "It looks like a piece of jewelry or something."

Charlotte picked up the piece and held it under the light, studying the steel link bracelet. "It's a watch." She dusted off the sapphire-blue dial, then turned it over. "And it's engraved."

"Can you make out the lettering?"

"I think so." She pulled it closer, squinting while trying to read the tiny inscription. "Hold on. Let me scrape the dust off the back. It says, *W, J…* WJK."

"WJK," Miles repeated. "That could be anybody. Let's send it to the lab and have the fingerprints lifted. You never know who—"

"Hold on!" Charlotte steadied herself against the car after almost losing her balance.

"What's wrong?"

"Those initials," she said, her skin growing cold. "They're Walter's. *Walter Jacobs Kincaid*."

Chapter Twenty-Five

Charlotte stared out the window at the long stretch of desert road.

"I am absolutely spent. Mentally, physically, emotionally…"

Miles covered her hand with his. "I know you are. Hang in there. We're almost at the finish line."

"I wonder why Chief Mitchell hasn't gotten back to us yet."

"Why don't you try him again? And maybe suggest that he publicly name Walter a person of interest."

"I like that idea—"

A sharp pang hit Charlotte's stomach when she reached down into her purse. She placed her hand over her belly, taking in several sharp breaths until it subsided.

"You good?"

"I'm fine," she lied, not wanting him to worry. "Just trying to get to my phone." Charlotte unlocked the screen. "Wait, how did I miss three calls from the chief? I didn't even hear my phone ring." Just as she tapped his name in the Contacts list, a notification popped up.

"Now he's texting me."

"What's he saying?"

Get to the Creosote River, now! Walter's body was found washed up along the shore!

Her phone slipped out of her hand.

"Charlotte? What's going on?"

"Change of plans. Head to the Creosote River. Walter is dead."

"Walter is *what*?"

"Dead!"

She jerked back in her seat when Miles slammed down on the gas. Bile burned the back of her throat. Charlotte inhaled a rush of air, forcing it back down while searching the floor for her phone. Soon as she found it, she dialed Chief Mitchell. He picked up on the first ring.

"Please tell me you're on your way here," he choked out.

She winced at the pain in his voice. It conjured a deep level of culpability. She'd been adamant of Walter's guilt. So adamant that she had overlooked the real killer. Now Walter was dead. Ella had almost died. *She'd* almost died on more than one occasion. And a slew of other innocent victims lay dead in her wake.

"Yes, Chief," Charlotte whispered into the phone. "We're on the road now. And I am so sorry. For all of this."

"Don't be. You've just been doing your job."

She switched the call to speakerphone. "What condition was Walter's body in when he was found?"

Chief Mitchell went silent as the crime scene chaos rang out in the background.

"Are you still there?" she asked.

"I'm here. Walter's, uh—his body was in pretty good condition, just like the other victims. And the...the number one was carved into his right cheek."

Charlotte doubled over, her head falling between her knees.

"The number one," Miles said, reaching over and gently rubbing her back. "Meaning he was killed today."

"That's what I'm assuming," the chief said. "And...that's not all."

Charlotte slowly rose up and rolled down the window. "What else?"

"There was a heart-shaped symbol carved into his chest."

"Oh, my God," she moaned. The sick feeling pooling inside her stomach intensified.

"Listen," Chief Mitchell said. "I need to go. Forensics is calling me back over. Thanks for the update on Ella. Glad she's okay. You two just get here as soon as you can."

"We will, Chief."

Charlotte glanced over at Miles. He appeared ashen, his expression immobile.

"This is unreal," he said. "The killer carved a heart into Walter's chest? He is doing everything in his power to break us."

"But it's not gonna work," she countered, feeling a second wind coming on."

Miles entered the Creosote River into the navigation system, then increased his speed along Interstate 50's desolate roadway.

Charlotte gripped the dashboard. Unsettling tremors crawled along her skin as she stared up ahead, then in the side-view mirror. They were surrounded by sand and tumbleweed. Aside from a pair of headlights in the far distance, there were no other cars in sight. "I guess they don't call this highway the loneliest road in America for nothing."

"It is pretty damn eerie out here."

The pair grew silent for several minutes before Charlotte spoke up.

"I cannot believe Walter is dead. Why would the killer

murder him?" She pressed her fingertips into her temples. "Wait, what am I saying? I know why. He's sending me a message by targeting everyone around me."

"And what do you think that message is?"

"That I'm next." Charlotte shivered at the sound of those words. "This case has taken us back to square one over and over again. But this time? We're a good ten steps behind square one."

Her cell phone buzzed. A notification from an unknown number appeared.

"Here we go." She held up the screen. "A text from an anonymous sender." Her thumb trembled as she swiped open the message.

ARE YOU READY TO DIE, SERGEANT BOWMAN? BECAUSE IT'S YOUR TURN NOW!

She gagged when a video of Walter's dead, naked body began to play. He'd been propped up on a pile of rough stones. Blood poured from the scar etched into his cheek. The top half of the heart carved into his chest was pointed, resembling a devil's horns. A zigzag line was sliced down the middle, as if it were broken. Sinister laughter could be heard in the background.

"What the hell is that?" Miles asked.

Charlotte shoved the phone into his chest. "I think I'm gonna be sick!"

He glanced at the screen before quickly turning away. "We don't need to see that. Just turn it off. We'll deal with the crime scene once we get there."

A pair of headlights flashed behind them. Charlotte jumped when a horn blared so loudly that it rattled the car.

"Why would some jerk be riding our bumper like that?" Miles asked.

She stared out of the back windshield. "I don't know. It looks like an eighteen-wheeler. I should flash my badge and tell him to pull over."

"I would under normal circumstances. But we've got a bigger situation to deal with."

The truck's horn roared once again, piercing Charlotte's ears.

Miles veered to the side of the road. "That almost blew out my eardrums!"

"Just let him pass us. He's obviously in a hurry. Maybe he's late on a delivery."

Miles let up on the accelerator and rode the shoulder. Instead of going around them, the truck slowed down while continuing to ride their bumper.

"*What* is he doing now? Didn't I give him enough room to go around us?"

"More than enough. Forget about it. He lost his chance. Let's keep going."

Miles got back on the road and sped up. Just as he drove a safe distance away, the trucker turned on his high beams and flew toward them.

"Now I can't see, and he's riding our bumper aga—"

Boom!

The car careened into the opposite lane.

"Did he just *hit* us?" Charlotte screamed.

"Yes! He did!"

Bam!

Another hit. Charlotte's head slammed against the dashboard as Miles struggled to regain control of the vehicle. They were lucky the airbags didn't deploy.

She sat up slowly. Blood poured from her nostrils.

"Charlotte! Are you all right?" Miles snatched a stack of napkins from the glove compartment while gripping the steering wheel.

She moaned, pressing them to her nose. "He must be drunk."

"Either that or we're under attack. Whatever the case, we've got two choices. Apprehend him or get the hell away from him."

Charlotte held the napkins in one hand while grabbing hold of her gun with the other. Just as she turned in her seat...

Pow!

A bullet shot through their back windshield and struck the touch screen.

"Get down!" Miles yelled right before a second bullet hit the side of his headrest.

The steering wheel jerked from side to side. He lost control of the car. Pellets of gravel slammed against the windows as a cloud of sand enveloped the car.

Charlotte gripped the door handle, watching in horror while they sped into the desert.

The vehicle jolted over jagged rocks and hardened cacti. Dust billowed everywhere.

Suddenly, everything lit up around them. Charlotte turned around. The truck had followed them off the road.

"Shoot him!" Miles yelled.

She steadied herself, rolled down the window and pressed her arm against the door frame.

Bang!

The bullet ricocheted off the truck's side-view mirror. She shot again. This time it hit the windshield, cracking the glass.

The semi shook so violently that the trailer teetered on its right side.

"Hit him again!" Miles shouted.

Pow!

The bullet hit a tire. The truck came to a stuttering halt. Sand swirled everywhere.

"Slow down!" Charlotte instructed.

Miles spun a one-eighty and came to a stop. They watched as the eighteen-wheeler's trailer fell onto its side. Miles shined the high beams directly inside the cab. It appeared dark.

Charlotte slid to the edge of her seat, struggling to see who was behind the wheel. The driver appeared to be dressed in all black. His face was hidden behind a ski mask.

"Police!" she yelled out the window. "Step out of the truck with your hands up!"

The driver didn't budge.

Miles cracked opened his door. "You've got one more time! Get out of the vehicle with your hands in the air!"

No movement. Just silence.

"Let's double-team him," Charlotte breathed. "We'll jump out together with our guns drawn but remain behind the car doors."

Miles pulled his weapon from the middle compartment. "And if that doesn't work, we'll move in on him. You ready?"

"I'm ready."

He reached over and placed his hand over her stomach. "Be careful. And I already know what you're gonna say, but you can stay here and let me handle this alone."

"Not a chance."

"Just like I thought. Okay, then. Let's go."

The pair stepped out of the car and crouched down.

"Either step out of the truck with your hands up," Charlotte warned, "or we'll come to you. And don't get it twisted. We *will* shoot!"

The driver slowly opened the door.

"Here he comes," Miles whispered. "Stay on high alert."

"I'm on it," Charlotte confirmed, her eyes laser focused on the semi.

A Timberland boot hit the step. The driver climbed out of the cab but remained behind the door.

"Now step in front of the truck with your hands in the air!" she commanded.

He didn't move.

"Walk out with your hands up!" Miles echoed.

The driver stood stoically behind the door.

"Should we move in on him?" Charlotte whispered.

"Yes. Follow my lead. But be careful. Keep in mind he's got a gun."

Miles crept from around his door. "Since you don't wanna come to us," he called out, "we're coming to you. Don't do anything stupid or else you will pay the price."

Charlotte bent down and moved around the back of the car, joining Miles. The pair stayed low, duckwalking toward the truck with their weapons aimed at the driver.

"We're moving in—"

The attacker took off running. Miles and Charlotte went charging after him. The darkness intensified as they ran farther away from the vehicles' headlights. She followed the sound of the assailant's footsteps, then took a shot. The footsteps continued.

"Dammit!" she hissed, angry that she'd missed.

Sand swirled as they stomped along the desert floor, further impairing their vision. Miles took a shot. Their attacker went tumbling to the ground.

"Stay back!" he told Charlotte. "I'm going in!"

She activated the light on her cell phone and shined it toward the man as Miles pounced on him.

"Put your hands behind your back!" he asserted.

A scuffle ensued as the assailant thrashed about. Clouds of dust enveloped their bodies, making it impossible for Charlotte to make out either of the men.

"Miles!" she screamed.

No response. Only the sound of limbs scuffling through the gravel.

Pop! Pop! Pop!

Shots rang out. Charlotte fell to the ground.

"Miles!" she called out once again. Still no response.

Panic pulled her off the ground and sent her running toward the men. Just as she reached their feet, Charlotte heard the sound of clanking metal.

"You're under arrest," Miles choked out, spitting a mouthful of sand. He cranked open a pair of handcuffs, struggling to contain the attacker's wrists.

"Let me help you!" Charlotte insisted.

"No! Stand down!"

The moment Miles slipped a cuff onto the man's wrist, the assailant reached up and cracked him in the jaw.

Charlotte stepped forward with her gun aimed at the man's chest. "Miles, *move!*"

"No!" he moaned. "Don't shoot!"

She knew he wanted to arrest the killer, not carry him away in a body bag. So she retreated.

Miles and the assailant rolled through the sand once more, throwing blows as the detective struggled to cuff him. Charlotte's legs shivered as she looked on helplessly. She was dying to jump in and assist. But she couldn't. She had a baby to protect.

Through the sound of crunching gravel, Charlotte finally heard the handcuffs click.

"Got him!" Miles yelled. He stood, pulling their suspect to his feet.

She ran over and yanked off his ski mask, shining her light in his face.

The man smiled brightly.

Charlotte jumped back, almost falling to her knees.

"Surpriiise," he sang. "Happy to see me, Char Char?" The man leaned in with his lips puckered. Miles yanked him back.

"Wait," the detective said, "you know him?"

"Yes." Her voice trembled with shock. "I do. This is Noel. Noel Reed. Ella's ex-boyfriend."

MILES FLOORED THE gas pedal, speeding down Interstate 50 toward River Valley's police station. Noel sat smugly in the back seat with his hands cuffed behind his back.

Charlotte activated the Voice Memos app on her cell phone and began recording the conversation.

"Why, Noel?" she asked. "What would possess you to kill all those innocent people?"

He leaned on his left elbow, his head cocked as he stared at her.

"The answer to that question is simple, really. I killed them because of you."

"Because of *me*? Why?"

"Why? Ha! You mean to tell me you don't know?"

Miles glanced in the rearview mirror. "Stop with the BS and answer the question."

Noel scooted over as far as his seat belt would allow and looked Charlotte directly in the eyes. "The reason why I killed all those innocent people was to get back at you. You! The one who talked the only woman I ever loved into leaving me."

Charlotte felt her rapid heartbeat pulsating out of her chest. "That's what this is about? You decided to become a serial killer because Ella ended your three-month relationship?"

"Don't talk to me like our union was nothing!"

"Hey!" Miles yelled. "Keep your voice down and show some respect."

Noel's head jerked back and hit the seat when Miles slammed down on the accelerator. "Slow down, man!" He glared at Charlotte. "You should've stayed out of my effing business. Let me and Ella be happy. But *nooo*. Her lonely, single, jealous big sister just had to butt in and convince her to dump me. So I did what any sane person would do. I found a way to keep you occupied, *Sergeant Bowman*. You know, interfered with your work since I couldn't interfere with your personal life. After all, you don't have one. Well, you do now, apparently. By the way, congratulations on the pregnancy, you two!"

"How do you know about that?"

"Now, Charlotte. Did you honestly think I wouldn't hack into my lady love's email so I could keep up with her every move?"

"You are a psychopath. Not to mention a raging freak."

"No, I'm just a man who wants what he wants. And when I can't get it, I do bad things."

"Evil," Charlotte whispered. "Just pure evil."

"Wait, let me get this straight," Miles said. "You attacked, kidnapped and killed innocent people just to take Sergeant Bowman's focus off your relationship?"

"Yep." Noel smirked. "That, plus payback. But then I realized that it wasn't working. I *still* wasn't getting what I wanted. So I had to beat Ella's ass—"

"Hey!" Charlotte yelled. "Watch your mouth!"

"Oh, what are you so upset about? At least I spared her life!"

Charlotte fought the urge to grab her gun and shoot him dead, right there on the spot.

"Why did you kill Corporal Kincaid?" Miles asked.

Noel snorted. "I bet you Charlotte was happy about that one. Ella told me she couldn't stand him. I even tried to do Charlotte a favor by pinning the murders on him. Planting his watch near Ella's apartment complex was genius, wasn't it?"

"*Why* did you kill him?"

"Because I caught him trying to get with my girl!"

"What are you talking about?" Charlotte asked.

"Oh, don't act like you can't remember. That day you all were at some coffee shop. I followed Ella there. Saw Corporal Kincaid walk her out, flirting and dancing peacock in heat."

"You *completely* misread that one," Charlotte said. "They were actually arguing."

"Even worse, Sergeant! What business did he have fighting with my woman?" Noel stared out the window, his upper lip curling into a scowl. "Nothing I ever did worked. The threats and murders didn't stop Charlotte's nosy ass from meddling in our relationship. Ella didn't reach out to me after she was attacked. And I waited, too. But she called the police instead. That pissed me off so bad that I *had* to kill Walter. I was ready, too. He'd been tied up in my basement all day. But don't worry, he won't be missed. He was a douchebag. Right, Charlotte?"

She ignored him, despite his piercing eyes scrutinizing her.

"No matter how hard I tried," Noel continued, "I couldn't scare you off this case. I should've killed you when I had the chance. But I didn't. Because of Ella. Now I'm probably gonna go to prison for the rest of my life."

"*Probably?*" Miles shot back. "With six counts of first-degree murder and two counts of attempted murder? You'll definitely be locked up for life."

"So how did you do it?" Charlotte asked. "How did you kill your victims?"

Noel threw his head back and unleashed a shrill cackle. "Aww, wouldn't you like to know."

"Yes. I would."

"Let's just say I drew inspiration from some of the greats. First I injected them, like Charles Cullen, aka the Angel of Death, did to his victims. Then I carved my numeric signature into their flesh, similar to my boy Roger Flender, aka The Deity."

"You were inspired by a fictional character on a TV show?"

"Why, yes, I was. *Bones* to be exact. Good job, Char Char."

"Do not call me that."

"My apologies, Charlala. Anyway, Roger Flender's modus operandi was brilliant. That, sprinkled with a bit of Peter Ballentine's method of carving a heart into Walter's chest, and *boom*! You've got yourselves a multidimensional copycat killer who kept River Valley PD befuddled for *months*!"

The weight of remorse crushed Charlotte's chest. While she and Walter may not have been on the best of terms, and he'd made some questionable moves during the investigation, his intentions were good. He just wanted to help solve the case. In the end, it cost him his life.

"Don't you all wanna know how I put my victims out of their misery?" Noel asked, his cartoonish tone oozing with glee.

"That was my next question," Miles said.

"Welp, after I held them captive in my basement until I got tired of looking at them, I injected them with, drumroll please, *da-da-da-da-da*...potassium chloride! Copious, copious amounts of potassium chloride. Wasn't that a brilliant choice? It's hard to detect, exits the system quickly, and most importantly? It's *deadly*. Learned all of that from the great Nurse Ella Bowman."

"So you used medication you stole from Ella to kill people?"

"No! Of course not. I may be a murderer, but I'm nobody's thief. Like I said, I learned about it from her. One day when I was digging through her medicine bag looking for aspirin, and by aspirin I mean percs, I saw a glass vial and asked what it was. She told me it's used to treat hypokalemia patients, then warned me to stay the hell away from it because it could kill me."

"Did my sister know that she was dating a drug addict?"

"I am not a drug addict, ma'am. I'm simply a man with needs."

"If you didn't steal the potassium chloride from Ella, how'd you get it?"

Noel bowed his head and batted his eyelashes. "Through the dark web, of course, where you can get virtually anything. Mi loco amigo had that KCl coming in *hot*!"

There it was. That phrase he'd texted to Charlotte. It resonated like sharp nails, penetrating her skin. How ironic that Hunter's use of the phrase had almost incriminated him.

"The dark web, huh," she said. "Duly noted. We'll be sure to inform our digital forensic investigator of that when we turn over your electronics. See if we can hunt down the owner of the site and hit him with charges as well."

Miles nodded. "Copy that."

"C-c-can we get back to that heart I carved into Corporal Kincaid's chest?" Noel sputtered at the detective. "That was a nice little personal touch, wasn't it? An ode to the entire Love family, if you will. I just love, no pun intended, how I combined the whole California serial killer thing with my own personal vendetta against you two."

Miles's stolid expression crumbled into an angry scowl. The moment he opened his mouth to speak, Charlotte grabbed his arm.

"Just tune him out," she said. "His words mean nothing, and he's going to prison for life. This whole ordeal is over."

"You're right. Finally…"

Epilogue

Two months later...

"Are you enjoying being here in Clemmington?" Miles asked Charlotte.

"I am. I'm loving it, actually. This is a nice change of pace from River Valley. And after all that I've been through—rather, *we've* been through—I needed a change of scenery."

"I agree."

Miles sat back in his lawn chair and glanced around his parents' backyard. The colorful philodendron plants and butterfly bushes surrounding the lush green lawn had blossomed since the last time he was there. So had the western redbud tree that stood in the middle of the yard, its magenta-colored blooms blowing gently in the breeze.

The entire Love family and a few close friends were there to celebrate Miles's return and welcome Charlotte, who'd taken a leave from the force. His heart was full, being back home with her by his side.

He kissed the back of her hand, then stood. "May I have everyone's attention, please? First, I'd like to thank all of you for being here today. I don't know how my mother managed to pull this little welcome home gathering off on such short notice, but nevertheless, I appreciate it."

"Anything for my son!" Betty called out.

"While my stint in River Valley was a success, and Charlotte and I managed to capture the Numeric Serial Killer, it feels damn good to be home."

His sister, Lena, raised her glass. "Us having you back in one piece feels even better!"

"Thanks, sis." He turned to Charlotte. "And to you. The woman I fell in love with some time ago and never stopped loving. It may seem odd that we reconnected over a murder investigation, but however it came about, I'm just glad that we did. Words could never convey how excited I am for our future together. You, me and baby Zoe. Thank you for reaching out on that fateful day and asking for my help. More importantly, thank you for not sending me on my way once the case was solved."

"Well, by that time," Charlotte said, pointing at her slightly protruding belly, "I was kind of stuck with you." She paused when the group broke out into laughter. "Seriously, though, you deserve all of my thanks. Not only for assisting me with the biggest investigation of my career, but for showing me that true love hadn't passed me by. I just had to open myself up to it. For that, I will be forever grateful."

"Aww," the crowd sighed as the pair shared a kiss.

"I love you," Miles whispered in her ear.

"I love you, too."

Miles's father, Kennedy, who served as Clemmington's chief of police, waved his hand in the air. "Thank you for those wonderful words, you two. Now that we've toasted to the happy couple, I have some news that I'd like to share. If I may…"

"Of course," Miles said. "You've got the floor."

Betty wrapped her arm around Kennedy, her eyes filling with tears.

"Um," Kennedy began, his voice wavering. "After working for the Clemmington Police Department for almost forty years, I've decided to…to turn in my badge—"

"Wait, *what!*" Jake yelled over the group's stunned gasps. "Dad, you're retiring? When did you decide this?"

"Your mother and I have been discussing it for a while now. It's time, son. I'm no spring chicken. Plus, your mother and I are ready to relax. Get out there and do some traveling. Enjoy life without the stress of an investigation hanging over my head." He pointed toward Miles and Charlotte. "Not to mention we've got our first grandbaby on the way. I'd like to focus on being a grandfather."

The family gathered around and embraced Kennedy. A few tears trickled down his cheeks. Betty patted them away.

"I'm so proud of you, honey," she told him.

Jake pulled away abruptly. "Hold on. Who's gonna take over as Clemmington's new chief?"

"Good question," Miles chimed in.

"As long as it's not my archenemy," Lena interjected, "better known as Detective Russ Campbell, then I'm good with whoever you choose."

Kennedy grabbed a bottle of champagne. "The person I've chosen to run the department," he began, refilling Jake's glass, "is you."

"Me?" Jake whispered.

"Yes. *You.* I've already confirmed it with the mayor."

"Congratulations, baby," Betty told him.

The crowd went wild as champagne splashed everywhere. Miles, Lena and Jake threw their arms around one another and hopped around in a circle. It was a gesture they'd been making since they were children.

Charlotte snapped a photo of the celebration. "Congratulations on your retirement, Chief Love. I can only imagine what life was like in your household back when these three were younger."

"Oh, there was never a dull moment, I can tell you that much."

"Charlotte!" Ella called out as she came running through the back gate. "I am so sorry I'm late."

"Hey," Jake whispered, tugging Miles's arm. "Who is that?"

"You don't recognize her from the video chat? That's Ella. Charlotte's sister."

Jake's mouth fell open as he eyed her. "Oh, yeah. It's all coming back to me now. She's even prettier in person. Is she single?"

"I don't know. Why don't you go and ask her yourself?"

"Smart-ass…" Jake muttered.

Charlotte barely introduced the pair before Jake handed Ella a drink and offered to introduce her to everyone.

"Your brother is a smooth one, isn't he?" she asked Miles.

"Not usually. But there's something about Ella that brings out the Denzel in him."

"Well, while they get to know one another, I think the baby and I are ready for a second helping of barbecue."

"Follow me," Miles said, holding out his arm and leading Charlotte into the kitchen. "I could use a few more ribs and a little quiet time myself. I adore my family, but they can be a bit exhausting to say the least. Are you sure you're gonna be able to handle all the madness that the Love family brings to the table?"

"Absolutely. In fact, nothing would make me happier."

He stood at the counter and stared at her, overcome by a tingling sense of elation.

"Why are you looking at me like that?" Charlotte asked.

"Because I can't believe that this is actually my life. You've gotta understand, I never thought we'd get a second chance.

Yet here we are. Together in Clemmington. After solving the case of a lifetime. *And* we're having a baby. I'm just so...so overwhelmed."

"With happiness?" she asked, running her hands along his biceps.

He responded by grabbing hold of her hips, their bodies swaying to the jazz music streaming from the deck. "Of course. And love. And joy. Because I get to spend the rest of my life with the only woman I've ever loved."

"Ditto," Charlotte said as her lips melted into his.

* * * * *

ON THE RUN WITH HIS BODYGUARD

TARA TAYLOR QUINN

For Tim. My RV partner. My life partner.
Before. Now. Forever.

Chapter One

"I know you. You're the guy who beat that huge fraud rap in California."

Securities fraud, tax fraud, money laundering. Crimes for which he'd been found not guilty. They'd become the nightmare from which he couldn't wake.

He'd had to give his driver's license to check in.

Keeping his expression completely neutral, Joe Hamilton asked, "Is lot nineteen available? I'd like to rent, with full hookup on a week-by-week basis." He paused, and when an immediate rejection didn't come immediately, added, "And I'll pay you extra to keep my identity between the two of us."

The older man eyed him with a mixture of cloaked fascination and obvious mistrust. "We're a quiet community here," he said. "No offense, but we'd like to keep it that way."

He'd specifically chosen the desert RV park for its remote location. "I keep to myself," he said, and then, because he really needed a place to hole up undetected, added, "If word gets out to the press that I'm here, you have my word that I'll leave immediately. And I'll trust you to keep your residents away from lot nineteen."

He didn't quite hold his breath. But pretty damned close.

"I'll need a money order or cashier's check."

Joe reached into the back pocket of his jeans, pulling out

his wallet. "I can do one better than that. I have cash." Retrieving bills, spreading them out, he laid down the advertised weekly rate with full hookup, adding in a hefty tip.

And saw the big, balding, slightly hunched manager shaking his head. "Sorry, man, but I'm not touching that. We're a small operation, just my wife and I, and this is all we've got. I can't afford to be passing bad money…"

The man's words were, in one sense, almost comical, in a dark sort of way. While Joe had been accused of ultimately stealing millions from unsuspecting investors, some of whom lost retirements, there'd been no counterfeit money charges in the long list of grievances against him.

"It'll have to be cashier's check or money order," the man behind the small, scarred counter said.

"How about I unhook my car, park my rig in spot nineteen and then drive the forty miles I'll have to go to get either one of those?" He didn't want to take a chance on losing the spot. He'd chosen the small year-round RV park specifically for its location just over the California border in Arizona, which was a good forty miles to even anything that could be considered a full-out grocery store. The area was known for its natural minerals—and once a year hosted an international gem show that brought in thousands of recreational vehicles—but was mostly just a small gas exit off the remote six-hour stretch of desert highway connecting Phoenix to Los Angeles.

The man wouldn't look him in the eye. Joe didn't back down. He stood there, a good several inches taller, with broader shoulders, and waited. Spot nineteen was in a secluded spot in the park, separated from view by a couple of paloverde trees, and the farthest spot from the park's recreational center that housed a couple of card rooms and an ancient outdoor swimming pool. Most of which he knew from the hours' worth of online perusal he'd done the night before, mapping out sites across the Southwest and finding out everything he could about Sierra's Web, the Phoenix firm of experts he'd hired by phone that morning while on the way to Quartz Landing—his current location.

When a guy was in hiding, he had to have a good, thorough plan. One that came with contingencies in case of default.

And when he was all alone in the world, with enemies and death threats on his trail, he could start to feel a little desperate. If he'd let himself.

"Please, I just need a place to find a little peace." The words broke out of him.

"Park it," the man—Bob, his name tag read—said with a single nod, handing Joe a key card to get through the security gate. But he still didn't meet Joe's gaze.

Joe pretended not to notice as he thanked the man, leaving his cash lying on the counter. He had to get the rig in place and hooked up before Bob changed his mind.

"YOU WANT ME to what?" McKenna Meredith screeched quietly into her phone.

"I know it's a lot to ask, but the guy's in real danger, Ken," Glen Rivers, forensics expert and partner in the nationally renowned firm Sierra's Web, came back immediately. "He hired the entire firm this morning, and in less than two hours, we've determined he's being traced, by what looks like multiple sources, but he has, thus far, moved before anyone actually found him. He's living out of one of those recreational vehicles and has no known address. Hud and I looked at video surveillance from areas he's stayed most recently, and yesterday someone was tailing his car. He managed to lose them before returning to his rig and was gone from the area, driving the rig and towing the car, within the hour."

"Yeah, but come on, Glen, Joe Hamilton? *The* Joe Hamilton? I thought Sierra's Web was in business to see that justice is done. To help good people out of hard places. Hamilton's a crook of the worst kind." Because he'd pretended to be anything but. He'd lived among, socialized with and appeared to care about the people he'd been robbing. "You want me to protect him?"

"He says he's innocent. That's why he hired us—the entire firm of experts if that's what it takes—to help him prove that he didn't inflate earnings or falsify reporting records. He says he didn't commit any of the crimes he was charged with. Which, by the way, is probably why there wasn't enough evidence to get a guilty verdict."

Walking around the staked-off and newly cleaned desert lot her dad and half-brothers were checking out on a mountain ridge overlooking Shelter Valley—the small Arizona town where she'd spent her happiest childhood moments— she hated the thought of leaving so soon.

"He was Bellair Software's chief accountant, Glen." She didn't follow crime cases in the news all that much, but the Bellair one…she'd been hearing about it for months. "And I don't expect he's going to want me on the case," she added then. "My grandparents hadn't invested, thankfully, but some of their friends did, and they lost millions."

"He's given us complete carte blanche, and you are our best choice for this one by far." Glen wasn't backing down. "Not only because you're one of the best bodyguards we've ever had on board, or because you fit the undercover portion of the plan perfectly, but because of your wealthy upbringing…you grew up in this world, Ken. You understand the inner workings. You'll see and hear things, pick up on things, that others might not…"

"I don't like him." At all. She'd chosen long ago to stay as clear as she could from people who thought that money mattered most.

"You've met him?"

"No. But the choices he's made, fraud aside...money clearly is what drives him." It had been all over the news how the man's entire life had consisted of making money, from his social interactions to the mansion he'd purchased in an elite neighborhood. Hamilton didn't seem to do anything, attend a party or play a golf game, unless he was there for moneymaking purposes.

The perp who'd kidnapped and killed her mother had been solely driven by greed for money, too. A fact that, many years later, Glen had helped her to prove.

"You seriously want me to find someone else?"

Of course not. She was going to take the job, assuming Glen still wanted her to have it. She'd known that, the second she'd heard Glen had an assignment for her—regardless of the fact that she'd just come off a five-week job for him. Sierra's Web hired and worked for the best of the best. She was proud to be one of them.

And she needed the money.

"You know better than that," she said, glancing across to the three dark heads bent over a site plan. "I just want full disclosure. And you also have to know...if I discover something that proves his guilt, I won't continue to work for him."

"We told him the same thing this morning—had him sign paperwork to that end, before we accepted his down payment."

When her father glanced up, his brow raised in question, she smiled, letting him know that everything was okay. But he'd know, too, that she was leaving. She might have only lived with him full-time for the first two years of her life, and then just for weekend and summer visits, but the man could read her like a book.

"What does he know about me?" she asked Glen.

"Only what you tell him. Or what he can find on the internet."

She had no social media presence. Kept a very low profile in general.

"Shouldn't he be told I could be perceived to have a conflict of interest?"

"I've talked to the partners, and we agree that your past is a help to this particular job, not a hindrance. We see no conflict of interest in terms of your assignment. We all agree that you're the best we have to offer for the task, and we have complete confidence you'll do it well. If you see a need to make him aware of any similarities in acquaintances between the two of you, that's up to you."

Seeing her father and brothers nodding in unison in their huddle over construction plans, she told Glen, "I'll be in Quartz Landing before dark," and rang off.

The men in her life were standing on the big break they'd been working toward for so many years—transitioning from construction workers to company owners. The years of training, sweating under the hot Arizona sun hammering boards for others, of certifying as electricians and plumbers, license applications, insurance payments, job bidding, and finally... a winning bid.

At the moment there was only a two-lane paved road from the end of Shelter Valley's Main Street up to the ridge on which the four of them all stood, but a developer had plans in place to grow the town right up the mountain. And wanted her family's new company to build the first phase. With an option to continue with phases two and three, assuming everything played out to the developer's satisfaction.

Her brothers both had wives. Toddlers.

She'd promised Meredith and Sons Construction Company financial help. They hadn't asked. Had actually refused. Several times. Until she'd had a hissy fit about family, about being a full-fledged member of the family, about wanting to invest in the family...but she knew they'd only capitulated because they thought she was using inheritance money that she hated.

Money that could have been her mother's.

What they didn't know didn't hurt them as long as they didn't find out. Which meant she was going to work.

"A new job call?" her father asked as she approached the threesome in their jeans and lightweight button-down cotton shirts—long-sleeved even in the nearly one-hundred-degree temperature—work boots, and Meredith Construction baseball caps.

"Yeah." She didn't bother to hide her disappointment at another visit cut short. But she was eager to go, too. And not just because she wanted to ensure that they'd have whatever money they needed whenever they needed it. But because she truly loved what she did. Protecting others from lives lived in fear gave her a rush of adrenaline like none other.

Because she was good at it. And being good at it reminded her that she was trained, qualified, licensed in nearly half of the US states to bear arms and protect, which meant that she no longer had to live her own life afraid of whatever evil could be lurking close by.

The new job, though…protecting a man she was certain was guilty…that put a whole new spin on things.

Chapter Two

Joe trusted no one. Not anymore. Maybe it had always been that way. Growing up alone with a lying, stealing, cheating father had taught him early.

He'd thought he trusted his high school English teacher. His tennis coach. His college financial adviser. He'd thought he trusted everyone he dealt with at Bellair Software.

He'd thought getting arrested alongside his old man had taught him the hardest lesson he'd ever have to learn.

He'd been wrong about that one.

And he was having some doubts about Sierra's Web, too. The firm that provided people who were the best of the best in every field was the only one of its kind, which didn't sit well with him—it meant they had no competition to keep them honest. On the other hand, they lived by reputation alone, and he'd been unable to find a single legitimate unhappy customer. If they didn't get the job done, they returned all monies charged.

Problem was, he needed the job done—not his money back.

And he needed it done by the best of the best in whatever field was necessary, and he needed all the best working together to make that happen.

One firm, unending experts—they seemed like his only real hope.

Then they'd called to tell him that he had more than one overeager justice seeker on his trail—kind of a no-brainer, that one, except that their in-house tech expert, a partner in the firm, had found evidence of some pretty savvy talent doing work to that end.

He'd stopped to get a flu shot and someone had tapped into the record of it. Knew where he'd been.

So the plan now was to provide him with a live-in bodyguard who was an expert in the field. Fine. But a female one? To share his one-bedroom home on wheels? Under the guise of them being married?

He liked the idea of catching anyone out to get him, though. In addition to proving his innocence. No matter how much proof he found, the case had been so sensationalized, there would be radicals who would still believe him guilty. At least for a time. And the only way to stop the stalking was to catch the stalker.

Stalker*s*, he amended silently as he paced the three-foot-wide lane that stretched between the back of his driver's seat, past plush captain's chairs and a couch, through the tiny kitchen, by the table and four chairs in the bay window slide out, across the shared bath and laundry room, to the bedroom door. And then back again.

There'd be more chance of hiding for the time it took to figure it all out if he appeared to be holed up with a woman, just enjoying life. And if someone found him, his potential assailant wouldn't be prepared for a bodyguard's defense.

With the undercover-bodyguard plan, Joe would also have more chance of going undetected, giving him some desperately needed privacy, if he appeared to be just a guy living on the road with his wife. It had become kind of a thing, he'd been told. Minimalistic living.

He'd agreed to the plan because it fit his main goal—other than proving his innocence—traveling undetected.

But having done so, he'd been fretting for the past hour, wasting precious investigative time, wondering how on earth he was going to share his small space with anyone, let alone a woman. His butt bumped the wall every time he showered in the confined space. No way he could get in there picturing hers having done the same.

She'd have to use the park's public shower facilities.

Which meant they'd have to stay in parks.

He'd spent the majority of his month on the road sleeping in a parking lot here or a rest area there. Finding dumping stations as needed.

But that meant the majority of his days were taken up with driving and he wasn't getting enough investigating done.

Not that he couldn't go over and over the evidence as he drove. Or slept, for that matter. He'd memorized every detail during the two months before his trial...

And... He stopped in tracks on the solid wood floor, bending down a tad to see out the window over his double ceramic kitchen sink. A small, light blue–ish SUV had just pulled up next to his car in the parking area allotted to spot nineteen. The passenger door opened, a body sprang out, grabbed a large duffel out of the back seat and shut both doors, and the SUV made a circle around their site, heading back toward the main park area, including its exit.

She'd arrived.

All small-boned, red-curly-haired, five feet five of her. Dressed in lightweight purple pants, a shortish white blouse and tennis shoes. Without socks. As a wife cover, he could see it. But how in the hell was this sprite going to protect him?

Had someone in the firm been financially ruined by the Bellair collapse? And this was the type of protection the firm was giving him for the exorbitant fee he'd agreed to pay?

Had he been set up?

Had someone tapped into Sierra's Web's plans for him? Sent someone in his bodyguard's stead?

Was she an impostor? Sent to gather intel?

Or poison him?

Maybe his mind was getting a bit dramatic on him, but Joe's dread increased. Not because he was afraid of one smallish woman or any harm she might have been sent to do, but because he was back to square one.

If this petite, fine-boned person was the best Sierra's Web could provide for his protection, he was once again going to be alone in proving his innocence and finding any hope of getting even a small portion of his life back.

So be it.

He wasn't giving up.

He'd send the visitor on her way, unhook the rig, hook up the car and head out.

As always, it was up to him to protect himself.

He just had to get better at it.

SHE SHOULD HAVE told the rideshare driver to wait. Joe Hamilton was footing the four-hour round-trip bill—he could afford the extra minutes. Feeling uneasy, reminding herself that she was in an RV park with other residents around, with an office where she could call for another ride if need be, she approached the shiny beige-and-brown rig, noting the three slide-out room expanders. A potential attacker could hide under any of the three and there'd be no way for occupants of the thirty-three-foot vehicle to know they were there.

First order of business was mirror additions, or better yet, cameras, positioned to show her all angles of the rig at all times, including underneath it—right from her phone, preferably.

Two electrically dropped metal steps led up to the door

of the rig. Standing to the side of them, she reached up and knocked on the tinny-sounding screen door. And when the more solid inner door opened, revealing a tall, slim man in cargo shorts that hung to his somewhat bony knees, she pulled open the screen door and climbed up. The two outdoor steps, and then onto the first step inside the rig that led up to the living area.

Wood floors, shiny and clean, were just below eye level. Better than looking up at the male crotch covered by a loosely hanging white T-shirt.

"Stop right there." His voice wasn't loose. Or slim-sounding. The deep, commanding tones dug into her, shooting her gaze straight up to her new employer's face.

What she could see of it through the long hair and beard.

No one had prepared her for the drastic change to his appearance. Good move, though, for someone trying to avoid recognition. She, along with a good part of the nation, had seen his short-haired, cleanly shaven photo all over the internet in the month since he'd been found not guilty.

Not to be confused with exonerated, which meant proven innocent.

Thoughts flew during the few seconds she stood there, gaze locked with his. "I'm McKenna Meredith, Mr. Hamilton," she said, drawing on years of polite public grooming at her grandmother's behest. "From Sierra's Web."

As she issued that last credential, she grabbed the wooden rail attached to the back side of the kitchen cupboard and lifted one foot to the second step inside his mobile home, stopping instantly when a hand of steel came down, capturing her forearm in a viselike grip.

What the...intruder? Not Hamilton. Heart pounding, she reacted with pure, carefully trained and honed instinct. Grabbing the arm of the hand holding her, bringing her own captured arm into her chest, she used both of her arms to hold his immobile against her while her free hand grabbed fingers and twisted with one smooth motion.

Arm bar. Wrist lock.

Twist and the man came down two steps—so close in the confined space that their bodies were touching, thigh to thigh. Their chins, hers tilted up to him, his tilted down to her, mere inches apart.

Ready to knee the man and ask questions later, she stopped herself as her gaze met his. He might have grown a lot of hair in various places, but the eyes were the same.

Way more vivid blue than the internet had shown her.

And…if she wasn't mistaken, they were glinting with humor. Or admiration.

Not the time to tell him she'd thought he was an intruder in his own home.

"We might be posing as husband and wife, Mr. Hamilton, but you ever touch me again without my consent, and I will not only quit the job, but I'll file charges. Do I make myself clear?" She gave his wrist one more little twist for emphasis, just in case.

"Loudly." The voice definitely held something other than menace. He had to be hurting. She wasn't breaking his arm—though she easily could—but she wasn't going easy on him, either. You wouldn't know it, though. She noticed teeth through the scraggly growth of hair on his face.

The man was smiling.

Feeling a smile of her own coming on, not liking the response, she let him go and stepped back down out of the rig until he moved farther up into it.

Which he did. Immediately.

Not exactly the way she'd envisioned their first meet, but, she supposed, considering the client, not all bad, either.

SHE'D HAD HIM at a disadvantage, him leaning down, being off balance…but she'd still been impressive. Rubbing his wrist, Joe backed up to the far end of the kitchen, as McKenna, large duffel still on her back, climbed up into his temporary home.

For such a small thing, she took up far too much space.

Distracted him.

Confusing him. He hadn't cared about anything but proving his innocence for months. Why in the hell should he care that her big brown eyes were frowning as she surveyed his place?

And then it hit him... Moving aside, crossing the three feet over to the sink, he said, "There's a bedroom, if you can call it that, back there." He pointed to his left, through the bath and laundry area. "I'll clear stuff out and won't enter it again while you're here. There's barely room to walk around the bed, and the nightstands are basically tiny counters nailed to the wall, but there's a TV mounted in a corner, and, most importantly, a door that locks."

"Does the door from the bathroom to here lock on the outside, too?" she asked, stone-faced, and he couldn't tell if she was serious or not. He used to think he was adept at reading people.

"It does not."

With a sideways jut of her head, as if to say, *whatever*, she said, "I'll just have to trust you to stay put, then," and slung her bag down on the floor behind the passenger chair up in the front of the rig. "I'm the bodyguard. I'll be staying out here, by the doors, in case of intruders."

She went on to inspect every inch of the rig's inside, asked questions about how everything worked, which had him leaning over her in very tight quarters to show her how to flush and hold the commode handle until material was gone. While they were hooked up to a water source—meaning while they were in parks—she could hold the handle as long as she liked. On the road, where the water source was limited to what they could carry in the hundred-gallon fresh water tank, she should release the handle as soon as possible.

The lessons then moved to the outside of the recreational vehicle—at her behest. She wanted to know how to hook up and unhook—both water and electric. How to empty tanks. Even how to connect the car for towing.

"I doubt a dangerous situation would require you to hook up and tow a car," he told her as they headed back to the door of the rig. Dinner would be next. Two of them, in a tiny kitchen. His supplies had been purchased with one eater in mind...

"I'm not expecting to have to do any of the tasks we've just gone over," she told him. "Other than flushing, of course. But I need to know the proper procedures so I can be on the lookout for any tampering with any of it..."

He'd been thinking about having to split his steak, and she was talking protection against assault. Pretty clear which of the two of them had it all together.

He needed to up his game. Substantially.

Back inside the rig, with the door locked and bolted, he fought the mental fatigue that had been slowly descending upon him. "I'm sorry," he said, dropping down to one of the upholstered kitchen chairs. "I know there are a lot of people who hate me. I've read the death threats...but I... I'm just not ready to accept that my physical person is in danger. People spew all the time. It's how they vent, get things off their chests..."

"You thought someone was following you when you were in your car yesterday. You lost them before getting back to your RV, but that doesn't mean they can't find it. Or you in it. That's why you called Sierra's Web—for help in keeping you safe and proving your innocence."

"I called Sierra's Web so that I can get my life back, not because I'm afraid of being killed."

"At least one of the IP addresses that has been on your trail can be traced to a man the FBI believes is guilty of a murder for hire. They just can't find enough evidence to prove it."

He didn't want to know how a private firm of experts had come up with that information so quickly.

"We work closely with local and federal police," McKenna, still standing in the middle of the living area, answered his unasked question. "I'm an expert bodyguard, not a babysitter. I wouldn't be here if there wasn't real cause for concern."

He wasn't ready to hear that, either.

But was saved from arguing the point when her phone rang. The call was brief. "Yes." "Yes." And "I'm on it."

"We have to go," she said before the cell was even back in her pocket. "I'll take care of the electric—you get the plumbing…"

He had to follow her out the door to continue the conversation, but he pushed the buttons for the slide outs to close inside the rig, bringing the kitchen table only a foot from the sink and shrinking the bedroom so there was no room to walk at the end of the bed, either.

"What's going on?" he demanded, his voice low in spite of the trees and yards separating them from the rest of the campers in the park.

"Glen Rivers, the firm's forensics partner, just found a message board on the dark web with your name on it. A group of extremely angry people—and if they're on the dark web, chances are they are extreme, period—are working together, trying to find you. They've just posted a picture of you with your long hair and beard getting into your car. The attached message says it's a possible sighting of you and that you might be in or around Quartz Landing."

The dark web was gunning for him? A whole new kind of terror hit Joe then. He'd never really feared for his life before. Only feared for the quality of it.

Getting the rig unhooked, the car loaded—with mud smeared on the license plate—and the two of them out of there didn't take long. With McKenna belted in the passenger seat across from him, Joe drove as quickly as he safely could out of the park and down the road. "Highway or back roads?" he asked when he hit the intersection where the choice had to be made.

He'd asked the question rather than just making the decision.

That's when he knew that he'd accepted the necessity of having a pretend-wife bodyguard in his sphere.

And he admitted, to himself, that he wanted her there.

Chapter Three

She had him take the highway. The lightless two-and-a-half-hour stretch east to Phoenix wasn't a length of road she wanted to be on in the dark of night, but it was better than equally dark, less trafficked single-lane roads through the desert where even a big rig could disappear without a trace.

She was good. She wasn't a superheroine.

"You do this often? Protect someone on the run?"

Staring ahead at miles of darkness, broken only by the headlights coming at them from across the median and the taillights ahead in their lane, McKenna assessed any answer she might give him. Not trusting your subject made it difficult to know how to interact with him.

If Joe Hamilton was innocent, she felt for him. If he wasn't, he'd brought his current situation upon himself. The latter seemed more likely. Was easier to believe.

The latter deserved nothing more from her than the best of her ability to keep him safe.

Answering his questions didn't fall under that jurisdiction.

Unless he didn't trust her enough to follow her orders if immediate danger arose...

"All of my clients are in some kind of perceived danger."

Both hands on the wheel, Joe's gaze remained pointed out at the massive expanse in front of them. He'd remained in the right lane, letting faster vehicles, less laden travelers, whiz past them. Any one of them could be someone out to get him. "Get over," she said.

"Excuse me?" He did glance her way then, but she looked away. She needed him focused on his driving, not on her.

"Get over and stay in the left lane," she said then. "I can't see what's coming up behind us, and someone could easily drive up beside you. All it would take is one shot…"

She watched him as she delivered the blow without any kind of couching or compassion, cringing inside at the rudeness that would most certainly hurt her grandmother's sensibilities. Something she still cared about…

With an obviously stiffened chin, Joe immediately signaled, changed lanes and stayed put. "I'm going to be pissing off a lot of people, clogging up the fast lane," he offered, but he didn't argue.

Which earned him a kudo and deepened the guilt she felt for how she'd talked to him. Truth was, the guy was…compelling. A mixture of she wasn't sure she could trust him and curiously wanting to help him.

"My most recent case involved an eighteen-year-old boy who was testifying at a high-profile gang trial." She wanted him to know that he was safer with her than by himself.

In a perfect world, she'd be able to promise him that she wouldn't let anything happen to him, but life didn't work that way.

"I'm assuming, since you're here, that the trial ended."

"It did."

"And the kid is safe."

Her hesitation came as a result of the clench in her stomach. She felt his glance, knew she'd failed to be the pure professional she'd sworn she would be around him.

Regardless of their unusually intimate circumstances.

"They got him?" Joe's tone held more compassion than

fear. Concern for the kid rather than worry that he'd just put his own life in her hands.

"No," she said.

"Then what?"

She should never have brought up the case. It was still too close, too raw. She'd been with the kid for five long weeks. Had, through daily electronic calls and meetings, grown to know his mother and younger sister, too.

"At the conclusion of the trial, in order to protect the mother and sister no one knew about, as well as himself, he had to enter witness protection. He'd been in New York using a fake identity at the time he'd witnessed the crime. If he assumed his old identity, his mom and sister would be exposed. And because his mom had shared parenting of his sister, she would have had to leave her behind to join him in the program. He knew that going in, as did his mother, and he still, with her blessing, chose to testify. To do the right thing and put away a murdering drug dealer for life." She broke off, briefly, then added, "The program has never lost a witness who abided by all the rules."

She kept reminding herself of the statistic every time she thought of Tommy getting in the car with the US marshal who would whisk him away to a new life.

A world where he had no family.

She couldn't imagine life without her family—both sides of it. And ached inside every time she thought about helping a process that ripped a kid's family away from him forever.

Joe's silence meant more to her than any platitudes he could have offered.

The tall, bony-kneed guy, even if he was guilty, had at least one good quality.

SHE HAD HIM stay on the same highway through Phoenix and then travel another two hours farther east, over equally deserted desert surrounded by shadowy mountain ranges, to Tucson, directing him to pull into the first twenty-four-hour big box store parking lot they came to upon reaching civilization.

The abundance of overhead lights—giving security to late-night shoppers—hurt his eyes with their brightness. Making him feel as though he was onstage, under a spotlight, but he agreed with her call. He'd recently spent more nights than not in parking lots exactly like the one she'd chosen.

Other than a directional conversation, they'd spoken little over the drive. She'd been alert, watchful, clearly on duty and—after the tidbit about her last case—silent.

He'd have thought that he'd want it that way. Was used to being alone. Until he was exonerated, he wanted to be alone. He needed to focus. To live and relive every move he'd made over the past two years until he found the key to where it had all gone wrong.

Until he knew who'd framed him, he couldn't trust anyone.

He also couldn't be bothered with inane chatter.

So why did her lack of conversation rankle so damned much?

"I need to get some things from the store," she said as he waited for her to exit the cab area of the rig so he could do the same. "And since I can't leave you out here alone, I need you to come with me."

Her directions were sounding more and more like orders. He'd taken a lot of them, from a lot of people, growing up. In the life he'd built for himself, he was the one who gave the orders.

And he generally issued them with a lot more respect than she'd had in her tone.

"Please."

One word. Offered with a glance that met his. And he followed her out the door.

McKenna did a quick sweep of the recreational vehicle's outside before they headed into the store. Theirs wasn't the only rig on the lot. It wasn't the biggest. And the sweeping brown tones blended in with the other camping homes that had stopped for the night on the edge of the desert. While the space inside was elegant almost to the point of opulent with ceramic countertops and porcelain tile and real wood flooring, the outside looked like any other of hundreds such vehicles on Arizona roads.

She'd taken stock of every inch of the interior, including the bedroom with its empty under-bed compartment, while Joe drove. Delivering up fresh salmon salad sandwiches for dinner from a container she'd found in the refrigerator, at one point. For which he'd thanked her.

And she'd noted that his silverware was the real thing. Silver. Noted the small dishwasher, too, along with the state-of-the-art microwave/convection oven combination, installed above the small glass-topped stove and conventional oven. All, along with the refrigerator, in stainless steel. Other than the miniature sizes, she could have been in the kitchen of the mansion in which she'd grown up. The home where she still had her own room, which she visited several times a year. Her grandparents were getting older.

And while she didn't agree with many of their choices, she loved them.

"We need eight cameras," she said as she headed to the electronics department as soon as they entered the store. "You can pay for them now, or Sierra's Web can bill you as part of our expense report." She would give him the very best of her ability.

She didn't have to like him. Or what he stood for.

And didn't want to admire the way he pulled out his card and paid the bill for the cameras and other groceries and incidentals without a word of dissent. Or even question.

He assisted her with installing the eight optical devices, too, and then helped her test them on her phone to make certain they were angled exactly as she wanted them.

Inside the rig, sometime after midnight, she stood by the couch, looking at her phone, held it up to him so that he could see all eight videos, in miniature, lined up side by side on her screen. And as he came closer, leaning in to get a better look, she...liked having him there.

Liked his warmth. The piney smell of his skin.

Shutting down her phone, she backed up immediately. "If you don't mind, I'd like to get some rest," she said then. Adding, "I'll only be a couple of minutes in the bathroom, and then you can have that whole back area to yourself."

Yeah, she was basically kicking him out of his living room. And not being all that polite about it. She wasn't proud of herself.

And knew she was doing exactly what she was being paid to do.

And doing it well.

She wouldn't be able to maintain a sufficient level of focus if she didn't get some sleep.

"You don't like me much, do you?" He hadn't moved from his stance by the couch, where he'd been looking at the phone she'd been holding out to him.

"I don't know you."

"So, you're just always this...distant...with your clients?"

Distant instead of rude. The kind of choice her grandfather would have made. Calling out without losing the face of congeniality.

Doing it softly.

"We're strangers dealing with forced proximity, with the added tension of posing as husband and wife, and your life could be in danger, with only me to protect it. Keeping a measure of distance is wise."

But getting to know him better, having actual conversations like human beings…that would not only help her understand better how to protect him, but it could give insights for the rest of her team, too. The sooner they completed their investigation, one way or the other, the sooner she could get out of there.

"It's not only you protecting me." His words broke into her thoughts, the tone of voice getting her attention most of all. He sounded…resolute. A man ready to go into battle with absolute certainty he was going to win.

He had someone working with him, then? An accomplice? Was he hoping to frame whoever it was, pin the blame elsewhere so he could get back to the cushy life, complete with acceptance and admiration, he'd so obviously enjoyed? Thoughts flew. She tried to harness them. "Who else?"

"Me." With that, he turned his back, headed toward the bedroom. Then spun around. "I've been looking out for myself since my mother died. I was four at the time. I've been in jail. Lived on the streets. Put myself through college, earned multiple degrees and worked my way up to CFO of a prominent, publicly traded software conglomerate. All while keeping the only eye there's ever been on my own back."

She'd hit a nerve. Was kind of surprised it had taken so long. And couldn't let herself believe that his implied aggrievement was sincere. The man had convinced a jury that he wasn't guilty. He had to be good at making people see what he wanted them to see.

He could also be giving it to her straight up.

And still be guilty.

Or not.

"I apologize for making it sound as though you couldn't take care of yourself," she said, scrambling for a way to get out of the conversation and have some time apart from him.

With his long hair and face full of hair, his bony knees, the man wasn't overly attractive. The rest of his body—maybe, in another life, she'd have a hard time ignoring it…but…physical attraction aside, there was something about the guy that kept calling out to her.

A warning?

Or a cry for help?

Used to relying on her instincts, her lack of conviction unsettled her. A lot.

He was paying her to be at her best.

And was standing there, as though waiting for something, without having so much as acknowledged that he'd heard her apology.

Silence. Waiting. Leaving an uncomfortable lull. All ways to get someone to talk.

If they had something to confess.

"I was disappointed when your jury found you not guilty."

Anger should have appeared on his face, and then he should have kicked her out of his home. His stance, expression, didn't change at all.

Reminding her, once again, of her grandfather. The man could keep up appearances through anything. Including his own daughter's funeral. McKenna had only been three at the time, didn't remember much of anything from that year, but she had a clear vision of standing between her grandparents at the grave site and looking up to see her grandfather's stoic face and then over at the tears running rampant down her grandmother's cheeks. Some of them had dripped on her…

"Friends of my grandparents put their major retirement investment in Bellair stock." The son of that same couple had been the man her grandparents had wanted her mother to marry.

"You're close with them?"

"My grandparents?" She shrugged. "Relatively."

"The friends."

"Oh." Another shrug. "Not particularly. I haven't seen them in years." Not since she'd laid down her own set of rules with her maternal family. No more society outings or big lavish gatherings. The time she spent with them was to be just them. Family time. Period.

"Glen Rivers is aware of this?"

"Yes."

"And he still called you to take this job?"

If they were being honest—"Actually, he said I was the best person for the job."

"He told me the same." Joe punctuated his words with a nod at the end, and she wondered if that was it then. The conversation was over and they could get some rest before dawn happened and they'd need to get going again.

The only movement he made was to put his hands in the pockets of his shorts. Drawing her attention to those knees.

Maybe to avoid looking at any other part of him. His eyes most of all. So much to read there. Real or fantasy, she wouldn't decide. Couldn't let herself get caught up in the answer.

"You think I'm guilty."

The quiet statement drew her gaze up in spite of her best choice not to look him in the eye. The vivid blue of his eyes seemed to point straight into her. "I did. I'm not sure what I think at the moment. Except that, either way, I've committed to keeping you safe as long as Sierra's Web is in your employ and your life is in danger."

Another nod. His chin jutted, drawing attention to lips that were mostly buried in facial hair. Bringing to mind a picture she'd seen of him in the news after his acquittal. His full lips had been upturned, but not enough to be considered smiling. His cheekbones prominent, in a strong face that she'd found far too attractive.

Such a waste on a man who'd bilk millions...

And...stop.

"You've been in touch with Glen today," she said then, the consummate professional. She had, after all, grown up in her grandparents' home, under their tutelage. "You know that the firm is just getting started and has more than a thousand pages of case file to assimilate in order to determine where to start looking for another guilty party. Or for evidence that definitely proves your innocence. Obviously, your safety is the first concern, so they moved on that immediately and will keep me updated anytime anything changes there, but this could take a while. From what I understand, the people after you...it could be any number of people who lost large amounts of money...could be overzealous zanies out to get anyone who's rich and seemingly getting away with massive fraud. And, if you're innocent, the real thief, or thieves, have good motivation to want you dead, as well. If you die without proving your innocence, who else will ever look for it? They continue to shine the light on you, and the likely scenario is the world believes them."

"They've been pretty good at it so far." His statement was fact...completely without any call for sympathy.

She needed to get him to talk about his case, from the beginning. Glen and others at the firm had already and would be speaking with him again, as well.

And none of it needed to happen that night.

She looked up at him. "You know I could be perceived as having a conflict of interest. If you'd like Glen to replace me, now would be a good time to make that call. He could have someone else here before daybreak and time to head farther south."

"Farther south?"

"There's nothing about you or your life that would lead anyone to think you'd head down to nothing but small towns swallowed up by the massive acreage of desert and mountains. Which means it's less likely anyone down there would be expecting to see you." Which wasn't the issue at hand. "Would you like me to call Glen?"

He perused her long enough to make her uncomfortable again. Personally so. And then he straightened, pulling his hands out of his pockets to plant them on his hips. Man, he was tall. And those hips…the arms that led up to muscular shoulders…

"In the first place…" His commanding tone brought her attention back to his face. To eyes that seemed not to miss much. "If a call to Glen Rivers is in order, I'd make it myself. Second, while I don't completely trust you, or Sierra's Web, for that matter… I've made the decision to put my future in the firm's hands, for now, which means giving you all free rein to do your best on my behalf."

She heard him. Knew that the fact that he was acting strictly from a place of carefully thought-out logic, not instinct or emotion, mattered, but couldn't delve into the whys. Not then. "You don't trust *me*?" That was new to her. And not a sensation she liked. At all.

"You just told me that you don't trust me."

Well, yes, she had, but… "You've been in the news for months and there's been no proof you didn't—"

She broke off.

Having someone not trust her felt…horrible. And she'd thrown that feeling in his face without even realizing what she'd been putting on him.

There'd been no proof that he wasn't a major criminal, but there wasn't substantial enough proof to convict him of being one, either.

What if he really was innocent? Life had to have been sheer hell for months…with everyone he knew, people he'd trusted, turning their backs on him.

She'd known the man less than a day, and she'd been insulted by his lack of trust. Multiply that by thousands and...

"Don't take it personally." His words broke into her thoughts. "I don't trust anyone right now. Probably wouldn't even trust myself if I weren't privy to the inside scoop."

He didn't quite grin. But there'd been a lightening to his tone that seemed to reflect from his eyes, too.

"I...um...need to apologize," she said then, moving closer to him, but only because she was heading for the bathroom so that she could get her ablutions done and be closer to desperately needed time to herself. "I've been treating you like a job instead of like a person for whom I'm working, and that was wrong. No matter what, you're a human being with feelings, and I'm sorry I lost sight of that."

"Apology accepted."

Warmth flooded her. Which wasn't good, either, for entirely different reasons.

Grabbing her duffel, she pushed past him and slid the pocket door into place behind her.

Until she could rest, think, get perspective, she needed his person separated from her person by a door, at the very least.

Chapter Four

Joe slept surprisingly well. Maybe better than he had in months. Stupid, really, kidlike, but having someone out in his living room, guarding his door—even though he didn't fear danger for an instant or he'd have kept guard himself—had given him a sense of security he hadn't known since the morning the FBI had stormed into his office and arrested him.

And who was he kidding? Having McKenna Meredith out there had distracted him from the messed-up reality his life had become.

For whole minutes there, she'd had him thinking about things other than the crimes it looked like he'd committed.

He heard her in the bathroom, less than four feet away from where he lay in bed, separated only by a pocket door, just before dawn. Heard her body knock against the wall of the shower, too. Swallowed hard. And gave himself an extra ten minutes after she'd exited the room before entering it himself.

As per the system they'd worked out the night before, both pocket doors—the one leading from the front of the rig into the bathroom, and the one leading from the bathroom to the bedroom—were to be kept closed during sleeping hours. And during the time either of them were using the facilities, both pocket doors would be locked from the inside, thus avoiding any chance of privacy invasion.

The plan was a good one. And didn't factor in the part where he'd been considered a pariah for months and so, had been without female companionship. To suddenly thrust him—a healthy heterosexual male—into a situation where there was only four feet and a very thin, medium-density-fiberboard wall between him and an intriguing naked woman... not the most comfortable happenstance.

And the way to avoid disaster was to keep his mind on the things that would make his life better and off the ones that would most certainly derail it even further.

At the moment, Sierra's Web was his best—and possibly only—hope of getting his life back. Acting inappropriately with one of their employees, one who'd warned him to keep his hands off her, would not only lose him his last hope of help but could very well land him in a deeper hell than the one in which he already resided.

Joe Hamilton, CFO of Bellair Software, the man who bilked millions and got away with it, strikes again. This time by hitting on a woman in his employ. One who'd already warned him to leave her alone...

The imaginary news lead knocking any sense of attraction out of his mind—and his body, too—Joe got up, showered and pulled on another pair of the cargo shorts and the short-sleeved shirts that were the only wardrobe of his long-haired persona. He noticed breakfast scents coming from the kitchen as he unlocked the door into the living area. McKenna had said she wanted to be on the road by daybreak, and the sky's deep purple color signaled that the moment was arriving imminently.

There was no sign of the sheets, blanket and pillow he'd pulled out of the under-couch storage the night before. The table was set for two, with a plate of toast in between, and

McKenna, in slim-fitting navy cotton pants and a sleeveless white blouse, that curly red hair still damp from her recent shower, was carrying a pan bearing omelet portions over to the table.

He'd told her to make herself at home. Had mentioned that he had provisions for omelets when they'd been in the store the night before. He hadn't expected her to cook for him.

"I'll make dinner," he said as he sat down and dug in. Forcing himself to think about the work at hand, not the intimacy of the situation, the two of them in the very small space, all blinds closed to block the light—and their privacy—from the parking lot outside.

He wanted to know if she'd slept all right. If she needed anything.

He didn't want to think about people on a site on the dark web targeting him. He was a numbers guy. One who liked everything in rows and columns and who chose to spend his life in a universe he could control.

The internet, most particularly the dark web part of it, was out of control.

Before he got around to deciding whether or not he should inquire as to her comfort, she sat down opposite him and said, "We need you to unhook your car as soon as you've finished eating. It's been decided that the car will be left here, key fob under the spare tire. You're to text Glen the electronic entry code. He's already got a driver, about your height with long dark hair and a beard, on the way here from Phoenix. He's hired the guy to spend the next couple of days driving around the western part of the state, north and south of Quartz Landing. You'll be billed accordingly."

He'd given them carte blanche. Told them to do whatever they had to do, at whatever expense. And he saw the plan immediately...whoever was on that dark-web site was going to be given chances for sightings of him right where they'd be looking—and far away from his actual person.

"Does the guy know he could be in danger?"

"He's a freelance bodyguard the firm uses on occasion."

"And he just happens to have long hair and a beard?"

He could have sworn, when she held her fork aloft with a bite of an incredibly delicious ham, pepper, onion and cheese omelet, that she was ready to grin at him. She didn't. But her tone had a hint of teasing when she asked, "You ever hear of wigs and costume shops?"

She took her bite. Finished it, then said, "If we get lucky, he catches someone watching him, or lures someone to approach him with intent to harm or hold him hostage, holds whoever it is, and calls the police. Hopefully he'll have a chance to question the perp himself before law enforcement arrives, but if not, we'll be privy to the report afterward."

He heard her words and realized the magnitude of the job he'd hired Sierra's Web to handle for him. Not only were they working on proving his innocence, but in order to protect him—and also perhaps find clues as to who'd framed him—they had to investigate any crazies who were after him.

He still noticed the full lips just a foot and a half away from his.

The thirty-three-foot rig had been small when he'd been there alone—with the slides pulled out. You didn't bother with such luxuries when you were only stopping for a few hours and needed to be prepared to leave at any moment.

Or maybe, just maybe, since he finally had someone taking on his worries, his mind was going a little bonkers with the first tiny bit of freedom it had had in months.

It was up to him to corral lip-type thoughts and keep his mind solely on the fact that had been running dizzily around in circles in his brain for months. "I was thinking I should get a haircut and shave," he mentioned then, not quite getting off the body parts sitting so intimately close together, but keeping the conversation somewhat case-oriented. "No point in keeping up my attempt at a disguise if my cover's been blown."

"To the contrary—" McKenna didn't miss a beat, or even glance over at his body parts, mentioned or otherwise, as she continued to eat as though if she didn't get her food down, someone would take it away from her.

Did she always eat so fast? Or was it just him she was eager to get away from?

"Glen said that it was determined during the teams meeting last night that the disguise is still best for now. They've been looking, and so far, the photo has only appeared on the one site on the dark web. Whereas—"

"My clean-shaven likeness has been plastered on every social media site from here to everywhere, not to mention placements on all national news sources." He wasn't prone to interrupting others when they were speaking to him, but the topic had grown...bothersome.

When he'd pictured unknown viewers following his case, the weight had been heavy enough to make a hermit out of him. But to think that the woman sitting so closely across from him that he had to keep his thighs opened so his knees didn't touch hers...to think that McKenna had been looking at those pictures, following the articles, the case...

Finishing the last bites of his breakfast in one forkful, Joe rinsed his plate, put it in the dishwasher and went out to unhook his car.

He hadn't had it for long. Bought it for its towing capabilities after he acquired the rig, but it had represented the beginning of life to him after his acquittal. Safe haven.

At some point he'd accept the fact that getting attached wasn't good for him.

GLEN KNEW SOMEONE who knew someone who owned vast desert land, and by late morning, McKenna and Joe, with the rig newly dumped and holding tanks filled, were parked on an acre of desert in the middle of hundreds of acres of desert, at the foothills of the Catalina Mountains. On private land they couldn't legally be bothered without a warrant— not that any law enforcement was out to get him. That horror was firmly behind him. His charges had been dismissed with prejudice—something his high-priced lawyer had managed to argue into fact—meaning he couldn't be tried again. And with Joe paying rent for the acre, making the property his in terms of the right to defend it from trespassers, they were planning to stay put for a day or two.

Unless something changed.

She'd spent the two-hour road trip fully focused on every vehicle that passed. Every one behind them. And all those in front of them, too. Looking for any sign of danger—expressions on occupants' faces, cars that lingered when the speed limit was faster than they were going, ones that showed up more than once.

She'd checked in with the camera app on her phone, too. Getting better looks, and saving images, of anything even remotely suspicious.

Maybe it was all overkill.

Could be that none of the death threats Joe had received since his acquittal intended real harm.

The experts at Sierra's Web thought differently.

And truth be told, so did she.

Watching the man as he'd driven, seemingly so calm, so intent and yet ready to comply without complaint to their every demand, her heart lurched a time or two.

Couldn't be easy, living life cut adrift from anyone and everything he'd valued.

Most particularly if, as he proclaimed, he was innocent.

She'd be a basket case if that was the case and she was in his shoes.

Was his calm, then, a sign that he was guilty? That he'd taken risks, knowing that there could be a price to pay, but determining the cost worthy the payout?

She hadn't seen so much as a wayward blink at the tally Sierra's Web was running up on his behalf. He had assets—she and everyone else who'd followed the news knew that—and she knew, too, that while everything had been frozen while he'd been on trial, his possessions, including all investments and accounts, were fully his again.

But he wasn't listed as one of the richest men in the world. Being an accountant, he had to feel the pinch when his money was flowing out fast with no work on the horizon.

Who wanted to hire an accountant whose company had been bilked of millions? Even if he hadn't done it, the crimes committed had all been under his direct watch.

And if he was guilty, if he had millions stashed away in some offshore account investigators had been unable to find…his perceived comfort with the current leak in his financial plumbing was more understandable.

Even so, she felt for him.

Which wasn't like her, at all.

Maybe because she was still so raw from the emotional conclusion of her last case?

Or a tad bit het up to be protecting a man who, even if innocent, stood for everything she avoided in life?

Who valued the same kind of wealth that had killed her mother?

There'd been a small blue car—a few years old and with a hitch for towing—waiting for them, marking their turnoff from the dirt road they'd traveled to their hiding spot. Unlocked, keys under the floor mat. Had it been stolen, they wouldn't have been safe and had been told to call in and keep driving.

Bony knees came in just as she was signing in to the application on her laptop for the videoconference they were due to have with the rest of the Sierra's Web team on his case. She knew some of them. Not all. In addition to the partners and full-time Sierra's Web experts like herself, they'd brought in some freelancers as well.

With Joe's life in danger, and so many intricacies to his case, they needed the manpower.

His tall, long-haired being seemed to suck up half of their living space. She'd hoped to set the laptop on the dash, with both of them sitting in their respective seats for traveling—with the good-size console in between them. There'd been no way to get the device far enough away to catch both of them on camera and still enable them to actually see others on the screen.

Which left either sitting side by side on the couch, with the computer balancing on their laps—or to sit side by side at the kitchen table.

The solution had been obvious—and her least favorite.

Scooting over to the chair whose side butted the wall of the rig in the cubby that held the table, she made room for Joe to take the chair she'd just vacated next to it. Their thighs touched. With the wall there, she had nowhere farther to scootch.

He did. And did. Have room, and scootch, that was. But the movement didn't take away his warmth, his piney scent or the branding of heat on her thigh where his had so briefly been.

Glen's serious expression popped up on the screen, offering instant distraction, and with quick introductions, the meeting of eleven began.

As the forensic scientist expert partner, Glen reported that he'd received the overnight courier package containing all physical evidence that Joe had, including the computer he'd used to work from home during his tenure as Bellair's CFO, his work cell phone, all personal files Joe had kept on his own financials and the death threat letters he hadn't yet turned in to the police.

Because Glen had been chosen by the partners to oversee all physical investigative experts, including bodyguards and PIs, he was the only partner McKenna knew well.

Hudson Warner, Sierra's Web's IT expert partner, spoke next. She'd met Hudson several times in the Sierra's Web headquarters in Phoenix. And was intimidated by the level of intricate technical stuff he knew.

The rest of the experts on the call were there to listen and learn. To brainstorm.

And every single one of them could see McKenna sitting next to her bearded pretend husband, knowing full well that they were strangers living in a very tiny space as a married couple.

They had to be wondering what her current job was like, what it was asking of her.

Or, at least, she felt as though they were.

And was incredibly tense all of a sudden as she worried about what nine trained experts might see or sense as she sat there fighting a myriad of feelings for their client.

Newest of which was overt sexual attraction. Yeah, she'd found him…decent to look at, someone who might garner a second look from her even in his current disheveled state from the moment he'd opened his door to her the day before.

But she'd been so busy not liking him for being some-one who made money the focus of life, and guarding herself against what she suspected was a brilliant criminal, that she'd managed, until he'd just sat down, to pretend that she wasn't attracted to him.

You could notice that a guy looked good without feeling any personal desire to have him for yourself, she told herself. But her thoughts fell short, even as she entertained them, since they didn't explain that intense awareness in her thigh or the tingling the sensation had sent to other places. The way it suddenly had her nerves sending jagged messages throughout her body.

"We're dual-pronged here, folks," Glen was saying after Hudson's introductions. "With different but connecting purposes. I'm going to be heading up the physical protection arm—including any and all investigations into who could be or is following Joe Hamilton, either physically or on the internet, who's sending hate mail, both snail and E, and why. Keep in mind, we aren't just looking at one doer here. There's big potential for multiple perps, some working together, but others working independently, too."

McKenna felt Joe stiffen next to her. Glancing at his face next to her on-screen, she didn't detect any noticeable change but couldn't help but feel for him right then. Sitting there listening to yourself being described as someone who had cause to have multiple people wanting you dead...

Even if he wasn't petrified for his life, just knowing that... so much hate coming at you... She wanted so badly to tell him that he didn't deserve it.

That Sierra's Web would clear his name.

But she didn't know yet if they could.

She didn't even know if it was possible.

And he knew even she doubted his innocence. Maybe not as much that day as she had the day before, but...

"And I'm the lead on the Bellair fraud," Hudson was saying. "Our main charge is to find out who committed the fraud and, assuming it wasn't our client, figure out how he was framed so that we can clear his name."

Joe's expression didn't falter even a little bit, though all on-screen gazes seemed to be pinned on him. A few team members nodded—whether in support of Joe or just a willingness to give their best to the job ahead, McKenna didn't know. She fought the urge to touch the bony knee under the table—just out of human decency, she told herself.

Acknowledgment that the moment might be difficult for him. A reminder that he'd get through it. She didn't know what...

What she did know was that he deserved better from her than a woman focused on her own personal reactions. That thought firmly in mind, she tuned in to the camera app on her phone, saw that they were still all alone in their desert hideout and focused fully on the screen in front of her instead of the bony knees beside her.

Chapter Five

Customer returns weren't reported in the right quarter, sales were inflated, inventory was shown as sold that wasn't, some storage and maintenance costs weren't reflected—four completely different departments in Bellair, with only one entity in common: his accounting department.

He knew the basic facts – he just didn't know how any of them had happened. How had quarterly earnings been reported in wrong quarters? How had sales been inflated? What made inventory show as sold when it wasn't? Why weren't storage and maintenance costs reflected? He'd never been able to figure out the how. Nor had the prosecution been able to prove how – which was why they'd failed to get a conviction.

What everyone did know was that the resulting inflated earnings report was like kindling to investors, who then lost millions when Bellair's payout wasn't at all what the earnings had projected they would be. Dividends produced less than half of their expected income. Stocks dropped, and while Bellair was still successful, still selling great products that consumers wanted, that many businesses across the country used, they now had a cache of unhappy investors who'd bought high, expecting high returns, and instead had to take a huge loss in dividends or sell at a loss.

Some bogus reports had been generated from their source database. And some numbers had been changed between their original databases and his final report.

He'd personally verified all the pertinent numbers that had caused celebrations to happen and stocks to rise. Had checked them against various company bank accounts.

He'd also been the one to figure out that partial returns from two quarters had been reported on a third, subsequent one. And to see when the company's bottom-line dollars started to come in as they'd done before the great rise. He'd suspected fraud, and hoped for mistakes, as any good accountant should. He'd tried to handle the matter himself. To research, investigate, talk to employees involved. Find discrepancies and the sources of them. All tasks that fell under his specific job duties as CFO of Bellair. He'd recorded conversations, had kept meticulous notes.

Without enough time to find out the cause of the changed numbers before quarter's end, he'd had to report the lower earnings to Bellair's major shareholder, president and CEO, the man he'd thought of as a father figure, James Bellair.

And had been arrested that night.

During the subsequent investigation and the trial that followed, evidence had been produced to show that discrepancies had come from his computer, or his computer log-in on other systems, all done internally, at the office, and he'd known they were done at times he wasn't there. But didn't have alibis, as he'd been at home alone. The prosecution hadn't had solid enough proof that he'd been at the office, either, as no cameras had him on view, and his key card to gain entrance hadn't been used.

Joe sat and listened while Glen and Hudson laid out the basics of his case for the entire team they'd compiled. He heard their words. Mentally verified the correctness of their facts as they relayed them.

And disassociated from any ownership of them. He'd never have made it through the past months, sitting in the front of the courtroom day after day, hearing himself maligned, if he'd bought in to the story that had been fabricated about him.

His defense lawyer had brought in a great trial-prep guy to work with him—Sam White. Sam had also been tried for a crime he didn't commit. He'd been found guilty and had spent five years behind bars before he'd been exonerated. He knew all about not buying in to the story that people told about you. And he'd taught the concept well.

But then, when he'd been under Sam's tutelage, he hadn't been holed up with a pretend wife. With the first woman to actually interest him, in a personal sense, for more months than he could count.

Ignoring the warm body next to his, the way she held herself at attention, her gaze either on the screen or her phone app, trying not to wonder what she was thinking-proved to be a whole lot harder than sitting in court had been.

But then, when he'd been at trial, and investors had thought he'd be found guilty and would be made to cough up the money they'd lost, when the real perpetrator had figured Joe would be taking the fall for him, he hadn't had so many people wishing him dead. Or hatemongers on the dark web hunting him down...

"I was able to match several IP addresses from the Bellair victim message board accessed through the company's social media pages to the Joe Hamilton board on the dark web," Hudson said then, continuing to speak as though Joe wasn't there. "But there are many other addresses out there that didn't match, so we're going to continue to assume that we're not just looking at victims here in terms of threat."

Joe had insisted on being part of the meeting. In case anyone had any questions for him, they'd be answered immediately, but also because he wanted every one of the people working on his behalf to see him—the person. To know whom they were working for.

"We've also put in a request to James Bellair, asking for access to some company files and databases, under the assumption that, with Joe being found not guilty, they'd like to know who is. If I were a CEO with no knowledge of how my company had been attacked, I'd sure want to know..."

"Thinking that if he doesn't comply, he's in on it?" Amelia, one of Hudson's computer experts, asked.

"Hoping that he will comply." Hudson's reply impressed Joe, though he couldn't say why. Except that maybe it was because he held the same hope.

"I've also made it clear to Mr. Bellair that we have a signed disclosure with Joe Hamilton that if we find proof he's guilty, we will cease working for him."

All eyes turned to Joe, then, and he looked at them all straight on, thinking about the dog he'd had for a while as a kid. Checkers. A mongrel who'd been lost until Joe had found him. Joe had been lost, too, until Checkers had wandered into the yard of the trailer his father had rented that year.

Until his attention was drawn to the nods—a few more than previously.

According to Sam, when speaking about the jury Joe would be facing, nods were good when you wanted the speaker to be believed.

It was to his benefit to have the Sierra's Web experts believing in the project their bosses were laying out for them.

And he couldn't help but notice that McKenna wasn't among the nodders. He knew from sitting next to her, but also from her face next to his in the little square on the screen.

"Hold it!" Joe's heart lurched as Bryce Armstrong, the expert private investigator Glen had hired specifically for Joe's job, popped on the screen. "Joe, take the SIM card and battery out of your phone," he said. "You two need to get moving. I've got tracers out and someone's accessing your phone's location…"

"My location services are off," he said, but he grabbed the phone off the table and immediately did as he was told.

"There are apps, a particularly expensive one used mostly by private investigators…it employs a conglomeration of things, including atmospheric pressure, to track a phone."

"Okay, gang, it's been nice chatting, but we're out of here," McKenna said then. "I'll be in touch." She was already pushing at Joe to let her out of her seat before she'd closed the laptop.

"I'm on it," Joe told her, at the door of the rig in two steps. Pushing buttons to retract the slides he'd just let out with breaths of relief, he jumped down the steps and headed out to hook up the blue car for towing. And wedged the phone between a rock and a wheel of the rig.

He didn't just want the damned thing untraceable, he wanted it smashed to hell.

As though he could somehow get vengeance from the unending hell his life had become by taking it out on the cell.

"It's a new phone, and new number, just a couple of days ago," he announced inanely, making him sound as though he was looking for reassurance, as he reentered the rig. His bodyguard already knew about his phone. She'd grilled him on it and made certain his location services were off in the first ten minutes she'd been formally accepted in the rig.

McKenna, who'd been securing a couple of the unattached kitchen appliances they'd removed from storage and put out on the cupboards, glanced over at him, met his gaze.

And nodded.

Giving him…something good.

Embarrassed, a bit pissed at himself for needing, or accepting, anything emotional from McKenna Meredith, Joe turned his back, jumped into the driver's seat of his thirty-three-foot-plus-tow-bar-and-car load and started the engine.

THEY WERE GOING completely off the grid—McKenna's call. If someone was using high-tech software to find them, they couldn't take chances. Arizona was filled with roads that ran for miles on end through desert and winding around mountains without even a gas station to refuel. Deciding to head back the way they'd come and then go west again, she had Joe stop at a remote service exit—used mostly by truckers going from the California ports to the eastern states—and bought a couple of burner phones, taking the batteries out of both of them.

Another long, silent hour down the road, on a flat desert stretch, she put one battery back in place only long enough to see if they had service and then make a quick call to Glen. He and Hudson would be the only two people in the world to have the number. And she'd only be putting her battery in long enough to check in a few times a day. She'd already disabled her laptop.

"What's the second phone for?" Joe's voice, deep and sounding somewhat loud in the silence she'd grown used to, startled her so much she jumped.

"Just in case," she told him, trying not to think about how he must feeling. Or wondering what he'd been thinking about during the past few hours on the road.

"If this phone gets compromised or destroyed, I'll have a backup." She was big on backups. "Being prepared gives me the confidence to concentrate on the dangers inherent in the moment, rather than having to worry about what could lie ahead."

She heard herself, felt...lacking...somehow, and amended. "Not that I don't think ahead. Of course I do. I always have a plan."

"You mind sharing our current one?"

"I told you we had to go off the grid." Maybe there was more tension in her tone than she'd have liked. Not work-related.

"Right."

"That's the plan."

Unless she thought of a better one. Or something changed.

She took a deep breath. Tried to instill kindness, or at the very least, politeness, into her tone, without getting all compassionate or weird again. "You planned to spend however long it took, hiding out on the road, until you proved your innocence."

"Yeah."

"That's what we're doing."

Hopefully as silently as possible. Though not talking to him hadn't lessened her awareness of him any, it *had* allowed her to instill mind over matter enough to keep her thoughts more focused.

"You aren't nervous, being out in the middle of nowhere, completed disconnected, with someone you think might be a criminal?"

"I'm disconnected, not unarmed," she told him before she could blurt out that she had no fear of him whatsoever.

"Good point."

She hoped the conversation was done, until he added, "Noted."

And then she thought to ask, "Are you armed?"

"I don't have a gun permit."

"Which doesn't answer my question."

"No permit, no gun."

She could look down past his bony knees and see that he didn't have a killer knife stashed in his slip-ons. And pretend that her heart hadn't warmed at his law-abiding proclamation.

He could be lying to her.

Would have to be a consummate liar to have committed the crimes he had and still be fighting so hard to prove his innocence.

"I half expected you to quit me after today's meeting."

Obviously the near-total silence she'd preferred hadn't been such a good idea after all. Gave the man too much time to think.

"I'm not a quitter," she said. Keep it all business. Impersonal.

Boundaries.

The way he'd told the guy at the gas station that his wife didn't want to travel across the desert to Tucson without both of them having cell phones had been all business. She'd known it at the time. Knew it as she sat there beside him with the huge console acting as a physical boundary to remind her that she wasn't setting out for an adventure in the middle of nowhere.

She was just having another day at work.

And still, she said, "Good move back there, by the way, telling him we were heading east when we're going west."

"Only good if he didn't see us pull out and head in the opposite direction."

"He'd have had to follow us out the door around the building and across the lot to do so."

Yeah, this was better. Light banter about the job. Reality instead of emotional chaos.

"I haven't seen you make any other phone calls, other than to Glen." His question lacked levity. And bordered on personal.

Raising an awareness of him as a person again.

"I haven't."

"Your people are used to you disappearing for days at a time without contact?"

Absolutely none of his business.

But it showed humanity, the fact that he'd thought about any toll his job could be taking on her life.

"If you mean family, personal people, then yes. If I don't check in with Glen, every top cop in this part of the country will be hunting us down."

Maybe a bit of an exaggeration, but not as much of one as he might think.

"I didn't do it."

"Whether you did or not isn't any of my business."

"I'm making it your business. Everything you heard today... I've heard it so many times, in court and out of it, during countless sessions with my attorney, and in my own head...but hearing it alongside you, out here... I'm telling you, I'm innocent."

He wanted them to be people, experiencing a situation together.

She couldn't do it. "And I'm telling you, it doesn't matter, either way. I do my job the same."

He glanced her way briefly. Nodded.

Some of the tension seeped out of her. And then he asked, "Is your mind open at all to the possibility that I'm innocent?"

Her head shot in his direction so fast it made it her dizzy. "Of course it is," she blurted out, exploding with the need for him to know that she wasn't sitting in judgment on him.

And she wasn't closed-minded, either.

She just...

Had to protect herself.

Most particularly with the unwanted feelings he was arousing in her. She couldn't go down that road. Because of the job—but it was way more than that.

"I'm hoping that Sierra's Web experts are able to give you the proof you need," she told him. "Really hoping. I want you to be able to get your life back." There. She'd given him the bit of herself she had to give.

Because anything more…even thinking about letting him be more than a job in her life, ever, was not an option.

No matter how much her body was tuning in to his.

Or how much her heart sympathized with his plight.

Because in the end, if he was exonerated, she still couldn't have anything to do with him. He lived in a world she could not inhabit.

Valued things she did not value.

He'd made his entire life about being wealthy.

And she'd refused the trust fund that was her birthright.

Chapter Six

Late in the afternoon, they came to a small desert community that consisted of a couple of golf courses, some housing developments, a few strip shopping areas and many RV and mobile home parks. Six of them that Joe counted from the signs coming into town. He'd exited the long, long road into nowhere to get gas.

McKenna thought they should stop for the night. At least. As husband and wife, and with his disguised looks, maybe they'd get to hang around a bit longer.

She chose the smallest, least expensive, least opulent park. And went in to register them as John and McKenna Meredith, using her driver's license as identification. They couldn't check in without valid state ID and he certainly couldn't use his.

So what if there was no luxurious built-in pool and spa, or clubhouse filled with billiards, card rooms and tool shops. It wasn't like he'd be frequenting any of the facilities. Their site was spacious, though it had other sites on all four sides of it, with only a road separating them from the site in front of them.

"We're here to blend in," McKenna told him as he pulled up to the site and hesitated before unhooking the car so he could back the rig into the hookups. "And unless someone who's after you is staying here in the park, there's not much chance any of your stalkers would be able to linger without being noticed. Not only do you need the key card to get back here, they have twenty-four-hour security patrolling on a golf cart."

He had to wonder about why that was…what kind of community were they in that would require such a thing? But, keeping his thoughts to himself, he got the rig parked and turned to see McKenna parking the car in the designated spot next to their RV. And while he hooked up to electric and plumbing, she pushed out the slides and, he found as he entered the rig, she'd already set the toaster, blender and small canisters back up on the counter next to the built-in coffee maker.

Just like he'd always imagined a camping trip with a wife would be. The two of them working together, just knowing what to do to complement the other and get the chores done without having to talk it through. Or ask questions.

"You've done this before," he said as he went to the refrigerator for a bottle of water.

"Nope. I've never been in an RV before yesterday. It's my job to pay attention to my surroundings and to know how to take care of them in case of emergency." She'd said something similar the day before when she'd been observing the hookup process. Thankfully, his embarrassing momentary lapse into something more personal was just between he and himself.

They were parked. Set for the night. Which meant it was time for him to get to work. Pulling out his laptop—he'd already disabled the battery and all internet capabilities—he started in immediately with a reorganization of his investigation, splitting it up as Glen and Hudson had during the video meeting earlier that day.

The chair across the table, and close to the wall, instead of directly opposite him, pulled out and McKenna sat down. He could have done without the flowery scent. It distracted him.

"I called Glen," she told him. "And hooked up to the park's free Wi-Fi, rather than the phone's internal connection to download the camera app. I'll be turning it on and off throughout the night, and someone will be monitoring my number in the event that anyone tries to track the phone."

"How would they know?"

She shook her head. "No real clue. Except they can see if there is more activity on the phone's data or number or something. I don't ask…"

They had all night together in that tiny space. Him, and this woman who drew him to her just by admitting that there were things she didn't know, and being okay with the not knowing.

He'd always felt like what he didn't know could kick him in the ass.

Ironic beyond any sense of humor at all that he'd turned out to be right.

Hands folded in front of her, McKenna looked at him—and panic flew. From his right side to his left, his head to his toes. He was massive nerves, sitting calmly. Placidly.

For the few seconds it took him to disassociate from emotions that were not going to get the better of him.

He should probably head to the bedroom. He didn't have to sit at the table to work on his computer. There was a television back there, too…

He'd never been much of a TV watcher.

"From what Glen reported, you've been over everything on your case multiple times," McKenna said, as though she knew he needed to be rescued.

Brought back to what mattered.

What he cared about most.

"That's right," he told her, glancing at the document he was starting—one that would include several spreadsheets as well.

"What do you think you're going to find? Staring at the same stuff over and over again?"

Panic again. Deep breath. Picture Checkers. He shrugged. "If I knew, I'd have found it already."

"So, talk to me about it," she told him. "I have nothing to do but sit here and monitor cameras, hopefully for days on end, if we're lucky. My dad always says that talking things over helps give different perspective, and while I'm not sure he's right all the time, I have found that talking to him definitely makes me feel better."

Her dad.

The first mention of family other than grandparents with whom she kept in touch.

The image he had of her changed with a father in her life. Not physically. Not even in turns of his attraction to her.

But...he was glad to know that she had the support...

And aware that he had no business feeling one way or the other about it. Thought about retreating to the bedroom. He couldn't stand completely erect in the back of the rig, due to underneath storage, but with the slide out, he could walk around the bed. And let his feet hang over the mattress without touching the wall.

"Right now I'm reorganizing," he heard himself say, relieved that he was staying put. Sleeping in that small space was one thing...having to spend unending hours there could start to feel like one step up from the jail cell he'd occupied. "The way Glen and Hudson laid it out on the video call this morning. My spreadsheets contain all the crimes together, looking for the similarity that would tell me who was behind them."

"You're assuming it's one person, then."

"No, hoping is more like it."

"Because it will be easier to prove and catch whoever it is?"

"Yeah." And because he wasn't ready to accept that more than one of the peers he'd trusted with his life had stolen it away from him.

In the end, he wanted to know that the people he'd cared most about, the people he'd considered family, had had his back, as opposed to stabbing it.

"Now I'm thinking maybe it's a difference I need to look for, not a similarity. Look for how each thing happened individually, rather than searching for one way one person somehow falsified all of the records. I'm going to separate out the departments involved and look at each one on its own."

He glanced at his spreadsheet again.

"Mind if I come around and look with you?"

Of course he minded. He was dry mouthed with minding. "Sure, go ahead," he told her, moving so that she could climb over his seat to get to the one in the smaller space against the wall.

"If I'm getting too nosy, just tell me," she said as she slid into the chair. "I'm here on business, and this is business. Maybe I'll see something that will help me nail a culprit at some point."

Busy trying to swallow as he sat back down, he didn't say a word. But understood the difficulty in not being able to get out, explore, play a round of golf or meet the neighbors.

"Tomorrow, if we're still here, I'll probably get out and meet the neighbors," she said then, again with the seeming to know what he was thinking. "You're going to be a writer, working on a book. We're newly married, and I took a month off to travel around with you but need to give you some quiet, alone time to write. But don't worry, I'll keep the rig in sight at all times."

His safety was the last thing Joe was worrying about.

The story she'd just told—he'd been right there, buying in to it, as a neighbor would.

Except that, for a split second there, he'd yearned to be a real part of the fantasy...

As he got to work, sorting and moving bulleted points, he had a whole new motivation to get to the truth. He wasn't going to last long, living side by side with the curly red-headed sprite who was getting under skin that no one had penetrated...ever.

THE INVENTORY DEPARTMENT of Bellair had reported shipping more inventory than they'd shipped. Just randomly. Not on any set schedule, or the same day of the week, or at the same time. It had even happened once on a weekend. Had to have been done manually. But by whom?

The sales department had added an additional, identical sale, every tenth sale. Joe had already caught that, but he couldn't explain it. The company had been using the database software program for years. Used it in other departments. Someone had to have manually doubled every tenth sale, which was certainly doable. But who?

Times didn't coincide between the two happenings, so it could be the same person.

The returns department had held reports of returns for six months. And then let them all fall at once. Which prevented the inflated promised dividends from paying out. And caused the stock to drop instantly. The news had been all over that one. They'd latched on and repeated. Again and again. Probably because the concept had been an easy one to grasp.

Online banking sessions, which had been downloaded as per Bellair practice, didn't match online statements collected later. Joe had no explanation for that one.

Prosecutors had claimed that he'd manipulated the PDF after the download. They'd had no proof, but it was a logical explanation. Joe agreed that the explanation was logical. But he wasn't the one who'd done it.

"It's also possible that whoever in the company was doing all this had an accomplice at the bank," he said as darkness started to fall outside.

McKenna reached up to turn on the light attached to the wall beside her. They could see his computer just fine without it, but sitting in close quarters in the dark with Joe was definitely out.

She focused on his case, engrossed far more than she'd expected to be. Her initial offer to listen had been more polite and for his sake than because she'd expected to get involved. Either way. If she didn't know the details, she wouldn't have cause to doubt him as much.

"There's something I don't get." She forced herself to keep her gaze glued on the computer screen.

"What's that?"

"I get how people who invested lost money—they bought when stock was just going up, so they paid more but expected it to continue to grow so they'd make a lot. And they were promised a five percent dividend, payable bi-yearly, and their five percent turned out to be far below projected income."

"Basically, in a nutshell, you're right. There's more to it, but yeah."

"What I don't get is where they think you got money from it all."

His hesitation gave her time to hear her own words, and she cringed. "Where whoever did this got money," she quickly corrected, realizing as the words came out that she was making matters worse.

He knew she wasn't sure about his guilt. She didn't have to keep making the matter front and center between them.

He got up. Helped himself to a beer. Offered her one, but, because she was on the job, she had to decline. After uncapping his bottle, he didn't sit back down. Rather, he leaned against the refrigerator, frowning in her general direction.

"I'm sorry."

His shrug drew her attention for a moment, allowing her to avoid his gaze. If the man was innocent, he deserved to have someone in his life who believed in him.

But to mean anything, the belief had to be real. And she wasn't quite there. He was free. Couldn't be retried, and yet he was spending a bundle to prove his innocence anyway.

And…without his innocence, his chances of continuing to make his fortune in his chosen field, his chance of living the überwealthy life, weren't good.

He hadn't answered her question.

The realization bothered her.

More and more as the silence stretched between them.

"Joe? What aren't you telling me?" She stared him right in the eye then. Fully aware that her need for an answer had nothing to do with the job.

And needing it anyway.

"When the stock prices first went up, I thought the inflated numbers were legitimate, and I sold my stock. Not the shares that the company gave me as part of my package, but all the shares I'd purchased myself over the past several years."

Oh. God.

Sick to her stomach, she stared at him. Openmouthed.

"So, you did profit from the fraud."

"Not knowing that it was fraud and in a completely legal manner."

She had to get out. Go for a walk.

No reason to feel that way. She'd thought him guilty when she'd taken the job.

"You didn't think it odd that the company was suddenly showing such an increase?"

"I did, yes, but we'd just released a major new product,

Stellar, a state-of-the-art gaming system that rivals anything that's ever been released before, and those were the sales numbers that had been inflated. And the returns that had been held. It took me a bit to catch on to the fact that we had a problem, and by then I'd already sold the stock. I knew, immediately, that they'd be looking at me. Some kind of insider trading suspicion was considered. I never, for one second, thought anyone would think I was guilty of fraud."

He sounded so believable. Or was she just falling prey to his charm?

Long-haired guy with bony knees.

"I buy and sell stock on a regular basis. Not just Bellair, but others, too." His tone, so conversational, broke into her thoughts. "It's a hobby, of sorts, but also a serious money-maker for me. And it's not the first time I've sold Bellair stock, which my lawyer proved in court with full documentation. Each time the company has come out with a major new product that exceeds expectation, I sell stock. And then buy it up again when things level off. It's a risk, but I believe in Bellair, and it's always paid off."

What he said made sense.

A smart man planning a crime would make certain that he'd crossed all his t's and dotted his i's. A company's CFO would likely be on first-name terms with bank managers and such.

All the back-and-forth…he was exhausting her.

Turning on her phone, she checked the outside cameras. Took a screenshot from each one and shut the phone back off.

"You want steak for dinner?" she asked. "We can grill…"

One way or another, she needed to get out. Have some space. Breathe fresh air.

Joe didn't reply. Or move.

"You knew going in that I had doubts," she reminded him, a tad defensively.

He nodded. Turned. Reached for the steaks. Seasoned them. Headed outside.

She had to go with him. Had to guard his body.

And what about the heart beating inside the body? Did anyone guard that for him?

Sitting in the lawn chair he'd set out beside the one he was using, she said, "Thank you for telling me."

He hadn't had to answer her query regarding his profits. Or tell her anything at all about his case. He had her on the job, doing what he needed her to do, regardless.

Sipping his beer, he looked out toward the other rigs filling the park. Nodded at a couple passing by on bikes. "I didn't tell you to try and manipulate you into believing I'm innocent."

"I didn't think you had." But she kind of had, hadn't she? The part of her that knew he could be guilty.

The way he nodded his head, his expression shrouded from her, from the world, told her that he knew she'd just lied to him.

And that the lie had disappointed him.

Chapter Seven

He'd withheld information.

Stupid thing to do.

And not his way. At all.

The woman was throwing him all out of kilter. Making him into less of the straight-up man he was. He couldn't have that.

"The prosecutors claimed that I'd profited in another way," he said, his voice accompanying the sound of grilling steaks. He spoke softly. There were neighboring campers all around them, some parked just yards away, all with lights on inside their rigs.

Brows raised, she glanced over at him, her eyes glints of white in the falling darkness. She didn't ask questions. Didn't look at him long, either, but then she never did. McKenna's brown-eyed gaze was always busy watching their surroundings.

"There were other shareholders who sold their stock during the brief boom."

"So?" She was watching a car moving slowly through the park, stopping now and then, as though looking for something. Or someone.

"With sales of Stellar so impressively exceeding expectations, it would have been smarter for them to hang on for the big payout."

"Unless they knew that there wasn't going to be one." She was still watching the car. It had turned onto another avenue in the park, out of sight, but her gaze was in the direction it was last seen.

"That was the prosecutor's claim." He could leave it there.

And if he wanted the possibility on the table of her someday believing in his innocence, he had to tell her what she could find out by other means.

"The story he laid out for the jury was that I tipped them off and then got a payoff from each one of them, a percentage of the profits they made by selling."

"A bank employee accomplice kind of fits that theory, doesn't it?"

Yeah, he'd known she'd put it all together.

"Get inside. Now." Her tone, while still soft, had noticeably changed. "Turn off all lights in there and stay down low."

He heard his chair fold up the second he'd vacated it. Saw her shove it under the rig as he entered the door.

Inside, with the door shut, he stayed right there crouched on the first step, down, as she'd instructed, but high enough to be able to peer out.

No way he was going to hide inside while she took a bullet for him.

He saw nothing on the road, no sign of the car he'd noticed earlier.

And…turning toward her…he was stunned to see her with her hands on the ground, at her feet, as though she was tying her shoe—not so much because of her hands on her foot, but because of the booty shot she'd pointed at the road.

Before he'd come up with any explanation for her odd behavior, the car drove by. The one he hadn't seen any sign of.

Drove by keeping its slow, steady speed.

He got a glimpse of the occupant. As much of one as he could make out in the near darkness and glare of dash lights. Male. Military haircut. Freshly shaven. Wrinkles around the eyes.

The PI that had been mentioned in that morning's video-conference?

Heart racing, he watched the man for any sudden movement, his hand on the door handle, ready to burst out and catch any bullet that might fly their way.

How in the hell was the guy tracking them?

And doing it so quickly?

Did Sierra's Web have a leak?

The driver passed, his scrutiny on the rig next door to them, studying it like he'd studied theirs. Joe didn't move, staying inside as ordered, but crouched right at the door, watching McKenna stand upright and calmly move to turn the steaks.

Maybe he wouldn't have noticed her watching the passing car surreptitiously over the top of the portable grill if he hadn't spent the past twenty-four hours right beside her. Seeing her work.

She wouldn't be out there risking her life if she was behind any leak.

Was she in the same boat he was? Being stabbed by someone with whom she worked?

Dropping back to sit his butt on the second step, Joe entertained the thought but didn't really buy it. Just didn't make sense. Life always came down to the money, and he was paying Sierra's Web a hefty fee for their services. He couldn't come up with a motivation for anyone there to want him dead.

Or to want the firm to fail. It wasn't like one botched job would tarnish the firm's eleven-year golden reputation.

The stress of being arrested, tried, hated and turned on

was getting to him more than he'd thought. Making him as suspicious of others as his father had always been...

He heard the click of the door a mere second before McKenna pulled it open and nearly took a lap full of hot steak as she stopped midstride so as not to step on him.

His hands on her hips were instinctive. Holding her upright as he stood, while she adjusted the steaks on her platter.

But somehow he didn't let go soon enough. They stood there, lower bodies an inch apart, her staring up at him with a platter of steaks between them. She'd held his gaze for more than a few seconds, and he got lost in those brown eyes. Mesmerized by the life in them. Maybe by a storm brewing there...

Letting go, he stepped back and asked, "What do you think?"

When she didn't answer right away, he added, "About the car. I'm assuming that's why you wanted me to come inside." He reached for the light switch so she wouldn't stumble coming up the steps.

"Don't!" Her tone stopped him instantly, as he was sure it had been meant to do. "Let's close all the blinds before we turn on any lights."

Uneasy, he did as she asked. At the same time, taking it as a good sign that they weren't leaving.

It wasn't until they were seated cattycorner across from each other at the table, her against the wall, him not, eating steaks and salad, that she said, "The car pulled in half a block down from here. The driver got out, and people greeted him. I'm going under the assumption he was looking for the right slot."

Good. His stomach allowed more room for the food he'd been forcing down.

"I checked in with Glen as soon as I heard the greetings down the way," she said then, and he slowed down his chewing as he read the serious expression on her face. "The front gate and pillars of your home were vandalized. Someone left you a spray-painted message."

It had only been a matter of time. Was just a stucco cement wall and metal privacy gate, both of which could be repainted. "Which was?" he prompted when she didn't dish.

"'Leave or die. We don't want you here.'"

Chin jutted, he nodded. Carried his plate to the counter, disposed of the uneaten food, rinsed his dishes, put them in the dishwasher and excused himself to bed.

There were some things a guy had to deal with outside the company of a woman he was starting to admire far too much.

THE FEEL OF Joe Hamilton's hands on her hips should not have been what kept McKenna awake. And shouldn't have been what she'd dreamed about, either. She might have worried more about both if she hadn't seen a shadow on the camera app during her 4:10 a.m. check.

Up and off the couch, in the pants and shirt she'd slept in, she slid into her shoes as she enlarged the one camera. Took a screenshot and continued to watch.

Someone was outside their rig. Not far from the grill. Down on hands and knees?

Could it be an animal? Brought in by the scent?

Yeah, they were in town—a small one, in a park—but the surrounding area was all mountainous desert. A mountain lion?

As she watched, the figure rose and she retrieved the gun she generally wore holstered to her ankle from under the pillow next to where she'd been sleeping.

If the intruder was animal, it had to be a bear...

Out of sight of the camera.

Stepping stealthily, so the rig wouldn't show any movement, she got to the side of the door, peering out the window.

Phone in one hand, gun poised in the other. She didn't have eyes on the intruder.

Not by camera, or through the window. He seemed to have just disappeared.

Enlarging all seven of the other cameras, she checked, one by one, looking for any sign of occupation, but saw nothing but the same cleared area she'd been watching for nearly twelve hours. Back to camera one—and nothing.

She hadn't imagined movement out there. She had the screenshots to prove it. And, glancing toward the back of the rig, knew she had to wake up Joe. She'd taken a couple of steps in that direction when he came stumbling through the bathroom, still buttoning the shorts he'd obviously just pulled on.

He didn't make a sound, but his expression said plenty. Wanting to know what was going on.

Motioning him down below window level, she crouched and met him at the table, showing him the images on her phone.

"I'm going out to take a look," she barely whispered. "Stay low."

When he shook his head, she raised her brow, and, with a resigned look, he nodded. Either he let her do her job, or she'd be gone.

It was the silent message she sent him. She assumed his acquiescence meant he got it.

McKenna unlatched the door slowly, silently and, inch by inch, eased outside, taking in every bit of space she could see. The park was well lit, even at night, but with dark rigs on all sides, there were still plenty of shadows in which someone, or something, could be hiding.

A sound behind her had her swinging with one breath, heart pounding, gun pointed, and she saw the rig behind them dip, as though someone had just climbed up inside.

A middle-of-the-night trek to the public restroom facility?

Or their intruder? Turning around more slowly, gun still held out in front of her with both hands, she did a thorough check of their site and was about to head back inside when she saw something move on the windshield of the car.

A piece of paper, brown, as it turned out when she retrieved it. Couldn't make out any messaging in the darkness, but as her toe caught on the wheel of the car, she noticed something else.

The tire was flat.

Both front tires were flat.

Watching on all sides, she hurried back inside the rig. And saw Joe, fully dressed, already packing up the kitchen by the light of one small battery-operated lantern.

While she itched to check out the rig next door, she couldn't waste the time. Her job was to stay with Joe. To assess current danger to her client. Not catch a tire slasher.

She carried the paper over to him, holding it out so they could huddle together and read it by the dim light.

The picture jumped out at her. Throat tightening, she studied the copied image from a popular social media site, including side-by-side likenesses of Joe. The short-haired, clean-shaved, business-suited shot that had been plastered all over the news, and a more recent version of long-haired, bearded Joe, in a pair of shorts she hadn't seen. The side of the legs were pocketed.

"When was the last time you wore those shorts?" she asked quietly.

"Three or four days."

Breathing a tad easier, she nodded. And started to read the inked and somewhat uneven note. "We don't need no liars and cheats here. Leave now and I won't respond to this post."

Moving closer, she barely made out the post itself. But she

got the gist of it. And the hashtag, #wheresjoenow. Someone had moved the hunt for Joe from the dark web to social media.

"Go shave," she said, following him back toward the bathroom to veer to the laundry side of the small space. She'd seen a small container of bleach there with some other household products.

"All I have are these trimming scissors to cut my hair, but we can get some..." He held up the small cutters he was using to cut his beard down, collecting the hair in a trash bag, before shaving. The single-blade travel razor and little can of shaving cream were going to be a challenge.

She shook her head, pretending that she didn't notice that she was standing in the bathroom with a man performing personal ablutions.

A man she was finding harder and harder to keep at a personal distance.

"We need to leave your hair long, but we'll bleach it. I did this once, when I was younger, and while I don't recommend it, for various reasons, it works. I just need to mix some shampoo in with a little bit of bleach." She moved to the kitchen, grabbing a plastic container they could throw away, all the while instructing him on putting on clothes he wouldn't mind discarding and draping his shoulders with a towel that he could do without.

She chattered to keep her thoughts from wandering off on her. She was pretty certain there was no immediate threat to Joe's life—the photo let them know that someone knew who Joe was, but the slashed tires were more in line with the words on the note. A warning rather than an immediate threat. They'd been given time to move on. And with adrenalin still pumping, with imminent danger gone, she was too aware of the man whose intimate habits were becoming far too familiar to her.

By the time he was shaved and ready for her, she'd put

away her bedding, moved in the slides and brushed her teeth and washed her face at the kitchen sink. Draping the floor with a sheet, she had him sit on an also-covered kitchen chair, put the rubber gloves she'd found under the kitchen sink, on her hands and grabbed a comb.

"We're only going to leave this on for a couple of minutes," she told him, imagining herself as any other hairdresser or barber he'd visited over the years. Nothing intimate about that. Just business. She couldn't even feel his hair with the rubber between her fingers and the long strands. It took her far too long to comb in the bleach. A good five minutes of keeping her mind occupied on tasks ahead, and off the shoulders the backs of her hands kept bumping into.

He never said a word through the entire process. Just sat there, leaving her to imagine what he was thinking. How he could possibly be feeling.

"Okay, rinsing's going to be a treat," she said, words forced as cheerfully as she could push them through her tight throat. Wanting to blame the bleach stench for the tightness, but knew she'd be lying to herself if she did.

"The only space big enough is the shower." It was a tiny combination unit with the tiniest tub she'd ever seen. But as a sink, it would do fine. "Sit down and lean your head back. We can't let any of this touch your skin." She handed him a thick towel. "Keep this over your eyes at all times."

Kneeling down beside him, she turned on the water, decided lukewarm was better than waiting, and, leaning over him, concentrated on getting the poisonous cleaning agent out of his hair without burning or otherwise hurting either one of them.

The entire project almost went to hell in an instant as, leaning to reach the ends of the long strands on the back of his head, her breast brushed up against his chin.

She jerked. He coughed.

She slipped, fell forward and, catching herself in the tub with both hands, left him face-planted between her breasts.

Chapter Eight

Joe's arms closed around her by pure instinct. Catching the weight of her upper body with his face and neck, he sat upright, holding her tight.

For a split second, he thought he'd died and gone to heaven. It was a light place, a warm place, and the scents were a mixture of glorious floral woman and...bleach.

And the softness. His face nestled into it—and the split second was over. His nose. McKenna's breasts.

He pulled away from her as voraciously as she drew apart from him, and the knee that she'd been resting on landed in his lap, just missing his misters.

The erection was there, though, pressing against her upper leg, for the second or two it took her to stand up and get out of there. The water was running, his hair was dripping and Joe sat, giving his body a second to recuperate.

Giving his good sense a chance to return.

And his heart to calm down.

"You need to wash your hair," she called from the front room, her voice sounding so odd he might have thought someone else was in the rig with them if there'd been even a realm of possibility of that being the case. "Fast," she called out. "We need to roll quietly out of here before daybreak."

Those last words shrank his penis and stole all good feel-

ing from his being as reality slammed him twice over. The
woman who'd just ignited him believed him to be guilty of
fraud, among other things. And he was being stalked on social media.

The fates that had borne him into the life of a criminal,
the fates he'd eschewed by making good, had to be rolling
in laughter.

Choking back the anger, the hopelessness, the bone-deep
sadness that hit him, Joe washed his hair.

He was not going to let the dark side win.

THEY WERE HEADING SOUTHEAST, still in Arizona, on another
two-lane highway through the middle of vast nowhere. Unending brush, cactus and furry Joshua trees, all landscaped
with mountains on the horizon, flew by in flurries of browns
and muted greens with the flashes of the various purple, orange, red and white flowers that brought the desert to life
beneath the state's almost constant blue skies and sunshine.

Predawn had moved through dawn and into early morning. McKenna wanted them out of town and lost in the desert before the area they'd been in came to life. Just in case
their vandalizer did not keep his word to remain silent about
Joe's identity.

So much for her thought that they could get lost in plain
sight.

She'd handed Joe a rubber band when he'd come out of the
bathroom with blond-streaked hair, telling him his heading
into the next phase of his life would be ponytail style. He'd
pulled the hair back without a word. Moved on to ready the
rig for immediate travel.

While she'd been left thunked in the lower region at the
sight of him—clean shaven, hair pulled back from his face—
whew. She'd been fighting attraction when he'd been hid-

den from her, but with his eyes and mouth right there…in full view…

She was slightly poleaxed.

Noted and would be guarded against. She'd given herself a bye on the first look and would prevent any further such reactions in the future. Knowledge was her tool. And the key to her defense.

Billboards started to appear, announcing a small town ahead, with a big box store, and she had Joe pull off long enough for them to run in and get him a pair of black, horn-rimmed glasses with only glass for the lenses.

And she got hit again. Who knew glasses did it for her?

That was new.

Joe also picked up a tire-repair kit. They had a full-size spare and he'd seemed confident that he could fix the other, less deeply damaged tire, as there was still a lot of air in it. Deeply surprised that he'd know anything about tires, or changing them himself, she was also relieved that they weren't going to have to spend time hanging around an auto shop.

Back on the road within minutes, she turned on her phone to check in with Glen. Chances were good that since the photo that their middle-of-the-night stalker had exposed to them had been taken prior to McKenna's advent into his life, it wasn't yet known that she was with him.

She heard the click of Glen's phone, took the breath she needed to get out her urgent message and was cut off with his "McKenna, get him out of public view."

"Done." She told her boss about the slashed tires and photo. "The fact that he slashed the tires that ride up on the tow bar trailer, allowing us to leave without needing to get them repaired, tells me that he really did just want us gone," she added, something she'd come up with during the couple of hours they'd been on the road.

Maybe because she was trying to find ways to keep Joe's spirits up.

She hoped not.

His spirits weren't her issue. His bodily safety was all she'd been hired to oversee.

"One of the team members is tracking the social media posts, attempting to get back to the original poster, but with instructions to everyone to copy and paste the post themselves, it's taking a while," he told her. "We've been on it since last night, when Hud was first notified of the posting. The #wheresjoenow hashtag has over seven hundred thousand hits."

She specifically did not glance at Joe.

"In one day?"

"We're seeing a slew of what appear to be new profiles, along with a mixture of profiles of the rich and powerful, and a couple of influencers have now picked up the post as well."

The only relevance to her in the turn of events was that in order to keep Joe safe, she had to keep him out of sight. They had provisions for a couple of weeks. But she was going to have to learn how to drive the rig, with him in the back with blinds drawn, and to gas up and dump and refill holding tanks.

They'd be fine.

"We've got other developments, Ken." Glen's tone warned her before his news came at her. "Bellair is cooperating fully with our investigation. They want their reputation fully cleared. Last evening, Hudson's team found a virus in the return-reporting software. It triggered returns of a couple of projects to hold reporting for six months, and then do a full dump all at once."

Okay. They were at least getting somewhere. Glen went on to say why the problem hadn't been discovered sooner. Something to do with the expertise involved in the discovery.

And some to do with the fact that prosecutors and investigators had been set on proving Joe guilty, not solving Bellair's company problems.

"The virus originated from Joe's computer."

Not a good development for Joe.

And not her concern.

"Do you want to talk to him?" she asked, keeping her tone neutral.

"Not yet. And we don't want you to say anything, either, as it's a conversation we'll want to have fresh with him. Hud wants to do some more looking, first, so we know what we're taking to him."

Which meant what? That the firm's partner thought there was a chance someone else had used Joe's computer? Or Glen wanted irrefutable proof before they fired him as a client?

The thought followed immediately with another. She didn't want him fired. No way she was going to just walk away from the man while he was being hunted like an animal. Or leave him to fend on his own in hiding...

Because...that would be inhumane.

He'd been found not guilty. What he did or didn't do before, and what he did or didn't need to do to make amends, was on him. His karma.

But what was happening to him in the aftermath...just wasn't right.

If people had beefs with him, they had to take them up in civil court. Or find something else to charge him with.

Stalking was against the law.

Threatening someone's life even more so.

And it felt like a crime to hang up the phone and not tell Joe about the newly discovered virus that explained how the returns portion of his problem had happened. A virus originating from Joe's computer. Her boss had given her a direct order—in as many words—and her loyalty had to come first for the firm for which she worked, the firm that was paying her, the job she'd agreed to do—not to the man who could be a criminal sitting next to her.

But her heart...it wondered who was loyal to Joe?

HE COULD THINK of worse things than being out in glorious country, periodically driving through mountains with views that most only got to see on expensive vacations. The desert expanses were good, too, in a more peaceful way.

And the view inside his rig, sitting just a couple of feet away in the captain's chair passenger portion of the cab...he wasn't in any way ready to be done with that.

Wasn't sure he'd ever tire of looking at the curly red-haired woman who exuded strength and energy and feminine soft-ness all at the same time. In lightweight black cotton pants and a white tank top, she'd just come back from taking care of the small load of laundry she'd run in the combo washer/ dryer unit.

Leaving him to inappropriately glom on her lingerie choices. He figured bikini briefs, but definitely no thongs. And unpadded, no-underwire back-closure bras.

Sensible. Durable. Strong. And...feminine.

Her.

At the time, with her in the back, his musings had been a way of passing the time so he didn't get off-kilter with con-spiracy theory–type thoughts regarding whatever Glen had told her on the phone that she hadn't told Joe.

Her "do you want to talk to him" had designated the end to conversation regarding the social media dilemma. After that she'd listened. A quick glance had shown him a frown on her face. She'd rung off without cheer.

And had only given him the social media update.

He wanted to trust someone.

To trust her. Beyond just her skill and willingness to do

her job to the best of her ability. Another irony in a life filled with them—he trusted her with his life.

But wasn't sure he could trust her beyond doing the one job he was paying her to do.

Really, what did he know about her?

"What?" she blurted into the silence that had once again fallen.

"What, what?"

"You're looking at me weird."

"I am not. If you have noticed, I'm driving a forty-foot load here. I have to keep my eyes on the road."

"You've glanced over three times in the past ten minutes."

She was counting. He found that…intriguing.

"What are you thinking about?" Her question…she was pushing and treading into waters that were far too personal.

He didn't much care. She'd given him entry, and he wanted to step inside the door. Not far. Just enough to have a look around.

"I want to know why you aren't more curious about me," he said, when what he'd wanted to ask was why she never talked about herself. His tongue had changed course midstream.

Her shrug couldn't be more insultingly obvious in its drollness. And before she could answer, he rushed in with, "That sounded narcissistic. I'm just curious as to how you can agree to travel around the middle of nowhere with a virtual stranger, one you half believe is a criminal, and not at least try to find out more about him. For peace of mind, if nothing else."

While it hadn't been the question he'd been meaning to ask—that had been a more basic inquiry into her life in a general sense—it was the one for which he most wanted an answer.

Because it led him past the foyer—the place strangers saw—and took him more deeply inside.

"I know what I need to know," she told him with another shrug.

He should have let it go. Was facing more than one hundred miles of vast desert with only an occasional vehicle passing by, and had nothing to do but sit and think. "What do you know?"

"Everything that was in the news."

"I'm rich and the world thinks I'm a thief?"

"I know your lifestyle. You wined and dined on yachts and in private rooms reserved for the wealthy in all the best restaurants. You golf at courses average Americans can't even afford to get a good glimpse of. You sail a boat that had to have cost twice what I paid for my house..."

He'd been mentally ticking off her tidbits, remembering them appearing in various news sources, though he was pretty sure they hadn't all been during the trial.

Meaning she'd looked him up? Since she'd taken the job with him?

He should have assumed as much. Knowing her investigation was all part of keeping him safe.

"And you paid way too much for a certain model-year Maserati because you'd always wanted one."

Whoa. Hold on.

First off, the way she'd said that last bit, her tone of voice, made him sound like a spoiled brat. And second, that information had never been in the news.

Seeing a rest stop ahead, Joe pulled off.

They did it occasionally, when he needed to head back to the can. He parked and didn't unbuckle. Or leave his seat.

"How did you know that? About my car?"

If he didn't know her better, he'd think she'd just squirmed a bit. Joe's mood lightened a tad. But not much. Was Sierra's

Web's private investigator prying into every detail of his life? Including a car sale that had happened years before any of his alleged crimes had been committed? Was the firm trying to find things on him that would prove his guilt, not his innocence?

"You bought it from a gentleman who told a group of people about you, and one of those people then invested in Bellair Software when stock started to rise last year."

"The friend of your grandparents?"

"Distant friend." The way she said that, as though the distance was what mattered, bothered him.

Dale Grammar, the man he'd purchased the car from, would only have had friends in the wealthiest of circles. Which meant...

Surely she wasn't one of them...the class of people who'd pretended to welcome him in as one of them and then had treated him as a pariah when he'd been arrested.

Joe frowned.

He should have trusted his instincts...

Not trusted her...

"Who are your grandparents?" He didn't ask politely.

"Neil and Glenda Whitaker."

He didn't know them. But they'd be two generations older than him, and since he was brand-new money, not likely to have run into him. Or vice versa. If what he was suspecting was even true.

"They live in Phoenix?"

"About two miles from you." She named a gated mountain community filled exclusively with multimillion-dollar estates. All part of the crowd that had eschewed him—whether they'd invested in Bellair or not. Bilking one of them was like bilking them all.

No.

"Who are your parents?"

She'd said her only connection to him or his case was a friend of her grandparents. Someone she hadn't seen in years. He hadn't questioned further. At that point, he wasn't sure he'd cared.

"Anne and Kyle Meredith."

He'd never heard of either one of them.

"And they live in Phoenix as well?"

She'd turned on her phone, was looking at the camera app and watching her rearview mirror. Glancing at his view of the same mirror, he saw a midsize sedan come into view, driving slowly, before pulling into a slot.

"Go," she said.

He had to follow her direction. Intended to. But something made him say, "I'll go as long as you understand this conversation is not over." Because cars came and went. People had to pee. And she could be using the sedan's appearance as an excuse to get out of telling him who she really was.

Her quick nod brought him a twinge of shame, and he pulled out as quickly as his load would allow.

One thing was for certain. McKenna Meredith, no matter who she was, had invaded his personal space in a big way.

And he wasn't all sorry.

Chapter Nine

She didn't feel comfortable talking about her family.

Most particularly not with him.

Every nerve in her body tightened, not in a good way, when, two miles down the road, he spoke again. "Do your parents live in Phoenix?"

"No."

"Where do they live?"

She could lie.

Or better yet, just not answer. What was he going to do about it? Fire her? Fire Sierra's Web? In his current state of affairs, he needed them far more than she needed this one job.

The imbalance in their circumstances pulled at her. The man was fighting for his life, for the freedom the courts had granted him. Even if he'd committed fraud, his sentence wouldn't have been a life on the run with viral social media after him.

"My father lives in Shelter Valley."

"The town built around Montford University..."

"Yeah, you ever been there?" She'd be much happier talking about Shelter Valley. She loved the place. Always had.

"No."

"It's only about an hour from Phoenix, depending on how fast you drive, and with light traffic, maybe less, but it's like its own world, surrounded by mountains. And the people…they're…"

The same car that had been in the rest area was behind them. Which it would almost have to be, since they were on a one-way side of a highway with a big desert culvert between them and the opposite side. Behind them was the only way a car could leave the rest stop.

But a thirty-three-foot rig, especially one towing a car, wasn't going to be able to go as fast as a sedan. Every car that came up behind them eventually passed.

Taking a little longer than she'd have liked, the car did eventually signal that it was going into the right lane, her lane, and came up alongside her.

She got a good look at the driver.

A brown-haired, white teenager who didn't even glance her way as he passed. But he gave them the finger.

"Guess he didn't appreciate me driving so slowly in the fast lane."

Obviously not. But if bullets were going to be flying out of a car at them, it had to come in at her side, not Joe's. There was no negotiating that one.

"You said your father lives in Shelter Valley." Joe's tone didn't sound very conversational as he restarted the conversation she'd hoped was over. "Your parents are divorced."

She might have looked for a way to avoid answering another question, but she couldn't let that one stand.

"No," she said. "My parents were soul mates from the moment they met, until the day my mother died."

Not that she remembered those times all that much. But she had a gazillion pictures of her mom and dad with her half-brothers, whom Anne had adopted. Had heard the stories over and over again. And never tired of hearing them.

"Was it recent?" His tone had softened considerably. Striking another chord of tension in her. One that begged her to let herself move closer to him.

"I was three."

He was going to get it out of her. She saw the reality.

Some of it, anyway.

Not all of it.

Only those she trusted with her whole heart got her memories of that last day. Those, of course, she'd never forget.

"So you grew up in Shelter Valley?"

"I grew up visiting Shelter Valley."

There were the grandparents. He knew about them. And she had to control that rhetoric, so she said, "My grandparents disowned my parents." She didn't have to say why. Or which one was their biological child. "After my mother died…" *Mama.* She could only think of Anne by the name she'd called her. "My grandparents petitioned the courts to raise me, as they could give me far more than my father could. He wanted the best for me, and he agreed to giving them custody of me as long as he got visits every other weekend and a month over the summer."

"You grew up in Moon Glow?" The housing development on the mountain.

"Until I was sixteen, got my driver's license and drove to Shelter Valley without my grandparents' permission." She kind of smiled, remembering the determination in her young heart that day. She'd known that no matter how much trouble she was getting into, she was doing the right thing.

"You got to stay?"

"Not quite that simply, but, in the end, yes. The custodial schedule remained intact, but the custodians flip-flopped. And only on the grounds that my grandparents did not take me to any social functions, or in any way expose me to their lifestyle, other than in their home. And my time with them was to be spent solely with them. No one was invited over when I was there."

She was telling him too much.

Far too much.

He'd wonder how the courts would have agreed to such a stipulation. She'd wonder, too, in his position, if she hadn't known about the counselor she'd been seeing, the expert testimony that had been given. A testimony that had been a major prompter in her applying to Sierra's Web once she'd garnered enough commendations in her field to be considered an expert. The firm hadn't yet been around when she was a kid, but the expert witness psychologist who'd changed McKenna's life for the better had been her eye-opener to what McKenna wanted to do with her own life.

Spend it bringing justice and hope, the possibility of renewed joy, to people who needed them.

And Joe Hamilton, from everything she'd seen, was most definitely in need.

JOE HAD MORE QUESTIONS. A lot of them.

And over a hill, he finally saw an exit for gas. "We need to stop here," he said, but McKenna, glancing at the two-pump station with a small inside counter, shook her head.

"We're only going to make it another fifty miles or so."

She nodded. "There's a truck stop about ten miles down the road." And then, as though realizing she'd been sounding autocratic, almost to the point of rudeness, she added, "That kid that flipped us off...his car was parked outside the little store," she told him.

He hadn't noticed.

But then, he'd been thinking about McKenna's childhood, trying not to compare it to his, not thinking about young punks who needed to learn some manners.

"I lost my mother young, too," he told her as he continued

to drive in the fast lane, watching as vehicles passed him on the right—silently apologizing to them for his rudeness. He could hardly tell them he was following instructions, keeping himself in the lane where any would be attacker would have to go through McKenna to get to him.

Watching her side mirror with more than general care, McKenna didn't respond. And he saw why. The small black sedan was behind him again. Far enough back that he could see the car from his side mirror as well. And then only from McKenna's. The kid didn't ride his ass as he had the last time. Just calmly passed, not even glancing their way as he sped on up the road.

"Guess he learned some manners." Joe spoke out loud and wasn't sure why. He and McKenna weren't on a sharing-random-thoughts basis.

As evidenced by her lack of response.

"I'm sorry about your mother." A full five minutes had passed since he'd shared his little tidbit. Five minutes of wishing he hadn't bared any part of his soul to her.

He nodded. Held his tongue against any further revelations that he'd later regret.

"How old were you?"

"Four." Old enough to remember her, though there hadn't been a lot of pictures. His parents hadn't been married and in love as hers had been. They'd just been living together.

There hadn't been any grandparents in the picture to fight for him, either, not that his father would have given him up. Mitch had liked the welfare money that having a kid brought in every month.

And he'd probably liked having a son, too.

Joe remembered some good times.

Mixed in with all the bad.

Mitch had never raised a hand to him. He'd always been thankful for that...

"Did you grow up in Phoenix?" McKenna's question, breaking their more common silence, startled him.

"No. LA area." According to his dad, his mom had left a not-great home in Michigan at eighteen and never looked back. And Mitch's's parents—his mom had been a drug addict and his father was in prison in Nebraska, doing life. The charges against him had changed depending on how drunk Mitch had been when telling the story. Murder was on there, but it wasn't quite clear if it had been intentional or a case of self-defense gone wrong while stealing a car.

Or robbing a bank, as the tale was sometimes told.

Joe had looked the old man up once—saw theft and murder charges—and the fact that Mitch Sr. had died in prison, right there in LA, when Joe was fifteen.

Feeling the stench of his past life fill up the rig, Joe offered one more fact about himself. "I graduated from college at twenty and moved to Phoenix to take the job at Bellair."

The life he'd lived as a child had been out of his control.

But by the time he'd legally become a man, he'd already become someone else. No arrest, no false charges, no social media, spray paint, slashed tires, death threats or ostracizations were going to change that.

He was a good man who'd amassed a fortune he was proud of through determination, dedication, unending hard work and carefully thought-out great choices.

Whether McKenna Meredith ever believed that or not.

WHEN MCKENNA SAW the menagerie of cars, semis, pickup trucks and recreational vehicles parked or snaking around the parking lot of the truck stop, she knew she'd made the right choice to bypass the smaller station.

Having Joe pull up at an outer pump, where the rig blocked the view of the pump from all but the highway, she instructed him to head to the back.

She could gas up quickly, using her card to pay at the pump, and then hopefully they'd be out of there before Joe was even seen behind the wheel.

Her driving lessons were on the schedule for whenever they stopped for the night.

Which would be as soon as she got a good sense of where that would be. Probably another box store parking lot. So, maybe Yuma. And the next morning they could head up north to the Grand Canyon, where there were hundreds of miles of parkland, plenty of private camping areas, and visitors were a norm, not something to be gaped at.

As soon as she heard the back bedroom pocket door slide closed, she opened the driver's door of the rig, her hip on the edge of the seat, ready for her foot to find the first step down, her gaze on the door's mirrors. The aisle between the rig and the pump were completely clear and…

A body slid under the door from the front and up to pin her to the side of the seat with one quick move. Metal pushed into her left kidney…a gun?…as a voice hissed in her ear. "Where is he?"

Heart pounding with anger and adrenaline, she used well-honed muscles to hold her weight steady in spite of the awkward position. "Where's who?" she asked.

Another jab to her kidney that was going to leave a bruise, and the cheek pushed up to hers moved again. "You know who. Now move slowly back inside. I have no beef with you. I want him."

He might not have a beef with her, but the sentiment was most definitely not returned. And no way was she giving him access to the rig. But with the door at his back, she had no real route down, either. And no way to get to her ankle holster.

Maintaining her position, she reached for the wrist holding the weapon to her back, felt it turn, and the tip of a knife pierced her skin. She was aware, but only peripherally, as she twisted, too, got the guy in a wrist lock and, switching positions with him, had him down in the seat, her body holding him in an arm brace, just as Joe came barreling out of the back room with a raised hammer in his hand.

Damn!

"Stop!" She spoke with more meanness than she knew she possessed, glancing at Joe. If he came any closer, she'd have to handle two men at once.

She could do it.

Just didn't want to have to.

SHE HAD THE arm in her grasp disabled but hadn't yet disarmed her attacker. She finally got a good look at him, though.

The teenager who'd given them the finger...

With another twist of the wrist in her grasp, and a tight flick, she saw the knife drop to the floor of the rig right by her foot, and then, with a knee in the kid's gut, right under his rib cage, she patted him down for further weapons before looking around for something to tie his hands.

A piece of cording appeared before her eyes—wrapped in a strong male hand.

Taking it without removing her gaze from her prisoner, she jerked him over, pulling his wrists behind him, wrapped them and tied a quick, very tight knot.

Other than a couple of grunts, the kid hadn't made a sound until she flipped him back over, let go of him, and he slowly slid to a sitting position behind the wheel. Joe appeared in the small space then, hauled the kid out of his seat and pushed him down to a sitting position by the door with his back against the kitchen wall.

"Who else did you tell where we are?" Joe asked, his tone pretty menacing, too. "You the one who put me on social media?"

"No." The kid's sullen tone didn't do him any favors. Nor did the hate spearing from his eyes to Joe's head. Joe took a step forward, reaching as though to grab the kid, and the boy looked down. "I swear, man, I didn't tell anyone. I saw the message board…"

"What's a kid your age doing on the dark web?" Joe threw out the accusation, and McKenna, who'd been standing there watching the scene unfold, stared at him. She had to call the police and get the kid in custody—hopefully without raising undue attention, or having Joe's likeness actually be seen— but she was kind of wanting to watch how he played things out with the kid, too.

For the moment, because he was on the right track, getting the information Glen and Hud were going to need, she left them alone—gun now in hand—watching for any sign that her physical skills were needed.

"I don't know…"

Joe stepped closer.

"I was looking for you, okay?" the teenager shouted, his voice filled with emotion. "One of the pictures, I knew the road, and I've been following you ever since."

"Following me?" Standing back, hands on his hips, Joe frowned. "Why?"

"I was working up the guts to kill you."

McKenna raised her gun. Saw Joe's frown out of the corner of her eye.

"Come again?"

"That's why I haven't told anyone where you are. I wanted you all to myself."

"How old are you?"

"Sixteen."

"Driving your own car?"

Seriously? They had an attempted murderer on the floor of the rig and Joe cared whose car he'd been driving?

"It is now."

Joe glanced at her then. "What are we going to do with him now?"

"It was my dad's car," the kid said then. Glared at Joe and finished with, "Until you killed him." Spittle shot forward.

"I killed him?"

"He had cancer, too, but losing the money… He'd invested his whole savings with Bellair so I could go to college, and then, when he lost all the money, he just gave up. He died before your trial ended."

"And you really think killing me is going to make any of that better?"

The fire in the boy's eyes was not even a little diminished then as he looked between the two of them. "You have to pay."

"What's your name?" Joe asked then.

"What's it to you?"

"Nothing." McKenna had had enough. They were going to start attracting attention, hogging the pump for so long. "The police will get it out of you soon enough." She pulled out her phone, waited for it to boot up.

"No police." Joe's tone was as firm as it had ever been.

Openmouthed she stared at him. What did he think they were going to do, keep the kid captive? Get rid of him themselves?

Even as she had the thought, she knew that latter part was ludicrous. And wasn't at all fond of the first bit, either.

"I'm going to teach you a thing or two about life, kid, but, first, you're going to tell me your name." Joe's tone was unrelenting.

Losing some of his belligerence, the young man looked up at McKenna, as though seeing any hope coming through her. She was pretty sure that the police sounded like a better option to him than the big, angry man standing before him.

A man the kid believed guilty of major corporate fraud, money laundering and God knew what else.

The kid believed...not *she* believed...

Shaking her head, she thought about the tip of a knife scraping her skin, ignored the teenager's plea and glanced over at Joe.

At the thought of her back, the first she'd had of it since her scuffle with the boy, she lifted her free hand back behind her and...felt blood.

The cut was surface, she could feel that, too, but her shirt had a small hole in it and was also wet.

"My name's William," the boy finally said. "What of it?"

"Does your mother know where you are?"

"She thinks I'm staying at my friend's house..."

"You ever been arrested, William?"

"No."

"Yet you were willing to spend the rest of your life in jail for murder..."

"No way I was getting caught." The bravado was back.

"You're caught now."

Silence fell again. The kind she and Joe had shared the first few hours they'd been on the road together. It grew. And suffocated you with the tension of not knowing what he was thinking...

Of course, in her case, she hadn't been the least bit afraid of the man.

Nor had she been on his bad side.

"Here's what we're going to do, William. You're going to give me your mother's name and number. I'm going to have a friend check it out, check you out, and as long as what you've told me is true, we're going to make a deal."

"I'm not making no deal with you..."

Joe stepped closer again, bending over the captured kid. "Your father raise you to be stupid, boy?"

"No."

"Then act like it. You're in a load of trouble here, you got that?"

With a sullen smirk, the kid glared at the wall in front of him.

"*If* you check out, and that's a big if, then we're going to deliver you to someone who will take you home. You will not say a word to anyone, not even a fly in your room, about seeing me or knowing where I am. And in return for your silence, you earn four years of college tuition. But only if you maintain a B average or higher."

"I'm not…"

"You're being stupid again. You got a choice—the cops or my offer."

McKenna watched as all fight seemed to drain out of the boy. His shoulders slumped, his head relaxed back and his mouth seemed to de-age, leaving him to look like little more than a grieving boy.

She still had a hand holding her shirt against the blood at her back.

"You're forcing me to let you go," the boy finally said. And then, the glare back in his eye, looked up. "So, no! I'm not doing it. You go ahead and call the cops. See if I care. You don't just get to ruin so many lives and then just walk away."

With a nod, Joe sat down.

Shocked, McKenna pointed her gun at William, praying that she didn't have to take a shot.

"I'm trying to help you," Joe said, his tone more calm. "And trying to do it quickly, because we really need to get going." He glanced toward McKenna, at the gun, and said, "She doesn't take kindly to her schedule being messed up."

William glanced at her, then back at Joe.

"I didn't do it, William. Some pretty powerful people are trying to help me prove that, and people like you, stalking me, trying to make my life miserable, are slowing us down. If you really want to get the people who hurt your family, then you need to take my deal and let us get on with what we're doing. I'm sorry your dad lost his money. I'm even more sorry that he died. I'd like to help. I didn't take your father's money, but I have plenty of my own—legally and honestly earned—and I'd like to put some in a trust for your college education. Assuming you go home. Don't say a word about me until this is all over, because if you do, you not only put McKenna there in danger, you also slow our process of finding the real thief. You stay out of trouble. And maintain a B average."

"I have a 4.0." William's tone was disgusted, but it had lost all its luster.

"Do we have a deal?" Joe wasn't letting up.

"You really didn't do it?" The short-haired boy looked him right in the eye.

Joe looked back. "I really didn't do it."

"Man, sucks being you then."

And that, McKenna figured, just about summed it all up.

Chapter Ten

McKenna had still thought Joe should call the police and have William arrested. When he'd first caught sight of the blood smeared all over her hand, he'd almost agreed.

If not for the horror on William's face when he'd seen what he'd done, and for the fact that the cut really was just a scratch—albeit one that bled a lot—he'd have stepped back while she notified authorities. Instead, he'd left William with his hands tied behind his back down in the stairwell of the rig, telling the kid not to move, and had gone to the bedroom to have a quiet session with his bodyguard. Asking her to give the kid a break – on Joe's terms.

Remembering those moments a couple of hours later, as he and McKenna were once again on a road to nowhere, through nowhere, actually heading toward Yuma, she'd said, Joe got a little buzzed down below. The two of them, behind the closed door in that tiny, tiny bedroom…he'd never ever thought that would happen.

She'd had to sit on the mattress he slept on, as there wasn't room for two of them to stand at the door, and he was pretty sure he'd remember her body there, like her heat had been transfused into his sheets, the next time he lay down to sleep.

Every time he lay down in that bed forevermore.

He'd tended to her back, ascertaining that it really was just the surface wound she'd claimed, but insisting on putting antibiotic and a bandage on it, just the same. Pretty much holding his breath, and setting his memory function to pause so that it wouldn't retain the paleness, or softness, of her skin.

He'd also always remember the way she'd capitulated to his wishes. Seeing the best in not calling the police. For William's sake first and foremost, though she'd been willing to forgo that because she thought the kid should pay for what he'd done. But for the sake of the case, they sure as hell didn't need any more publicity, and he could only imagine what social media would do when it got wind of another Joe Hamilton run-in with the police...

She'd called Glen before giving her agreement to his plan. But he'd heard her talking to her boss. Heard her arranging details to bring William's mother up to speed, and then for legal contracts and signatures and to have someone chaperone William home. And knew, when she'd said, "Yes, I do," that Glen had been asking her if she agreed with the plan.

She might not fully trust him, but she was keeping an open mind to his thoughts.

He'd take it.

And wanted more.

So now...reaching one pinnacle and heading straight up the next incline...

"You know, you and William have something in common," he said when the silence was getting to be too long again. They weren't strangers anymore. Hours of no talk between them...not as good as it had been.

"What's that?" As always, her attention was on the outside of the rig, on mirrors and landscape and vehicles on the road.

"You both followed your heart at sixteen, leaving home without permission, but uncaring of the consequences for having done so because you were so sure you were on the right path."

Of course, William hadn't been—on the right path.

But his motivation, standing up for his father who could no longer stand up for himself, had been.

He wasn't all that surprised when she didn't respond. But, feeling empowered by the way the thing with William had gone, he pushed more.

Pushing himself to reach for what he wanted, to refuse to settle for less, to give everything he had, had made him a near multimillionaire by the age of thirty-one, he reminded himself. He drew a breath and asked, "Why were you so eager to leave your grandparents' home?"

"How do you know I wasn't just eager to be with my dad?"

"Because of the stipulations you put on your visits to the home you grew up in," he said. She had to have known he'd read the nuances. "And the fact that the court allowed them."

Her pause gave *him* pause. She wasn't going to tell him the truth. At least not all of it. She was calculating what to tell him. He knew it before she started speaking.

"I'm guessing you wouldn't understand." The answer, when it finally came, was a huge disappointment. He hadn't expected everything, but he'd been counting on something.

Another clue, at least, into the life and mind of the woman who intrigued him more than any other human being he'd ever known.

And not just because she'd single-handedly taken down an armed and emotionally distraught kid set to kill him.

"Why would you say that?" Yeah, still not content to just sit still and take it, as he'd been doing for months while quietly trying to figure out what in the hell had happened at Bellair. To figure out *who* had happened was more like it.

"True or false. You love big-city action, glitz, schmoozing with people who are wealthy or wealthier than you are."

"True." No shame for being proud of what he'd built. Or for enjoying his success.

"I like small towns, evenings where the only cacophony is the raucous laughter at the table while I drink beer and play card games. And small gatherings where I know and care about everyone who's present. I want to be able to let my hair down, so to speak, and trust that I won't get slapped later for having done so. Expensive things make me nervous, not happy. Having to watch what I say, or the volume with which I say it, when I'm in a private, nonbusiness gathering, makes me tense. I abhor parties that are thrown as a guise for business to get done, and I most definitely can't stand knowing that every time I attend a function, I'm being judged for what I'm wearing, how I'm walking, how much I eat or if I get drunk or not."

Wow. She'd pretty much chewed up and spit out the entire lifestyle that energized him. Motivated him. Challenged him. The life he'd spent his youth envisioning. The world where he thrived and intended to grow old.

Leaving him sorry he'd asked.

Very sorry.

Note to self—in the future, he needed to be sure of the direction he was headed before he pushed.

And the bright side…his bizarre sense of connection to her should, from that moment on, be severed. Leaving him to give one hundred percent of his focus to assisting Sierra's Web in any way he could. To prove his innocence so he could get back to the life he craved.

Like looking outside the box for the person who'd had access to his computer, as well as those in other departments, even on nonbusiness days.

The list, as far as he knew it, was short.

He'd been over it again and again.

Narrowing down, to within hours, when access would have had to have been gained, for someone to have physically changed the databases. Cross-checking with times he'd been away from his computer.

Searching social media for anything that might tell him where any of the individuals on his list had been any of the times when changes to databases would have had to be made.

He'd managed to weed out all of them.

Which was why he'd called Sierra's Web in the first place.

He had different angles now for gaining inspiration. And as soon as he figured out what he'd been missing and had access to the internet, he could begin the weeding-out process again.

His time driving would be far better spent to that end.

Just in case Sierra's Web didn't come through for him.

And McKenna?

She was one hell of a bodyguard. He was thankful.

And would leave it at that.

THE AFTERNOON SLIPPED from early to mid, on the road, after they'd handed William over to a Sierra's Web associate who'd been an hour away and met them at the truck stop. McKenna, having served up tuna sandwiches, which she and Joe had eaten in silence as they drove, was getting closer to stir-crazy.

A state so unlike her she wasn't sure what to do with it.

Emotions roiled within her, making it difficult for her to find her work Zen, though she was definitely focused on seeking out any possible dangers lurking around them. There just wasn't enough for to concentrate on outside the rig to keep all other thoughts at bay.

Bits of conversations kept drifting in. Him wanting to know about her family. Her life.

Her aversion to wealth. He'd wanted personal details.

She'd slammed his way of life instead.

Joe had been reaching out to her. She'd rebuffed him.

It was the right thing to do.

And hurt way more than it should have.

His fingers, warm and tender, on her back, brushing healthy skin as he'd gently placed the antiseptic-coated bandage over her tiny cut...she kept feeling them there. Hours later.

Their situation...living together in such cramped quarters, him in hiding, in real danger from multiple sources, him being so engrossed in a lifestyle that used to give her severe anxiety attacks...of course there'd be emotional overloads.

Her not fully trusting him, even as she was growing to admire many things about him.

William's brief moment in their lives just seemed to set it all off for her. To frame it. The caring, compassionate, astute way Joe had handled the aggressively surly teenager—seeming almost to identify with him—to the point of being able to find the exact carrot to dangle in front of William to prevent him from ruining his life—her heart filled every time she replayed those moments between the two males.

But at the same time, she was equally aware that Joe had served his own end. That he could have manipulated William, used the boy's own needs against him, in order to get what Joe most needed—no police on scene.

And William's continued silence.

Two huge reasons to work the boy.

And with a payoff attached that was less than he'd be paying Sierra's Web.

Her heart eschewed the negative thoughts every time they came to her. But they eventually found their way back.

And...his mom had died when he was little, too. She craved details. About his mom. What had happened. Most importantly to her, how it had affected him.

She couldn't ask, though. Because she couldn't tell.

Not without giving away the deepest parts of her heart, and that most definitely was out where Joe Hamilton was concerned.

About an hour outside Yuma, she saw what looked to be a long-ago-deserted planned development. There were roads, overgrown lots that looked like they'd been staked out for homes and nothing else but dust. She had Joe take the exit and circle back to the abandoned community. After his tutelage on how to drive the rig, she had him work on the cars' tires while, in the rig alone, she drove in long circles around the property, making both right and left turns, and eventually, attempting to back up the rig.

She ran off the road a time or two. Her neck stiff with tension, she kept at it, and before nightfall, she was proficient enough that she could drive them if she had to.

And it looked like the car was back in service as well.

So, maybe...in the interest of mental health...

"What do you think about parking the rig at the first big box store we come to and then taking the car and going somewhere for dinner?" she suggested.

Probably a huge mistake.

But the alternative—the two of them cooped up inside a rig with no slides out, in a public parking lot—seemed to carry the most danger at the moment.

"You asking me on a date?"

Yep. Definitely a mistake. She knew she shouldn't have...

"I'm sorry." His apology came softly, with warmth. "That was uncalled-for, inappropriate and wrong. I would very much appreciate the opportunity to get out of this tube and have some semblance of normal personhood, even if it's only for an hour or so."

"I'm not talking about sitting in a restaurant," she quickly clarified, afraid, just that quickly, that she was about to disappoint him. "I was thinking more about ordering something, picking it up and finding a place to picnic. Maybe from within the car."

"We're at the border. We could cross over and have some great, authentic Mexican food."

Was he serious?

"And show your passport?" she asked, frowning at him.

The way his face fell, as energy seemed to drain from his expression—and him—he admitted, "Believe it or not, for a second there, I forgot."

As soon as he said the words, his second hand moved from his thigh to join the first up on the wheel. She saw the whites of his knuckles as he gripped with both hands.

And she knew.

What he obviously feared she'd figured out.

The idea of a time out with her had completely wiped away thoughts of why they were together at all.

She had that much power.

Or the idea of time out did.

Needing to rescue him, needing him to be allowed to feel good for a second without regrets, she went with her most immediate thought and admitted, "I'm about to crawl out of my skin here. And I've only been cooped up in this thing for a couple of days. You've been in it for over a month. As your bodyguard, I have determined that it's in the interests of your mental—and thereby physical—safety to have a night out."

His desire to have dinner with her had nothing to do with her in particular. He'd seen her offer as a brief break from the luxurious prison he'd been living in. He couldn't go anywhere without her. It was strictly business. And nothing more.

It was the story she offered him to go with.

The story she was going with.

"Fine."

His brief answer in no way indicated to her whether he was going with the story or not.

HE DIDN'T GET the dinner he'd envisioned. When McKenna had suggested getting her check-in with Glen out of the way before they unhooked the car and headed out, he'd seen the suggestion as a sign that she wanted their evening to be open-ended, with no need for anyone else to be aware where they were, how late they were up, out or together. She'd have her camera check-ins and someone would be monitoring that, of course, but otherwise...they'd have the night free.

He was envisioning it that way whether she'd timed the call accordingly or not.

They'd pulled into the busy parking lot where they'd be spending the night—parked at the farthest point from the store for privacy purposes—and before he'd stepped down from the rig to unhook the car, she'd wanted to check cameras and then make their call.

As eager as he'd been to get going, he knew the connection with Sierra's Web was most important. He might or not be a part of the call, but he had to be present in case anyone at Sierra's Web had questions for him or something to tell him.

It wasn't like they could contact him. Standing right next to McKenna, he'd heard Glen Rivers' raised voice the second the call connected.

"Destroy your phone and get out of there, now. Turn on your other phone at ten and I'll call you."

There'd been a click, dead air, and once again they were on the road into nowhere. A dark nowhere completely unlit by any form of streetlights. If not for the brightness of the clear moon, they wouldn't have been able to see anything except the road illuminated by the rig's headlights. And, occasionally, the lights of other vehicles passing by.

McKenna didn't say much, but he could tell by the terse expression on her face, the unnaturally straight posture, that she was tense.

She had him head northwest, toward the Colorado River,

which ran along parts of western Arizona, a section of the state with which he wasn't familiar, and maybe that was a good thing. No one would have reason to associate him with the area.

And then she left her seat up front next to him long enough to put a chicken-and-potato concoction in the convection oven and then to serve it an hour later. They'd stopped long enough for him to use the restroom, but he ate while driving. Until they knew what they were running from, he wasn't giving it a chance to catch up to them.

"Obviously, they saw tracking movement on my phone," McKenna had said early on in the evening.

But telling her to have her spare phone on at a precise time? And them calling her?

She was watching the road with focused care, which he was paying her to do, and appreciated her for, but shortly after dinner was done, and there nothing more to do but drive into the night, he ran out of ways to keep his mind from concocting bad scenarios involving his lack of life.

He just couldn't come up with a viable scenario for someone to randomly change inventory numbers and have every tenth sale of Stellar double without getting caught. The six-month hold on returns had been hugely detrimental, but not as hard to do. The program allowed holds on returns to allow the returns department to verify that the return actually arrived back to Bellair and that the quality issue was indeed apparent.

And as far as the Bellair bank accounts showing proceeds that matched the lower inventory and higher sales…then suddenly not showing them? That one sent him into the twilight zone every time. His trial attorney, the man's investigative team, unable to explain the phenomenon, had merely used the prosecutor's lack of proof that he'd somehow manipulated bank records to get a not-guilty verdict on the bank fraud charge.

But lack of proof didn't give him his life back.

It was like someone at the bank *was* involved in the fraud.

And there he was again…circled back around to the who. Looking at the what, trying to figure out the how, was still contingent upon the who.

"How do I log on to a bank's portal, download PDF versions of bank statements and then have them be fraudulent?" he said aloud.

McKenna's lack of response didn't help.

"There has to be someone at the bank who's involved, and how in the hell do I prove that? Just start accusing every employee who worked there? It's not like I, or anyone, is going to be awarded a warrant to check their personal finances without at least some cause to do so other than place of employment."

Still nothing. Which bothered him.

It shouldn't. He didn't blame her for not engaging in a personal battle that had nothing to do with her assignment.

But…sadly enough…she was the closest thing he had to a friend at the moment.

Seriously. Had he really lowered his standards so far down that he'd settle for his only friend to be someone who didn't even believe in him?

"I need internet access to research social media accounts of known bank employees to see if there was any indication of a financial windfall in terms of new purchases, or expensive vacations."

He'd long ago done so for all Bellair employees who could possibly have been involved in the scheme.

"You've got a team of proven experts working pretty much around the clock, Joe. I'm sure Glen and his computer forensics team took care of that on day one. And Hud's IT team… they'll be looking at every line of coding in every program to do with every single one of the known fraudulent postings, comparing them, running searches for similar crimes and all kinds of things you and I can only imagine. One way or another, they're going to figure this out. I can promise you that."

One way or another.

He got her message. She still doubted his innocence. And yet he trusted her. And the confidence with which she'd voiced her certainty in her team's abilities and the successful outcome of his case—because if they did figure it out, they'd be exonerating him—was enough comfort to recharge his sanity for another few hundred miles.

Calmed, sitting back, trying to enjoy being out on the open road with no deadline or bottom-line pressures, Joe was more than a little startled when McKenna's voice broke the silence.

"I can't even begin to imagine how it feels, being you right now." The words themselves weren't at all comforting, but the warmth in her tone got his full attention.

Not that he showed her that. Or allowed himself to soak it in.

"I just want you to know that you aren't fighting this alone."

Unfamiliar spouts of emotion welled within him. Emotion that had no good outlet. Which reminded him why he should have just kept his mouth shut.

Even if, by some weird twist of fate he and McKenna ever did actually become friends, there was no future for them.

With her adamant abhorrence of his lifestyle, they were far too opposite to attract.

Chapter Eleven

"I'm assuming you've been to Lake Havasu?" They'd been on the road for a little less than three hours, and McKenna was eager for them to be safely stopped for the night before their call with Glen. Whatever was up, it couldn't be good.

Joe deserved time to process without having to simultaneously keep a forty-foot load on the road. To have a beer if he wanted it.

The man had more to deal with than most could handle, and he was still right there, doing whatever was asked of him.

He had a much more powerful arsenal of self-control than she did.

"I haven't been to the area," he said after a pause. "Why would you assume I had?"

"It's a popular hangout for wealthy kids."

"I wasn't wealthy as a kid."

There'd been nothing about his childhood in the news of his trial. Or on the Bellair website biography of their CFO. She knew he'd graduated from University of Southern California with honors, had a master's degree in finance.

"I'm assuming that's where we're headed?"

Signs had been appearing for a while. Didn't mean she'd been planning to stop. "Just north of the lake, there is a plethora of private RV stops. Some are parks, but not all. There are just random spaces to rent along the river. On both the California and Arizona sides. There's one that I know of where we don't have to physically see anyone to check in. Just leave payment electronically and hook up."

Funny the things you remembered…

Now if only the site still existed. And she could find it.

"I take it you and your friends partied here?"

More like she had been held captive at a New Year's event with her grandparents. She'd overheard someone laughingly talk about parking a troublesome in-law at the site with a cooler of beer so that the someone could enjoy the weekend celebration they were all attending that was taking place across multiple yachts.

"I was invited to, but no" was all she said.

"Because you were with your father?"

That again. No more personal talk. She'd given herself a stern warning on that one. Most particularly after feeling those tender fingers on her skin earlier that day.

Hard to believe it had been only that morning that she'd stopped William from attempting to murder Joe…

"Because I didn't want to," she said when she realized his question was still hanging out there. And yes, because every chance she'd had to get away, she'd spent in Shelter Valley. And… "I didn't really have many close friends growing up," she told him—because her heart had spent the past hours hurting for him, and she wanted him to know that he wasn't the only one who knew what lonely felt like. "With my life being split into two places," she affirmed what he already knew.

And was gratified when, other than directional discussion, he didn't push any further conversation between them. She needed every ounce of her focus on whatever Glen had to tell them, and then spending the night alone with the man who'd be affected by the news.

What if Glen's forensic team had proven that the virus causing the glitch in the returns database was Joe's work?

Would someone be coming to get her out of there that night?

Tamping down her wayward mind on that one, she quickly reasoned that wouldn't be the case. He'd have had her stay in Yuma, at the busy public big box store, and wait for a ride home if that were the situation, not have her destroy her phone and head back out over the road.

But the urgency in Glen's voice, his command for her to wait for him to call her—no way that boded good.

Which would probably mean more work for her. But while she absolutely needed to know as soon as possible, she didn't worry so much about the job. She was up for it. And good at it.

But she wasn't sure how much more bad Joe's big shoulders could take without starting to crack.

At which point, she strongly feared she'd feel a compelling need to step in and offer to help take some of the weight off—because keeping those shoulders, part of his body, safe and well was, after all, the job he was paying her to do.

IT WAS ALMOST eerily easy to find a pay-by-card site to stop for the night. The space they chose, accessed by a service road just off the two-lane state road they'd turned on to at Lake Havasu, was just yards from water's edge. The space they chose, while big enough was largely hidden from the road by the mass of trees surrounding it.

She'd expressed pleasure that it was that last space on-site, so there'd be no reason for any vehicles to approach.

Joe liked that it was at the end of the road. And hoped the privacy meant it would be their last stop.

That they could stay put for however long it took the Sierra's Web experts to unravel the tangle his life had become.

Still in travel-weary clothes, they were sitting on opposite ends of the couch, all shades drawn, including the one that covered the dash and driving windows, as well as the one that pulled down to hide the driving cabin from view of the living space. Precisely at ten, she turned on her phone. He watched her do it, seeming to notice every second of movement, of sound.

She didn't glance his way. Or acknowledge him.

Less than ten seconds later, her phone rang. "I've got you on speakerphone," she said as soon as she clicked to answer.

Warning her boss not to say anything he didn't want Joe to hear?

Considering the urgency with which she'd done it, the motivation seemed pretty obvious.

"Good." Glen's response came loud and clear into their small quarters. "We're looking at your phone now, but we're pretty confident that number hasn't been compromised."

"But you obviously think my other one was."

He'd had her smash the phone and ditch it.

"We didn't see any trace on it yet, but based on what's going on here, we are assuming it would've been."

Joe didn't want assumption. He wanted answers. Sierra's Web had been on his case for three days, two nights and...

"Someone was watching my and Hud's phones," Glen continued. "Could be related to another case, but as a whole, the partners agree that nothing else we're working on at the moment would warrant an illegal trace. This is the only case we're on together, and no other phones are being tracked."

"Someone knows I hired you," Joe confirmed, agreeing with Glen's assessment immediately.

"We have to assume as much. So...we both now have burner phones as well. Only you two will know the numbers. And we only communicate with the phone you're currently on."

"Got it." McKenna's tone was firm. "Do you know yet who was tracking you?"

"No. Which means we're dealing with someone highly skilled in the technical field."

"Another expert." Joe couldn't keep silent any longer. He was a take-charge guy. One who worked as hard or harder as anyone worked for him.

Maybe if he was doing more, he'd be wanting less from the woman sitting a small cushion away from him.

"Someone who at least has the skills to track phones illegally, to hack into accounts and see numbers called, times and durations of calls, at the very least."

"What's more concerning," Joe said, "is that someone knew I hired you."

"Exactly."

"William's the obvious answer," McKenna said, still not making any kind of eye contact with Joe. She'd stared at the phone she held between them. At the door. Even the floor.

"Our thought, too," Glen's tone didn't sound…confident.

Which prompted Joe's thoughts to an out-loud version. "No way. That kid is—"

"You're right, Mr. Hamilton," Glen interrupted. "We've already confirmed that not only has William not been unsupervised for one second since he left you, but he's lost all electronic rights for the next month, at least, and was made to turn over his cell, his tablet and his computer."

"I'm guessing that didn't go over well." McKenna's comment made clear what Joe had already known. She didn't like that the kid got off without punishment for his intent to murder a man.

Joe didn't think the kid, once faced with the opportunity to finish his plan, would actually have done it. He'd been William's age once…

"Actually, according to his mother, William volunteered

to turn them over. And to pee with the door open and sleep on the floor of her room if that's what it took to earn her trust back."

Joe didn't realize he was grinning until he caught the movement of McKenna's gaze swinging in his direction.

"So that leaves who?" she asked then, looking at Joe for another few seconds before turning away once again.

"Unless either of you have told anyone, that's us and whoever was told at Bellair."

"It's pretty clear that whoever framed me had a high-up position at Bellair," Joe said, his tone finding real conviction for the first time in a while. Sitting forward, his heart pumping with new life, he said, "So there we go. Why would anyone from Bellair be trying to find me, illegally no less, unless they knew I'd hired you to find out the truth?"

"Which means exposing them," Glen said. "We're ahead of you on that one. And have decided to let the situation ride for the time being. Unless, Joe, you can tell us, with your life on the line, that James Bellair can be one hundred percent trusted..."

"I can't. Not anymore." The words left a bitter taste in his mouth. "It could also be someone at Bellair who bought stock when they first heard Stellar's reports and then lost a life's savings," he added, as though to take the heat off James at the same time he'd put it on. "Someone in middle management. Maybe someone whose life took a downturn after the crash." He'd been searching for people who'd had sudden upticks, but what if...

"With Bellair's permission, we're checking out every single employee, including any lifestyle or obvious emotional changes, on the payroll, both current and during the year before the fraud started," Glen stated then. "Kelly Chase, our expert psychiatrist partner, already has an expert specializing in corporate relations on scene conducting interviews."

He was impressed. Relieved. Almost grinned again.

No one mentioned the other possibility—someone from Sierra's Web, someone who wasn't, perhaps, happy that the firm had taken on the case of a believed criminal and had leaked the information to the rabids out to get him.

He couldn't see anyone wanting to put McKenna—one of their own—in more danger. But the goal could be to get the firm off the case...to avoid the negative publicity.

Keeping those thoughts to himself for the time being, Joe thought they were done when Glen said, "We've got some other things to discuss," in a tone that sounded less friendly and more...like a cop investigating a crime.

When said cop wasspeaking to a person of interest.

Holding his judgment, Joe waited.

"You know anything about computer viruses?"

"You're speaking to me, I presume?" Joe asked, trying to figure out in a blink where the conversation could be heading.

"Yes."

Without time to figure out what was obviously a problem coming at him, Joe went with the only truth he had available. "I know that I go through a lot of irritating authentication steps to avoid them. And that the company pays a hefty sum, with my sign-off, to be protected against them."

"I meant in terms of creating them."

What? "I know nothing about that," he blurted. Firmly. And then, more slowly, "Why are you asking?"

They were working for him. He had a right to know anything they'd found on his dime.

Glen didn't give any indication of arguing with Joe's unspoken thought as he relayed that they'd found a virus written into the return software that caused the system to automatically hold reporting on returns of Stellar for six months. At which time there'd been the major dump in the system that had first caught his attention. The database hadn't been physically changed by a person, as Joe and others had thought, but by a virus created by a person? A virus that could act on its own accord when any of them were present in the office?

"The virus was sophisticated," Glen said. "It took Hud's team, with Hud working on it himself, a couple of hours to figure out what was going on and how. A small, thirty-second-to-implement code in the software was all it was."

"And you're going to tell me that it looks like I did it."

"I'm going to tell you that it was done from your work computer." Which should not have been a surprise to anyone.

"Just like inventory numbers were randomly changed from my computer," he reminded. "Or by someone hacking into my computer and using it remotely."

Which was what he'd always contended-that whatever had actually happened, had been done by someone hacking into his computer-but he couldn't explain who, when or how. Couldn't prove it, either. "Since the night I was arrested, I've been trying to figure out who had access, capability and motive," he said, not even caring at the moment that his weariness, his clearly disheartened spirit, filled his tone.

"Right," Glen agreed easily. If there was judgment in the words, Joe couldn't find it.

And...he reminded himself when it occurred to him that McKenna hadn't moved, or said a word, one way or another, they were all still on the phone, having this conversation.

Which wouldn't be happening if the firm was convinced of his guilt.

If they were on the way there...if something Joe said in the next moments got them there...

"Is there a timeline for when this was done?" He asked a question he'd posed before. And hadn't ever received an answer to. "Surely they can tell when the computer was accessed?"

"The computer's internal clock was overridden. The randomly changed inventory numbers, and the virus creation, both show as having happened when the computer was brand-new."

He hadn't even known someone could do such a thing.

"And there's more. The virus was a miniscule, few-stroke change in code, one that could only be seen by comparing hundreds of lines one by one, and still then, a couple of experts missed it..." *Get on with it!* Joe wanted to say. But he maintained control.

Because, no matter what the world made him out to be, he would not be his father's son.

"In addition to that virus, Hud's team found a command embedded in the sales program itself that ordered every tenth sale of Stellar to double itself. To make it harder to find, the command wasn't in the part of the software that handled numbers of orders, but rather, was down farther, after payment had been made, added to shipped orders."

"But they never really shipped." If he hadn't been sick to his stomach with panic, he might have been impressed as he assumed where the story was leading. "This guy's good," he said, feeling like ashes sitting there.

"Just to confirm, you're telling me you had no knowledge of the change." He heard Glen's words. Considered them fair. Opened his mouth to respond but heard McKenna's voice first.

"If gray skin tone and glazed-looking eyes are anything to go by—and in my line of work, they are—I'm going to say that's a definite no."

That gaze she'd called glazed swung to her—wide-open and aware.

Had she just stood up for him? Expressed a measure of faith?

As grim as his prospects looked from what Glen was relaying, Joe's entire future seemed brighter in that moment.

And he answered, "I had no idea, but it sure explains a lot." And then followed up, "I'm guessing you aren't now going to tell me you have a clue who's responsible." He wanted to head off the bad news at the pass. And go for the worst, too. "But it happened from my computer, right?"

"We can't confirm that yet." Glen's response surprised him, but not nearly as much as McKenna's speaking up for him had done. Not even close. "This one's odd. The software that runs the sales database is a Bellair product, one that's used by thousands of companies, and the change is in the product itself."

Oh, God. Blood drained from his face again. "You're telling me thousands of companies have been affected?"

"No. Apparently Bellair uses the prototype, and that was all that was changed."

So, what? A designer was behind the cluster that had become his world?

Joe needed a beer. "Can I interrupt with a prosaic question?" he asked.

"Of course."

"Are McKenna and I staying put for the night?"

"That's up to her."

He glanced her way. She nodded.

Joe got his beer. Uncapped it. Swallowed half a bottle. And heard Glen say, "We're closing in, guys. Which likely means that whoever is behind all this could be pulling out all the stops to close in on you."

"Which would explain the Sierra's Web phone hack," McKenna said, whether to take up Joe's slack, or just because he didn't know. But he was grateful to her for it as he sat back down.

"And the #wheresjoenow hashtag has also spread like wildfire."

"You think there's a connection there?" Joe asked.

"I think it's possible. My team is working that angle now. But even if the doer is behind the onslaught, a whole lot of people have been riled up into thinking that they can somehow help see justice done."

"Which means there will be completely-unrelated-to-the-case righteous-cause fighters on our trail as well," McKenna summed up.

"Right." Glen's sigh came clearly over the line. "The partners met tonight and all agree that we should keep up the same protocol for now. You always check your cameras at the designated times whenever stopped, and you call for check-ins at least twice daily, using only this number or the one I gave you for Hudson. We're going to continue to monitor your phone 24-7. Good news—yes, there is some—no recent pictures have popped up on either #wheresjoenow or the dark web. There've been suspected sightings being reported all day long, in various states, but none in the Yuma area. And no mention of any companions or an RV. Good job, Ken."

Ken?

Joe glanced at her. She was staring at the curtain between the living room and the cab, clearly avoiding his view.

"William found us," she pointed out.

"He'd been hanging out online nonstop, watching the board, saw the second the photo of Joe in the green shorts, long hair and beard posted. Recognized something in the background and has been following Joe ever since."

"That was days ago." Joe made a point of making sure the others got that. If the kid had wanted to kill him, he'd had ample opportunity.

"There could be others," Glen pointed out.

Doubtful. The kid had been filled with rage, panic, driven by grief. But he hadn't been a killer. Which was why it had taken days for William to make his move. Joe was pretty sure anyone else who worked so hard to find him wouldn't hesitate to do their worst. Even if that just meant smearing his current situation, including the rig and McKenna, all over social media so anyone who wanted him dead would find him.

"I've got this," McKenna told her boss, but when Joe looked over, she was looking back at him. Telling him.

"Stay safe" were Glen's last words before the call disconnected.

For the first time since McKenna Meredith had descended upon him, Joe had doubts about that. Not for his physical safety. He'd never been worried much on that score. But emotionally...he had no idea how much damage the woman was going to do to him before the job was done.

Chapter Twelve

Bony knees. Bony knees. Bony knees.

Not soft fingers, or a warm gaze that seemed to want to tell her things.

A tone of voice that had prompted her to assure him, within her boss's earshot, that she had his back—literally, if not figuratively.

The firm, experts that they were, seeing what they saw, weren't quitting him.

She wasn't alone in her sense that there was more to Joe Hamilton's story than a chief financial officer trying to make money with fraudulent activity.

More to the man than the thief he'd been labeled.

"The evidence that Hud and Glen are finding isn't exonerating you." She had to get right to the part of the conversation that had bothered her most.

Because it hadn't convinced her to quit him?

"No, but they're getting closer than anyone has to date. I knew the what. Couldn't figure out the how. And while we don't know how my computer was compromised, at least we know in what form the desecration took place. We know we're looking for someone within Bellair's ranks who's a tech whiz…"

For all she knew, he could be. Just because he'd said he wasn't didn't mean…

"Ken."

Automatically glancing up as she heard her name, McKenna's gaze collided with Joe's. "Don't call me that."

He nodded. "Reserved only for friends and family, huh?"

"Only the ones who want to piss me off."

Eyes widening, Joe looked like he was holding back a smile. Which did kind of raise her ire.

"Glen Rivers is the only one who calls me that. When he'd first been told that I was coming in for an interview, he'd only heard Ken Meredith—there'd been some remodeling going on in the home office—that day. He'd been expecting to meet with a man and he made kind of fool of himself when I showed up. Doubted my ability to do the job..."

"I'm guessing he made the same mistake I did," Joe said with a quirky twist of his lips.

If he meant seeing her size and misjudging her capabilities, then, "Pretty much."

"Did he get the same response?"

"Oh, no. He decided the interview would be a physical one, coming at me quickly to show me why I wasn't right for the job, and landed on his back."

"You flipped him, and he hired you anyway?"

"I let him down gently. And he's called me Ken ever since. His way of telling me that I'm as good as any man at what I do." Or so she chose to think. Could also be that Glen was reminding himself not to underestimate people.

Either way, she was happy to comply.

And they weren't dealing with the job at hand. Straightening, she put her hands, still holding the phone, in her lap, and said, "We're going to have to go to the box store in the morning and purchase several hundred dollars' worth of prepaid credit cards. My name isn't on the Sierra's Web site, nor is the expert list made public anywhere, but there's no guarantee with tens of thousands of internet users jumping on #wheres-joenow that someone won't know that I work for the firm."

It was a stretch. But also an easy situation to imagine.

"You're thinking whoever is after me would hack credit card usage?"

Again, could be overkill. Her instincts were telling her to move forward with the plan anyway. "We've just established that we're dealing with someone who's highly tech savvy within Bellair. We also know we've got someone savvy enough, and unscrupulous enough, to put up a Joe Hamilton message board on the dark web. It stands to reason that either of these folks, and any number of others, have motive to find you. And the skills to hack credit card usage. You willing to risk them being successful?" she asked but didn't wait for a response. "Never mind answering that. I'm not willing. End of story."

"You aren't going to tell me we have to close up and leave again, are you? Because you already said we didn't, and I've had a beer." As if to signify the point, he emptied the bottle he still held. And turned to her wearing a stony expression.

"I always carry a prepaid credit card, just as a precaution, and after Glen's call earlier, the need for dumping my phone and waiting for him to call us, I decided to use the prepaid to check us in."

His almost grin was back.

The man was being hunted by tens of thousands. Someone wanted him badly enough to be illegally tracking a company's phones. Someone who knew he'd hired Sierra's Web. Proof was appearing that made him look guilty.

By McKenna's estimation, the world was completely closing in on him.

And Joe was…seemingly glad just to be able to stay put for the night.

She didn't know whether she should admire him or worry

about his sanity. And didn't seem to have much choice in the matter, as her heart was already busy thinking more highly of him.

The whole thing with William… In the midst of his own trauma, Joe had had the patience and wherewithal to think of another, to try to right a wrong he claimed he hadn't even committed.

But her heart wasn't a part of her current equation. As she checked the outside cameras and then turned off her phone, she would have liked to have had more of a view than the darkened area around them, or to have a chance while it was still light to get a better sense of their immediate surroundings.

And she'd like for Joe to excuse himself to bed.

To be locked away from her for a few hours so she could have a few private words with herself. Refocusing on head over heart.

And maybe get a little rest, too.

In his shorts and white shirt, with those bony knees right there for her to concentrate on, he headed for the door, all right. The one leading outside.

"What are you doing?" Her tone was sharp. It needed to be.

"I've got to get out of here, to walk a bit. Even if it's just around the rig. As dark as it is outside, and as secluded as we are, and while there are no pictures or mentions of you or the rig on social media, I'm as little at risk as I'm going to be."

She hated to disappoint him, most particularly since she understood his need for exercise, but, "It's just too risky, Joe. I have no idea what's out there. If it'd still been light when we'd driven in…"

With a shake of his head, he took another step toward the door before turning back to her. "I'm not asking, I'm telling, McKenna." His tone wasn't nearly as sharp as hers had been, but it brooked no argument. "I'm more of a risk to myself if I don't get out for a minute or two."

"I can't let you just go wander off alone into the night."

"So come with me."

"It's not smart." She had to stop him. "You can't evaluate risk level without knowing what you're walking out to."

"Look—" His shoulders relaxed, and for a second she thought she'd convinced him. "I'm following all of your commands, taking your advice, but right now, if I don't get out of here, I'm going to be climbing some serious walls. Or attempting to jump your bones."

He just put it right out there. Stark. In the open.

And, wrong as it might be, she flooded with desire between her legs. Something that, thankfully, was not apparent to him.

As his suddenly clear erection was to her.

"I'm the client. You're the bodyguard," he said, turning abruptly away from her. "My choice. I'm going outside. You may come with me or not as you choose."

He was going to say something like that and just…walk out?

She couldn't let him do that. He'd walk back in and his words, the attraction clearly building between them, instead of just inside her, would still be there.

The door lock clicked, and McKenna sprang up. She had two choices—physically restrain the man with a neck hold.

Or follow him out the door.

Deciding that not touching him was the less risky choice, she followed him out.

Maybe he'd been an ass. Had just shot himself in the foot. Joe just knew that he'd been too cornered, for too long, to maintain his healthy equilibrium without a break.

He got that having a bodyguard was probably the best

choice—she'd not only saved his body from William's knife, she'd prevented a kid from ruining the rest of his own life.

On his own, Joe had been followed and photographed.

With McKenna calling the shots, they'd stayed days ahead of everyone stalking him.

It was possible that the guy who'd slashed their tires as a very clear warning to get out had taken that route because he'd seen Joe with someone.

A woman posing as his wife.

For whatever reason, the man had been as good as his word, based on the lack of new photos on Twitter.

She'd gotten him out of the park he'd paid cash for, too, before anyone had time to get a picture of him. Or knew about her.

And...she was right behind him, within half a step, as, hands in his pockets, he walked slowly around the rig. He wasn't an idiot. Didn't intend to embark on some adventurous midnight hike.

Fresh air, even with the temperature still pushing seventy, felt good. He could hear the river, along with McKenna's footsteps. And the sky for a ceiling...much more freeing than the room he'd be bedding down in soon.

A room where, if he stood upright on the far side of the bed, he'd hit his head on the ceiling.

A bed where, earlier that day, McKenna had sat with her shirt raised, exposing the soft skin of her side and back to him.

The room where, after he'd left, she'd changed her shirt.

The walk was supposed to be giving desire a chance to drain out of him...

Step, step and there she was. Beside him. Close enough to brush shoulders. Closing in the space he'd sought by escaping to the outdoors. "As your bodyguard, I'm supposed to be in front," she said, and then, pointing to the right, behind and past their rig, she added, "Can we head over there? Since I'm out here, I'd really like to get a better feel for our surroundings."

Didn't matter to him where he walked. And being out, with her, while not calming him, was definitely dispelling the impending sense of doom that had threatened during the phone call.

What had appeared to him to be a thick mass of woods behind them turned out to only be a few yards in depth. The trees were densely situated, but they made it through them in a couple of minutes. Stepping carefully since they couldn't see much.

He mentioned wildlife.

She had her hand on the butt of the gun sticking out of her waistband. The woman was always aware, prepared, ready.

Qualities that he held dear.

Her left hand suddenly flew out in front of him, stopping forward motion and catching him across the crotch. Though he was instantly inflamed again, he wasn't sure she'd even noticed what she'd touched.

That's when he heard the crackling sound she'd obviously already noticed.

Motioning at him to stay behind, she crouched and moved silently forward a step and then two, then stopped and flagged him forward.

The scene was...nice. A fire on the beach, and what looked like two couples sitting around it. He couldn't make out voices, but they were obviously talking. Having some libation.

Normal life.

He couldn't remember a time he'd had one.

Couldn't picture himself ever sitting around a fire on the beach. Past or future. Not unless it was a manned bonfire and the beach was a lavishly catered private party.

But for that moment, he was glad to be sharing a small part of someone else's good time with his bodyguard.

"I'M NOT A sexual predator."

McKenna missed a step, not even sure at first she'd heard Joe right as they walked slowly along the outer side of the woods that filled the cliff above the river. She'd allowed herself to slip into the moment. The rapidly cooling night, the moon above, the river, friends on the beach, peace, quiet, privacy and her, walking along the edge of some woods with a man she liked.

Then she really heard his words and stopped walking altogether, putting him between the cliff edge several feet away and her. "Why would you say a thing like that?"

If he was about to confess some other crime that he was suspected of committing...

Even as she had the thought, she dismissed it. No way she was going to believe that one.

"Back there...my comment about jumping your bones... was beyond inappropriate."

Oh. Yeah, she'd known they had to get back to that.

Had been enjoying their time away from their reality.

"To the contrary, I found it honest. And in our situation, commendable, even. You were struggling with something specific and you gave warning."

"I've never, and would never, touch a woman without her consent. Not purposefully. In a sexual manner."

She stepped right up to him, head tilted to meet what she could see of his gaze in the moonlight. "Joe, you don't have to convince me that you're a decent man."

His gaze was hot. Sliding through her skin to the inside no one got to share.

"I don't fear for my physical safety with you at all."

"That sounds like you do fear something else."

She'd hoped her tone hadn't left that hanging there.

"I do."

He stepped around her, as though to head back to the rig, and she caught at his forearm, pulling him back to her. "I fear that I won't be able to stay on top of my attraction to you, and then we *would* have a problem."

His head tilt was...endearing. Made her want to smile.

"Well, I guess we got that out into the open," he said, sounding so casual she wanted to laugh out loud.

She didn't. She started back to the rig by his side, instead.

And wondered what it would be like to not be on a job, but rather to be taking a moonlit stroll in the woods, her fingers interlocked with Joe's.

"I won't take advantage."

They'd gone several yards before he spoke again, all levity gone from his tone.

"I know."

"I need you on this job. You know the case. Know me. And I trust you to do the job well. You've proven your abilities and I find it...not impossible...to take orders from you without the fact that I have to do so getting too far under my skin."

"I'm not leaving, Joe."

He gave a half grunt. She took it as a thank-you.

"Hypothetically, what would it look like if, say, you happen to lose your battle and your attraction gets on top of you?" She'd told him she had to stay on top of it. Did the man remember every word she uttered?

Was she surprised by that?

He paid attention.

Which made it so hard to understand how someone could have used his computer, multiple times, to commit fraud without him picking up on it.

The thought crept through.

Because no matter what, she was on the job.

And still, his question hung there…needing an answer. For both their sakes.

"Hypothetically, how? In what sense?" She had to tread like cotton, choose her words with acute care.

"Would you lose your job?"

"Absolutely not." The words rushed out, maybe because he'd allowed her an easy answer. "In the first place, I'm a commissioned expert, not on staff. In the second place, as long as I keep you alive and as free from the danger threatening you as is humanly possible, I'd be doing nothing wrong. Assuming you were consenting, which you would be or nothing would happen anyway. I'm not a predator, either."

"What about conflict of interest?"

"You think, if I took personal interest in you, I'd be less interested in keeping you alive and free from danger?"

They'd almost reached the rig, which brought a pit of disappointment to her gut.

"I think I could be a distraction…" His tone, that hint of audacious humor, made her want to laugh. She was working. Contained herself.

"Well, I know that, if anything, I'd be more invested in protecting you, if that were possible. Because I'd be protecting a part of me, as well."

She heard the words. Stopped in her tracks. "Oh, man, I swear, I did not mean that at all, in any way, like it sounded," she said, her eyes so wide with horror, she could feel the night air drying them.

And then had to take a quick visual sweep of the area around the rig, before they stepped into the clearing, just because…that was her.

"No worries," he told her, but he sounded pleased with himself. So much so that her brain was scrambling for the words to take him down a step or ten.

"And for the record," he added, before she got there. "If I

ever do get to know what it feels like to share…bones…with you, you can bet that you would be a part of me as well."

McKenna glanced down. Around. Behind them as they reached the rig door.

She did what she had to do so her client absolutely did not see the smile on her face.

Chapter Thirteen

Joe was on his way to bed, to go over spreadsheets and employees, job responsibilities and time schedules, in light of the new information he'd received that evening, when McKenna called him back.

He stopped at the door into the bathroom. Was she going to suggest heading to the back with him? Growing hard at the thought, he said, "Yeah?" Trying not to sound too eager.

Or needy.

"I just need to be clear about something…"

If the clarity would lead her to bed with him…

"What's that?"

"If we ever do, you know, do the bone thing…and I'm not saying that I'm up for it, just if…it would only be for the moment…"

He'd already figured that one out. She was a two-couple beach fire and he was a catered-bonfire gathering of two hundred.

Beyond that, even if he found that he could do the beach fire, he was still a very rich man to whom the security of wealth meant more than he could give up, and she'd made it very clear that she wanted no part of that life.

"Can I ask you something?" Leaning his shoulder against

the edge of the pocket door he was about to close, he watched her settle back into a corner of the couch, phone in hand.

"Of course."

"Those stipulations you had the court put on your visits with your grandparents…"

"Yeah?"

"Do you still require them to abide by them?"

"It's no longer a matter of needing to require it," she told him. "Once they really understood how I felt, they've made certain that they don't ever put me in a position of having to ask."

He had no idea how much he'd been hoping for a different answer until it didn't come.

And yet, with the completely solid understanding that even if he and McKenna took their relationship to a personal level it wouldn't be anything long term, Joe had less trouble concentrating than he'd expected when he sat up in bed half an hour later, spreadsheets in front of him.

He still wanted McKenna, but the differences between them weren't going to be breached, which meant that anything that happened between them would only open the door to one of them getting hurt.

He wasn't worried about himself. Normal relationship hurts would almost be a welcome change from the majority of the pain he'd suffered in his life. And holding her in his arms, knowing her intimately, would be worth any resulting heartache.

Knowing that, because of him, she was hurting…not so easy to dismiss. That would eat at him, and he'd end up not liking himself.

Reaching that point, his thoughts were finally able to be consumed by the information he'd received from Glen that night. He had to find the evidence that had been eluding him for months and get McKenna out of his life before anything more happened between them.

In the past two days, Sierra's Web's experts had given him not only new information regarding the fraud at Bellair, but new insights, as well.

He had no timelines—except that he knew when he'd been in the office. With sixty hours a week being his norm, and the office closed most of the time he wasn't there, that left very few windows.

He began narrowing and then stopped as something else struck him.

A virus might hit at any time, by various means, but an actual change to the sales program for which Bellair had become nationally known—the program the company still used itself—could only have happened when the program was down. Anything else would have sent several alarms across the desks of all top management. Ditto, even a momentary, few-stroke hesitation. A glitch in the program could cost the company millions, even billions of dollars, and so extra protocols had been put in place and were aggressively monitored. And with online sales, the company had to carefully schedule maintenance time to service the program or install updates, generally in the middle of the night when fewer sales were generated, with carefully monitored employee involvement. Heightened security protocols were also in place during those times.

And the CFO, while not present during program maintenance, had a complete list of personnel who were, as well as time and date stamps for every change.

Sierra's Web experts had his computer, but Joe had saved everything on an external hard drive, which he plugged into his laptop with hands that, while not shaking, were buzzing with nervous energy.

A few clicks and he had the list of sales program updates.

Found one that closely coincided with Stellar's release. Copied the list of people who were paid overtime to be present that night, carried it over and pasted it in the fraud investigation portion of the spreadsheet he'd started after the video meeting with Glen Rivers and Hudson Warner.

And then pasted it again to the stalking portion—his list of people who could possibly have a motive for either wanting him gone or a need for extra money to line their pockets and might have found him to be the likely scapegoat to help make it happen.

If he couldn't get online, he needed someone at Sierra's Web to do so—to check social media accounts, if that's all they could access, on everyone on the list.

There were a few names new to his investigation there.

He no longer had access to company files that could tell him specifics about the employees—not all of whom he knew—but it stood to reason that anyone who'd been vetted to help with such a sensitive software program update would have a high level of technical skills.

Beyond that, they finally had a real starting place. The rest of the fraudulent activity could have happened at various times, but this...a change in the actual sales program... their pool of possible perpetrators had just been narrowed considerably.

Alight with the first real hope he'd had in months, Joe sprang up out of bed, nearly banging his head on the ceiling as he stood on the raised bed portion of the room and, stepping down, threw open the pocket door. McKenna had the only usable phone in the place, and he had to connect with whatever techs were working the night shift at Sierra's Web...

She'd left on the dim running lights along the floor. He saw the edge of the couch pulled out to a bed, heard quick movement from that direction, and before he'd taken another step was staring down the barrel of her gun.

Jaw dropping open, Joe recognized his mistake at the same time he took note that she slept in her clothes. That night? Every night?

"Joe, what the hell…" Her voice groggy from sleep, he saw the weapon drop as, pushing hair back out of her face, she climbed fully out of her makeshift bed.

"I'm sorry," he told her, then glanced down at the hand still holding her gun. "Seriously sorry."

She was staring at him—he couldn't make out a lot from her shadowed expression and the three feet separating them—but her face was pointed as straight in his direction as her gun had been.

And he realized he'd come charging out of his quarters wearing only the basketball shorts he'd started sleeping in the night she'd arrived. Before awkwardness could stifle them completely, he blurted, "I need to use the phone, to get with experts on the night shift. I've got something that—"

She was shaking her head.

"The numbers we have are only for Glen and Hud—phones they'll have on their persons. If this isn't a matter of immediate life and death, we need to wait until the morning."

Of course they did. Had he been more himself, rather than feeling like a caged and hungry tiger, he'd have realized that.

"Right," he said then, turning back to the door of his cave. "Good point."

"Joe?"

"Yeah?"

"I'd like to know what you found."

It was two in the morning. He had to be ready to drive the next day if the need arose. And she needed rest, too.

Things he should have already considered.

"In the morning," he said, and leaving her standing there looking all accessible and gorgeous, he put himself to bed.

THAT CHEST. OH LORDY. Even in near darkness, she'd noticed nipples peeking out of dark hair.

And the broadness—his shoulders seemed to expand, his muscles thicker, when he took off his shirt.

But his belly button was what had done her in.

She'd actually had a thought to stick her tongue in it.

Which sent her diving back for her covers. And her phone. Looking at the cameras would get her focus back on track.

Joe was counting on her to keep him safe, and she was damned well going to do it.

And…what had he found?

Would it really clear his name?

Her wealth of wanting that for him startled her as she lay there, ensuring that there was no movement in the vicinity of their rig.

Of course she wanted a successful end to the job for all involved, but her feelings went way beyond client/bodyguard care.

In a few very long days, the man had grown on her.

Felt like a real friend. Someone who'd touched her life in a way she'd never forget.

Someone who hadn't touched her enough yet.

If his case was solved, the job complete…she'd never know what it felt like to lie with him. To be touched by him, more than just fingers attaching a bandage to a scratch.

She'd already removed the bandage, but she reached her fingers back to rub the area, remembering his soft warmth doing the same.

Should she go knock on his door?

Make the bone thing happen?

Before it was too late?

She was still in clothes from the day before. She changed after her shower early every morning. And if they had to be on the run again, he needed his rest.

Did she really want her time with him to be rushed?
Did she…

MCKENNA WOKE UP before dawn, realizing she'd fallen asleep still contemplating sex with Joe—and was hugely relieved that she'd done so.

Fallen asleep.

Without having sex with Joe.

She showered and was already dressed in her traditional work clothes of lightweight pants, blue that time, and short-sleeved white top, outside, circling the area, when she heard plumbing working inside the rig. And hurried inside to fix breakfast.

Joe was up, which meant the day had officially begun.

And she needed to hear his news.

To get the job done, and herself home, before she made a total fool of herself.

FULLY DRESSED IN tan cargo shorts and a short-sleeved black shirt, Joe told McKenna about the scheduled sales-program maintenance over breakfast, keeping things between them strictly business. The fact that she'd chosen the cattycorner chair, at the wall opposite his side of the table, told him that she intended to do the same.

And while a part of him was truly disappointed, he was a realist through and through and felt a whole lot more comfortable with the situation as they took their seats at opposite ends of the couch for the call to Glen.

The conversation went even better than he'd anticipated, as a time he'd pinned for the sales program change coincided with one of the suspects Glen's computer forensic team had been looking at for the virus coding.

"Coding is kind of like a fingerprint in the digital world," Glen said. "Hud can tell you how to write programs to make computers do things, and my guys know how to pick up on coding differentials—ways programmers write their commands…"

Heart pounding, Joe glanced over at McKenna. And lost a breath when her gaze, moist with emotion, stared back at him.

He'd known all along he was innocent. He'd never been certain anyone would be able to prove it.

"You're saying the commands in the virus and in the sales program change were written by one person?"

"I'm saying that we were looking into the virus compared with work one employee has done legitimately for the company…and that employee is on the list you just read off to me."

Had he been standing next to McKenna, he'd have grabbed her up and twirled a circle. Had he been outside, he'd have let out a loud whoop!

Joe took a sip of coffee, put the cup on the table back in front of the couch, rubbed his hands on his legs and noticed McKenna's sockless ankle, leading to the foot enclosed by her tennis shoe, bouncing up and down, almost in rhythm with his hands.

They had something—the two of them. Even if it was just the sharing of a few bizarre, unforgettable days. He was honored to have known her.

And glad that they were ending it as friends—no hurt feelings involved.

Joe thought they'd be ending the call as his report conversation wound down, maybe with the hope expressed that it would all be over that day.

Most particularly when he heard Glen's "We've got more here." The firm was living up to its reputation. Getting the job done.

"Something we need to talk about," the man continued,

his tone changing to one more akin to doom and gloom than celebration.

McKenna glanced at him. He nodded, as if to tell her all was good. And was still gazing into her eyes as Glen said, "You didn't tell us you had a criminal record."

He heard McKenna's hiss but didn't see her expression. Or the shock he was sure would be in her eyes as his eyes closed, and then, turning his head, opened again to stare at the floor by the kitchen sink.

"I don't have one," he said, but he knew the words, while technically true, were pointless. They'd obviously dug up something during their search.

The possibility had always been there.

"Not as an adult," he amended. Glen had seemed eager to get the information Joe had given him about the sales program. Had vowed to get everyone to work on it. The firm wasn't quitting him.

It kept coming back to that.

Maybe because it felt like it was all he had.

Watching as McKenna stood by the door, looking out the blinds she'd raised, staring at her back, he figured he'd lost the only other thing he'd been valuing lately—her friendship.

"I had an…unusual childhood," he admitted, watching that straight, forbidding posture by the door. "It has nothing to do with my life now."

"I have to disagree with that," Glen said. "On several levels. One, we're sitting here blindsided, unaware that our client has a past conviction…"

McKenna's head swung enough for her to see him. And she saw him looking at her and just as swiftly turned back.

"Second, fraud and theft are…"

Holy hell. "What!" He jumped to his feet, picking up the phone she'd laid on the couch between them. Dropped it, ungently, on the table and stood there, glaring at its silent self.

"Theft?"

"You were convicted? Did time? You telling me you were innocent then, too?" McKenna hurled the words.

Warmth drained from him. And surged back in the form of red-hot anger. "That record was sealed!" His raised voice on the last word shocked even him.

He glanced toward McKenna, ashamed of his outburst, wanting to apologize. The look of betrayal in her eyes as she stared at him kept him silent.

"It's all over the internet," Glen said somewhat softly, as though trying to mediate more than anything. "Popped up some time after midnight, the team tells me. The #wheresjoenow hashtag has more than tripled in hits."

"The record was sealed," he said again, but he felt more like an abandoned dog than the strong, capable, determined man he knew himself to be.

If he didn't know better, he'd think the past fifteen years of his life had been a fluke.

"Which means we have an even bigger problem." Glen's tone held warmth and professionalism. At least one of them was staying on task. "How did someone get into sealed records?"

"I'd like to know about the charges before we go any further," McKenna said. "I'm assuming there's been no activity on either this line or yours," she said, clearly to Glen. "We're safe to stay on the phone?"

"No activity. And I was getting to that, as well," Glen said. "If we're going to figure this out, Joe, we need to know all relevant information."

"It's not relevant," he said, certain of that. "Except as a way to put the squeeze on me by getting more and more people hunting me down until I'm found."

"It's relevant to me." McKenna sat at the table by the wall, pulling down the shade next to her. One she'd raised less than an hour before.

Looking at her, Joe got it.

She wasn't sure she was going to stay. Regardless of what the firm decided.

Part of him, maybe the larger part, wanted to show her the door. Let her go. Take his chances guarding himself.

Probably better for her if he did, before she got any deeper into the black hole that had become his life.

Sitting down on the opposite side of the table, he took a deep breath.

And made a decision he'd thought he'd never have to make.

Chapter Fourteen

"My father was a two-bit thief."

McKenna's heart stopped and then went into overtime as Joe's words, said in a low, resigned voice she didn't recognize, fell to the phone on the table.

"Who went on to rob a bank," he continued, dropping his bombshells into the early-morning silence.

"When I was eight, he started using me to score goods, which he'd then return for cash. We'd go shopping. He'd let me pick clothes, a toy that I wanted, and told me I could carry them while he went to the counter and paid for them. I didn't find out until I was caught walking out with a video game console that he wasn't actually paying anyone for any of it. I was arrested. Charged. Convicted. I told everyone I thought my dad had paid for the items. He testified that he knew I had a problem. That he was getting help for me. He was charming and convincing, and they believed him. I served six months in detention and was then released to his custody. I grew wise overnight. He did his own stealing after that, got caught when I was fifteen, and I haven't seen him since."

Tears filled her eyes. She couldn't help them. Didn't even try. Joe hadn't looked her way since he'd started talking. Was staring at the phone to which he was speaking.

"I have never knowingly broken the law," he said. "Not even to break the speed limit the first time I drove my Maserati."

He could be playing them. Growing up in crime...he'd been bred to make things seem different than they were. To con people into believing him when he lied to their faces.

And she believed him.

Because her instincts knew she could?

Or because she was too personally close to see reality?

"Fine." When Glen's response, clear and strong, came over the phone, she'd actually forgotten her boss was there with them.

And then drew in air more easily as his reply fully resonated with her.

Glen believed Joe.

Glen, whose team of experts was digging into every aspect of the man's life, from the things he spent money on, how much he spent and how often, to the places he frequented. They knew far more about him than she did.

And Glen believed Joe.

Something tripped in her heart. A switch she hadn't known was there.

Before she could even fully acknowledge or identify any change in her, Glen continued, "So that leaves the bigger problem...how did this information make it onto social media?"

And she tuned in. Fully tuned in. To the case. All business.

With fear striking at her, she told them. "Someone in law enforcement had to put it there. Someone getting caught up in the social media hunt, who happened to have access... Everyone wants to be involved these days...to be a part of whatever chase is on... It's become a major form of entertainment, and for some, a way to get noticed and gain influence."

"Law enforcement is our first guess, too," Glen said. "It's the obvious one. But it could also be someone from your past,

Joe, who's looking for their sixty seconds of fame. That's what I need to hear from you. Who knew?"

"No one," he said, then added, "People who worked for the court, of course, or in juvie. The records were sealed. And I have not spoken of it, other than to law enforcement personnel, since the day I was arrested."

"Were you in counseling?"

"Yes, while in detention. Not afterward. The only issue I had was being blamed for something I didn't knowingly do." His harsh chuckle almost choked her.

"I've kept my nose completely clean ever since," Joe continued before she could say anything, do anything, to make the moments better.

"Which meant that my past never had cause to surface again."

He'd walked the straight and narrow so that he never had to go through what he was going through in that moment. The unfairness of it caught at her.

Pushing away the emotion that welled up in her, McKenna sat up straighter. He'd hired a professional. At the same time, anger at a world that had dealt the man a second unfair blow reignited her backbone. And her determination to stay by his side until he was not only exonerated, but safe from the rabids who were making a pastime out of hunting him down.

The rest, any attraction between them, would just have to sort itself out.

"WHAT ABOUT YOUR FATHER? He knew."

Joe took a deep breath when Glen got to the question he'd been waiting for.

Could the old man have caught wind of his son's apparent downfall and jumped on the bandwagon with information no one else could give?

"Last I checked he's up in Alaska, living in some remote

place, fishing for a living. I guess his one stint in prison after the foiled bank robbery convinced him a life of stealing wasn't for him. After he testified against me as a kid, he'd said he let me take the blame to save us, save our family. He'd known that if he went away, there'd be no more us, that I'd be sent away from him for good. I believed him at the time. I'd like to believe him still. And to hope that there's no way he'd do this to me, but how would I know?"

There. It was all out. Every sad, sorry detail of a life he'd escaped. He'd thought permanently.

"What about your mother?"

Joe heard Glen's question. He could feel McKenna's gaze but avoided it completely. Hated what she'd just heard. Didn't want to think about what any of it meant.

"My mother died when I was four," he said. And left it at that.

He'd been wrong. Not every sad, sorry detail had escaped. There were some he got to keep to himself forever.

"And there was no other family?"

McKenna's impatient sigh, coming from across the table, hit him funny. In a way that didn't hurt.

"No other family," he said, liking that his bodyguard was ready for the excruciating questions to be done, too.

"I'll get someone checking out your father as soon as we're off here," Glen said. "If he's still living remotely in Alaska, once we locate him it should be an easy enough task to see if he's behind the leak—most particularly if he's in one of the areas without cell and internet service. And don't worry, we'll be discreet. If he *is* involved, we don't want to alert him that we're on to him."

"Which leaves us most likely dealing with someone in law enforcement." McKenna sounded...capable. Ready. "And that tells me that Joe and I have to blend in more. Keeping our distance, but not seeming to hide at all. At least until something tells me differently, I think we'll stay put right here. Spend some time at the river, a married couple on vacation, maybe renting a fishing boat, waving at other couples..."

On one hand, Joe liked everything about her plan—so much that he was fine to never have it end. On the other... every word she spoke spelled disaster.

The last thing he needed was more intimacy with his bodyguard.

"If we're on the road, and there's someone out there with access putting BOLOs on radios—"

"Hud's team has already put out an anonymous post from a new account saying that you all were seen heading up toward Utah," Glen interrupted.

"Okay, good. We'll unhook the car, make it look like we're comfortable, settling in. Keep the rig off the grid, if we can. And, based on what you're seeing...do we think it's safe for me to keep the phone on? I need to be alerted the second anything changes on your end."

"It's a risk," Glen's response came back. "But maybe the lesser of the two?"

McKenna's touch on his arm brought Joe's gaze straight at her for the first time since she'd heard he was a thief. "It's your life, Joe. Your call."

Such a small thing. Turning to him.

And it was everything.

Giving him back a semblance of the control that had been stripped from him. As though she knew...and was there, having his back, even on that.

"Keep the phones on," he told them, without any hesitation. "Have someone tracking them both 24-7—I don't care how much it costs. We need you to be able to contact us immediately if you find anything."

And if someone found them...

If a cop stopped them, they had to respond in the event that the cop was legitimate and had reason…

McKenna was an expert at keeping her clients out of danger. She had a weapon and was trained to use it.

He didn't and wasn't.

And if someone got too close, it was him they wanted, and he was willing to die before he'd let anything happen to her.

End of story.

SHE'D BEEN THINKING about protecting her client. Period. Staying put meant he was exposed to fewer people who could recognize him.

On the road, he was on display, sitting up in the driver's seat of the rig. Every single person passing by could get a look at him.

When posts on the hashtag to find him had only numbered in the thousands, the chances of someone having seen the posts and recognizing him had been minimal, and the need for him to throw off anyone on his tail had been paramount.

But once the hashtag had gone viral, there was no telling how many people had seen his photo or joined the hunt to get their own picture of him to post. Most of the lookers were harmless.

And at least some of those who'd crossed over from the dark web were not. Game players, entertainment seekers could lead a killer straight to Joe.

Either an angry, out-of-control, desperate person out to make him pay for the loss of their life savings, or the person who'd framed him for fraud, expecting him to go down for the crime, needing him dead before the truth was exposed.

Without Joe, no one would be looking for the true culprit. Bellair and prosecutors were certain they had their man.

For the job, she'd made the right choice.

As soon as they were off the phone, she and Joe drove to

the closest box store, him with a bandanna tied around his head, and the start of a mustache, to quickly pick up a pair of matching straw hats, several prepaid credit cards, cornstarch, food coloring and packets of powdered orange punch drink, paying at self-checkout. They were back in the car within seven minutes, and she'd noticed no one giving them a second glance.

"You have a sudden penchant for orange drink?" he asked as they left the parking lot. She'd known the question was coming.

Who bought food coloring while guarding a live body?

Taking a deep breath, she told him, "You're getting a few homemade henna tattoos."

"A what now?"

"I'm not a great artist, so your choices are going to be limited, but I'm thinking one on each forearm and one where your neck meets your collarbone. We don't want you looking like a gangbanger, but the tattoo will not only draw eyes away from your face, it will also definitely not match the photos of you going around."

She spoke quickly. Ready for his arguments. And ready to get her way—even if he threatened to fire her over it.

When he said nothing at all, she glanced his way—their faces much closer in the closer confines of the car—expecting to confront his frown with convincing arguments.

He was shaking his head. And had that funny little almost grin on his face again. Needing to keep her gaze outside the car, making sure there was no one tailing them or staying close enough long enough for camera shots, she quickly turned her attention back to the road. But felt the growing-familiar tug in her groin area.

Seriously? Just from a not smile?

"You have all kinds of tricks in that arsenal of yours, don't you?"

"I take my job seriously. And prefer to get the work done without physical battle whenever possible."

"So...this tattoo, exactly how does it happen?" he seemed to be musing—just a guy on vacation—though she knew a whole lot more had to be going on in that brain of his.

He knew anyone could recognize him at any time.

If he needed distraction to help get them back to the rig, she'd give it to him. He just needed to drive safely.

"I'll mix powdered drink mix with cornstarch, food coloring and water. And I've got a little eyeliner brush in my cosmetic bag that will work fine as a paintbrush."

Tattoo talk was much better then thinking about being alone in the rig with him, leaning over him, painting on his neck.

"You planning to do this every morning? Because if you think I'm going to forgo a shower, with us in such close quarters, you're going to want to think again."

Showering. Close quarters. All parts of the plan she'd deliberately not contemplated when she'd announced on the phone that morning . Instinct told her that her idea was the best way to keep Joe safe.

"We let the paste sit for twenty minutes, maybe a little longer, and the dye stains your skin. We'll treat it with lemon juice and sugar—both of which we already have on hand—to keep it moist, and that will help it last longer. If we're lucky, you'll still be wearing them when you head back to your real life."

The words started out in jest.

As she heard them, her stomach tightened, and her spirits took a dive.

He would be leaving. Probably very shortly.

And she was emotionally attached to the event.

But then, she'd been emotionally jumbled by the end result of her last job, as well. Sending a young man off to live without his family for the rest of his life. She'd hurt for him. For his mom and sister. And she'd moved on to her own life.

Wanting to believe leaving Joe would be the same, McKenna really tried, but she knew if she bought into that theory, she'd be lying to herself.

Chapter Fifteen

Just no way to hide the evidence. She'd had him sit in the chair behind her captain's chair up in the cab, because it swiveled, giving her easy access, and because it had arms upon which he could place his own upper limbs so they were steady while she painted. And didn't move while the paint dried.

Only problem was, when the light touch of her brush on his forearms raised tingles across his body, and his lower member grew in response, sticking out with obvious formation beneath the shirt resting across it, he couldn't move a hand to cover himself.

The pain grew as she lowered her head to her work, making him want things he should not be wanting from her, things he hadn't had in too many months.

Things he hadn't even wanted in more months than he could count.

The fresh soapy scent of her, those red curls, all just right there, taking up his view, leaving him with nothing else to concentrate on.

He'd chosen to have the word *Freedom* on one arm. Was thinking maybe he should have shortened it to *Free*. Or even *F*.

She was going to do a vine with the word *Truth* crawling up his other arm.

And the one on his neck would be an infinity sign.

At the rate they were going, he was going to be embarrassing himself with leakage before she finished with the *F*.

"Tell me about your mother." McKenna's statement, so out of the blue, shocked him a bit.

"What?"

"You said she died when you were four. I'm assuming you have memories of her. What was she like?"

He could almost feel her breath on his skin as she spoke, but the words...they took him in a whole other direction. A road he would not normally have traveled.

"She laughed a lot, I think," he told her, not quite eager but willing to let his mind wander back as it distracted him from his most immediate discomfort. "I remember her laughing. In the kitchen. And in the car. She'd run with me out in the yard and laugh when she caught up to me. I think I let her catch up."

It had been so long since he'd called any of it up...things had faded.

"She made the best chocolate chip cookies," he said then. "I'm not sure I actually remember what they tasted like, but I remember her handing me a cookie one time when I was upset. I have no idea what about. And years later, my dad still talked about those cookies."

It was about the only time his old man had mentioned his mother.

There were other memories, though. "She took me to a public swimming pool once. I wanted to go off the diving board. I don't think she was into it, but I remember her standing at the edge of the pool, ready to jump in if I needed her to."

"Did you jump?"

"Of course."

"Did she?"

"Nope. I swam to the side just fine and went right back up on the board."

"You still swim?"

"There's a pool in my backyard." It had been months since he'd done any morning laps. Months since he'd lived any semblance of a normal life.

The light touch of bristle against his skin had normalized some.

"How'd she die?"

About to prevaricate, Joe wondered why. She already knew the worst. And it wasn't like he was ever going to see McKenna again after he was exonerated and free from public scorn.

The news wasn't sealed. It could come up.

Her company could find it in their search for other things.

He'd rather she hear it from him.

"An overdose of sleeping pills."

"Prescription?"

"Over-the-counter. She swallowed two bottles of them."

"Wow. I'm so sorry."

He'd have shrugged if he could move his arms. "It was a long time ago."

"Where were you at the time?"

"Home alone with her."

"You found her."

"Yep. They'd made her sick. She died on the bathroom floor. I thought she was just sleeping."

Because some things just didn't fade, no matter how many years had passed.

She was still painting. Slowly. Meticulously. He could feel the strokes.

Couldn't see for her bent head.

And wasn't watching, anyway.

Even when his vision wasn't inward, he'd been staring at

the back portion of the rig. The conversation wasn't pretty, but his body wasn't hard anymore, either.

"I was there when my mom died, too." The words were so soft he'd thought maybe he imagined them. The brushstrokes hadn't changed. There was no indication she'd just told him something so significant.

No sense that she'd just given him an intimate part of herself.

For a second, he didn't know what to do with it.

But he couldn't leave something so significant just hanging there. It mattered that she'd shared with him. Far more than what he'd revealed that day. His ruminations had been a part of the job.

"You were just three." The response wasn't his best. Didn't please him overly much. Repeating something she'd already told him.

He couldn't imagine…a little three-year-old McKenna processing something like that.

"Had she been sick?"

"No." The brushstrokes stopped for a moment. "She was killed. A robbery gone bad."

Joe felt like he'd been kicked in the gut. Turning toward her, needing to offer…his empathy at the very least…he saw her head still bent over his arm. Brushstrokes started again.

She was calling the shots. Telling him she didn't want any more from him.

She'd just wanted him to know.

They'd both been present at their mothers' horrific deaths.

A god-awful thing that they had in common.

SHE'D BEEN DOING tattoos for years, ever since learning them as a form of disguise in a class she'd taken after completing her criminal justice degree, and then bodyguard training from a nationally known tactical and security program. She'd even had a booth where she'd painted on children at Shelter Valley's annual festivals. They were an art form she oddly enjoyed.

Until Joe.

Painting on his skin, being that close to him without touching him elsewhere, in other ways, had been one of the more difficult physical exercises she'd ever done.

When she'd seen evidence of his similar struggle, shortly after she'd begun, knowing they had to get through at least three brandings, she'd grabbed at the one thing she could think of to save them from imminent disaster.

Brought up the mother he'd so clearly not wanted to talk about that morning.

The fact that she knew so much about him, and not that, had bothered her then. Hearing the truth had certainly solved the tattoo-as-a-precursor-to-sex problem.

And had only drawn her closer to him in a far more dangerous way.

Physical cravings they could take care of if necessary.

Matters of the heart between them—never.

Her artwork pleased her, though, turning out even better than she'd expected.

Joe had seemed to find his new tats not too hateful as he looked them over and then complimented her on yet another talent.

Their gazes had met—and she'd had to get them out of there. Instantly.

He'd been as agreeable as always, maybe with a hint of desperation mirroring hers. With their new hats on their heads, shading their faces, his lightened hair in its new ponytail style, they'd set out to be a couple enjoying their early-October vacation in the vicinity of others along the river, walking the beach, in sight but far enough away to keep facial features unrecognizable.

She'd taken his hand as soon as they'd headed out. "We're a married couple enjoying alone time," she reminded him, and herself, as she felt his fingers close around hers. "We need to appear engrossed enough in each other to not offend others by our lack of interaction, and to discourage others from engaging with us."

She could feel her pulse racing, even as she said the words. Wondered if he could feel it, too. Talked about the water as they got down toward the shore, grassy land interspersed with beach areas, all dotted with people. Mostly families. Set apart in individual groupings here and there.

No one paid them any attention, just as they passed by others in the distance without looking at them. They were all just part of the landscape.

Just as she'd hoped.

But with the job going so well, she was left walking along the river in balmy eighty-degree sunshine with a gorgeous man at her side, holding her hand.

"Do you have a woman in your life, back home?" she asked, maybe a little out of desperation, but definitely as another reminder to herself that she most definitely was not it.

"No one serious."

"What does that mean?"

"I dated. Not seriously. When I get back and am exonerated, those women will still be there. Maybe attached now. Maybe not."

"Did any of them stand by you after your arrest?"

"Not that I'm aware of."

Sounded exactly right to her. Based on what she knew of the keep-up-appearances society in which he lived.

And yet, he couldn't wait to get his life back. Was spending huge amounts of money to that end.

"How about you?"

His question made her sweat. Or the exercise did. Quite suddenly.

"This isn't about me."

"It's not about my dating life, either, but you asked."

Valid point.

"It's easier when we're talking about you. Since you're the client, the one this whole situation revolves around…"

"Easier for you, maybe. And you haven't answered my question."

They'd been walking for half a mile. Another mile at least of unfettered ground stretched before them. She watched a speedboat pass. Saw some brave kayakers riding the wake.

"I date. Not seriously. Most guys who ask me out aren't as enamored of me once they find out what I do for a living." Okay, she hadn't meant that to come out.

"What about the ones you ask out?"

Yeah. "I don't tend to do that much." She'd grown up in two worlds, with two sets of friends, which left her on the outside looking in with both groups.

And with her families…the same.

"I'm a bit of a loner," she said aloud. Finding the words kind of sad, though she was perfectly happy with her life. "Not everyone has to grow up and get married and start a family to be happy and fulfilled."

"I agree with you completely on that one." When he gave her hand a squeeze, as though to shake on the agreement, her groin came to life again.

From a hand squeeze.

Added to the entire situation into which they'd been thrust.

"What made you want to become a bodyguard?" His question disappointed her. Mostly because most men asked it with a tone that said they just didn't get it. Like she wasn't normal for making the choice.

It took her a second to realize he hadn't had the tone. And so, for the first time, she answered the question rather than parrying it.

"My dad says it's because of what happened to my mother, and he's probably right. From my point of view, I like the idea of being able to protect people, not just with brute strength, or guns, though I can do both, of course, but by using a whole-life approach."

"Like disguises."

"Like disguises," she agreed.

There was more. She'd grown up afraid. Petrified to be alone in society—not just her grandparents' society, but in public, period. Until she'd run to Shelter Valley and found her own strength. From there, training to be a protector rather than a victim had seemed like a natural course. She was the person she'd been meant to be.

And if that meant she never married or had children of her own...

The whole concept was one she'd left for the future to figure out. Hadn't been bothered that it wasn't happening for her yet.

Until Joe had asked her about dating.

Speaking of which, a couple was walking toward them. One they'd passed half an hour before. Going in opposite directions then, too. Only now they were much closer.

Close enough for her to tell that she'd seen them once before. Getting off a boat that had just tied up at the one long dock attached to the far end of the road filled with pay-as-you-go campsites. The woman couldn't seem to take her eyes of Joe.

While she was holding hands with another man...

Her foot lifted to take her next step, but she swung around instead, slamming her body into Joe's, pushing him up against the closest tree. She lifted both of his arms, tats showing, positioned them so that his newly inked neck was in full view and planted her lips on top of his.

There was no time to warn him, to tell him to play along.

Keeping her eyes half-closed, she turned her head, as though to better fit her mouth to Joe's, but kept her gaze intent on the couple.

The mouth beneath hers opened. Joe's tongue, warm, but not sloppy wet, pushed at the opening of her lips. It had to look real. Believable.

Moving her body against his, their arms still both raised against the tree, she opened her mouth, too. Letting her tongue mingle with the one that had gained entrance.

Saw the young woman glance immediately away, out to the water, and then lean in, as though saying something to her partner, after which the two of them immediately turned and went back the way they'd come.

And... Joe's mouth was devouring hers. Small kisses in between deep, intimate thrusts, until their mouths seemed to become one entity, meant to keep them together forever.

It took her a full minute to drop his wrist down from the trunk of the tree.

To pull her body away from the rock-hard heat against which she'd been pressing.

And another few seconds to get her mouth apart from his.

She'd done the right thing. Followed the plan exactly.

And it had worked perfectly.

Disaster of recognition by some young social media user averted.

But one look at Joe's face, at the shock in his eyes before he turned away, and she knew that another disaster had just fallen upon them.

Between them.

The disaster *was* them.

The couple who had just had hot, undeniable sex with their mouths.

Who had burning bodies that were careening toward total coupling.

But who knew that if it happened, it wouldn't be anything more than a side effect of the job.

Just like the kiss had been.

Chapter Sixteen

Had Joe's life been his own, he'd have walked back to the rig alone, fired it up and headed out. As it was, all the way back, walking hand in hand, in total silence, with the woman pretending to be his wife, he formed the words that would get her out of his life within the hour. Over and over. In differing versions.

"Look out at the water." The command came with purpose, and he followed it immediately, felt a jerk on the hand holding his as McKenna waved in the direction away from the river with her free hand.

"That couple was watching us. Now they aren't," she said without speeding up their slow, steady pace.

"Wouldn't it look more like we're a couple enjoying an engrossing time together if we were talking to each other?" he asked, somewhat to be perverse, but also because the question was valid.

"Yes, it would. I'm just not sure what to say. And it's taking most of my energy at the moment focusing outward. One missed bit of interest and you could be splashed all over the internet…with our location right alongside the picture."

And…he felt like an ass. All worked up over a little kiss that he'd known could happen. That had happened for good reason. She'd been working. Doing her job.

And he'd...forgotten for a few seconds that she was on the job. Forgotten that he was paying her.

"You're free to go as soon as we get back," he told her. "I'll tell Glen that having a bodyguard is driving me crazy and I'm willing to take my chances without one."

"Aside from the way that reflects on me, are you telling me to leave?"

One word. *Yes.* All his rehearsing and he couldn't come out with one word? "I'm a good man, McKenna," he said instead. "I live by a strict code of ethics, which most definitely includes zero sexual anything in the workplace, not because we're so socially conscious about it now, but because that's who I've always been." Not that he'd given her any reason to believe him. Just the opposite.

And there was the rub.

Coming from the life he'd been born to, he had to stand straighter, work harder, live cleaner than others to live beside them.

He couldn't carry on an affair with his bodyguard and come out liking himself.

"So, actors, who have to come together with costars onscreen, or in the theater, you think they're bad people?"

"Of course not."

"How is this different? Other than the camera crews and overall coolness of being a movie star. We're doing a job here. As planned." Her words sounded forced.

And he couldn't pretend.

"It's different because I wasn't working. Or going along with the plan to keep me safe."

"Of course you were." Her immediate response, the adamant way she said it, riled him up more. He couldn't afford to live in shades of gray.

"No, I—"

"If you hadn't been following the plan, you'd have had

your arms around me, not staked up to a tree exposing your tattoos," she interrupted.

She could have been right. Except that he'd been turned on by the whole pinned-up-on-the-tree thing, too.

"Your body's reaction was natural, Joe. As was mine. We're human."

As was mine. He'd known, of course. But to hear her admit she'd been as turned on as he'd been...

"And we still got the job done. That young social media influencer wannabe, or whoever she was, had been following us, staring, getting closer, studying...and with one kiss at a tree, we lost her interest."

He hadn't known. About the woman. He'd known why McKenna had kissed him—to make their relationship clear to anyone around the campsites along the river. That there'd been someone suspicious, ready to expose him...

He'd been lost in her kiss. She'd been working the whole time. Watching some woman he hadn't even been aware of.

"Besides, I'm the one who made the advance, not you. It's me who, in your scenario, would have been wrong. I'm also the one who came up with the plan. All you've done is follow orders."

If only it were that simple.

"So if I crawl into your bed tonight and proceed to have sex with you, it's all your fault?" He was being facetious. Completely. And still felt the pull. "I have carte blanche just to take what I'm driven to need, because there's a *plan*?" He had to make her see that she was playing with fire. That he was.

And that he wasn't sure he could keep them from getting burned. If it was just him at risk, he'd bear the scars, as he had the others. But if he knowingly let himself hurt her...

She had to go.

There was no other option.

As soon as they were back at the rig, they were parting ways.

SHE WANTED HIM.

In the worst way.

More than she'd ever thought about wanting a man.

It would only be for the moment—during the job—while they were playing a part. But realistically, her life choices didn't accommodate any more than that, anyway.

Yards away from the rig, her mind was spinning. What was she doing?

Thinking?

Who was she kidding?

It was going to happen.

Either that or Joe was getting ready to fire her, and she couldn't let him do that. Not if it meant leaving him out there on his own.

Or even finding someone else to take her place.

Someone who didn't know the job. Or him. Who wouldn't be able to protect him as well as she could.

Chances of him letting another bodyguard in were slim.

There'd been nothing but a strained silence between them in the five minutes since he'd challenged her with his mock threat to climb into her bed and ravish her body.

"I think a better plan would be to do it in your bed," she put out there, knowing that she was crossing a point of no return. "That couch isn't long enough for your legs and doing it all scrunched up could get a little awkward."

He didn't miss a step, just kept forward motion toward the rig, but she was pretty sure his hand was sweating.

"That way I come to you," she continued, "which lets you completely off the hook in terms of harassment accountability."

Of course, he could then have a case against her...

"Which I will not do without your prior consent," she amended.

They'd reached the rig. Pulling her behind it, where they'd

set chairs in the trees on the lot, out of view, he lowered her to her chair and then took his.

"Enough with the craziness," he said. "You might think this is all fun and games, but—"

She kissed him. Quickly. Instinctively. To silence him before he could make a bigger mess of things.

"I'm being serious, Joe," she told him, looking him straight in the eye. "I can't explain this thing that's sprung up between us. I've been on plenty of jobs with men before and had absolutely no desire to get any closer to them, in any way. And I'm guessing you've worked with a lot of women and also not had this problem, or you'd have been quitting jobs."

"I've never worked with a woman in as intimate quarters as this," he said. She noticed, right away, that he hadn't denied the main gist of her assumption.

What he was feeling for her was new to him, too.

But he wasn't closing up the rig and driving away from her. Yet.

"Answer me this…do you think you could have sex with me—in a world where there was no reason not to do so—and be okay leaving me behind?"

"That's the whole point," he told her, sitting forward, frowning at her. "It can't lead to anything. And I'm not going to start something that I know I'm not going to finish."

"Right."

"Which means you need to—"

"It means that we're on the same page," she interrupted, feeling as though she was fighting for life.

His life.

"Because I fully believe I can have sex with you and be okay when the job ends and…we do."

His stare was intense. She just couldn't tell if it was in her favor—their favor—or not. The man was certainly a stickler for doing what he thought was right.

To the point of sacrificing himself maybe a bit too much.

"Don't you see? You wouldn't be starting something you aren't going to finish, because we know there is a finish—and what it is—before we start."

Was she really sitting there begging a man to have sex with her?

It was a new one, that was for sure.

One she'd never in a million years have seen herself doing.

"Ground rules." His blurt sounded a bit guttural. Not at all as though he was convinced. Or capitulating.

"We'd have to have ground rules," he said while she was scrambling to figure out what he needed so she could give it to him.

And it came to her. "I've got one. We only have sex at night, after we'd normally part to go to bed, and I don't sleep in your room. I have to be on alert out front, and checking cameras, every two hours."

He didn't respond.

"What about you? What are your rules?"

Did he have any? If he had some, did that mean he was going to agree to her plan?

Stomach clenching, chest tight, she waited. Not sure if a small part of her was hoping he'd refuse. What she'd proposed, what they'd do, carried some risk.

Which scared her.

Like, what if sleeping with him didn't cure what made her ache? What if she was really falling for the guy? Would having sex with him make it harder for her to leave him behind?

Did she want to have to wonder, for the rest of her days, what his lovemaking would have been like?

And what was life without taking risks?

She'd had that one drummed into her for most of her life. Mostly from the counselor she'd seen during her early teens.

Joe's silence was making her far too edgy.

Were they going to do it?

Were they?

"You have any rules, Joe?"

"One."

Oh, God. They were going to do it.

They were going to do it!

While her crotch flooded with wanting, she asked, "What's that?"

Who the hell cared? They were going to do it. That night. Leaving them a good part of a day to get through without doing it first.

"That it only happens in the rig. Period."

Kind of confused, based on her one rule, she said, "Of course."

His nod wasn't a happy one.

"Why?" she asked.

"Because I'm getting rid of the thing the second this is over."

Ah. He'd drawn boundaries.

Good ones.

Probably wasn't good that she was hurt by them.

Chapter Seventeen

Hell. He was in more hell. A different kind of hell. His body ached for one thing only, and he had about twelve hours to get through, undetected by anyone around him, surrounded by temptation on steroids, before he could get lost in whatever sublime universe McKenna took him to. She'd said nighttime only. Who knew the rule might kill him?

On the one hand, he couldn't believe his good luck.

On the other...sheer torture to a man who'd never felt the kind of connection he did to his temporary bodyguard. It was physical, for sure. With added sugar on top in that the woman herself intrigued him.

Unlike anyone he'd ever known or even imagined knowing.

He'd just gone inside for his laptop, thinking he'd spend the day sitting outside in their makeshift hideaway, focusing on the only thing that would be able to engross him at that point—getting his life back—when McKenna's phone rang.

Gut clenching, he took his seat beside her under the trees and waited, all thoughts of sex a distant memory.

"Yeah, hang on a second," she said, standing, motioning for Joe to precede her inside.

He knew when she put the phone on speaker and sat on the couch that Sierra's Web had more news for them. Weight settled upon him, as it did anytime his fraud case was involved.

Would his innocence ever be proven? Or would he go to the grave thought to be the man who'd cheated Bellair Software and its investors?

He had to believe in himself.

Believing was all he'd ever had, and he'd used it to climb out of some pretty deep hellholes.

"We've got a list of time stamps of fraudulent activity," Glen said as soon as McKenna let him know he was speakerphone. "Since we can't email, Joe, I'm going to read off the list for you to take down."

His laptop already on in front of him, Joe opened a new document.

And typed quickly, efficiently, as Glen read off names. Some known to him, some not, waiting for one to pop out. Just one. That was all they needed. A clue to who. Or to why.

When Glen finished, Joe looked back over the list. Nothing stood out. Not a single name on the list represented anything untoward.

"All of these people have better-than-average technical skills," Glen said. "Working with a tech company, one would expect that, so it's not surprising that the fraud was done with electronic modifications."

Yeah, but he wasn't a techie. He was an accountant. The boring guy behind the scenes crunching numbers so they could all create and sell innovative software solutions.

"Our problem is the timelines." Glen broke into his thoughts. "Based on what we know about the software updates for sales and narrowing down potential times the returns virus would have had to be loaded, based on when it hit, cross-checking with employee time cards, interviews and social media posts, we've determined that not one person on this list could have done this."

And they were back to him.

He was the one person who'd had access to his computer

any time of the day—or night, if he accessed it remotely. Yada yada. He'd heard it all in court. Over and over.

"Hud's team is looking at the theory that there's more than one employee involved." Glen's words came like all the others he'd shared on that call. Professional to the point of prosaic. Yet they hit Joe as an avalanche.

Looking back at the list, he read it again, not for any memories of anything that could have been considered questionable—even someone getting caught trying to cheat on overtime—but rather, for associations.

Others at Sierra's Web, like the personnel manager, would be better equipped to know who hung out with who—or had a beef with who, for that matter.

"Anyone on there you knew personally?"

As in, someone who'd been his accomplice?

"No." Again, not a techie. But he kept the thought to himself. Could be, probably was, that the experts were looking for someone with an axe to grind against Joe. He'd already been down that road long ago and had come up blank.

Back to square one.

The only way to get his name cleared was to find out who'd framed him.

Joe looked at the list in front of him so hard his eyes hurt. He could feel McKenna's presence on the other end of the couch as she listened to the conversation.

He needed to find something.

Anything.

That needle in the world's largest stack of hay...

"Colin Emerson and Jerry Webb worked on Stellar's lay down," he said as the two names seemed to meld together in front of his eyes. "They were team leaders during the trial period, given special overtime. And bonuses..."

And their names on that list meant they'd been present during the fraudulent activity...

"Got it," Glen said. "We'll dive deeper with them. See what we can find."

A flood of relief sailed through Joe. Even if the names brought nothing, he felt as though progress was being made.

"One other thing," Glen said and, steeling himself, Joe waited for the *here it comes* news. "A couple of people on my team are leaning harder and harder toward the Bellairs. I know they were completely cleared from the very beginning, but it's worth another conversation. I'd like to know your take on them."

"James, CEO, father to Julius and uncle to Mark, who are both VPs, and have seats on the board." Opening his mind to the trio wasn't easy. He'd spent months trying to wipe out the years' worth of memories he'd thought they'd built together.

If they'd framed him, though, he wanted to know. Had spent many, many sleepless nights going over facts and records, schedules and functions, more so than the investigators had done, and had come up empty.

As had all financial forensics regarding their bank accounts and spending habits.

Glen had Joe's notes on them, as well as the investigative case files.

He was asking for Joe's personal opinion. Everyone knew he'd hung with Julius and Mark like family.

"It makes zero sense that it would be them," he said, clearing his mind to find the facts—unhampered by pain of rejection. "Their company took a big hit over the scandal. They stood to make much more money just by continuing to do what they were doing."

If the teams were throwing out theories... "It seems to me that whoever did this felt as though they weren't getting their fair share of the wealth. Why else would you sabotage your own employer?"

"It's an angle we're looking at."

"And you'd see me, right?" Joe said before Glen could come right out and point the obvious finger. He'd asked the company to give the case a complete look—with carte blanche to investigate him as well. He'd figured it was the only way to prove what he hadn't done.

He'd never figured for having a woman he intended to bed sitting there hearing it all.

"You weren't being paid commensurate to CFOs of other Fortune 500 companies."

"I was young and new—they gave me, a nobody fresh out of college, a chance. The opportunity to excel and advance, and I did so more quickly than most in my field. They paid me far more than I'd have been worth anywhere else."

"In the beginning, yes, but where you were when all this went down?"

"I wanted stock options beyond what I could afford. That's what I asked for and what I got. What I still have, actually. I bought and sold Bellair stock with my own funds but never touched the shares the company gave me."

Glen, McKenna and the other Sierra's Web experts would believe him or not.

"I became quite wealthy working at Bellair. It makes more sense that whoever did this—you know, to take so many risks, tampering with various departments…it's like they went overboard to make the company look…vulnerable."

"It made a dent in their earnings, but they've already bounced back," Glen pointed out. "Notwithstanding whatever might happen in civil court with investors who lost millions."

Another fact he couldn't refute.

"All I can tell you is that James, Julius, Mark—they were like family to me, treated me like a son, a brother. They were always checking in to make certain I was happy, to be sure someone else wasn't going to steal me away from them…"

And it appeared that he'd burned them.

Hard as he tried, he couldn't show the lie to that image.

And was starting to wonder if he should just accept what was, cut his losses and get on with the rest of his life. He had his freedom. He had his health. He had his wealth. He had his degrees.

From there, he could choose any multitude of endeavors that would support the lifestyle that made him happy.

He just wouldn't have the respect that he'd fought tooth and nail to earn.

And McKenna would leave thinking she'd protected a criminal. Believing she'd been turned on by a thief.

The thought kept him glued to the fight.

Joe stood as McKenna disconnected from Glen's call. Phone reports were good, so far. There didn't seem to be any activity tracking their lines.

And while the #wheresjoenow hashtag was growing ever more popular, the Sierra's Web experts had found no credible recent photos or mentions of sightings that were close enough to their true location to be of concern.

There were more details surfacing about the game console Joe had stolen as a kid, along with new private sale listings of the type of games that he'd had on him when he'd been arrested. And an upsurge in the search for those old games. Some thought the key to where he'd be, and to proving what he'd done, would be found in the games he'd played.

As if he'd actually had a chance to play them before his father sold them for cash.

McKenna found the entire witch hunt excruciating. People didn't seem to care that Joe had been found not guilty, didn't even afford him the reasonable doubt he'd had before and during his trial. The hunt for Joe was a game in and of itself. A dangerous, debilitating game for the man whose life wasn't a game at all.

Sierra's Web had verified that Joe's father's last known residence was Alaska. Verified employment records for a fishery, and a Sierra's Web expert would be arriving in the little village to investigate further yet that day, under the guise of vacationing away from it all.

Before they'd ended the call, Glen had given Joe time stamps on various computer activities that his crew had compiled with the list of names, and Joe had agreed to go through them with the hope of finding a solid alibi for himself during any of the times mentioned.

Some of it was information that had already come out in court. Some of the times were newly discovered. Glen's team had already marked off the times coinciding with proof that Joe had been in the office. His list, the times they couldn't verify, was shorter.

And there he stood, open computer in hand, leaning against the counter as he studied the screen.

Feeling caged?

She would be.

Though, ironically, with him there, and in light of their recent conversation, she wasn't feeling at all shut in. Or trapped.

She was yearning to connect with him. To be there not just to protect him from death or physical harm, but to help with the mental/emotional tension if she could.

To protect his overall health as well as his life.

Not her job description. And yet...not entirely a stretch, either. Compassion was as much a part of the human experience as breathing.

"You're free to go if you'd like."

Startled, not in a good way, she looked up to see him watching her. "I thought we were through with all of that."

His shrug didn't seem to carry a lot of oomph. "Every report seems to sink me further," he pointed out. "I know you've never been convinced of my innocence, and with what happened out there... I just want it clear that you don't have to stay."

"I'm always free to quit my job," she said. "Or to take myself off a case."

She wasn't going.

"You're okay with sleeping with a thief?"

Those words, even given the circumstances, sent fire to her crotch.

"Okay, well, we won't be sleeping together. Rule number one. And beyond that, I'm attracted to your bod, Joe, not to..."

She wanted to keep it light. For both their sakes. But she couldn't finish the sentence.

"I know what I see," she said then. "The choices you're making, to pursue this case when you could take your money and run. The calm and control you exhibit every single time the phone rings with more inculpatory news. The way you thought of William—a total stranger—before yourself. The way you—a powerful, wealthy, self-made man—follow orders without question or complaint..."

The tender yet undeniable hunger in his kiss. She had to stop. If she didn't, she'd convince herself to fall in love with the guy.

"You said the Bellairs were like family to you..." His voice had changed when he'd mentioned the three men with whom he'd worked. There'd been...real emotion there. Hurt?

Sorrow?

For their betrayal?

Or his own?

The facts definitely pointed to the latter, but she couldn't put stealing from the family who'd given him his opportunities on the man she'd come to know.

"Yeah, they were like family."

"Just at work?"

Shaking his head, he glanced at his computer for a long minute, then set it down. And sat down in a chair pulled out from the kitchen table. Turning sideways, he leaned his hands on the back of the chair and faced her.

"You grew up in that world," he told her. "You know how the holidays go, the celebrations. There aren't many small family gatherings."

He was right, to a point.

"But you always have your inner circle."

He nodded. "I was invited, by James Bellair, CEO and others, to pretty much every gathering—didn't always choose to go."

But he went to all the big affairs. So not her. Completely opposite of her, in fact.

"James's wife died when Julius and his sister, Priscilla, were in grade school. He remarried when they were starting junior high. Sheila's nice, kind—she's just much younger than James and is a jet-setter. She's gone more than she's home. But then, he lives at the office. It works for them. Not so much for Priscilla. Julius and James both said she was a handful through high school—drugs, drinking...as she got older, her antics got more sophisticated, but last I knew, she was still out drinking all the time. The pertinent thing here is that she found it a fun pastime to flirt with me whenever Sheila wasn't around. Sheila would have called her out for it because she knew how hard I fought to be accepted on my own merit – not as the love interest of the daughter of the company's owner. So I avoided any smaller functions when Sheila was gone."

Wondering how Sheilia knew what mattered most to Joe, swallowing back the instant flash of jealousy, she asked, "Was Priscilla older or younger than Julius?" Hoping she sounded kindly interested. And nothing more.

"She's a year older."

She'd gone to school with a Bellair but didn't remember a girl. Or a Priscilla among any of the crowd she knew.

"I'm sure you know what I'm talking about," he continued. "The entitled, spoiled girl who thinks she can do no wrong, gets into trouble and generally makes life hell for her parents."

"I knew a few uppity kids, male and female, but there were a lot of nice kids at the club, too," she said.

"The Biltmore Country Club?"

"Yeah. Some of those kids grew up to be philanthropists, educators. One girl I knew fairly well is a neonatal specialist at one of the largest children's hospitals in the world, and another founded a Doctors Without Borders–type foundation, sending doctors all over the world to help communities that don't have regular medical care…"

Standing, he went to the refrigerator, grabbed a beer, nodding. "You don't have to sell me on the all the good done by society people in Phoenix."

Of course not. He was one of them.

And…it occurred to her, for a few minutes there, they'd been almost like normal people who could have met at the club. Chatting about things they knew. A society they both understood.

Except that she hadn't been to the Biltmore since she was fourteen.

More, she had absolutely no desire to ever go back. To that club, or any other part of that lifestyle.

Chapter Eighteen

By late afternoon, Joe was not only accepting of what was to come that night, he was champing at the bit to get to it. Every time McKenna moved, he thought about moving with her. Watching her face as he filled her with pleasure.

Mostly, he tried not to watch her at all. With his back to her, he spent most of the afternoon at the kitchen table, plugging times into various spreadsheets, all organized differently to give him clear, simple looks at situations. A spreadsheet for the returns virus, one of the sales program change, another for inventory changes—all cataloging times, employees on duty and ones with known technical skills who could have completed the job, whether they were on duty or not. After his call with Glen, he added Julius, his cousin Mark and James onto all three spreadsheets, just to compare timelines with times he knew for certain the three of them had been occupied at social gatherings.

Golf games.

Fishing expeditions on the yacht.

Just before the sun started to set, he added another spreadsheet for timelines. Listing all fraudulent activities across the top and filling in all applicable time frames into the rows below.

And then added one that listed all the downloaded online

banking transactions he'd amassed that did not match up to ones the prosecution had collected after his arrest. James, Julius and Mark were on those, too, along with him. That one was blankest of all. Only the four of them ever accessed online banking for the company.

Which meant that the only thing that made sense was the theory that whoever had defrauded Bellair had had an accomplice at the bank.

"Can you call Glen and have them check to see which employees have known association with Bellair's bank?" he called out without turning around to see what McKenna was doing.

"Yep." Her reply came right away, and he forced himself not to turn around.

Dusk had fallen, and McKenna had pulled all the blinds and turned on the lights by the time he found something. An anomaly he hadn't seen before.

Because he'd never seen timelines side by side on one sheet.

McKenna had put a plate of fresh-cut veggies with some ranch dip in front of him at some point. He'd munched away and turned to see an empty plate on the coffee table in front of her, too. He should have thought about dinner.

She could have mentioned it. Was writing on a spiral-bound tablet he hadn't seen before.

"Every single one of the fraudulent activities, including the many random changes made to inventory databases, either took place when the office was open or on Sunday mornings." He said the words aloud, felt energy coursing through him, but didn't know how to translate the information. "We need to call Glen again," he said.

McKenna tossed him the phone. He saw the opened camera app. Noticed a rabbit munching on a leaf in the corner of camera seven, minimized and pressed the numbers.

HE'D PUT THE phone on speaker. As soon as McKenna heard Joe talking about timelines adding up in accordance with him, but not in the way one would think, she put down her drawing pad and headed over to the table, uneasy without the cameras in front of her after a day of studying them intently.

Hundreds of thousands of hunters with Joe in their sights gave her a bad feeling.

Possible cops on the road with a BOLO bearing Joe's likeness was even worse.

And she felt the weight of them all more deeply, more personally, than any other danger in any other job she'd ever taken.

"Take out all times when the offices were open," he was saying to Glen. "Then take out the incidences that happened at night during scheduled maintenance hours. And what are you left with?"

"Sunday mornings."

"Right." Joe was nodding as though that explained everything.

"I don't get the significance." Glen voiced McKenna's own confusion.

"Unless there's an important function that I need to attend, a golf outing or breakfast where important business is set to take place, I am always home on Sunday mornings," he said. "It's sacred time."

Eyes wide, McKenna stared at him. He hadn't said religious or church time, but sacred time. She wanted more.

"Can you prove it? Phone calls? Home security system?"

Her heart started to pound as she continued to watch Joe, who was mostly studying his computer but was also shaking his head.

"That's just it," he said. "Sacred time is off time. No electronics. Obviously, my security cameras would be on, but I wouldn't be on them. I don't come and go from eight until eleven thirty on Sunday mornings."

"That's why you never had an alibi in court."

"The prosecutors gave my attorney a list of possible timelines. They all included hours in which I could have made the changes to the reports myself. They didn't know about the virus, the program rewrite. It was assumed I changed reports to reflect those anomalies that we now know were created by the techie stuff. But with this more specific information, with times nailed down...there's a definite pattern."

Nervous energy flowed through her. She could feel his excitement. She just couldn't find a good cause for it.

"Being home alone, without an alibi, doesn't help you, Joe," she blurted, tense from a day of calm in the midst of the bigger storm brewing around them.

If they didn't get him exonerated soon, the tornado was going to find them...

"It points to someone framing me," he said, looking at her for a second and then back at the phone. "There were other times the office was closed, Saturdays, Saturday nights, Sunday nights, but no, all the out-of-office incidents happened on Sunday mornings. A time when I would be home without electronics, meaning I'd have no alibi."

She sort of got it, but...

"It's the time I was sure to be most vulnerable."

He was so certain he was on to something big. She wanted it for him—wanted him to find the key that unlocked his invisible cell.

But...

"So, who knew?" Glen's question, his thinking tone, gave her hope.

"Only one person in the world would know that," he said, and her chest tightened. He *was* on to something. "My father," he said.

And then, hardly taking a breath, he continued, "I have no idea how any of this happened, how my father would ever gain access to anyone at Bellair or why he'd bother. It makes no sense to me. Not yet. But this is big," he said, sounding as though he'd bet his life on the fact. "My mother created sacred time. It was the one thing that never changed in my life. The one thing she fought for in our lives. No matter what my dad had going with us, no matter where we were, Sunday mornings from eight until eleven thirty were sacred. Off time, she said. No TV. No phone. No computers or games or cars. It was time for quiet, for peace, for rest. After she…died…sacred time was the one thing I fought my dad about. I didn't care what he did to me, I was observing sacred time…"

It was a stretch. A big one. But she did see that someone knowing that—someone who wanted to frame Joe for something—would see Sunday mornings as an opportune time.

"Someone could have just noticed your pattern of not being available on Sunday mornings," she pointed out when Glen said nothing, silently hoping that her boss would at least consider Joe's information possibly valid. Joe was so sure he was right. He'd come so alive, become so vital…a man who was making her feel more energetic just sitting with him.

A man whose hope was so fragile.

"I never told anyone I wasn't available. To the contrary, when something important came up, I accepted invitations. Yet none of the fraud happened at those times—when I would have had alibis. Only the Sundays when I was home. I already checked my schedule," he said. "Add that to the fact that someone knew what was inside my sealed record. It could be unrelated, I know. Could be someone in law enforcement eager to be someone in the #wheresjoenow game, but what if it isn't? There are two things now that seem to be coming into play that only my father would have known."

"I'll get the team delving into every person on our list, looking for any connection to Bellair Software and your father..."

"Thank you." Joe nodded, his expression alight and yet calm, too.

Raising her curiosity about the man he'd been. The man he would be again. Not the wealthy background, not the lifestyle, but the man.

And her whole body tingled, thinking about how much better she was going to get to know him...that night.

HE WANTED TO romance her with wine and a warm, gooey chocolate dessert. To undress her and soak in a tub that would massage them with spray nozzles.

To take her to eat at the Top of the Mountain. And dancing in the Buttes.

Or on a dinner cruise out to Catalina Island off the coast of California.

Just for starters.

Instead, Joe made spaghetti, his mother's recipe, and poured his beer into a glass instead of drinking it out of the bottle while she sipped on ice water, keeping constant watch on the camera app on her phone.

He'd gone over to turn on some good romantic mood music; the sound system had state-of-the-art speakers built in throughout the rig that could be turned on or off separately, as needed. But without the ability to stream, he had nothing to play.

For the first time in months, he felt like he was on the upswing.

Was in the mood for ambience. For the niceties he'd worked so hard to provide.

McKenna's brow was creased. Not with an all-out frown, but with the way she was watching her phone...

"You seem uneasy. Have you noticed something going on? Something suspicious?"

Shaking her head, she looked over at him and...smiled. An actual, natural, very real expression of...goodness.

It took his air, and his ability to swallow with it.

Desperate to maintain decorum, to not just grab her hand and pull her back to his bed, he glanced around the table. Alighted on her spiral notebook.

"What's this?" he asked, pulling it forward. When she shrugged and didn't argue, he opened it, expecting to see lined notepaper.

Curious as to what she'd write...notes about the job, he'd imagined.

Instead, the pages were originally blank and thicker than regular lined paper.

She'd been drawing. Views from outside the rig.

All done with minute precision.

And a soft beauty.

"Wow. These are great," he told her, totally impressed.

"They're how I commit to memory the area I'm protecting," she told him. "When I have to spend long hours sitting and watching. So my mind doesn't wander. So I don't get bored. And so I'll notice if even the smallest thing changes."

Like she stared at the camera images, now that she could keep them on full-time.

Reminding him that no matter how much of a breakthrough he felt he'd had that day, the danger still lurked, every bit as fueled as it had been, in the world all around them.

"Hopefully Glen will have some answers by morning," she said then, obviously thinking on the same wavelength as him. Not too difficult to figure out, with them discussing the fact that she was there because one of almost a million people could be lurking right outside their door at any moment.

Or a police officer could pull up to the door, demand access and be on the take.

With the amount of money involved in his case, the amounts the prosecution had thrown about that he'd made on his stock sale, his bonus proceeds, someone could be willing to buy a corrupt cop for the bigger payout.

Or worse, as Sierra's Web pushed more into the case, the real culprit could be desperate enough to stay anonymous that they'd pay a dirty cop to kill him.

There were people out there who'd be willing to justify the killing of a bad guy who'd been set free without paying for his crime…

"Sierra's Web experts are the best," she said then. "You know their story, right?"

He shook his head, picking up his fork again. No matter what the morrow brought, he had the now.

With her.

"The seven partners, they were friends in college," she told him, her eyes glowing with…fondness? Admiration?

Was it wrong to want her to look at him that way?

"That's nice," he said, more to please her than anything else. He'd had friends in college, too, Julius Bellair being one of them. But that hadn't won him his job at the company.

The right skills, work ethic and dedication had done that.

McKenna shook her head, sobered. "They met in a communications class. Had been put together as a team on a project but grew personally close. There'd been an eighth member. Her name was Sierra…"

He sobered then, too. Tuning in. "She didn't make it to a scheduled meet after a school break and they reported her missing, but no one took them seriously, saying she'd probably just changed plans. Her father wasn't worried. When she didn't show up by start of class, they went to a professor of theirs and told her their concerns. Long story short, the seven of them ended up working with the police, each bringing their own perspectives to the case. It was those seven different views of Sierra, the seven different interactions, that helped the police solve the case."

Joe's fork stopped on the way to his mouth. He'd had no idea… "So they found her. Obviously, she's part of the firm…" Even as he was saying the words, the truth hit him. There were only seven partners.

"They were too late." He guessed.

"She'd already been dead before they'd been due to meet. There was nothing they could have done at that point. But the important thing was that because of them, and their refusal to stop looking for answers until they found them, they solved her murder. They brought Sierra justice."

He sipped his beer. Feeling suddenly as though he had something more than just money on his case. Something more powerful.

Fanciful, and yet…

"They're going to bring you that same energy, Joe. That same refusal to quit until they find the answers they seek. That's just how we are."

We. She'd changed from *they* to *we.*

Because she was a part of them. She had her calling in life. Her place. Her family.

And he was lucky enough to have her sitting at dinner, alone with him, eating his spaghetti.

If all he got was that one dinner, he'd be forever thankful for it.

Chapter Nineteen

McKenna waited for Joe to finish in the bathroom and close himself into the back of the rig before heading to the shower. Normally she would have waited until early morning, since she was sleeping in her clothes, but no way she going to Joe's bed without fresh-smelling skin.

They both knew what was coming. He'd barely been able to contain himself after the dinner dishes were done. Sitting, jumping up to adjust a shade, or open the refrigerator only to close it again, and returning to his seat.

He'd lasted about fifteen minutes and then excused himself to shower and head to bed.

She didn't question his early retirement. He was beyond ready.

She was beyond the point of trying to rationalize or question. They'd established rules meant to protect them from residual emotional attachment. And she was so on fire, she knew she'd regret not experiencing everything Joe had to give her.

Her nipples tingled as she washed them, the water sluicing over her body massaging already-sensitized nerve endings. She'd never known a desire so all consuming, so compelling, that it took her over—body and mind...

"McKenna!"

Startled, with her head under the water, she slipped in the small tub, grabbed hold of the washcloth bar and shivered, mouth open as Joe opened the glass door and shoved a towel in at her.

"Glen called," she heard as she shut off the water. She'd left her phone on the sink, which was right outside his bedroom door.

"We have to get out—now."

She felt the whirr as the bedroom slide moved inward, and she catapulted into action. By the time she'd hurriedly dried off and pulled clean clothes on over her still-damp body, Joe, in a clean pair of tan shorts and a brown shirt, was already outside.

"You don't ever leave the rig without me checking things first," she bit out, completely out of sync, as she scrambled to get from sensual woman to bodyguard in a matter of seconds.

"Glen said leave now," he relayed, his near whisper filled with urgency. "I'm figuring it's less of a risk for me to get the car hooked up than it is to wait around for someone to get here."

She handled the hookups. He got the car's front tires ramped. By the time they'd climbed back into the rig, the slides were in place.

"Leave the kitchen stuff," Joe said as he climbed behind the wheel of the rig.

Doing as he said, she buckled herself into the captain's chair beside him. "Tell me exactly what Glen said."

He was pulling out, using only the rig's less bright driving lights until they'd reached the end of the access road and were turning on to the entry ramp for the highway. As he switched on the headlights and sped up, he said, "Someone noticed tracking activity pinging off the cell towers, and subsequently the numbers, used by Sierra's Web. And then traced those to numbers called..."

Going cold with dread—a little bit of wet hair fallout—she guessed, "They've got my number."

"I've already destroyed the phone—Glen's orders. They're pretty sure the tracking got only as far as the cell tower we were pinging off, not our exact location."

Keeping a watch for anything and everything, including police cars, McKenna felt sick. Her entire body tensed as she thought over facts, tried to figure out a plan.

If they were stopped by a dirty cop, she had no way to alert anyone.

No emergency contact method.

She had a gun. Her knife.

Her training.

The cop would have all three as well.

They couldn't live on the road as they'd done the first couple of days they'd been together. With possibly billions of peoples on the hashtage now, that would be too much risk.

Another obscure park somewhere?

Could they get lucky enough to find a place, in a hurry, that offered the same privacy as the one they'd just left? What were the chances of finding a site buried in trees at the end of a road?

She knew the answer even as she silently asked it. Slim at best.

With both hands on the wheel, Joe sat up straight, staring at the road ahead. He hadn't said a word since he'd entered the closest highway ramp, which would lead them to a major east-west highway.

Grasping for the best plan, even a good plan, in the twenty minutes she had before they reached the expressway, she suddenly just knew.

With a calm that was more her style, she told Joe to turn left before he reached the major highway. Perhaps they'd have less chance of someone coming to their aid if they were attacked on a dark two-lane country highway through the desert, but they'd also have that many fewer eyes on them.

"This road connects with one other and will lead us east, and then in about an hour and a half we'll be heading south," she said, all business. "We're keeping to side roads and should reach our destination not long after midnight. The route is often traveled by RV vacationers who want a more scenic route and less traffic to deal with, so our passing shouldn't raise curiosity. Plus, no semis."

She was half thinking out loud. Half giving him the explanation he deserved.

"Where's our destination?"

Right. She'd failed to mention that part. "Shelter Valley."

His glance toward her was quick, turning sharply back to the road. "The town where your father lives?" She could see his frown from the lights on the dash.

"And my brothers, actually, too. They've got land at the edge of town. We can camp out there, at least until we have time to assimilate."

"I'm not bringing my danger to your family."

"It's our best chance, Joe. We'll keep our distance from them, so if anyone does find us they don't also find them. The land is outside town central, off a dirt road. Dad has a cabin out there, so we'll have electricity to hook up to. The biggest problem is going to be dumping and filling the holding tanks, but we'll figure that out..."

Mind buzzing with details—like how she was going to alert her family—McKenna kept her eyes focused between mirrors, the terrain on both sides of them and the road ahead. Energy sluiced through her as she sat poised to fly into action at any provocation. Her gun was loaded. Her seat, higher up than any other vehicle's would be, gave her a better vantage point for shooting.

"You have brothers."

Seemed so long ago that she'd told him the little bit about her private life she'd been willing to share. Hard to believe that she'd been so closed off to him that he didn't know about Jackson and Kierland.

"Two," she told him, wanting him to know on a far more personal level than because he was heading toward their hometown. It felt wrong, Joe not knowing her as she knew him.

"They're biologically my half-brothers," she continued. Their old way of driving in total silence wasn't right anymore. They'd become a team, the two of them.

A professional, working team.

One with enough trust between them to share certain confidences.

Like partners on the police force, putting each other's lives in each other's hands every day. Living in such close quarters, as they'd been doing, you get to know someone more quickly.

And if maybe her life wasn't in his hands, only his was in hers, the difference seemed minimal out there in the dark of the middle of nowhere...

Silence had fallen again. He hadn't asked any questions.

Which bothered her, where before, she'd have been appreciative.

"My dad was a widower when he met my mom," she said. It was fair that Joe know some of what he was getting into. "He owns a small construction company, but back when Mom and Dad met, he worked as a framer. My grandparents were adding a small garden cottage to their property, and Dad was foreman for the job. That's when he met my mom."

"And your grandparents didn't approve," Joe said then, understanding in his voice. "They gave her an ultimatum, and when she chose him, they disowned her."

Like she'd known, he understood that world.

"Thinking, of course, that she'd eventually come to her

senses," she added. "Instead, she married my dad, moved to Shelter Valley, and adopted Jackson and Kierland."

"How old were they when you were born?"

"Seven and nine," she told him. "They're both married, with kids, and in business with my dad, Meredith and Sons Construction."

He'd settled back in his seat, had one hand on the wheel, one on his thigh.

For a second there, with a brief flash of memory of what she'd thought would be going on that night, she was jealous of that thigh.

But mostly, as they traveled alone through the night, she welcomed the easy talking between them.

In a strange way, the conversation seemed almost as intimate as having sex.

As much as Joe disliked being on the run, having anger and the threat of death constantly at his back, as unsure as he was about his reception in the town McKenna loved, about the rightness of him even agreeing to go there with her, he wasn't hating the drive.

They'd gotten far enough away from any cell tower they might have pinged that it would be anyone's guess where they'd gone. And with the twists and turns McKenna was having him take on various winding back roads, he didn't even think he would be able to follow their tracks. Meaning, it wasn't a route anyone would expect to find them on.

Or be looking for them on.

"So technically, your brothers are your grandparents' step grandchildren," he said, trying to absorb as much of McKenna's dynamics as he could in their short time together. To figure her out enough that she didn't linger as the mystery she'd been to him since the moment she'd pinned him at his own front door.

"Technically." The one word spoke volumes. None of them good.

"I take it they didn't welcome them into the fold?" He understood why moneyed society had to remain closely protective. There were always people out to bilk you out of it. And if they'd gotten bad vibes from Kyle Meredith, thought he was out to use their only child for her money...

"That was my second hard lesson in life," McKenna told him, still diligently watching their surroundings.

The woman didn't ever stop—which would lead to her expert status, he recognized, trying to take a step back from the pain he'd just heard in her voice.

They were mind and body mates for a brief time.

Not heart-to-heart mates, ever.

He didn't ask for details.

But couldn't stop himself from listening, or ask her to stop, when she started telling him anyway.

"Jackson was always really artsy," she told him, filling in more blanks for him. "He got involved in a modern dance company in high school and won an opportunity to spend the summer in New York, training with one of the greats. He was eighteen at the time..."

"Making you nine?"

"Yeah." Glancing over her right shoulder, she was silent for a moment, then turned back.

"Everything okay?"

"Just a coyote."

Because she checked out every single movement.

"Anyway, Kierland was only sixteen, and in baseball, and Dad just didn't have the money to pay for New York room and board for the entire summer. To me it was a no-brainer. I was so certain my grandparents would at least loan him the money—they never spoke poorly to me about Dad or my brothers when I was little—that I told him they would."

Joe took a deep breath, knowing where the story was going. "They refused," he said.

"They gave me a lecture about the kind of life I was born to live, about being responsible to the wealth, about how I'd be a target, that there'd always be someone wanting handouts and that it was my first lesson in how to be strong enough to say no. I was so shocked, I went to my room and refused to come out until the next morning," she said, her reminiscence laced with sadness. "By that time I had a plan," she told him. "I'd already emptied all the piggy banks on my shelf—I got one each year for my birthday—and for the next couple of months saved all of my allowance, and went without lunch at school so I could save all of my lunch money, and then, with the help of our housekeeper, I took it all to the bank and cashed it in. I collected enough that Jack could come up with the rest. He took a custodial job and worked nights and weekends after dance classes."

Joe smiled, admiring her innovativeness, her sacrifice, at such a young age. "Your dad and brothers knew what you'd done?"

"Of course not. Neither Dad nor Jack would have taken the money if they'd known. They still think my grandparents sent the money home with me."

"Didn't they thank them? And find out then?"

"Jack sent a letter. I never heard about it arriving."

If it were possible for Joe to hold her in any higher esteem, picturing the nine-year-old girl who'd found a way to live two lives with an open heart, did it for him.

Just as he sometimes ached for his eight-year-old self, the hard lesson he'd learned that year, he ached for little McKenna.

There had to be a reason they'd been thrown together. Two kids who'd lost their mothers young.

Who'd learned tough life lessons a year or two before they'd turned double digits.

Maybe, just maybe…

"I later realized that they'd been scared to death about my exposure in Shelter Valley, a young girl with a big heart. And they'd also been bitter. They blamed my dad for taking my mother away from them. It was either that or blame themselves for disowning her when it was too late to do anything about it…"

And…there was the rub. His world, her eschewing it.

It had to have been impossibly difficult for that little girl, living and loving in both lives. Had to have taken a huge toll. One that had culminated in the restrictions put on her time with her grandparents. They could see her but no longer expose her to their society. Their lifestyle.

She'd reached a point where she'd no longer been able to live two lives.

And she'd chosen the one she wanted.

With a resigned acceptance Joe had mastered far too young, he saw more clearly than ever why he and McKenna would never, ever have a life together outside their shared moment in time.

She was working for him.

And when the job was done, they were going to part ways forever.

Chapter Twenty

McKenna thought she'd be a lot more nervous driving into Shelter Valley with Joe. While on edge due to the danger, she was feeling fine about introducing him to her dad and brothers. They were proud of her abilities, respected the work she did, and if ever she was going to bring a client to meet them, it would be Joe.

Because he was a client, not her man, that made it much easier.

They'd been so overtly pushy in their grilling of any guys she'd brought home during high school and college that she'd made a point of keeping her dating and family lives separate.

She had a lot of practice at it—living separate lives, and keeping the various sides of herself apart.

Where she got edgy, oddly enough, was in Joe's reaction to the town that she loved like none other. Directing him straight toward her father's cabin, rather than through town, given that it was after midnight and her number-one goal was keeping Joe anonymous, she found herself chattering.

"Shelter Valley is known for acceptance. No matter who you are or what your past might have been, if you want to live an honest life, among people who help each other out, this is the place to be. Our sheriff, Greg Richards, he's taken on mountain men, thieves, a kidnapper, a member of the mob, you name it, and he manages to rally troops and keep everyone safe. Greg's wife, she just showed up in town one day with a child, and without a single memory as to who she was, who the child was or why she had a little one with her...and one of our college professors came to town on the run from her abusive ex. She pretended to be her older sister, taking her sister's new job, after he'd killed her sister..."

Why should it matter to her what he thought of them? Or how his wealthy eyes would view them by light of day?

They passed a mansion softly lit in the distance, an estate that could easily rival any that McKenna had ever been in, and she quickly pointed that out to Joe, as though she needed him to know that even by his standards, her town could measure up. "The Montfords live there," she told him. "They founded Shelter Valley. Their daughter-in-law, Cassie, is the town's vet. She was their son's high school sweetheart, but before they were even engaged, he left her pregnant and went to join the Peace Corps. She subsequently miscarried their baby. He had a lot of nerve, coming back years later with a child in tow, but he'd grown up. Learned about life and begged everyone to give him a chance to make amends. Turned out the child belonged to friends of his who'd been killed, and he'd adopted her. He's now on city council. And married to that high school sweetheart."

She could go on and on about the lost and hurting souls who'd been welcomed and healed in her hometown. "Becca, our mayor of more than twenty years, is married to the president of Montford University," she told him, remembering that he'd asked her about the school. "They had miracle babies in their forties, and those kids are now students at Montford."

All the while she talked, she kept every single thing in the immediate vicinity outside their rig on her radar. Knowing the area like she did, she'd notice anything out of place.

"I'm not taking any chances, mind you," she told him, uneasy about his continued silence. "I can't vouch for every kid on social media, nor am I going to risk your life by making your presence here known..."

So why had she just babbled about how the town protected those who came needing help? His personal opinion couldn't matter to her.

She couldn't let it.

It wasn't even like she lived in Shelter Valley anymore. She'd moved to Phoenix when she'd joined Sierra's Web.

She didn't quite breathe a sigh of relief when they made the turnoff to her father's cabin without anyone on the road behind them. Or coming at them, either. There'd be no good reason for anyone to be out on the dead-end rural road that late at night.

"Stop," she told Joe just after he'd made the turn. Jumping down out of her seat, she went to the trash barrel that sat at the side of the road and put the ten-pound boulder that sat on the ground beside it up on the barrel.

And that's when she started to feel...a bit less worried. "My dad lives right down the road," she told Joe. Because he'd need to know soon enough. "He bought this property after I graduated from college. He's had plans drawn up to turn the cabin into his dream home but hasn't had the money to make it happen yet. But he drives by it every day on his way to work. The rock on the barrel is the sign to him that someone is using his place."

"Meaning?" With both hands on the wheel, Joe was sitting forward, moving at about a five-miles-an-hour pace over the washboard road—and frowning.

She was just glad that he'd finally spoken.

"He'll be knocking on the door at daybreak," she told him, "which is when he generally heads into work. I intend to ask him to get to Phoenix, to the home of a friend of mine who works for the firm, someone he knows, and have that person let Glen know where we are. Unless someone is tracking my dad, no one will know about the contact. I'll have him pick up another burner phone for us. There are several people here in town who commute to Phoenix daily. We'll set up a communication chain from there—so that no calls will track from Sierra's Web to Shelter Valley, but from people who work in Phoenix home to Shelter Valley. Except that they'll be calling us, not home. There's only one cell tower in the area, so it'll all ping the same."

Driving around a small mountain peak, a hill by Arizona standards, they'd reached the cabin. McKenna rolled down her window, heard the creek flowing. "In the summer, the creek's nearly dry, but after the monsoons, and through the winter, there's water flowing..." she said, having a hard time keeping the smile out of her voice.

Joe turned off the engine and was out of his seat, putting out the slides. Probably eager to get to bed and sleep. They'd been up since before dawn. He'd been driving for hours under tense situations.

And she'd just told him her father would be there in what amounted to less than five hours.

"We're good with the generator until morning, right?" she asked. They'd be one night without access to the cameras. She'd need to do at least two perimeter checks and set an alarm on her watch.

"We've got a built-in natural gas generator. We're good for a few days, at least."

He'd said *we've.*

Coasting off her *we're,* but still...he'd gone with it.

She'd liked hearing it.

And then he moved toward the back. She'd known he

would. Had been expecting it. Waiting for it so she could brush her teeth and get some rest, too. Her spirits still dropped.

All day long she'd anticipated that they'd be sharing a bed that night...

Probably best that fate had intervened.

A sure sign that she'd been on the wrong path.

And when the pocket door closed him in the small bathroom, as it had done every night they'd been together, she told herself she was thankful she'd been saved from making a grave mistake.

Waiting for her turn so she could get to bed.

The forward door opened, bathroom light still on, as Joe slid his own door open. She glanced up at him. Saw him standing there.

Completely naked. And clearly not focused on sleep.

"You coming?" he asked, his gaze boring into her.

As though in a trance, her body flooding with desire and her heart floating somewhere outside herself, McKenna smiled and was already pulling her shirt off as she headed toward him.

THE WOMAN WAS every fantasy he'd ever had rolled into one and coming true. She'd said she had to come to him, and so while his hands yearned to help her undress, he remained at the door of his room, watching her strip as she approached.

Her shoulders, soft–looking, slender, hid such strength, and the dichotomy aroused him. Mouth dry, he watched her reach back to unhook her bra. Waited. Aching so hard he started to spill.

Stared.

And stared some more.

The soft mounds were...everything a man could want. Not huge, but more than a handful, which was as large as he liked them. Her nipples, hard for him, pointed straight at him, as though naming him as their pleasurer. He was right there, reaching, as she approached him, and he brushed those nipples, but his hands slid around her bare upper body, pulling her into him, warm skin to warm skin, as his mouth—starved since it had left hers at the tree—sought life-confirming sustenance.

So much danger, so much hate and betrayal. Someone framing him. His father... None of it mattered when McKenna's arms closed around him.

She knew it all. She held it all. And wanted to take him into her, too.

Pushing him down to the bed, she climbed on with him, her knees straddling one of his legs, those breasts moving toward him, but he staved her off. Wanted a level playing field. And reached for the waistband of her pants.

Undid them. His penis giving a jump as he saw the lace edging on the low-cut pink panties she wore. With two fingers, he played with that lace. Reached to both hips and started to pull downward. Her hands covered his, helping him until he saw pubic hair, and part of a butt cheek, and then halting his motion.

He swallowed back a choking sound as everything in him cried out. And he lay there, hands off.

If she needed to stop, so did he.

No questions asked.

She didn't slide off the bed, just rolled to her left hip beside him, reached down to her ankle, and...came up with her gun. Handing it to him.

Oh hell...what the sight of that unholstered gun did to him...what it shouldn't have done to him. It wasn't a toy. Was absolutely not there for anything fun. Hard as a cement wall anyway, he took it and set it gently on the nightstand.

And donned a condom.

Getting her pants the rest of the way off her was a joint venture. He took care of the ankle holster, kissing up her leg as he did so.

And then she was on top of him again, pushing his shoulders back to the mattress and then running those incredibly strong, so slim fingers all over his chest, playing with his nipples, running through his chest hair.

He was going to die before they finished. Nothing that exquisite could exist on earth.

So much to touch. To explore. To taste.

She planted her lips against his, her thighs straddling him, and way before he was ready to be done, plunged herself down on him.

Crying out with pleasure, he felt her soft, warm cushion against his engorged penis, taking all of him deep inside. He forced himself to remain still in spite of the need to pull out and head back in, to get that embrace again and again.

"Oh, Joe, you're… This…" Throwing her head back, she arched, giving him a different angle inside her. And thrusting her breasts out to his happy-to-accommodate hands.

"Move with it," he urged softly. Wanting her to take every ounce of pleasure she could.

"I don't want it to end." Even as she said the words, her body pulled up on his, and he grabbed her hips lightly, not guiding, just riding along as she plunged back down, and then again.

And again.

He couldn't think. Could just see her. Feel her. Want her more than he'd wanted anything in his life.

And needed the moment to last forever, too.

He heard her cry.

Felt her pulse.

And exploded.

MCKENNA COULDN'T LOOK at him. Couldn't fall down to his chest and hold on tight. She hung her head back as she recovered a sense of self, blinking back the tears that welled from an overload of incredible emotion.

The one thing that wasn't allowed in that room.

As soon as she could trust herself to speak, she sat up. Smiled at him—a saucy smile befitting the moment. Because she couldn't let it go bad.

She might only have the one memory, and she would not have it smirched.

"Duty calls," she said, sliding off from him.

Grabbing her clothes and gun, she scooted to the pocket door and into the bathroom. Had it almost closed behind her when she heard his soft, deep, "Come again, anytime."

And filled with a need she feared was never going to leave her system.

JOE HAD THE most incredible night. Dreaming awake—and sleeping deeply, too. His bodyguard visited him a second time, after she'd made rounds, lying down next to him, already naked, and stroking him awake with distinctly mimicked moves on his penis. He'd been on top that time. Had shown her his moves. And she cried out even louder than their first coupling when he coaxed the finale out of her.

He'd hated having her leave him.

Knew that her doing so meant she could come back again, and sent her a sleepy invitation to repeat at her pleasure.

The next thing he knew, there was a loud banging on the door of the rig.

Flying out of bed, getting into shorts, sans underwear, and pulling a shirt from the drawer by the bed, he grabbed his hammer and ran the three steps into the kitchen.

Getting there just in time to hear the door of the rig shut. His bodyguard was nowhere in sight.

If McKenna was in trouble...

Throwing open the door, he prepared to take whatever action necessary, and found himself looking down at the curly redheaded woman who'd had sex with him during the night—twice—hugging a man every bit as tall as and broader than Joe was.

Quite a bit older than Joe, too, based on the gray-peppered hair that was otherwise pretty much the same curly red as McKenna's—just shorter. The eyes—brown and every bit as expressive as his recent lover's—were fixed on him.

Clearly sizing him up.

"You're up!" McKenna turned, probably hearing the door open—or maybe sensing the immediate change in what had to be her father. "Let's get inside, then," she ordered, leaving Joe little choice but to back up as she charged right for him.

Sliding his hammer along the wall by the sink, Joe headed for the bathroom. Gave father and daughter time to greet, to acquaint. Gave McKenna the chance to explain Joe in whatever way she felt a need to do.

He could hear their voices, but with the bathroom's exhaust fan blowing couldn't make out the words. Didn't want to.

Still stinging from Bellair's rejection, and trying not to think at all about the possibility that his own father could be complicit in the hell that had become Joe's life—again—he wasn't feeling all that favorable toward fathers.

Not for him.

Ablutions done, including a fresh shave, hair back in its ponytail, tats still going strong, Joe added underwear beneath his shorts and went to meet the man who'd fathered the most incredible woman he'd ever met.

The man his bodyguard hoped would agree to help them get Joe out of one hell of a mess.

Chapter Twenty-One

McKenna might have felt a bit…nervous…having her father and Joe meet after the night she'd just spent with the accountant who'd fallen from grace, but one look at Kyle Meredith's face once he'd stepped into the rig and all thoughts of anything personal fled.

The second she'd told him Joe's name, he'd let her know he'd heard about the case.

She'd quickly filled him in on what she and Joe were doing there, what they needed from him.

"Give me the address and I'll get there," Kyle said, and then, his gaze tightening, added, "Just tell me one thing. Do you believe he's innocent?"

She didn't doubt for a second that her father would do whatever she asked of him, regardless of her answer, and she told him honestly, "My heart believes he is."

It was more honesty than she'd given herself.

Or Joe.

The latch clicked on the pocket door and the door slid open before her father had a chance to respond. He reached out a hand to Joe, though, as Joe came to stand by them in the doorway.

So odd, watching her father—in his jeans, work boots and T-shirt—shake hands with Joe Hamilton. In all the years she'd lived in two worlds, she'd never, ever seen her father's hand clasped by her grandfather, or anyone else from that world.

"We need to talk," Kyle said then, glancing between the two of them. "Your brothers—" he nodded toward McKenna, but kept Joe in the conversation with eye contact as well "—have been following the #wheresjoenow hashtag since it came out that Sierra's Web was involved. They figured, with your familial associations…"

He didn't finish the sentence. Just shrugged.

"It's okay, Dad, Joe knows about Mom. He knows who my grandparents are."

With a nod, and a concerned frown, Kyle continued, "A new post went viral overnight. Said that though it's not listed on their site, Sierra's Web has bodyguard experts on staff and asked if anyone knew who Joe's was."

She swore. Loud and clear. "It won't be long before I'm the prime suspect," she said.

Joe followed up immediately with, "That's it, you're fired and I'm out of here."

"I'd think twice about that if I were you," Kyle said, standing shoulder spread to shoulder spread with Joe. "You're in a world of hurt, and there's nobody better able to protect you than McKenna and her team."

While McKenna glowed with love for the man who'd fathered her, he turned to look at her. "I'll stop by and see the sheriff on my way out of town. He'll get a group together to assist you in whatever way you need."

Her nod was as firm and professional as always, but her smile trembled a little. Kyle probably noticed but didn't call her on it as he turned back to Joe. "I have one requirement from you."

Gaze piercing and yet respectful-looking, Joe said, "I'm listening."

"Don't go getting all he-man here and barreling out with

hammers to fight bullets. You do that, you put my daughter's life at stake, 'cause then the subject she's protecting is in open range. Got it?"

"Yes, sir."

"You'll follow every order she gives, no testosterone-induced superhero antics?"

"I will."

"Good, then I have another question."

"What's that?" Hands in his pockets, Joe seemed to relax a bit, and McKenna bit her lip when the thought struck that Joe seemed to like her dad. A wave of happiness shot through her.

She shoved it away sharply. When it lingered, she allowed that her dad deserved the respect Joe was giving him, and it just felt good to see that.

Tuning back in, she heard something about Joe having a pair of jeans and wore a size-ten boot.

"Good, we'll get you outfitted. The boys are working on a new build, up Old Hill Road. They'll put you to work. Kenna can get you there."

What! "Dad! What's Joe going to do at a construction site?"

"I'm a licensed plumber and electrician."

Mouth wide-open, her gaze shot to him. "You're a what now?"

With a shrug, turning back toward his tiny bedroom, he stopped long enough to say, "I didn't have a scholarship to college, and no way was I going to start my life out in that much debt. I worked all through high school on construction sites. Just made sense to get licensed and keep working part-time…"

Joe shut the pocket door behind him, and she turned to her dad.

"Your brothers did a deep dive on him. The licensing came

up. Could have been a different Joe Hamilton, but they found an address that confirmed it was him."

"You want me out at the site where Jackson and Kierland can keep an eye out in case I need help," she challenged, trying to hide her shock—and hurt—at not knowing such a huge thing about Joe. She'd told him her brothers were in construction. That they had their own business.

"I don't sell you short, Kenna," Kyle said. "You've proven over and over that you're fully capable, an expert in your field, by Sierra's Web terms, but you're still just one person and this Joe guy—he's got armies out after him at the moment."

"Most of whom are just playing an online game for their own entertainment."

"But if there are even two angry people who take this up, who both find out from the same post where he is, and head up here at the same time from opposite directions..."

He didn't have to tell her what she was up against. She already knew.

"The idea is to not have to take any of them on," she reminded him. "My job is to keep Joe away from them. To stay one step ahead."

"And where better to do that than a construction site up on a mountain?"

He was right, of course. Completely right. Her view of anyone approaching would be extremely valuable.

And if Joe was busy with her brothers, she wouldn't have to worry about keeping her hands off him, either.

Watching him in a hard hat and jeans, though...

With a nod, she hugged her father, whispered in his ear to be safe in Phoenix, and heard his own whispered "be safe" back.

She might not share her home with anyone, but as far as family and love went, she was one of the wealthiest people she knew.

JACKSON AND KIERLAND Meredith didn't start out to be as open to having Joe around as her father had been eager to have him on their site.

Having just made the twenty-minute trip straight up—maneuvering sharp turns around the mountain the whole way—with McKenna more distant than she'd been in a while, he might have been a bit more sensitive to her brothers' lack of enthusiasm than he otherwise would have been.

"What's eating you?" he asked her as, after stiff introductions, he sat down to put on the new boots that he'd just paid Kierland back for.

"You knew my family was in construction but didn't bother mentioning that you share their skills? You think it's beneath you or something? Or maybe I'm just such a brief blip in your life that you thought finding similarities in our lives wasn't worth the time?"

Had their situation not been so fraught with tension, with watch-over-your-shoulder-every-second fear, with mistrust abounding from all directions and with the memory of the most incredible night that wasn't supposed to mean anything—he might have teased her out of the frown she was wearing.

"I helped build the home I live in," he told her instead, giving her a straight stare and total honesty. "And if you saw the inside, you'd see that I'm constantly making improvements, even where they aren't needed. It's what I do in my private time. In my alone time. My me time. It's how I both honor and remember the young man who grew me into the man I am today."

She blinked. Looked like she might be tearing up. Nodded.

And he made his escape only to find himself flanked by the two older Meredith siblings. They were at his side, at least one of them, for most of the day—giving him up to McKenna during lunch as they shared catering-service sandwiches that her brothers had brought up with them that morning.

"I'm guessing you're a little bored," he said as he hungrily devoured a roast beef and tomato on thick, freshly made bread.

"No," she told him, eating more slowly, keeping a watch on the road leading up the mountain. "I've been using the new burner phone Dad brought up to speak with Glen via a very busy coffee shop he never goes to. And I've spoken with Sheriff Richards, as well, via the new phone. So far, things are going according to plan."

She gave no more. Sensing her unusual mood—hoping it wasn't induced by their activities in his bed the night before—he didn't ask questions.

They ate in silence after that. She didn't elaborate on her report, nor did she ask how his day was going, what he was doing or anything about her brothers.

So he didn't offer the information.

He did thank her, though, as he stood up to get back to the faucets he'd been installing. The house had twelve of them, all told, laundry room included. He hoped to have them all complete by day's end.

"Just doing my job." McKenna didn't even look at him as she replied. He caught a glimpse of the phone she was studying, though. And understood when he saw that she'd already loaded the camera app and was currently checking the screens showing her the rig by her father's cabin.

The woman left nothing to chance.

Mostly, he was glad about that.

But where it left them, as two bodies comingling, he didn't want to guess.

McKenna watched Joe saunter back to the house where her brothers and the rest of their crew were sitting on a half wall eating lunch.

She would have to get the sexiest man alive as a client.

Waiting to hear from Glen, she'd had to force down her sandwich through a dry throat. Because every time she looked at Joe's hands, his legs—hell, any part of him—she flew right back to the night before. Feeling what she'd felt.

And Glen had stopped midsentence during their call, saying he'd have to get back to her.

Something had happened. She didn't know what.

So had no way to know if Joe was in further danger or not. Figuring the top of the mountain, with her brothers—both of them fit enough to take most men—close by was about as safe as she could get him, she did what she could.

Kept keeping watch.

While intermittently thinking about life. Her life. Her future. The summer Jackson had danced in New York, he'd met a lot of important people. Six months later, at home in Shelter Valley, he'd had a call, a job offer, a part in a Broadway play. Her father had just taken on a new, bigger project with the construction company and needed Jackson's help to keep costs down. And Jackson was in love. He'd turned down the job, eventually married, become a partner in Meredith and Sons, and had a son of his own.

She, on the other hand, was living her dream. Doing the work she loved.

Making her life count in the way that most mattered to her. Saving other people from the horror her mother had suffered. Because the world should be a place where good, loving people could be happy...

Staring at the road down the mountain, she had her phone in hand and was pressing the answer button the second it rang.

Two minutes later, she was in the partially built house, interrupting what looked to be a pretty intense private conversation between Kierland and Joe in a very luxurious upstairs bathroom.

"Joe." She announced herself before she got close enough to overhear them. The last thing she needed at the moment was to have to tell her brother to back off.

Joe was a client. Not a potential 'Kenna suitor.

The two broke apart equally, as though both were guilty of doing something that would anger her. She didn't have the energy for it.

"Let's go," she said, the urgency she was feeling creating a tightness in her gut that wasn't good. "Glen needs to speak with you." Barely sparing an apologetic glance at her brother for stealing his worker, leaving him with a job undone, she led the way out to the little car.

Having him sit in the back passenger side, hunkered down, just in case, she took the driver's seat and said, "He's getting to another location, to avoid tracking, since all anyone will get is the one Shelter Valley cell tower. There'd have to be multiple calls to or from one other tower to even get their interest..." She was babbling. Just sitting there. She'd drive if she had to, but until then... She glanced back at him, saw him lounging on a diagonal slant so that he was facing her. Watching the side of her face when she wasn't turned toward him.

She could feel him there.

She so badly needed to connect to the man who'd played her body so beautifully the night before that it scared her.

And lashed out with, "What were you and Kierland talking about back there?" For good measure, she pinned him with her stare that brooked no argument.

Expected him to prevaricate, and was shocked when she was held with an equally powerful stare.

"Why didn't you tell me why you can't be around wealthy society?"

She needed to swallow. Couldn't swallow. Couldn't look away from him.

And then did.

"He had no business telling you about that."

"He thought I already knew."

That brought her gaze back to him. "Why would he think that?"

"He started to grill me, like I was…let's say…more than just a client—a big brother routine unlike anything I've ever seen—even on television."

With a downturned smirk, she harrumphed. Rolled her eyes. Would have apologized except that… Kierland went from protective big brother to spilling her beans?

"And?"

"I couldn't very well look him in the eye and deny that we might have…noticed each other…so I said what I thought would end the conversation immediately. I told him that we'd established from day one that our worlds won't ever converge. I told him I knew that you wanted nothing to do with my lifestyle."

She saw it coming. Felt her lower lip trembling.

"You were there. You heard what the guy was saying to your mother. The man had done some gardening at your grandparents' place. Knew who she was. He wanted money. A lot of it. Insisted that he was being reasonable. What he was asking for would be nothing compared to the Whitaker fortune. She kept telling him that she'd been disowned. That she didn't have anywhere near the kind of money he wanted her to withdraw from various automatic teller machines…"

Tears welled. She was on the job. Couldn't let them fall.

"Your mother was killed solely because she came from wealth."

EVEN AS JOE said the words, he was hoping McKenna would tell him they weren't true. The only way…he didn't know what…but to never see her again…

She didn't deny them. Sitting rigid, facing the windshield

that pointed toward the road down the mountain, her shoulders stiff, she just sat there.

"And after years of being forced to live in that same wealthy environment, you had a breakdown." He said the rest. "That day you drove to Shelter Valley without permission...you refused to leave your father's house ever again, threatening to kill yourself..."

"I wouldn't have done it. Mom's killer would have won." The words held dead certainty. No emotion.

And were the death to his last hidden hope that maybe there'd be a future for them.

Even just as friends.

HER PHONE RINGING jarred every ounce of air in the car.

And there were no niceties as Glen's voice came over the line. "He's there?"

"I'm here," Joe called from the back, and McKenna turned, putting the phone on the console so they could be equally heard. And alternated looking between the phone and keeping watch out the windshield.

She hadn't looked at him since the death knell had sounded on any kind of them.

"A program was written to reroute the three Bellair computers with access to the company's online banking system to another site set up to look like and act like you were on the legitimate bank site. The transactions you saw, and statements you downloaded, were all fake. That site has since been taken down. Erased."

McKenna's gaze shot to Joe. Was this it? They'd found the piece that would clear Joe?

While her used-up heart soared for him, it cracked a bit more, too.

"Turns out, no one from the bank was involved."

If they caught the real thief...

He'd still need her for another day or two at least, right? Until there was time for the news to hit social media and put an end to the #wheresjoenow witch hunt.

Maybe that would even take a week or more…

Joe wasn't moving. Or asking questions.

Was he sorry to be seeing his time with her end, too?

"When you hired us, you gave us access to your sign-in password," Glen continued. Something was wrong with her boss's tone of voice. She'd never heard quite that tone before.

"That's right," Joe said, more statue than man.

"But there's another one, isn't there? One that has to be used to access secure documents that you create. It's called a signature. You send a secure document along with a password to those authorized to access it. But they can't manipulate it in any way. It takes your private password to do that."

What in the hell was going on?

Tell them they're wrong, she wanted to scream at Joe while still trying to piece together the significance of what she was hearing.

What it all had to do with the pirated banking log-in and bogus website.

Silent, waiting, McKenna stared at Joe, who suddenly looked ashen. She hoped it was only the sun moving in the sky, hitting the car differently, putting him more in the shade.

"There is another one, yes." Joe's words sounded, and felt, like death.

"I need it now."

"M-y-f-a-t-h-e-r-k-i-l-l-e-d-m-y-m-o-t-h-e-r."

M-y… *My…father killed my mother?*

Mouth open, she sat there. Stunned.

Afraid.

"Who else has that password?"

She held her breath. Waiting for the answer. Who'd done this to Joe?

And where were they now? In custody, she hoped.

He was talking a long time to answer. She couldn't reach back and touch him. But she poured her heart into the look she gave him.

"No one," he said.

"No one."

"I've been using encryption since I got out of juvenile detention. It was something I learned there, and with my father…knowing he lied about me, hanging me out to dry… I wanted everything I did on my computer kept separate from anything he might do."

Her heart reached out to him. Needing to soothe him.

"What about someone seeing you type it? Someone in your office, maybe, while you were signing in?"

"Never," he said, sounding adamant and completely unemotional. "I don't ever enter it when anyone else is in any room I'm in, and I always cover my hand as I type in case of a hidden camera. After so many years living with my dad, it became habit. One I've never broken."

And her brain froze, as she realized there was way too much significance in what he'd just said. She was missing something…

Until Joe said, "You're about to tell me that the fraudulent log-in and scam bank site were created by my computer, aren't you?"

"As soon as I get back to the office and have my team type in the password to verify that what they're seeing from the back door is truly accessible by the front door."

She felt sick. Throwing up imminent, sick to her stomach.

Sierra's Web had somehow traced the fake bank site back to Joe's IP address. Found some encrypted something stopping them from accessing it through his computer. And now had the password to do so.

"Is there anything more you want to say?" Glen asked, sounding a bit more like himself.

Say something! She stared at Joe, who was looking right back at her through eyes that looked like glass. *Say something, dammit!*

At least tell me you're sorry.

He shook his head.

Eyes wide, she implored him.

"I didn't do it." The words carried no punch.

"We'll be in touch," Glen said and dropped the call.

Chapter Twenty-Two

Joe waited for her How could you?

For a few seconds there, when the phone and subsequently the car fell eerily silent, he didn't much care if he lived or died.

He couldn't be recharged for any crimes related to the commission of the fraud. His lawyer had made certain that those conditions were airtight.

The assurance was of little consequence at the moment.

"Stay down." McKenna's tone back to day one, she started the car. Headed down the hill faster than he'd have done.

Made the turns with the precision of a race car driver.

He didn't ask where they were going. Could barely see out the front windshield from his vantage point.

Halfway down, she pulled off onto an embankment and turned around, pinning him with a look blaring so much emotion he couldn't decipher any of it.

Other than to know she was deathly upset.

"Look me in the eye and tell me you did not do this. Not any of it." Definitely day one.

And, just as he had that first day—after she'd proven herself to him—he did as she ordered. He looked her straight in the eye. Thought of her body together with his the night before, the second time, when she'd come into his room and crawled into bed, spooning him. "I did not do it." And then he went rogue. "I know how to create a signature. Period. You think they're going to teach a juvenile delinquent, a thief, how to create computer programs? That's giving drugs and a needle to an addict."

"You could have learned programming in high school, college or at home from the internet in your spare time."

He took her blows like a man. "I could have. I didn't."

She seemed on the verge of going one way or the other. He might as well have been on the precipice three feet away—teetering between staying on solid ground and catapulting over the outer edge of the cliff down to the city below.

He wasn't a man who gave up. Who quit trying. "Think, McKenna," he demanded. "All the months before my trial, during my trial, the month since my trial before I called Sierra's Web...if I'd known about the programs, known how to create them, wouldn't I have uncreated them? Or, say I hired someone to do it, wouldn't I have known they were there and done something to protect myself from them?"

He was grasping. He could hear it. Was pretty certain she'd heard it, too.

Her gaze still trained on him, she seemed to be trying to figure out his game.

And his life was on the line—more so than ever.

"I made mistakes." He admitted to her what he'd not dared to say out loud to anyone. "I should have verified the reports I was looking at against actual inventory. I should have made trips to the warehouse more often..."

While he sat trying to convince McKenna of his innocence, his mind was also scrambling to figure out how anyone had gained access to his encrypted files to save the fraudulent bank program there.

"Glen told me earlier today that their expert in Alaska

has confirmed that your father hasn't left the island in over a year. He has no registered cell phone and no internet access."

So, he had nothing.

Whoever had framed him was better at getting things done than Joe was. And the better man would win.

"There's snail mail," she said next. Then turned, put the car in gear and started back down the road.

There's snail mail.

He heard the words over and over. His body lighter, his breathing sporadic, he half lay there, taking every turn along with the car.

There's snail mail.

An open possibility for someone to have contacted his father to find out about sacred time. And his juvie record. Cash could have been sent through the mail in payment for the information.

But, McKenna had said, *there's snail mail.*

Meaning…she was looking for a way for him to still be innocent?

Finding the answer to that question was reason to stay alive.

Showing her that she was right to want to believe in him became his life's goal.

And Joe was a man who'd made a success out of the ashes his childhood had heaped upon him by honestly pursuing what he wanted in spite of the odds against him. By not giving up.

Maybe there wasn't a future for him together with McKenna Meredith, but if he could go into his own future leaving her with the knowledge that the moments she'd shared with Joe Hamilton, that the faith she'd wanted to have in him, were justified, real and true, then he'd be…satisfied.

MCKENNA FELT SOMETHING wrong the second she pulled onto the long dirt drive leading to her father's cabin. To the rig.

No way she could know if there were fresh tire tracks—theirs and her father's were fresh that day. It wasn't like she'd notice if some desert brush had moved—wind blew. Coyotes and rabbits, snakes and even a stray bobcat could have been by. Things got moved. Or stepped on.

And then, as she turned a corner into the clearing, she saw the tire track off to the left, as though someone unfamiliar with the area hadn't known about the slight dip...

Before she'd even fully registered the information, movement caught her eye. Someone at the rig. Running toward them.

"Get down to the floor," she told Joe, reaching for her gun as she put the car into Reverse.

"Wait!" The scream was female, and frantic-sounding. Not lethal.

"Joeeey!" Another loud cry, coming faintly into the car.

"I know that voice," he said from the floor. "It's Priscilla Bellair." Sitting up far enough to see through the windshield, he continued, "She's upset, McKenna, not angry. Maybe she knows something. I can't afford not to speak to her."

She didn't like it. At all.

The beautiful woman, in skinny black jeans and a white cropped top that left her perfectly flat belly, complete with button, in view, was almost at the car.

Clearly crying.

Holding her hands up.

Against her better judgment, she put the car in Park. "Let me check her out first," she said, unbuckling her seat belt and opening the door of the car, gun pointing at their intruder.

McKenna didn't like her, at all. All up in those heels and the makeup, calling her client *Joey*. Like they had something special... She approached, daring the woman to give her a reason to shoot.

Filled with...jealousy.

Her bad feeling…she was jealous of the woman who was a part of Joe's normal life. His chosen life.

"Don't move," she said as she approached Priscilla Bellair—a woman who could have been one of her classmates, for all she knew. With her gun never leaving a clear point on Priscilla's body, she used her free hand to pat the woman down and checked her purse for weapons.

Finding nothing but cell phone, wallet and makeup, she asked, "Why are you here?"

"I need to talk to Joe. I know who framed him. It's big, and I have no idea who else is involved. I'm going to be in danger if I say anything, and I'm hoping Sierra's Web can protect me, too." She spoke in a rush, clearly agitated, as McKenna noted by the other woman's pulse—something she'd purposely sought out as she gave her arm a supposedly warm, calming squeeze.

Still, she wasn't convinced.

Wasn't eager to have Joe and the woman in contact, let alone working together like McKenna and Joe had been doing. Both of them in hiding together…

Stop.

She was a professional.

"How did you know he was here?" she asked in a kinder voice, lowering her gun but not her guard.

"I'm on the board of Bellair," Priscilla said, sounding more…confident…for a second, and then, as if remembering her current circumstances, she took a shuddering breath and said, "I see all the reports. I know Joe hired Sierra's Web to prove his innocence. And I knew it was all going to come out. I just didn't know who to trust. I had someone check into registered bodyguards, and when your name came up, I had a friend I trust touch base with your grandparents. As soon as they heard what was going on, they agreed to speak with me and told me that the one place you'd feel safe was here with your dad. They gave me directions. Please, I need to talk to Joe! I don't know how much time I have…"

McKenna felt the urgency, from Priscilla, and from Joe, back in the car, too. She didn't trust him to hang back for long.

Her grandparents had led the woman to them? Neil and Glenda Whitaker might not like McKenna in Shelter Valley, but they always, always put what they thought was best for McKenna first and foremost. They'd never have sent Priscilla her way if they hadn't felt she and the story she had to tell were fully vetted.

And how else would Priscilla have found them so quickly?

Still, there was no vehicle visible on the premises other than hers. "How'd you get here?"

"I hired a rideshare in Phoenix. We went by your dad's house, and then here. I knew, when I saw the rig, that Joe was here. He was always talking about running off for a getaway on the beach in one of those things."

She hadn't realized Priscilla and Joe had known each other well enough for *always talking about*.

And, feeling like she had a rock in her gut, McKenna nodded. "Stay there," she ordered.

Gun at the ready, she walked slowly backward to the car, hearing Priscilla crying softly the whole time.

"She says she knows who framed you," she said as she opened the back passenger door. "She's spoken to my grandparents and is afraid that when she goes public with what she knows, her life is going to be in danger, too."

He was out of the car and heading toward Priscilla so fast, McKenna had to do a double take. And hurry to get ahead of him.

As long as she was on the job, she would damn well do it right.

And she'd deal with the emotional fallout—the searing sense of ownership, of wanting what was not hers to want—when she'd completed her assignment.

Her step filled with purpose, she reminded Joe, quietly, that he was still under obligation to follow all orders.

And promised herself that she'd put personal feelings aside and do her best by him.

She could feel his excitement as he approached the gorgeous woman. And didn't blame him. He was about to be handed the exoneration he'd been searching for these last many months.

Joy filled her heart as she thought about that aspect of what was going down. Thrill at the thought of Joe getting his reputation back.

Of him being able to live his life happily again.

Keeping her sights on that goal alone, she heard Priscilla ask if they could go inside. In spite of a fully armed, expert bodyguard standing right there, the Bellair heiress was looking around nervously, as though she expected machine guns to come barreling out of the desert or over a hill.

"Of course," Joe answered without waiting for McKenna, or even looking her way, which shot a sharp bullet of betrayal through her.

After all they'd been through, Priscilla Bellair shows up and McKenna's so easily forgotten?

A second later, she flamed with shame. If she couldn't get in the game, someone could die. Was she willing to live with that on her shoulders for the rest of her life?

If what Priscilla was saying was true, who knew who could have followed her? Or be on their trail?

Determining that Joe and Priscilla were right, they'd be safer in the rig, she left the car where it was, slowing down entry to the clearing, and hurried them both inside.

S<small>OMETHING WASN'T RIGHT.</small>

The moment he made eye contact with Priscilla, standing by the couch in his RV, Joe got a bad feeling.

Because of who she was about to tell him had framed him? Her father? Her brother? For a split second he was't sure he wanted to know.

Her gaze dropped from his almost immediately, and she started to cry again. "I'm so sorry, Joe," she said.

And that tone. He recognized it. Had heard it too many times before.

When she'd been playing on her father's sympathies.

"What did you do?" He couldn't help the sharp tone. If she'd already gone to the press with the news...or told James or Julius that she was on to them and given them time to get out of the country...

Ideas flashed. Sympathy for Priscilla Bellair did not.

McKenna had left the door of the rig open. Was standing by it, keeping watch. Inside and out. She had the camera app open on her phone as well.

"I found out who framed you during your trial, Joe. I knew it wasn't you. I overheard a conversation. But no one was supposed to get hurt, you know? Bellair Software stock had already rallied—the company would be able to pay back investors who were defrauded, cheap marketing money, really, as doing so would show incredible goodwill from the company and get it a lot of great press. And there was no way you were going to be convicted. There was no hard evidence, no solid proof of anything. And if I said anything..."

Someone *would* go to jail.

"Who, Priscilla?"

The woman he'd known for years, and had never liked, opened her purse.

McKenna raised her gun. Pointed it straight at Priscilla's chest.

Raising perfectly manicured and glossily painted fake nails, Priscilla held up her cell. "I'm only getting my phone out," she said quickly, bringing on more of that scared-and-so-sorry tone of voice with the frightened expression to match.

The act—she wasn't cutting it, and that worried him.

Was she stalling? Until someone else could get there?

Or…it hit him…until she got the text that told her they were safely out of the United States?

McKenna's gun stayed up, both of her hands holding it steadily on Priscilla. Whether his bodyguard knew Priscilla was acting, or if she was just being precautious, he didn't know, but he was thankful she was there.

Holding her phone but not looking at it, Priscilla bowed her head.

"Tell me who, Priscilla," Joe demanded. "And then get out."

Her head shot up. "See, there you go again," she whined. "That tone of voice. Why do you do that? Why do you always act like you think you're better than me?"

The cry sounded different. More…real. And he shook his head, confused.

"What are you talking about?"

"Who are *you* but some thief kid, the son of a thief, to come into my family, my life, to have my father treating you like more of a family member than his own daughter, and then, when I tried to find a way to make it all work, had graciously decided to make an honest man out of you, a real Bellair, you turned me down…"

He had no idea what she was talking about. "Other than meaningless flirting, you came on to me one time, at a party, and you were out-of-your-mind drunk."

"It took that much alcohol to get me to a point where I could do it…"

Tears flowed out of the woman's eyes, and he stared at her.

"Are you telling me that you knew I was innocent, that you let me take the blame, because you resented me?"

He couldn't get there. That someone valued life so little that she'd stoop to spending her time on something so petty?

"Tell me who framed me, Priscilla."

"Now," McKenna spoke for the first time, a biting tone he'd never heard. "Or we're done here."

"Ah…" The tone was almost eerie. The look that came over Priscilla's face even more so. "That's where you're wrong. You can't hurt me. I'm the only witness. Joe's only chance to be exonerated." And all signs of tears were gone as she cocked her head and opened her mouth to run her tongue along perfectly red lips. "It turns out that I'm the one who gets to call the shots after all. Because the only way I'm testifying is if Joe comes with me, stands by me…"

"Fine." He stepped forward. "If that's what it takes to make this end, I'll do it." He'd stand with Satan himself if the devil were willing to give him the name of the man who'd tried to ruin his life.

Even if it turned out to be James Bellair.

Made a sickening kind of sense.

Priscilla had spent half her life trying to get one up on her father…

"Over my dead body…" Pushing Joe back so suddenly she threw him off balance, McKenna stepped forward.

"Point your gun all you want, sweetie—" Priscilla's ugly was out in fuller force than he'd ever seen. "Truth is, Joe needs *me* to save him, not *you*."

She was right. With his private signature code…no way he'd ever be able to prove someone had stolen it from him. Glen was ready to quit him.

Clearly McKenna had known that, too.

As soon as Joe's private code got them into his encrypted

files and they found the bogus bank site there, he'd be fired as a client. Because they would find the programs they were seeking.

Just like they'd found everything else incriminating on his computer.

He had no idea how or why…or who…but Priscilla did.

She'd glanced at her phone. Pushed a button on the side, likely turning on the screen? Watching for the text?

If he went with her, he could still be a dead man. But he'd rather take his chances than live the rest of his life thought of as a thief.

He'd been there. Couldn't go back.

"Tell me one thing." McKenna's voice broke into the tense, waiting silence. With her standing half in front of him, he couldn't see her face.

"What's that?"

"Was Joe's father involved?"

He stared at the back of that curly red head. What in the hell did that matter?

Was she asking for his sake? Did she think he wanted to know?

"Yes."

He wouldn't have thought his heart could sink any more with the confirmation. And yet, crazy as it was, it did.

"You know what you were worth, Joe? A measly forty thousand dollars to sell you out. I couldn't believe it when I heard that part. That bit about your sealed record, that was a shock to hear, but I can honestly say it made me admire you more, the way you made good."

He wasn't falling for her flattery. Didn't give a damn what she thought of him. That she'd known, all through his trial, sitting there with her dad and brother and cousin…

Cousin.

"It's Mark, isn't it?" Made sense. The cousin who'd felt

outed when Joe was made CFO and given more shares of stock than Mark had.

"Uh-uh." Priscilla shook her head. "It's not going to be played that way. You and I are going to walk out of here together. I've got a rideshare due to arrive anytime now."

That was why she'd taken out her phone.

"You and I are going to take a ride back to Phoenix, and in exchange for my testimony, you're going to convince my father to make me a vice president of Bellair."

His jaw dropped. *What the*...

Her laugh was about the ugliest sound he'd ever heard. "See, Joe, right there. That's the problem. You're shocked. What, you think I don't have what it takes? I'm not as good as Julius and Mark...and...and *you*? I've got multiple degrees. I'm more capable than any of you...and yet I'm never even considered for a place in the company."

"You have a seat on the board."

"A complimentary seat. No one listens to anything I have to say, and with Mark, Julius and my father's votes all going the same way, mine doesn't even matter."

All true. With controlling stock, the Bellair vote counted two to one and always won.

Over McKenna's shoulder, which had to be getting tired holding up her gun, he looked Priscilla straight in the eye. "You really think you can do the work?"

"I know I can. I grew up in the Bellair household," she said. "I've been programming since I was a kid..."

The world stopped. No noise. No air. Just whirring.

It was Priscilla. She'd done it.

And she needed him out of the way.

Their little trip, whoever was arriving imminently... He'd be dead before he left Shelter Valley.

And so would McKenna.

He couldn't let that happen. Not because of him.

"Fine, you deserve the chance," he told Priscilla, pushing past McKenna, forcing her arm down.

She elbowed him. "Joe."

"No." He shook his head. "I've made my decision. All I've wanted all along was to be exonerated. To have the guilty party exposed. If this is what I have to do..." He shrugged. Looked straight at Priscilla. "If you've been feeling this way for so long, why didn't you just come talk to me years ago?" he asked. "I've always known that if you'd stop your partying and gallivanting, you'd be one hell of a businesswoman..."

Two could play her game. And he had to buy himself time to figure out if there was a way to save McKenna and keep himself alive, too.

Priscilla held up her phone. Nodded.

Her ride was obviously there.

"Let's go," he said, reaching for the woman's arm, pulling her toward the door.

"No!" Throwing a foot out in front of him, entangling her ankle in his with a huge thrust up, McKenna tripped him. He saw Priscilla raise a hand...to catch him?...then saw her arm outstretched, before he hit the couch. Flat on his back, he watched as McKenna aimed, Priscilla held her phone straight out, pushed...

And shards of electricity hit McKenna. Her entire body convulsed for a brief second before she dived, caught Priscilla around the waist and rolled with her down the steps of the rig, landing on top of the evil woman, knocking the air out of her.

Priscilla hadn't been looking at a phone. She'd been holding a Taser.

Jumping into action, Joe grabbed McKenna's fallen gun and jumped from the rig to the ground in one leap, aiming at Priscilla's perfect blond curls on the ground.

Both women were lying there, still, but if they were only winded…

"The rig…" McKenna's voice was barely coherent. He saw blood dripping from her lip. "Get in…drive…"

Ordering him around, even then.

His heart filled with more fear than he'd ever known, he held the gun steady. He wasn't a great shot. Needed McKenna to move before he dared…

"Driuh…" Was she trying repeat her order to drive?

He was losing her!

She couldn't die!

He cocked the trigger.

Oh, God, he couldn't miss. A fraction of an inch and…

McKenna dropped her head on top of Priscilla's, bleeding on the blond hair he'd been aiming for.

Moving forward, planning to move her, he heard tires behind him… Priscilla's hit man? And then his head exploded with sirens.

Before he was even sure what was happening, having the thought that Glen had called the Shelter Valley brigade on him, he felt someone clasp his shoulder, squeeze it and take the gun. He heard a strange voice say, "Good work, Joe. We'll take it from here."

Chapter Twenty-Three

McKenna heard the sirens through a haze of pain. Being tased was no good. No matter how much training…

She couldn't breathe. Couldn't let herself pass out.

Felt the body beneath her start to move. Made herself dead weight to keep it down. Had a flash of Joe's naked body beneath hers. Joyous.

Gasped in air.

Heard footsteps. Joe?

Voices fading in and out.

Felt warm fingers at her throat. "Alive," she gasped.

"Medic! Now! I need a medic over here!"

Running feet. Confusion.

Joe?

No, don't move me yet. Hurts too much.

Please.

Hands on her body.

Joe's?

His hands, gently, along her whole body. Touching her. Giving her life.

Reason for life.

Joyous.

She was lifting.

Excruciating pain.

Floating.

Joe?

FILLED WITH DREAD, with fear, Joe watched as McKenna was put on a stretcher, a stream of blood running from her mouth down to her chin beneath closed eyes.

"Her pulse is good, man." Kierland was there, hands in the pockets of his jeans, staring at his work boots.

Joe braced for the blame, the hate…the man's beloved sister was lying comatose because of him.

"There's blood coming from her mouth…" That couldn't be good. And he was always the guy who gave it straight up.

To counteract the thief gene.

"Looks like she split her lip on her landing. Or bit it. That's really going to piss her off. As much as she's practiced falls…"

He glanced over, the first time he'd taken his gaze off from McKenna. The guy wasn't spewing.

Gaze back at the ambulance, he could see two paramedics loading her in.

And then her father climbing in beside her.

Saw the bottoms of her tennis shoes just before the door slammed shut.

And prepared to get through whatever lay ahead.

MCKENNA CAME TO with a dry mouth, an itchy chin and an inability to get her fingers up to scratch it.

Pulling at the straps holding her wrists down, she heard someone say, "She's waking up," and opened her eyes.

"I haven't been asleep," she announced, saw her father bending over her. "I was just resting," she explained.

Saw the smile break out on his face…and the tears in his eyes.

"Oh, good Lord, girl, you gave me a scare this time."

She tried to move, winced and fell back as her midsection met strap and pain seared her.

"Priscilla Bellair..."

"Is in custody," her father said as a paramedic hovered, taking her blood pressure.

"I think I broke a rib," she told him.

"And split your lip."

"Damn. I know better than that. It was the tasing..."

And it hit her. She sprang forward again, fell back and pinned her father with a demanding stare. "Where's Joe? He didn't do it," she said. "Don't let them—"

"Shh." Her father smoothed her hair back from her forehead.

Which was what told her how very scared he'd really been.

"We're in the ambulance, moving," she said with some level of superiority.

He nodded, watching her with a still-worried frown.

"From the cabin to the hospital is only fifteen minutes."

"Right again."

"I was conscious when they loaded me on the stretcher."

"I know."

"Means I've only been out, at the most, ten minutes."

"Yeah."

"I'm not hooked up to oxygen."

"Your levels were fine..."

"Because I am fine," she told him. "And I need to get to Joe. He's in danger—"

"No, he's not," her father said. "Not anymore. In large part thanks to you."

She frowned. They'd just established she'd only been out a few minutes. The world didn't spin on a dime in that amount of time.

"Priscilla's the one who framed him, not Mark" she said,

eyes wide and urgent. "They need to know... Give me your phone, I have to call Glen..." She'd suspected something was up almost right away in the rig, partially based on Joe's reaction to Priscilla's histrionics. But when the woman had started talking about her programming degrees, after having just given them plenty of motive...

But Joe, he'd been going with her, to talk to Priscilla's dad...

It all came rolling back with frightening force. "Sheriff Richards..." She glanced at the paramedic. "You got a radio in here? Get Sheriff Richards on the line."

The lack of action in the small space was about to drive her to breaking some gurney straps.

"He already knows everything," Kyle told her, confusing her. Was she really losing her mind, then? Had he been humoring her about the ten minutes she'd figured she'd been out?

"And Joe?"

"Is fine and on his way back to Phoenix, I suspect. Or will be soon."

"So..."

The ambulance stopped. Doors flew open, and she slid away from her father. Into a cubicle, curtains closed around her and her clothes were cut off.

All overkill.

But she lay there, letting the professionals do their thing, answering questions, submitting to X-rays, whatever it took to get her ribs taped up so she could get out.

Knowing that as soon as she was free, on her own two feet, Joe would stand up from his chair in the waiting room, he'd get one look at her, and the worried look would leave his face.

They'd walk into each other's arms. Even if just for a cursory so-glad-you're-okay hug, and he'd tell her where Priscilla was and what happened next.

Even if she was right, and Priscilla was the one who'd framed him, there was still the social media fallout to deal with. Until word got around that Joe was innocent. Not just not guilty. But innocent.

It all happened pretty much like she'd figured. She had a couple of cracked ribs and a split lip but was otherwise in perfect health. She hadn't hit her head, had just passed out due to the tasing, which constricts air flow, and having the wind knocked out of her right afterward. She'd just needed a minute to catch her breath.

Which, with cracked ribs, and lying on top of a bad woman, had been a bit difficult.

So with taped ribs and donated clothes from a hospital closet filled for that purpose, she walked out of the ER and into the waiting room just a couple of hours after she'd been brought in. Out before dark.

But there things got confusing.

Wrong.

Four men got up out of chairs to come meet her. And a woman, too.

Her brothers. Her father. Her grandfather. And her grandmother.

Shockingly together.

But no Joe.

SITTING IN HIS RIG, still hooked up to electricity at Kyle Meredith's cabin, Joe drank a beer and watched the sun go down over Shelter Valley.

Waiting.

Kierland had assured him that as soon as there was news of McKenna, someone would give him a call on the brand-new cell phone Joe had purchased first thing after leaving the police station.

McKenna's brother, whose number he'd obtained from

Greg Richards, the sheriff of Shelter Valley, had been his first and only call.

He'd cleared things up with Glen Rivers at the police station. Thanking the man profusely. He'd get a final bill within a few days. Mailed to his home address in Phoenix.

It was all still surreal.

He could go home.

The sheriff was the one who'd suggested he wait until morning. Just long enough for news to hit nationally. Sierra's Web marketing experts were all over the internet slamming the #wheresjoenow hashtag with truth and a whole lot of mentions of more to come by morning, and to watch the news.

He'd been amusing himself with following the viral spread of the posts while he waited on news of McKenna.

Mostly, he'd been...numb.

Sitting alone, trying to comprehend.

He'd been right about Priscilla. She'd been the one to frame him. Other than his bribe-taking father, she'd been the only one involved. Had concocted the plan herself, had written programs, implemented everything.

Down to the minute detail.

With one exception.

She'd failed to protect herself from a curious kid taking a picture of the famous-looking woman visiting Joe's father's small, remote Alaskan village.

A photo the Sierra's Web investigative expert who'd flown to Alaska had lucked onto when asking questions of every villager...

Priscilla wouldn't have known that, but she'd known that Sierra's Web was closing in on her. She had a seat on the Bellair board. Got every report.

She was the one who'd started the #wheresjoenow hashtag. Had gotten all her friends to help her spread the word among influencers in an effort, she'd apparently told them, to save her family business. Interviews of those and others would happen. The investigation was only in its beginning stages, but with Sierra's Web's help, the Phoenix detectives would have an airtight case to present to prosecutors.

And the missing link, the one he hadn't known until Glen Rivers had told him in the sheriff's office—his private password...

His father, not trusting him when he got back from juvenile detention, had had a keystroke monitor put on his computer.

Something young Joe would never have known existed.

Something thirty-one-year-old Joe had never considered.

Sipping his beer, thinking about a second one, but wanting to be completely sober and able to drive if McKenna wanted to see him, Joe watched as lights came on all over the city.

Telling himself that emergency room visits always took forever.

If McKenna was in life-or-death trouble, someone would have called to let him know.

Half an hour after Glen had gotten off the phone with Joe and McKenna that afternoon, he'd had a call from his expert in Alaska. Giving him both key pieces of information—Priscilla and the pass code. With one phone call, Glen had alerted Sheriff Richards, who'd already had a frantic call from McKenna's grandparents. They'd raced up the mountain just in time to see Joe standing over McKenna and Priscilla lying on the ground.

Priscilla's hit man driver...he was still an unknown, at least as far as Joe knew. Priscilla might turn on the guy, she might not. Depended on what suited her own interests best.

Either way, the guy better hope that she hadn't paid him in any traceable form or her financials were going to lead law enforcement right to his doorstep.

Guy had probably wet his pants when he'd driven up the

mountain expecting to make a kill and finding the place ablaze with police cars and other emergency vehicles. If he had any sense at all, he'd be crossing the Arizona/Mexico border within the hour. If he hadn't already.

Priscilla had left the scene on a stretcher, but she'd been cuffed to it. Oddly, he hadn't taken any pleasure out of the sight.

James Bellair was going to be hurting over that one for the rest of his life.

The man had already called Joe.

Offered him his job back.

Seeing headlights coming up the road, he stood, set his empty beer can on the counter and went outside, heart pumping as he waited. He hadn't dared hope that McKenna would be back with him that night, but he'd...wanted her to be.

The white truck that came into view made sense. Meredith and Sons Construction. She'd need a way back. Either of her brothers or her dad.

Even if she was just there to pick up her things...he was beyond relieved to see her—anxious to see her. To look her in the eye, and know she really was all right.

To thank her for...so much more than guarding his body.

Only one person got out of the truck.

Kyle Meredith.

Not McKenna.

Glancing toward the passenger door, waiting for it to open even though he couldn't see a head or shoulders on that side of the truck, he finally turned to the older man walking toward him.

"How is she?" That was all that mattered.

"Good. Great. McKenna," the man said, as if that explained it all. Knowing her, her strength and determination, he figured it kind of did.

Got a little weak-kneed with relief.

"We all thought you'd be home in Phoenix by now," the man said, kind of shocking Joe. And making him suddenly embarrassed as well.

"I apologize, sir. I need to get off your land... I just, if McKenna wanted her things..." He wasn't a blubberer. He didn't usually find himself in humiliating situations, either.

Or have his heart in his throat.

"No need." Kyle sounded more pleased than anything. "I'm glad to have a chance to thank you, personally, for standing over that...with a gun." Joe heard the expletive the pause covered.

Agreed with it completely.

"You're welcome to stay as long as you'd like, Joe. You're a good man. And a helluva construction guy from what my boys tell me."

He glowed like a little boy. Until he recognized what he was doing, straightened his shoulders and nodded.

"It's I who owe you, your family... You raised one helluva woman. I owe her my life. Several times over."

Kyle's shrug, his headshake, seemed to convey perplexity—and understanding at the same time. "I never would have figured her for a bodyguard—growing up she was afraid of her own shadow, but there you have it. She found her calling. She won't let what happened to her dear sweet mama happen to anyone else on her watch."

Because she'd been on watch the day her mother had died. A three-year-old trapped in her car seat, overhearing the killer, watching it all go down.

"They're keeping her overnight?" he asked then, figuring maybe he could see her in the morning before he headed out.

"Hell, no. She's already halfway to Phoenix by now, I'd imagine. Said she wanted to get home, sleep in her own bed. Caught a ride with her grandparents..."

"What about the blood?" He'd been trying to forget the sight ever since the ambulance carrying her had pulled away. Resetting his mind every time it sent him a replay.

"She bit her lip on landing. And if you talk to her again, I wouldn't mention it," the older man said with a chuckle. "She was grumbling about that even before she got to the hospital. She ended up with a couple of cracked ribs, which she took with a shrug. They taped her up, and she walked out of there."

Joe smiled. Expressed his relief, and his thanks. Gathered up McKenna's things from his rig when Kyle offered to take them for her, and when Kyle told him he'd be seeing him, he agreed that he would.

Knowing that he would never see the man again.

Feeling like a fool, standing there in the RV alone after the man left, he pushed the button to pull in the slides, unhooked the electric, got his car on the tow bar and drove himself down the hill and out of Shelter Valley.

James had told him to take some days off before he came back to work, but Joe had just had his head put on straight for him.

No matter what he and McKenna had shared, his life was his life, and she wanted no part of it. She needed to have no part of it.

Leaving his RV outside the gated entrance to his property, he went inside, turned on his computer, found a program, typed, printed and walked the quarter mile from his house to the road, taped the For Sale signs all over the rig, locked the doors and went in to shower and sleep in his own bed.

He had to get up for work in the morning.

Work had always been the panacea for what ailed him.

He was sure it would soon put McKenna out of his mind.

Or, at least, bury her in a private space that he'd have to visit from time to time.

Just to remind himself of the incredible completeness he'd once known.

Chapter Twenty-Four

McKenna lay around for a full day. Used her ribs as an excuse. Babied herself. Her grandparents had tried to get her to go home with them, but she'd known she wouldn't have been able to handle that with aplomb. She'd needed her own space.

Her grandmother came to see her—twice—that first day.

She'd heard everything that had happened. Her greeting party outside the ER had filled her in on all the day's details.

With both of her grandparents tearfully apologizing for having sent Priscilla her way in the first place. They'd been on their way to a doctor's appointment to hear test results for her grandmother—a possibly life-threatening screening for something they hadn't even told McKenna about that had, thankfully, turned out completely benign—but talking after the appointment, they'd both felt off about the morning visit. Her grandfather had made a call to a high-ranking official he knew who filled him in on Priscilla Bellair's run-ins with the police over the years, and they had immediately called McKenna's dad to let him know that they might have sent danger McKenna's way.

Kyle had called Sheriff Richards first, and then his sons, only to find that McKenna and Joe had already left the construction site—half an hour before.

Everyone had scrambled, come together, and they'd all come to a happy ending.

The best of all endings for Joe Hamilton.

Maybe not for James Bellair, but that was life.

Her father had called several times that day, too, as had her brothers. Wanting her to come home to recuperate. Telling her that Joe had left her things with them.

And she'd received his private message through his lack of any kind of attempt to contact her at all. The job was over, and so were they. He didn't want to see her again.

As her male family members had cajoled her, in triplicate, on different calls, she'd remained strong in her need to be in her own home, sleep in her own bed. Eventually, they'd capitulated.

What they didn't know, what she couldn't tell them, was that it might be a while before she could be in Shelter Valley again. The town that made everyone welcome, whose residents helped hurting souls heal, was the town where she'd given away her heart.

And had it broken.

Her grandmother had told her, during the afternoon visit, that James had offered Joe his job back. She'd said that from what she'd heard, he'd presented himself in his old office before opening that morning.

A big part of McKenna's heart soared for him.

Knowing that Joe was safe, had his life back and was happy made her happy.

And the smaller part, the selfish part that wanted more time with him…she'd get over that. Just like she got over every other pain in her life.

When you learned at three how to recover from tragedy, it became an integral part of you. Was just kind of something you did.

And when you lost it at sixteen, trembling in your room

and threatening death if anyone tried to make you go out, you learned your limitations, too.

Joe's life was what he needed.

And it wasn't a life she could live.

But as she lay in bed that night, longing for him—his body, but just him even more—she admitted to herself that she just might have fallen in love with her wealthy, framed accountant client.

She couldn't be sure, analyzer and planner that she was, but she knew for sure she'd never hurt like she was hurting, never cried like she was crying every time she thought about never seeing him again for the rest of her life.

But on the second day, she quit wallowing.

And she quit her job.

Because the one thing she'd learned during her time with Joe—and maybe on the job before his as well—was that she needed more out of life. Had to find another way to help people live safe, happy lives. Because she needed a real home—and family—of her own.

She wanted to get married. To have a man in her bed at night who welcomed her with open arms and cried out when she pleasured him.

A man who had her back when she was in danger, even though she was perfectly capable of taking care of herself.

She wanted children.

And there was the true stopping point. No way she could bring little people into the world and expect them to just deal with her continual absences, knowing that every single time she left home, she'd be risking her own life to save another.

She'd had a good run of it. Had made a true difference.

But she'd always known the job wouldn't last forever. Bodies got older.

And hearts needed different things.

By the third day, she was meeting with Glen Rivers

again—at his behest. Sierra's Web wanted to offer her a new job—part of a new venture for them. Instead of just hiring qualified-in-their-field experts, they wanted each field of expertise to have a full-time staff member who put every qualified expert through initial and then continued training to make certain that Sierra's Web's highest standards were always maintained.

They wanted her to train and manage all the bodyguard experts who took on Sierra's Web jobs.

She accepted the position on the spot.

And made her life plan.

She was going to work. Date.

Fall in love. Get married.

And be pregnant by the time she was thirty-three.

That gave her a year for the dating and loving part. And a year to get pregnant.

She had her work cut out for her.

But when it came to the falling in love part, she'd be able to quickly cut through the crap. She knew what she wanted. What she needed. What she deserved.

She knew the kind of man she wanted as the father of her children. The integrity, the ability to be honest even when it made him look bad, the loyalty, to himself, and to those who'd betrayed him—not by framing him, but by disowning him when he'd been framed.

She wanted the kind of man she could walk out on after sex and still have him call out to her that she was welcome back anytime.

She knew it all before she'd even begun looking.

She'd had the absolute best teacher.

JOE MADE IT a week. Long enough to accept dinner invitations, to be patted on the back so many times it was a wonder he wasn't bruised, to be welcomed back into all his folds with open arms—and to realize that he didn't give a crap about any of it.

He didn't want to work for a man who'd had him arrested without giving him even a moment's benefit of the doubt.

He wasn't all that fond of a society that had shunned him, either.

And he was even less fond of the same world of people who welcomed him back, thinking they'd all just be friends again. Expecting him to not only understand the rules of the game, but to play by them.

Life wasn't a game to be played.

It was real. And precious.

And he feared he'd lived the best it had to offer during his purgatory.

In the arms of his bodyguard.

So he quit his job.

He made some phone calls.

A lot of them.

Bought a plot of land in a new development up on a small mountain above a little town and then purchased a storefront on the main street of that town; got his permits and licensing for private accounting; had designers come in to make the space right; conducted interviews; had a logo, stationery and signage created; and spent a lot of nights drinking beer with two particular guys he'd grown to like a lot.

Maybe even to love, like a guy would love a brother, if he'd ever had one.

Then they started to irritate him like brothers. Know-it-all, think-they-knew-better-than-him brothers.

"You need to call her, man," Kierland said one night just before Thanksgiving. "No way she'll refuse to come home for the holiday, and she's going to figure out something's up."

"Dad's not going to keep secrets from her forever," Jackson added.

The three of them were at Kyle's cabin, where Joe was temporarily living until his home was built in the new development Meredith Construction was building.

"There's no need for secrets," he said then, speaking aloud a truth he'd figured out over the past week or so. "I'm not doing all of this for her..."

Jackson snorted so hard beer dripped from his nose.

All three of them laughed.

And then sobered.

"I'm in love with her, yes," he said, not even feeling weird admitting the truth to her brothers before he'd even told the woman involved. "And the changes are because of her, but I made them because they were right for me. I just needed her tornado to come through my life for me to see that it was time to rebuild."

He heard a sound, a door in the back of the cabin, his bedroom door...

Just as he realized someone else was in the cabin, Jackson and Kierland stood and, without even a good night, headed out the front door.

Standing, he thought he was hallucinating at first, that he'd had more beer than he'd thought, when he saw the body in leggings and a long-sleeved Lycra shirt coming toward him. It was the curly red hair that told him he didn't want to wake up.

That he'd agree to live in the drunken stupor for the rest of his life if he could just keep seeing the vision before him.

"I love you, too."

He didn't want to wake up, ever. So he went with the fantasy. Stood up.

Walked toward his ethereal angel, daring her to disappear. She just kept coming toward him instead.

"How long have you known?" he asked.

"Since you quit Bellair."

That long. He shook his head. "Your grandparents?"

She nodded.

"You know I know about Sierra's Web?"

"No," she said, frowning. "I was actually looking forward to telling you that."

They were standing, toe to toe. Their faces inches apart.

"Why didn't you contact me?" he had to ask. Maybe because a part of him was always going to be that little boy who'd been sent to jail on a lie from his father.

"I could ask you the same question."

"You knew I was here. I didn't know you knew."

"I needed to know that you could be happy here," she told him. "It couldn't be for me, Joe, or it wasn't right for you."

He broke. Everything inside of him just came crumbling down. More than two decades of walls, whose construction had started in a juvenile detention hall, just cracked and fell to ash.

With tears brimming in his eyes, and a penis that was so hard it hurt, he pulled her to him. "I love you, McKenna Meredith."

"I love you, too, Joe Hamilton."

"You know we have to get married."

"You know I'm probably going to bark orders from time to time. For the rest of our lives."

"Yeah."

He glanced at the door. Needing to kiss her, to haul her to bed, in the worst way.

"You think they left?"

"If they know what's good for them. And if they didn't, they will," she told him, pushing him backward toward the bedroom door.

Not sure how much time he had before he exploded, Joe took her hand, dragged her behind him the rest of the way to his temporary quarters and, as they saw the reflection of taillights heading down the hill, he started to laugh.

To cry.

And to kiss her. Hard.

"This is forever."

"I know."

"We're going to make babies."

"Yep."

"I'm home, McKenna."

"I'm home, too, Joe. Finally."

And with that, they spent the rest of the night, two souls becoming one, body, mind and heart.

Knowing that love would protect them both, no matter what came, for the rest of their lives.

* * * * *

COMING SOON!

We really hope you enjoyed reading this book. If you're looking for more romance be sure to head to the shops when new books are available on

Thursday 8th June

To see which titles are coming soon, please visit

millsandboon.co.uk/nextmonth

LET'S TALK

Romance

For exclusive extracts, competitions and special offers, find us online:

 MillsandBoon

 @MillsandBoon

 @MillsandBoonUK

 @MillsandBoonUK

Get in touch on 01413 063 232

For all the latest titles coming soon, visit
millsandboon.co.uk/nextmonth

MILLS & BOON

THE HEART OF ROMANCE

A ROMANCE FOR EVERY READER

MODERN

Prepare to be swept off your feet by sophisticated, sexy and seductive heroes, in some of the world's most glamourous and romantic locations, where power and passion collide.

HISTORICAL

Escape with historical heroes from time gone by. Whether your passion is for wicked Regency Rakes, muscled Vikings or rugged Highlanders, awaken the romance of the past.

MEDICAL

Set your pulse racing with dedicated, delectable doctors in the high-pressure world of medicine, where emotions run high and passion, comfort and love are the best medicine.

True Love

Celebrate true love with tender stories of heartfelt romance, from the rush of falling in love to the joy a new baby can bring, and a focus on the emotional heart of a relationship.

Desire

Indulge in secrets and scandal, intense drama and sizzling hot action with heroes who have it all: wealth, status, good looks…everything but the right woman.

HEROES

The excitement of a gripping thriller, with intense romance at its heart. Resourceful, true-to-life women and strong, fearless men face danger and desire - a killer combination!

To see which titles are coming soon, please visit

millsandboon.co.uk/nextmonth

JOIN US ON SOCIAL MEDIA!

Stay up to date with our latest releases, author news and gossip, special offers and discounts, and all the behind-the-scenes action from Mills & Boon...

 @millsandboon

 @millsandboonuk

 facebook.com/millsandboon

 @millsandboonuk

It might just be true love...

MILLS & BOON
A ROMANCE FOR EVERY READER

- **FREE** delivery direct to your door
- **EXCLUSIVE** offers every month
- **SAVE** up to 30% on pre-paid subscritions

SUBSCRIBE AND SAVE